Acclaim for *New York Times* bestselling author
Robert K. Tanenbaum's "richly plotted, tough,
funny crime series" (*People*) featuring Butch Karp
and Marlene Ciampi

FURY

"Tanenbaum's most explosive legal thriller yet. *Fury* unleashes a
deadly mix of politics and criminal justice, taking the reader on a
riveting ride to its brilliantly plotted conclusion."

—Linda Fairstein, *New York Times* bestselling author of *Death Dance*

"In this nonstop thriller, Tanenbaum tells some very harsh truths
about the politics of crime fighting while confronting new terrors
the nation must face."

—Catherine Crier, former judge, *Court TV* host and author
of *A Deadly Game*

"*Fury* once again shows us Tanenbaum's special working knowledge of crime and the legal system in America."

—Vince Bugliosi, former Los Angeles district attorney and author
of *Helter Skelter* and the acclaimed *And the Sea Will Tell*

"A fascinating story. [His] ability to weave several seemingly
unrelated plots together is truly masterful."

—Cyril H. Wecht, M.D., J.D.

**Also available from Simon & Schuster Audio
and as an eBook**

ALSO BY ROBERT K. TANENBAUM

FICTION

Hoax
Resolved
Absolute Rage
Enemy Within
True Justice
Act of Revenge
Reckless Endangerment
Irresistible Impulse
Falsely Accused
Corruption of Blood
Justice Denied
Material Witness
Reversible Error
Immoral Certainty
Depraved Indifference
No Lesser Plea

NONFICTION

The Piano Teacher:
The True Story of a Psychotic Killer
Badge of the Assassin

ROBERT K. TANENBAUM

FURY

POCKET BOOKS
New York London Toronto Sydney

POCKET BOOKS, a division of Simon & Schuster, Inc.
1230 Avenue of the Americas, New York, NY 10020

Copyright © 2005 by Robert K. Tanenbaum

Originally published in hardcover in 2005 by Atria Books

ISBN-13: 978-0-7434-5291-5
ISBN-10:   0-7434-5291-7

This Pocket Books paperback edition July 2006

10 9 8 7 6 5 4 3 2 1

POCKET and colophon are registered trademarks of
Simon & Schuster, Inc.

Cover design by Carlos Beltran

Manufactured in the United States of America

For information regarding special discounts for bulk purchases,
please contact Simon & Schuster Special Sales at
1-800-456-6798 or business@simonandschuster.com.

To those most special,
Patti, Rachael, Roger, and Billy,
and to the memories of my legendary mentors,
District Attorney Frank S. Hogan and Henry Robbins

FURY

Prologue

Then . . .

TWENTY-EIGHT-YEAR-OLD LIZ TYLER WOKE in the dark moments before her alarm clock would have chimed. Reaching over to the nightstand, she turned it off. She lingered for a moment, enjoying the warmth of her husband, who slept soundly next to her, half hoping that he'd wake up and make love to her.

She'd never been more in love with him in their seven years of marriage. There'd been a rough spot three years earlier—a meaningless fling with the cliché tennis instructor to get even with her husband for his workaholic hours as a stockbroker—but he'd forgiven her and understood that he'd played a role in her infidelity. Wading through a flood of tears and self-recriminations, they'd reached a new level in their relationship and were stronger and more loving as a result. They'd conceived a baby, Rhiannon, named in memory of their first meeting at a Fleetwood Mac concert, and the child, now two, had cemented them to each other still further.

Sighing but getting no response, Liz decided to move on. This was her favorite time of day—just before the dawn, a precious few minutes to be alone with her thoughts before the demands of mommyhood and domestic engineering drove all other considerations from her mind until after the last bedtime story.

Liz slid from bed and into a sports bra, baggy sweatshirt, running shorts, socks, and running shoes. She walked around to his side of the bed and leaned over to kiss his cheek, rough with a day's growth of beard.

"Going running?" he mumbled, finding and stroking her long muscular leg with the hand that hung off the bed.

"Yeah, lazybones, want to join me?" She didn't really want him to go—this was her time—and knew he wouldn't but it was polite to ask.

"Maybe next time." He sounded more than half asleep, but his hand had continued to explore up her leg until it was reaching suggestive levels.

She moved away from his fingers, raising a muffled complaint. "You missed your chance five minutes ago, tiger," she said, laughing. "I'm up, dressed, and off to the beach. I'll be back before you go."

Leaving the bedroom, she'd tiptoed into her daughter's room and peeked over the rail of the crib. Rhiannon lay on her stomach, a thumb stuck in her mouth. She was dreaming, judging by the small sounds of discovery and joy she made in between sucks. Liz leaned over until her nose was less than an inch from her toddler's neck and inhaled deeply the sweet and sour smells of childhood.

With an effort, she straightened and left her daughter's room. Time to start or you're going to miss the sunrise, she thought, grabbing the lanyard, with the whistle on it, off the coatrack and heading out of her Brighton Beach apartment.

She quickly made her way over to the boardwalk and down the steps to the beach. Crossing the loose sand over to the shoreline where it was harder and more compact, she then headed up the beach toward Coney Island. She could just make out her destination in the growing gray of the dawn—a big insectlike pier a mile away.

Liz liked running in sand. It gave her a better workout and was largely responsible for her shedding the twenty extra pounds she'd gained during pregnancy. Only five foot six, she was down to a lithe, trim 110 pounds with just enough breast to give her cleavage. She was proud of how she treated her body and had adopted a tan, athletic look with short, spiky black hair that framed her green, almond-shaped eyes nicely.

Pounding up the beach, scattering the seagulls, who complained obscenely about the intrusion, she was mostly alone. She could see the occasional beachcomber in the distance and the early riser or two along the boardwalk, but this stretch of beach was all hers. It gave her a chance to think about an issue that was troubling her—whether to return to work.

She didn't like the idea of leaving Rhiannon with a babysitter. But on the other hand, she'd had a career she enjoyed before she got pregnant—working as a florist after getting an associate's degree in horticulture at Brooklyn Community College. She missed the work and she missed getting to socialize with adults during the day. But that just made her feel even more guilty, like she was being a bad mother.

The dilemma consumed her so much that as she approached the pier, she didn't notice the shadows moving beneath the weathered, barnacle-encrusted pylons. That was unusual, because she really didn't like to run beneath the hulking structure. As a little girl, she'd been afraid of *dark places—those spaces beneath the bed, in closets, and down in basements where monsters were said to hide.*

The dark places beneath the pier frightened her as an adult. But she always forced herself to finish this half of the run by racing beneath its beams, timing the sprint to match the waves receding enough to allow her a clear shot to the other side. In part, the idea was to conquer a childhood fear, but it was also similar to the reason people enjoy watching horror movies—they like being scared.

Liz was so caught up in the internal debate over going back to work that she didn't see the real monsters until she was halfway under the pier and one jumped out at her and yelled, "Boo!"

She veered and tried to sprint away but stumbled, giving him time to cut in front of her again. He wasn't horrible-looking for a monster, just a tall, gangly black teenager with mocha skin, nice, white teeth, and hazel-colored eyes. But he talked like a monster. "Say, where you going, bitch? Me and the homeboys was partyin' and thought maybe you should join us."

Standing as a wave came ashore and soaked her running shoes, Liz noticed that she was surrounded by a half-dozen teenagers—some of them leering, others looking uncomfortable. "Leave me alone!" she said forcefully as she'd been taught in a rape-prevention course she'd once taken at the YMCA, but the teenagers just laughed and smirked.

Liz tried to push her way past her tormentors. She could see the light on the other side of the pier and thought if she could just get there, she would be safe. She almost got through them, too, but then one of the boys, who seemed to be their leader, grabbed her by the arm and spun her around.

Terrified, she reached out and clawed his face. He

looked at her with surprise and then rage. He lifted his hand, which held a piece of steel bar, and struck her on the side of the head. It felt as if someone set off a big firecracker inside her skull. There was a flash of white light accompanied by a searing red pain, and she sank to her knees.

"Fucking ho," the boy snarled and grabbed her by the hair. He began dragging her up the beach, farther into the shadows beneath the pier.

The pain of being pulled by her hair and her fear of what would happen in the dark brought Liz partly to her senses. She stuck the whistle in her mouth and blew as she lunged up, scratching for his eyes.

She saw fear in his eyes and even dared to hope that she might fight her way to freedom. But then someone kicked her in the back, crushing the wind out of her and sending her sprawling headfirst into the sand. She pushed herself back up on her hands and knees. Then another firecracker went off in her head.

The next thing she knew she had been turned over on her back and someone was yanking her shorts off. "No, please," she begged. She couldn't see out of her right eye and her left caught only a blur of images as her dazed mind tried to reject what was happening to her.

"Hold her," the first boy shouted. Hands grabbed her shoulders and legs, pinning her to the ground as he got between her legs. She felt him trying to penetrate her and willed her mind to some other place where the world was still safe and good. The sun shone on a field as her daughter ran toward her laughing and her husband looked on.

The firecracker went off again. Then again. She drifted in and out of consciousness. Faces appeared. Some angry. Some frightened. Voices taunted her and urged each other to . . . *violate her.* "Yo, Des, your turn." Their voices sounded like crows in the cornfields of Iowa, where she'd grown up before she'd moved to New York to become a writer, fell in love at a Fleetwood Mac concert, married, had a baby, and named her Rhiannon.

"Fuck her, homes, ain't you a man?" There was a terrible pain on her right breast. She heard herself scream, but it sounded as if it was coming from some other woman.

There was a moment's respite. Then the first boy spoke again. "Hey, ratface, you want some of this bitch?"

Another voice entered her head. An evil voice, laced with malice. "Show you boys how to treat these bitches," the voice said. "If you want to teach them a real lesson, you got to fuck them dirty."

A man with a pockmarked face and foul, rotting breath leaned over and grinned in her face. Someone rolled her over. She felt the cool sand on her shattered face; it felt good and she wondered if these boys would now allow her to die. But the nightmare wasn't over. She felt herself penetrated again, ashamed to be used so horribly. Filthy, dirty, so much shame that she welcomed the new blows to her head, hoping that they would put her out of her misery. Die, she told herself.

In the distance, sirens wailed. The boys shouted words of alarm, indistinguishable from the screams of the sea-gulls and the whispering condolences of the waves.

Then the monsters were gone. She felt their running footsteps recede across the sand as she waited for death to release her from the humiliation and pain. But death was not so kind.

Slowly, painfully, she rose to her knees, then to her feet. She couldn't see much, just a light and a green moving field she knew was the water. Dirty. Filthy. She had only one desire—to cleanse herself before she let the sea take her.

They found her standing in the water up to her waist, scrubbing furiously between her legs, trying to wash away the shame of what the monsters had done to her. Someone summoned a police officer, who waded into the water to escort her back to shore.

When he got close, he had to look away for a moment to compose himself. Her face was covered by a sheet of blood, her left eye swollen shut, her right eye hanging half out of its socket. Her lips were split, a black hole where her front teeth had been.

She screamed when he first reached out for her arm and pulled away from him. "Please, ma'am, let me help you to someplace safe."

Turning a sightless face toward the officer, she'd cried, "Don't you know, there's no such place!"

1

HUGH LOUIS SHIFTED UNCOMFORTABLY IN THE chair next to the desk of the television talk-show host. He'd once played tight end for the semipro New Jersey Packers football team as he worked his way through law school. But those days were more than twenty years under the bridge, and the chair complained like a bitter housewife beneath his bulk.

As he waited for the taping to begin, Louis mopped away with a handkerchief at the interlocking streams and tributaries of sweat that coursed over his broad face. The stage crew bustled around, including an intent young woman who dabbed away at his host, Natalie Fitz, with last-minute applications of makeup to disguise encroaching wrinkles and a chronic fatigue that had settled in when she realized some years before that her chances of anchoring network news were slim and none.

Unless, she thought with a glance toward Louis, making nice with this fat shyster gets me an Emmy. Then who knows, maybe not the evening spot but one of the news magazines or a morning show. She turned up the wattage on her smile when Louis caught her looking. He returned it with the same show of teeth and lack of sincerity.

The other reason for Louis's prodigious amount of sweat was that he always started producing it when he was preparing to lie. It didn't matter that he lied all the time and, in fact, had made it the hallmark of his legal career. But his body never had gotten used to going along with what his mouth was saying. He guessed it had something to do with the strict Baptist upbringing his dear departed mother had beat into him while he was growing up poor and black in Brooklyn's Bedford-Stuyvesant neighborhood.

"Damn, it's hot in here. You folks never hear of air-conditioning?" he said to Fitz, adding a chuckle just to let her know he meant it in a friendly way. Like hell I do, he thought. Bitch probably had them turn up the heat to put me in my place. Well, won't be long, and I won't need the skinny old bag. Then we'll see who turns up the heat.

Louis never worried about the ethics of lying. He'd hated his mother and despised her for working at menial jobs—and for being dark as roasted coffee beans, whereas he'd inherited the milk-chocolate complexion of the father he'd never met.

As a kid, he'd dreamed of the day he could leave Bed-Stuy and his mother. Fortunately, his size and an early athleticism had been enough to get him a football scholarship at a small Virginia college. He'd hoped for an NFL career but an affection for fast food had buried whatever slim chance he had beneath rolls of fat. So he'd accepted his "wink and a nod" diploma given to less-than-deserving athletes at the school and moved on to Plan B. His mother had wanted him to join the ministry. "Like hell I will," he told her. "I'm going for where the jack is; I'm going to be a lawyer."

Subsequently, he'd been turned down by the finest law schools in the land. But a small, nondescript institution in New Jersey that faced probation with the national law school accreditation board had happily accepted him under its "nontraditional students" program and had even given him a partial scholarship. The Packers (regrettably not the team in Wisconsin) had paid him enough to handle the rest. He'd graduated with a law degree mostly by cheating and plagiarizing. But he'd already developed a reputation for playing the race card when things weren't going his way, so none of his professors were about to challenge him lest they find themselves defending a lawsuit instead of teaching about them.

Louis had perfected the art of sliding through holes to advance himself. He took and passed his bar exam in New York under a program that allowed for a certain amount of leniency for minority students, "recognizing that these tests have certain cultural biases that preclude such students from a fair opportunity."

His luck continued when he was snapped up by a mid-Manhattan white-shoe firm looking to enhance its positioning in the black community. He'd put in his time, taking advantage of his status as one of three young lawyers of color to work half as much as the young white attorneys, and for that matter, the other two minority colleagues. But then he'd noticed that while his color bought him a certain favoritism among the peons, he wasn't going to go much farther up the totem pole. The firm had only one black partner—an older, quiet, Harvard-educated tax attorney named Harvey Adams, who was about as black, in terms of how even he viewed himself, as Donald Trump.

Adams had been added to the partners list the same year that Louis was born. It dawned on Louis that he might be Adams's age before the next black would gain that distinction, so he'd quit to hang his shingle in Harlem and took his constituency with him.

When the firm's partners complained that he'd signed a no-competition contract and therefore had to return their clients to the firm's fold, Louis had gone to the newspapers and cried racism. The big white bully—who by the way had a glass ceiling when it came to minority partners—was trying to prevent the oppressed, young black victim from succeeding. It was his first experience with cultivating the media, which loved a race baiter nearly as much as it loved serial killers, adulterous politicians, and dirty cops. He rather enjoyed the experience and promised himself to employ the technique whenever necessary to achieve his ends.

Louis did not particularly believe that The Man was holding down his people. In fact, he thought a large percentage of his people were too stupid to walk their dogs. He much preferred the company of the fawning white liberals who peed all over themselves to coax him into accepting invitations to their parties—living proof that they weren't racists like those Nazis in the Republican Party. His monthly quota of invitations doubled after he started getting involved in politics and quickly made himself one of the top power brokers of the black vote.

Early on, he'd found it advantageous to keep a cadre of young black thugs on his payroll who could be counted on to show up at any staged event and work their way in front of the television cameras. They'd angrily denounce whatever Louis had decided and shout slogans and look for all the world like the beginning of a race riot, until Louis showed up to calm them down and bring peace to the situation. The white liberals, who feared unruly blacks the same way the antebellum South used to view a slave uprising, would then breathe a sigh of relief and extend their invitations so they could tell him in person that they were relieved they could count on his "voice of reason" when all looked lost. Their hearts spilling over with gratitude, they'd ask what could be done to prevent such further uprisings, which was his cue to suggest that they contribute to various charitable organizations in the black community. He didn't bother to tell them that most of these were controlled by his employees, who were adept at siphoning off the biggest share for his private bank accounts. Of course, a small number of "good works," as his hated mother used to say, served to keep up appearances but these were mostly used whenever the media needed a feel-good feature with some black faces in the photographs and videos.

As a result, Louis had grown fatter and richer, not necessarily in that order. He'd bought a palatial home on the Upper West Side—close enough to Harlem to appear to be still in touch with "my people," but far enough away to alleviate the fears of whites he invited to dinner at his house.

On occasion, someone in the black community—especially those pesky ministers who declined to be bought and were his biggest critics—would question his choice of neighborhood and friends. But he'd piously explain to his sycophants in the media and from friendlier pulpits that it was important for black men and women to see other successful black men and women living in fine estates as good as any white man's, and collecting fine art and finer automobiles. "I see myself as a role model for young men and women of my community. They see me and know there is no height to which they cannot aspire with hard work and perseverance."

Those who persisted in their criticism would find

themselves looking down from their pulpits into the angry eyes of those same young men who mugged for the television cameras. Nobody seemed to notice that an unusually high number of outspoken ministers and other conscientious community leaders became victims of crime—assaults and robberies, after which they tended to grow strangely quiet, although not always.

Such drastic measures weren't always necessary. Several ministers earned a better part of their "salaries" from monthly deposits set up at banks in their names, and were happy to invite him to deliver the occasional sermon—or call to action—in his fine, stentorian voice that added to the grandeur (as he saw it) of his three-hundred-plus pounds.

Louis kept a small, plain office in the heart of Harlem. It was the quintessential poor man's lawyer office furnished with chairs, desks, and tables that looked as if they had been taken from a high school cafeteria. He put in an appearance two days a week and did a certain amount of pro bono work, especially if there was a possibility of publicity. White cops shooting black teenagers. White slumlords evicting old Puerto Rican tenants.

Occasionally, he even managed to break into national headlines, such as during the case of a fourteen-year-old girl from the projects who claimed she'd been abducted by three white men who'd raped her and then branded her arm with a swastika before letting her go. Louis had appeared on the steps of 100 Centre Street with his arm draped around the girl, decrying "the racists in our midst" and lambasting the New York City police for not trying hard enough to catch the criminals.

During subsequent questioning, the girl had given conflicting reports. The NYPD spokesman indicated that the investigation was "ongoing" but that the BOLO (Be on the Lookout) for the suspects had been canceled. Louis held another press conference, this one outside his Harlem office, where he suggested that a "white, Catholic-controlled police department" was reluctant to pursue the case because of "racists in their own midst, and where that might lead." Sopping up a monsoon of sweat, he even suggested that the perpetrators were police officers.

"My client, who is only gradually recovering from this traumatic event—including, with the aid of a counselor, regaining memories she had understandably blocked—remembers that her assailants 'talked like police officers.' I'm not saying that they were police officers, but it is certainly a possibility." His Greek chorus of young hoodlums mugged ferociously for the television cameras and jeered a couple of cops who'd shown up to see why the crowd had gathered.

When it finally came out that the girl made up the story because she got pregnant by her twenty-one-year-old boyfriend and had simply been afraid to tell her parents, Louis did not offer an apology. Instead, he went on the offensive. The girl, he said, was the exception, not the rule.

"For every mixed-up child who tells a little fib to get out of trouble, there are hundreds of young black women who have been abducted and raped by the sort of men my client described, and the police do nothing."

Undaunted and logically incomprehensible, he then threatened to sue the City of New York because one of the detectives had slipped up and actually referred to the girl as "a liar" in the *New York Post*, which had, of course, used the statement as its main front-page headline. For once, J. Samuel "Settlement Sammy" Lindahl, the city's attorney known as Corporation Counsel, held firm under pressure from the Police Benevolent Association, the powerful police union, and because anybody with the vaguest idea of the law knew the city had no liability.

Although publicly he'd expressed outrage at Lindahl's refusal, privately Louis smiled, slicked back his heavily pomaded hair, and moved on. Didn't hurt to try. He laughed to himself.

Louis's favorite office, however, was actually in a Fifth Avenue high rise. The interior had been tastefully furnished in rich leathers, dark woods, and lots of polished brass by the city's hottest professional designer, who'd charged a cool million dollars for her services. That was where he spent the bulk of his working hours, meeting with his "money clients"—many of them white businessmen who merely wanted him to "smooth the way" for their ventures into the black neighborhoods of Manhattan, as well as across the rivers in Brooklyn and New Jersey.

Of course, such favors came with a price. After all, he had expenses that went beyond maintaining two law offices, the dozen or so classic automobiles, a condominium in Aspen, Colorado, that he rarely visited because he didn't really like snow, and frequent vacations in five-star hotels around the world. His most expensive possession, however, was Tawnee Renoso, a pretty little sixteen-year-old child of a black woman and a Puerto Rican man.

Louis was married. In fact, he'd been married since shortly after getting out of law school. Back then, Bobette Jones had been an attractive, light-skinned young woman who'd actually bought into his line that he was an idealistic lawyer out to champion the cause of poor people.

She'd borne him three children—none of whom

seemed to think much of him—but life with Louis had taken the life out of her. She seemed to have lost the weight he'd gained and was a disenchanted, dried-out husk of the woman she had once been.

There had been numerous women over the years but none had captured Louis's attention like Tawnee. He considered her his property; her father had been one of his clients, and when he couldn't pay, he'd offered up his then fourteen-year-old daughter.

Initially, the girl had been frightened and cried out in pain from his "attentions," but she was clever and had soon turned the tables. Two years later, he was paying for a penthouse apartment in SoHo and had just given her a BMW for her sixteenth birthday. Now she wanted a second one in a different color so as not to clash with some of the expensive clothing he bought her.

As for his wife, she was happy enough to let someone else have to struggle beneath his weight. She raised no complaints when Louis stayed out of the house for days at a time.

On the set of the television talk show, Louis closed his eyes and happily pictured the lithe, barely brown body of Tawnee. But his reverie was soon interrupted by the angry voice of the young man sitting on the other side of him from Fitz.

"What the fuck? Keep that shit away from me."

Louis turned in time to see his client, Jayshon Sykes, swat at the makeup girl, who was attempting to pat dry the sheen on his forehead. The girl nearly dropped her kit as she hastily backed out of range.

Summoning a "boys will be boys" laugh, Louis patted Sykes on his knee. "Now there, Jayshon," he said. "This pretty young lady is just trying to do her job. Remember what I told you about these people being our friends.

They're here to see that justice be done. Ain't that right, Natalie?" His chair screamed in agony as he turned his mass to look at the talk-show host.

Natalie hardly heard him. She was musing over opportunities lost and how to still find a way to the top. There'd been a time when she was a real beauty—the *New York Times*'s media columnist had called her "a sure thing for the big time." Then again, she'd slept with him for the publicity, just as she'd screwed every executive producer who might possibly help her achieve her dreams. But it didn't help. No man trusted a woman who faked orgasms so poorly that he was able to tell.

She had pretty much resigned herself to the fact that a late night local talk-show gig was as far as she was going to get. She'd even taken to hanging out at TriBeCa bars, hoping that some wealthy divorced doctor or stockbroker looking for a second chance would settle for a still good-looking, if fortysomething (she wasn't saying exactly how something), Number Two. But then a friend who owed her a favor had introduced her to Louis, and she'd landed the interview that all the major networks, including CNN and Fox, were clamoring for. In a few moments, she'd have an exclusive not only with Louis but the leader of "The Coney Island Four."

"That's right, Jayshon," Fitz beamed. "That's the job of the Fourth Estate—the press—keep an eye on government, especially an exploitative, racist justice system." She beamed at Sykes.

He returned her smile. "I'm sorry," he apologized. "It's just that when you are as young as I was, wrongfully accused but sent to prison anyway, you have to adopt a . . . how should I say this . . . a tough persona in order to deal with the sort of men who truly belong in a place like that and would do you unspeakable harm. I've been

under a lot of stress lately, and I'm so sorry if I reverted
to prison mentality."

Hmmm, Fitz thought. Articulate and well spoken. I
guess our researcher was right about him having been his
high school class valedictorian. Fitz smiled and tried to
let her eyes suggest what her mind was thinking. "That's
quite all right, Jayshon," she said. "Understandable, considering all you've been through. It's amazing that you've
done as well as you have and come out so . . . strong
and . . . I don't know . . . almost noble the way you handle
yourself."

He'd gone to prison a skinny, six-foot-three nineteen-
year-old, hit the weights, and come out ten years later at
250 pounds of muscle. He gave the television host his
most winning smile.

Fitz began daydreaming about a reinvigorated career.
She'd worked out an exclusive deal with Louis and had
already arranged to have her interview aired on the
national affiliate. The station's managers were also trying
to get her on *Larry King Live*.

The director called for everyone to take their places.
Fitz turned to the camera and put on her best "this is an
important story" face. In the chair next to her, Louis
wiped one last time at his brow and practiced his righteous scowl. Sykes practiced being contemplative,
thoughtful—the aggrieved young black man, set upon
by a racist police department and district attorney's
office, perhaps because he was too smart, too articulate,
and they'd wanted to slap him down. How'd the bitch put
it? Oh, yeah, noble.

Someone cued the techno music, as a stagehand
counted down and at the right moment pointed to Fitz.
"Good evening," she responded, looking at the camera,
"and welcome to this edition of *Brooklyn Insider.*" She

expertly stopped talking to one camera and turned to the next. "A little more than twelve years ago, a twenty-eight-year-old woman named Liz Tyler left her Brighton Beach home one morning and went jogging along the shore toward Coney Island."

On the monitor in front of her, the picture shifted to a scene of a long, wooden-legged pier that jutted from the sand out over the water. The camera zeroed in to an area beneath the pier, as Fitz continued her voice-over. "However, beneath this pier, Liz Tyler was brutally beaten, raped, and left for dead."

The camera zoomed in on Fitz's face. "That much is a fact. We also know there were no witnesses to what happened, except whoever attacked Mrs. Tyler. But Tyler suffered memory loss—probably due to the savage blows she received to her head that fractured her skull, blinded her in one eye, and left her in a coma for nearly three months."

The monitor now changed to old footage of a young Jayshon Sykes and three other black teenagers being led into a courtroom in handcuffs as Fitz droned on. "No witnesses, but that didn't prevent the New York City Police Department from identifying five young black men from Bedford-Stuyvesant—one of whom would become a witness for the prosecution—arresting them and, significantly, after several hours of intense questioning, eliciting alleged confessions to having committed this heinous crime. The four young men, who maintained their innocence—all of them fifteen years old when arrested, except for the eighteen-year-old Jayshon Sykes—were convicted nearly two years later of rape and attempted murder."

Fitz turned back to the second camera. "During the trial, defense attorneys tried to raise questions about the serious doubts they had regarding the confessions, saying that the police had coerced, intimidated, and threatened the boys. However, perhaps the most damning testimony came from one of the five original defendants, Kevin Little"—the monitor showed the thin, handsome face of a young black man—"who managed to work out a sweet deal for himself by turning on the others. Kevin Little was allowed to move to California, while his former friends were sentenced to thirty years in prison."

The monitor showed a file tape taken of the walls of Auburn State Prison with a few inmates wandering around in an open area beyond the fences and guard tower. "The irony is that Kevin Little was gunned down in gang-related violence three months later. But Jayshon and his codefendants—Desmond Davis, Packer Wilson, and Kwasama Jones—were sent to Attica, where they spent the next ten years behind walls and razor wire, guarded by men in towers with guns. And there they thought they would remain for the next thirty years of their lives, until one day this man"—the monitors flashed to the pock-marked face of a man with beady eyes and buck teeth, whose greasy black hair had been combed back, giving him the appearance of a rat—"Enrique Villalobos, stepped forward and confessed that he alone had committed this crime."

The monitors cut away to a taped interview with Villalobos, wearing a gray inmate jumpsuit and sitting in what was obviously a prison setting with a sterile, white cinder block wall. "All I can say is that a positive prison experience has left me a changed man," he said with a lisp to an off-camera interviewer. "I was a terrible sinner, but I have accepted Jesus Christ the Lord as my savior and know that I will be forgiven. . . . My conscience troubled me and so I have decided to come forward now to tell the truth, and that is I alone did these horrible things to that woman. I ask her forgiveness and that of the young men whose lives were stolen to pay for my sin."

The camera returned to Fitz, who had molded her face into a mask of moral indignation with a trace of anger. "During the trial, the prosecutors lightly brushed over the fact that the only DNA evidence found on the victim's body did not belong to any of the young men who had been charged. Instead, they chose to concentrate on the so-called Coney Island Four, presumably because they'd been involved in a minor altercation that night in the boardwalk area, as well as the questionable confessions.

"However, in a startling revelation, Brooklyn District Attorney Kristine Breman, who will appear on this show later this week"—Fitz had a hard time keeping the gloating look off her face . . . Emmy, here I come—"announced last spring that the mysterious DNA matched one man . . . and one man only . . . Enrique Villalobos.

"Hailed by civil libertarians as having made a 'bold move in the cause of justice,' DA Breman agreed to the demands of one of my guests tonight—noted Manhattan attorney Hugh Louis"—the camera panned to Louis, who nodded solemnly—"and released the Coney Island Four and followed that by exonerating the young men. The prosecutors who led the charge to convict the four teenagers and, it would appear, jumped to a tragic conclusion, have since been placed on administrative leave pending a full investigation of the Brooklyn Sex Crimes Bureau's actions, as well as those of the New York police officers and detectives assigned to the case."

Camera One cut to Fitz's face. "Not too close . . . soften the shot . . . we don't want those crow's-feet showing," the producer whispered into his mike for the cameraman. Fitz's expression changed to one of deep regret, as if what she was about to say offended her journalistic sensibilities. "We should point out that the prosecutors in this case—assistant district attorneys Robin Repass and Pam Russell—were asked to appear on this show, or to at least grant an interview in the interests of fairness. But regrettably, perhaps understandably, they've declined."

Fitz let the moment sink in and then turned to her right to face her guests as the camera panned back. She smiled. "Good evening, Hugh."

Louis allowed himself a small can't-we-all-just-get-along smile. "Good evening, Natalie."

Fitz shook her head. "I guess your counterparts from the Brooklyn DA's office didn't want to talk to us, but we're glad to see you and your client tonight."

Louis combined a laugh with a sneer. "And the liars shall be known by their . . . lies," he said, patting his forehead with his handkerchief and hoping that he'd gotten the biblical phrase right. "Perhaps they're afraid that the truth will be exposed beneath these bright lights."

Fitz nodded as if she'd just been listening to Solomon himself. She looked beyond Louis. "Indeed. And good evening and welcome, Mr. Sykes, we're glad you could join us."

Jayshon Sykes looked at the camera and smiled shyly. "Good evening, Ms. Fitz," he said. "And thank you for your interest in justice. I'm afraid not all of your counterparts in the media are as willing to admit that the justice system might not be as color blind as we'd like. Unfortunately, it cost myself and my friends ten years of our lives. Ten horrible years that can never be reclaimed."

Ten miles away across the East River, sitting on a swaybacked mattress in a dark, shabby hotel room on the island of Manhattan, a haggard, gray-haired woman recoiled from her television, clutching her stomach as if she'd been punched. She gasped and fumbled for the channel changer, but it slipped from her hands and bounced off the floor and under the bed.

She should have known to turn off the television when the pitted face of Enrique Villalobos had first appeared . . . *a positive prison experience* . . . but she'd turned away as if slapped. However, as though forced, she'd slowly looked back and then watched in horror as Jayshon Sykes smiled at the camera, and she looked into those eyes for the first time in ten years. . . . *Ten horrible years that can never be reclaimed.*

Unable to move or look away, she'd watched as the big black lawyer went on with comments about the "lazy white cops and venal white prosecutors" who had conspired to deprive four innocent young men "of their liberty and the flower of their youth." No amount of money could give them what had been stolen, he said, "but they will be asking—no, demanding in the interests of justice—$250 million to give these African-American men a fresh start and to punish the system that perpetuates the sin of racism."

As the man talked, a series of memories like slides from a projector flashed into her mind. She remembered waking up that morning when the world was still a good place . . . the warmth of her husband's body . . . the sweet-and-sour smell of her child.

After that the images grew more jumbled. She recalled jogging along the beach toward Coney Island. A pier, then shadows moving in the dark beneath the pier. Daylight on the other side, if she could just reach it. Hands reaching for her. Black faces . . . drunk . . . shouting . . . laughing. *"Hey, bitch, want some of this?"* The daylight on the other side of the pier. Safety. Hands groping, pulling at her clothing. Scratching at that face . . . the face on the television. Maybe not. I don't know. A brilliant flash of light, the horrible pain. Impossible to fight them all. Their voices like crows in the cornfields of Iowa . . . *"Fuck her, homes, ain't you a man?"* Violation.

The face of the other man from the television, a face cratered like the moon, only greasy. *"Show you boys how to treat these bitches. If you want to teach them a real lesson, you got to fuck them dirty."*

Violation . . . feeling so filthy, hoping they would kill her, disappointed when she realized they were gone and she was still alive . . . staggering into the ocean and washing and washing and washing and never getting clean . . . never again clean . . .

In the motel room, Liz Tyler's body shook as if she were being beaten again. The memory slide show stopped just in time for her to look again into Jayshon Sykes's eyes as he repeated his assertion—this time prompted by the fat man—that a terrible crime had been done to him and his friends. Another blow to the solar plexus. She couldn't breathe.

Tyler forced herself up from the bed and staggered toward the bathroom. She got only halfway there before she fell to her knees and vomited. Her stomach kept heaving as she hovered on her hands and knees above the growing pool on the filthy carpet. Finally, she had nothing left in her stomach and the dry heaves subsided. She shuddered and whispered to no one, "They're going to get away with it."

Saturday, December 11

ROGER "BUTCH" KARP LOOKED UP SHARPLY FROM his Sunday *New York Times* when the door to his Crosby Street loft in lower Manhattan flew open. A hooded figure stepped into the room accompanied by a draft of frigid air. He shivered but also felt a familiar warmth when the woman in the doorway stripped off her sweatshirt.

The woman, his wife, Marlene Ciampi, brushed a dusting of snow from her dark curly hair and stomped the moisture off her running shoes. She flung the sweatshirt with its faded Cal Berkeley logo at the coatrack; she missed but left it lying. Turning toward her husband, she blinked the moisture from her one good eye—the other having been lost many years before to a letter bomb. She caught the approving, puppy dog look on her husband's otherwise tough and craggy face and assumed a tough girl from Queens stance.

"Hey, whaddya staring at, ya big palooka," she snarled with just the right amount of sauce. "If you like it so much, why doncha take a picture?"

Karp laughed but kept looking. Twenty-five and some odd years earlier they'd both been neophyte assistant district attorneys for the New York County DA when a drunken roll in the hay after an office party had turned into an enduring love affair. The letter bomb had been intended for him—courtesy of one of the myriad of killers who would cross his path—but Marlene, jealously thinking it might be a note from his ex-wife, had opened it. The invasion of privacy had cost her an eye and a couple of pieces of her fingers, and one side of her face was laced with small white scars.

Karp knew that early on she'd wondered if he'd married her because he felt guilty about the injuries. But when his amorous intentions hadn't waned, and in fact grew more pronounced and eventually resulted in three children—twenty-one-year-old Lucy, who was currently working in New Mexico, and the twelve-year-old twins, Giancarlo and Isaac—she'd accepted that if there was one thing she could count on in her life, beyond being a lightning rod for danger, it was the constancy of his love for her.

There'd been a lot of rough spots along the way, both in their relationship and professionally—including enough run-ins with terrorists, psychopaths, mass murderers, and the usual scum of the earth to make a pretty decent action film. He wasn't quite sure if there was some sort of psychic target attached to his family's back or if it was just bad luck. Part of it was the job, but he knew plenty of prosecutors who'd led much quieter lives.

Marlene had eventually left the DA's office but, except for a brief foray into private practice, he'd remained, and that past summer he had been appointed to fulfill the term of District Attorney Jack X. Keegan, who'd jumped at the chance to become a federal judge.

Being the top law enforcement officer for Manhattan could certainly make a guy enemies big and small.

Just that past summer, he'd tangled with one of the wealthiest men in the country, a dilettante, white-shoe lawyer named Andrew Kane, who had appeared to be the runaway favorite to become the next mayor of Manhattan in that fall's election. At least that was the public's perception. However, Kane turned out to be a villain of Machiavellian proportions. He'd done his best to kill Karp and his family, but they'd escaped through a combination of good fortune and equally lethal friends. Karp, aided by a Manhattan grand jury, had charged and indicted Kane with capital murder. But the trial was still some months, perhaps even a year, away, delayed by the usual flurry of pretrial motions from Kane's lawyers.

Yet his job wasn't the only reason for the Karp-Ciampi marital discord that only recently had begun to turn the corner and appear as if the couple might weather the storm that had been tearing them apart. After leaving the DA's office, Marlene had gone through a number of incarnations. She'd created a firm that provided security for high-profile luminaries—such as movie stars, athletes, musicians, and diplomats—and became an instant multimillionaire when the company got bought by a larger firm that then went public with its stock. She currently owned a farm on Long Island that raised and trained Neapolitan mastiffs for security work, including defense and bomb sniffing. One of her newest protégés, a monstrous 150-pounder named Gilgamesh, was at that moment lying under the kitchen table keeping Karp's feet warm.

Outwardly Marlene could be flippant and casual about the violence that found her the way sharks follow blood in the water. However, psychologically she'd been deeply conflicted, a former Catholic school girl who could not totally justify her decision that if the justice system couldn't protect the helpless, then someone else had to—no matter what the personal cost.

Her husband was the opposite. The law, safeguarded by due process, wasn't something to follow when it was convenient. The law was sacrosanct, a thing of beauty precisely because of its rules. Yes, there was latitude within the law that a clever attorney could work with to his advantage—and he'd skirted the line himself on numerous occasions but never stepped over it. He also insisted that the lawyers who worked for him abide by the same standards. "Do it right or we don't deserve to win," he told them. So it had troubled him greatly that his wife skirted the law in a way he would never have allowed one of his employees to do.

Knowing what her actions were doing to him and haunted by her own conscience, Marlene had distanced herself from her family, especially after one of her efforts to exact revenge for the murder of a family in West Virginia that she had befriended had nearly gotten Giancarlo killed. She'd retreated to her dog farm and seemed on a path that would lead only farther and farther from her family in Manhattan.

However, Marlene heard about a program in New Mexico that used art therapy to save women who suffered from post-traumatic stress disorders—most of them the victims of domestic violence, although there were a couple who, like Marlene, had killed. She and Lucy, who herself was only just recovering from extreme sex abuse and torture by a psychopath named Felix Tighe, had left for New Mexico in early summer.

The program seemed to work wonders for Marlene— that and the friendship she'd developed with John Jojola, the chief of police for the Taos Pueblo. A Vietnam combat vet whose native skills at hunting and tracking had been used by the U.S. Army to stalk Vietcong leaders and kill them, Jojola had emerged from years of alcoholism to make peace with his own violent past. He'd recognized a kindred spirit in Marlene and had led her down the path he'd taken out of the darkness.

It was a better fall than it had been a spring. Surgery to remove a shotgun pellet from the blast that had nearly killed and blinded Giancarlo had been a success; he could see again, though there were moments when the disconnect between his eyes and brain acted up. Lucy was living in New Mexico, still working for a Catholic charity at the pueblo, and was apparently in love with some young cowboy she'd met.

Marlene was living at the Crosby Street loft again and seemed more at peace with herself than she had been for years. However, she'd warned Karp that while she felt as if she was making progress, she was not "cured."

"It's not as simple as that. Let's just say I'm in remission," she told him as she lay in his arms one night and he'd remarked on the change. "It's like a cancer. Maybe five, ten years down the road, if there are no more spots on the X-ray, I might be considered a 'survivor.' But like cancer, if it comes back, it could be worse than ever."

Karp was just happy to have her around as a wife, a lover, and the mother whom the twins had missed terribly. Watching her untie her running shoes, he thought she was still the most beautiful woman he knew.

The effects of the bomb had never bothered him. She was still a lovely woman with dark, curly hair framing her face, and he sometimes caught other men appreciating her classic Italian features. Her body had matured from the almost teenage physique she'd kept through three births; she was a little thicker around the middle, no matter how many sit-ups she did and miles she ran, and the once-perky tits no longer pointed up like flowers following the sun. But neither had they wilted, and if she had to work a little harder to keep that fine rear end as round and solid as a pair of bowling balls, he was well aware from her exuberance of the night that she was as passionate a lover as ever.

Karp especially loved to watch the way her hips moved when she walked, and she was walking toward him now with a half-smile on her face. "What's the matter, Karp, cat got your tongue . . . or maybe you're just too tired from your rather mild exertions last night? How about offering a lady a cup of that coffee and the sports section of the *Times*?"

Karp tilted his head toward the full pot of coffee. "For that unkind remark, you can help yourself, Ciampi," he pouted. "Mild exertions? I don't remember that there were any complaints last night."

"How could you? You rolled over and went to sleep as soon as you'd had your way with me."

"Lies . . . spurious innuendo and unsubstantiated rumors," Karp sputtered good-naturedly. The banter had been a part of their sex life from the beginning; neither took it seriously as neither had ever had cause to complain. Still, his "hurt look" had its desired effect, as Marlene circled around behind him, gently kissed him, and began massaging his shoulders, which elicited a deep groan of pleasure.

"Hey, don't just sit there while I do all the work," Marlene demanded, "tell me what's in the paper."

Marlene's command brought Karp back to the moment, and he remembered what he had intended to show her even before her wintry arrival. Usually he picked up the *Times* outside the justice building at 100

Centre Street at Dirty Warren's newsstand but had given in to the local newspaper boy's relentless campaign to at least have him deliver the Sunday paper.

Karp pointed out the top story of the day, which ran beneath the headline "Judge Backs Plaintiffs in the Coney Island Four Case." The city's last attempt to have the lawsuit dismissed had been denied by U.S. District Court Judge Marci Klinger. The Coney Island Four case would go forward unless the city settled.

Like most of the general public in the five boroughs, Karp had followed the story predominantly through the newspapers and television. There'd been a little of the intraoffice gossip and rumor between the DA offices in Manhattan and Brooklyn that floated around any big case, but he'd pretty much ignored it. He'd been flipping through the channels looking for a basketball game when he stopped to watch the *Brooklyn Insider* show. But he'd been so repulsed by Natalie Fitz's fawning over Louis and Sykes that he'd soon moved on to ESPN.

However, the newspaper story had sparked memories of the crime when it occurred some twelve years earlier. He recalled the horrific nature of the attack—young woman, set upon by a gang, raped, and nearly beaten to death—and how he'd felt a personal connection just because it had happened beneath the pier at Coney Island. He'd spent countless summer days at that beach, wandering the boardwalk with his buddies, riding the Ferris wheel at the amusement park and, best of all, wolfing down hot dogs at Nathan's Famous on the corner of Surf and Stillwell Avenues. He took it personally that a gang of vicious thugs had sullied the place.

He recalled that the trials had seemed pretty much a slam dunk. The perps had confessed, and they'd been linked to other assaults on the boardwalk that night. He'd given no more thought to it over the years, until the *Times* broke the story about the inmate who had come forward to confess that he had done the crime by himself. The inmate—Karp glanced at the newspaper for the name, Enrique Villalobos—had apparently "come to Jesus" and wanted to make it right.

When Karp first read about the confession, he'd rolled his eyes. Inmates were constantly finding religion, which they all apparently believed would help them out with the parole board. The fact that Villalobos was serving a true life sentence as a serial rapist/killer didn't change Karp's skepticism. Sometimes inmates confessed to crimes they didn't commit as a favor, or out of fear for another inmate, and thereafter received favored treatment by Corrections.

However, in this case, he'd been willing to concede that perhaps this time an inmate had told the truth when a little later the *Times* again reported—and the Brooklyn District Attorney's Office concurred—that Villalobos was a match for the DNA evidence found on the victim's clothing. It certainly warranted an investigation.

However, he was surprised when Brooklyn DA Kristine "Just call me Krissy" Breman immediately agreed to a motion filed by Louis to vacate the rape and attempted murder convictions of his clients. Karp figured that some details were being withheld that would explain the rush to the judgment. He was, however, disgusted when Breman appeared on the steps of the courthouse in Brooklyn with Louis and apologized for "this terrible miscarriage of justice."

Then again, the more he thought about it, the less surprised he'd been by her behavior. He'd known Breman almost as long as Marlene. They'd all joined the New York DA's office within a couple of years of each other, but Breman had almost immediately gravitated to management. He thought of her then and now as an empty pantsuit who'd never tried anything more challenging in her life than a misdemeanor Peeping Tom.

However, her family was connected with the Brooklyn DA, who gave her a sweetheart deal to become his spokeswoman and attend all the political functions he had long ago tired of. She'd schmoozed her way up the party food chain until her boss retired, when she'd been a natural with the clubhouse pols to assume the top spot at the DAO.

Karp had to hand it to her in one way; she could sidestep blame better than most matadors avoided a bull. Following Villalobos's confession and press conference, the press, as well as the demagogues and race baiters like Louis, had pilloried the former DA—a decent if burnedout man named Steve Colella—and the NYPD for the "racist railroading" of the poor young men. Breman had quickly gauged the sentiment and joined the chorus. Anxious to distance herself from any association with her predecessor, she had been outspoken regarding "this travesty of justice . . . which, unfortunately, occurred before my tenure or it would have been stopped in its tracks."

Breman had reminded the press that in her younger years with the New York DA's office she'd prosecuted sexual assault cases—a stretch, as she'd never actually gone to trial in the three months she was with the Sex Crimes Bureau. The "overzealous and callous prosecution" of the Coney Island defendants, she said, had "set back the course of sexual assault prosecutions a hundred years."

Along with the rest of the public, at least judging by the letters to the editor, Karp had assumed that the assistant DAs and cops had botched the case. The DNA evidence was pretty difficult to refute, and he assumed that even Breman would have taken a pretty good look at the case files, as well as questioned witnesses, including Villalobos, under oath before jumping on Louis's bandwagon.

One thing had bothered him, though, about the stories in the press. The two suspended prosecutors—Repass and Russell—were formerly protégées of his wife's when she ran the New York District Attorney's Sex Crimes Bureau. As they were junior assistant DAs, he had known them only in passing, but they had reputations as solid, aggressive litigators who'd modeled themselves after his wife. Only after Marlene left did they agree to cross the river and work for the Brooklyn DA, lured by the opportunity to start their own sex crimes bureau.

After the stories naming them broke, Marlene had refused to believe that they'd messed up. "They're as good, as thorough, and as honest as anyone who has ever come through that office."

But the Brooklyn DA didn't seem to have the same opinion. "Looks like your two ladies are going to take the fall for the Coney Island case," Karp said, and pointed to where the story noted that Breman had placed Repass and Russell on "administrative leave" until an investigation by her office could be completed.

Karp read the next paragraph aloud for Marlene. " 'An investigation,' Breman said, 'that will include aggressively pursuing any malfeasance on the part of her office staff or actions by members of the NYPD that resulted in "coerced false confessions" from four innocent young men of color.' "

Marlene stopped rubbing his shoulders and leaned forward to peer down at the newspaper. There was a file photo of her former assistants leaving the courthouse after the convictions ten years earlier. They looked satisfied, but there were no smiles or gloating; they had still followed her admonition, given when they were working for her, to remember Vince Lombardi's quote that he expected his players "to act like you've been there before" when they scored touchdowns.

"They may have made a mistake . . . it happens," Marlene said of the newspaper allegations. "But Breman seems awfully anxious to just let them swing in the wind."

Karp turned to a column he'd read earlier on the editorial page. "Listen to this: 'It is clear to us that the representatives of our legal system in this case—the prosecutors and the police officers—conspired to deprive these young men of their basic rights to liberty based on the color of their skin. Such indifference to the constitutional guarantee of a fair trial borders on the criminal.'"

Marlene gave him a sour look. "Since when do you quote editorials in the *New York Times*? Are we going to start believing the same paper that labeled you KKKarp?"

"I don't," he replied. "That paper lost its credibility a long time ago . . . after its liberal agenda left the editorial page and started showing up on page one. But a lot of people believe everything they read."

"I remember when the confession story broke last spring, there was a sidebar article about the victim," Marlene said. "Liz Tyler. Apparently, she suffered permanent brain damage that affected her speech, and she also has amnesia—she can't remember a thing about the attack or the assailants. She's like an 'inspirational speaker' that these rape-awareness groups trot out, but really, her life was pretty much ruined. She got divorced after the trial and lost custody of her little girl . . . something to do with a suicide attempt."

"I thought it was the Coney Island Five, not Four," Karp mused. "And why does the press always have to come up with idiotic names for these things? Like they're sports teams."

"Because it sells newspapers," Marlene replied. "And it *was* five, but one of them flipped, copped a plea, and testified against his comrades. If I remember correctly, he was later killed in a gang shooting."

"In Brooklyn?" Karp frowned. He couldn't recall the incident.

"No, somewhere in California. The story I read when this other joker confessed said the cops didn't think it had anything to do with this case. Just a drive-by . . . wrong time, wrong place."

Karp reached up and grabbed his wife's hands that still rested on his shoulders. "Sorry about Robin and Pam," he said. "I know you liked them."

Marlene withdrew her hands from his grip and moved around to sit down, elbows on the table and chin in her hands. She sighed.

Karp realized the conversation had just changed direction; this wasn't about the Coney Island case. "What's up, babe?"

She sighed again. "Nothing really. I just promised Dad that I'd stop by this morning to help a little with Mom, and I'm just not in the mood."

Karp waited to see if she wanted to go on. Marlene came from a close-knit Italian family and as the youngest, it had fallen to her to do most of the looking out for her aging parents. Despite her tough exterior, when it came to her mother and father she was still a little parochial school girl who was unsettled by the thought of her parents getting old. She tried to hide it, but he knew that she was disturbed to distraction by her mother's slow surrender to Alzheimer's and her father's growing inability to cope emotionally with his wife's ailment. Going to visit her parents at their home in Queens—formerly a pleasant experience that she'd welcomed as often as she could get away—was now something she avoided if possible. Only to beat herself up with guilt afterward.

Although he already knew how she'd answer, Karp suggested, "Call and say you can't make it. Find a better day . . . when you're feeling up to it."

Marlene shook her head. "No. Dad needs to get out of the house for a few hours. And there really aren't any 'better days.' In fact, it seems that she gets a little worse every day, and he gets a little angrier." She wiped at the tears that had formed in her eyes and smiled at him. "The boys still sleeping?"

He nodded. "Ever since the holiday break began, they've been staying up all night and sleeping until noon."

"Do you still have to go in today?"

He nodded again. "Yeah, I have a meeting with the next mayor of our fair city that he wanted at a time when there weren't a lot of eyes around . . . especially the press."

Marlene looked surprised. "The new mayor of Gotham wants to thank Batman for handing him the election by taking the Joker, Andrew Kane, out of the picture?"

Karp tried out his best comic book superhero voice. "No, ma'am. His honor knows that the Caped Crusader was simply doing what needed to be done in the interest of justice and the American way." It wasn't a very good impression, so he dropped the voice and continued, "It's nothing. He just wants a little quiet time to more than likely run the latest anticrime public relations campaign by me."

"Want me to call for the Batmobile?" she asked.

"No thanks, Cat Woman," he said. "I think I'll fly. I'm not fitting in my bat tights like I used to and can use the exercise."

3

AT LEAST THERE'S NO WIND, KARP THOUGHT AS HE left the five-story building on the corner of Grand and Crosby that housed the family loft. Sometimes gales blew up off the harbor and funneled down the stone canyons with such force that it could be difficult to walk. During the winter, the winds stabbed through the thickest coat like ice hooks, and the gray, overcast sky could make it seem colder yet.

Even on a day like this one, when the skies were bright blue and the air still, the temperature could dangle in the single digits. Karp pulled his long, dark-blue wool peacoat tighter around his neck and tugged a Russian Cossack hat down over his ears as far as it would go. The boys had bought him the hat for his birthday, and at the time he'd thought privately that he looked ridiculous in it and would never wear the thing. But now he was grateful for its protection and wished it could also cover his nose as he strode quickly south across Grand Street.

Despite the bite in the air, the walk was not an entirely unpleasant one. A few last snowflakes floated in the sunlight like leftover confetti from a parade and lent an air of authenticity to the Christmas decorations that hung in the various shop and loft windows along his route.

Karp loved this time of year with the wreaths and ribbons and the Hanukkah candles in the windows. Even the string of blinking lights the Chinese butcher at the corner of Centre and Canal had dangled around the row of plucked ducks in the viewing case brought back fond memories of holiday strolls with his parents to look at the lights and listen to the carolers in his Brooklyn neighborhood. He made a mental note to take the boys and Marlene, and maybe Lucy, if she made it home for the holidays, ice-skating beneath the Christmas tree at Rockefeller Center and to gawk like tourists at the holiday scenes in the windows along Fifth Avenue.

Centre Street on a chill Sunday morning was quiet, with only a few people scurrying from one destination to the next. Karp reflected that most of the wiser members of the public were hunkered down. But as he drew near Worth Street he saw that a small crowd of people, including several wearing dark blue coats with NYPD stenciled on the back, were gathered around a man who stood on a milk crate.

As Karp drew closer, he realized that the speaker was Dirty Warren, the guy who ran the newsstand where he usually bought his *Times* before heading into the courthouse at 100 Centre Street, which also housed his office. He would have recognized the vendor even if he couldn't see the long, pointed nose that protruded from the orange ski mask that otherwise revealed only a set of watery blue eyes beneath thick glasses and a blue-lipped mouth. It was the mouth that gave the owner away, not its appearance but what came out of it.

Dirty Warren had received his nickname, the only name Karp knew him by, because he suffered from Tourette's syndrome, a short circuit in his brain that was manifested by profanity-laced speech the likes of which was rarely heard away from sailors' bars. Karp sometimes suspected that Warren took advantage of his affliction to hurl invective at people he might not otherwise have dared confront. But proving it was difficult—sort of like demanding that someone in a wheelchair stand up to prove that he was indeed handicapped.

As he stood on top of the milk crate, Dirty Warren's diatribe had attracted the usual street people in their colorful array of cast-off garments and Salvation Army blankets, as well as a few curious tourists, who stood in slack-jawed amazement at the man's dexterity with foul language.

"Sh-sh-sh-shit, p-p-p-piss cocksucker. L-l-l-leave him al-l-lone!" Warren didn't normally stutter, as well as cuss, but it was d-d-damn cold. "D-d-didn't they ta-ta-ta-teach you pigs about the r-r-r-right of the pa-pa-pa-people to assemble or . . . ma-ma-ma-motherfucker vagina . . . the fah-fah-fah-freedom of speech at the academe-me-me? D-damn ass-wipe, ball-licker sons of wh-wh-wh-whores!"

Whatever had prompted the newspaper vendor to hold forth originally had now degenerated into a rant directed at the NYPD officers, who were trying to figure out a way to come at a large man they had surrounded.

Small wonder, Karp thought and smiled when he saw the man, whose massive head was covered with a filthy mane of dark curly hair that seemed to sprout over most of his face as well, and what wasn't covered with hair was nearly black with dirt and grease. The man was wearing what appeared to be four or five coats, the colors of which had long since faded. He'd stuffed his hair into a filthy Santa Claus hat and was waving his arms wildly as he shuffled back and forth in front of the cops like an enraged bear, which he resembled. He bellowed, "Back

ov, 'u fuggin' pigs. Let Warren 'peak. Freedom ov 'peech!
Freedom ov 'peech!"

The officers seemed reluctant to close and Karp knew
why. Even from the back of the crowd—maybe twenty
feet—he could smell the Walking Booger, another one of
the legions of homeless street wanderers he'd known for
years. Legend had it that Booger, whose explorations of
his nasal cavities with any one—and sometimes two at a
time—of his sausagelike fingers had earned him his nickname, had neither bathed nor washed his clothes in the
nearly two decades since he'd first shown up on the
streets. Not unless standing in the rain counted as a
shower or a visit to the laundromat. His breath alone
might have qualified as a weapon of mass destruction.
Every way he turned, the cops and the crowd on that side
took two steps back with horrified looks.

Karp would have walked on, but Warren spotted him
from his milk crate and yelled to him. "H-h-hey, Karp.
Would you p-please . . . scumbag piss drinker . . . explain
to New York's finest that th-th-there's such a thing as . . .
fa-fa-fuck me naked . . . a Constitution?"

One of the older officers with the chevrons of a sergeant on his sleeve turned to see whom Warren was
yelling to and looked relieved to see him. "Hey, Mr. Karp,
Sergeant Seamus, nice work this summer nailin' that
slimebag Kane and the slimebag cops who was doin' his
dirty work—gave us all a black eye," he said, removing a
glove and sticking out a big, meaty hand.

Karp shook the proffered hand. "Thanks, but there were
a lot more people involved than just me. Not to mention that
I think the reputation of the NYPD isn't going to be dic-
tated by a few bad apples."

"Thanks, I appreciate the sentiment," Seamus said with
a nod. He turned his attention toward Warren and Booger.

"Would you mind explaining to these gentlemen that they need to settle down before one of my boyos decides to end this 'peaceful assembly' by busting heads?" He nodded to a steroidal-looking younger cop who already had his night-stick out and was growing redder in the face with each pro-fanity launched from Warren's mouth.

Karp grimaced. "I'd call off the dogs, Seamus. The last time someone hit Booger—the big one there—that I know of, it was with a crowbar right between the eyes. Would have killed a cow. Instead it only made him mad enough to stuff his assailant—some skinhead bully who had a thing for homeless people—down a storm sewer. . . . Not to men-tion I don't know that your boy could get close enough without being overcome by the fumes."

Seamus wrinkled his nose. "Know what you mean. Still, we need to move this crowd along."

"I'll see what I can do," Karp replied. He turned and walked up to the soapbox orator. "Yo, Warren, come down from there. I need my paper."

Warren hurled a few more epithets toward the police, who shook their heads and moved on, then stepped down from his perch. Booger held up his arms as if to give him a hug. " 'arp, boy am I glad a see choo."

Karp sidestepped the hug and instead shook Booger's filthy hand, making a mental note to burn his glove as soon as he got home. "Glad to see you, too. What was all this anyway? The sergeant says his guys were trying to move people out from in front of storefront doors. They've been doing that since Tammany Hall."

"Yeah, piss face," Warren replied. "But they've p-p-p-picked up the pace, and on a Sunday morning in w-w-eather . . . ohhh SHIT! . . . like this, harassing street people like B-b-b-booger and the others when they're just t-t-trying to stay warm. It's all about the c-c-city's image . . . bitch son of a ba-ba-ba-bitch . . . so that the tourists won't have to be exposed to guys like Booger here. Ba-ba-but they don't want to do anything . . . lick my nuts . . . to help, just sh-sh-shove them out of sight, the darker the hole the better. Tiny-brained wipers of other people's bottoms."

Karp narrowed his eyes. "Wasn't that a line from a movie?"

"You . . . you . . . you tell me?" Warren grinned, playing their old game of "guess the movie" trivia.

"Monty Python and the Holy Grail," Karp said.

"Too easy, th-th-that one didn't count," Warren giggled while Booger guffawed.

Karp tried not to smile. No sense encouraging them. "Tell you what, if you can keep this on the QT, I'm on my way to meet with the new mayor, and if I get a chance, I'll quiz him about his plans for the homeless."

"Yeah, right," Warren said. "They're all the s-s-same. The more things change the more things remain the same . . . or . . . butthole . . . get worse."

" 'ah, worse," Booger chimed in.

"Well, we can always hope," Karp said. "I kind of like this guy."

"Yeah, we'll see. H-h-hey, you need a paper, right?" Warren said, as they approached his newsstand.

"Yeah, I need the *Post*," he said, handing over a ten. "Keep the change and maybe go get yourself and Booger a cup of coffee and a couple of doughnuts. And try to behave; the Cossacks are right around the corner waiting for you two anarchists to act up again."

Warren grabbed the bill and stomped off, muttering, with Booger shuffling alongside him, loudly repeating every third obscenity and raising his fist like a Cuban revolutionary.

Karp shook his head—never a dull moment in the Big Apple. He walked on past 100 Centre Street, the gray monolith that housed the city courts, the grand juries, the Manhattan house of detention—known affectionately as the Tombs—and the NY DAO.

He climbed the stairs and saw a familiar figure waiting for him at the door. "Why, Harry, what brings you to City Hall on a Sunday morning?" he asked.

Harry "Hotspur" Kipman was tall and thin to the point where he would have made a good Ichabod Crane for a stage production of *The Legend of Sleepy Hollow*. He had a pair of piercing blue eyes set a little too close together over an eagle's beak nose, but they saw through bullshit better than anyone Karp had ever known.

It was Karp who'd given him the nickname Hotspur for his temperament. Harry wasn't one to pull punches. He was a crusader against hypocrisy, and his directness was sometimes more off-putting than he intended. But he was at heart a good, gentle man with a dry wit and quick mind that made him a pleasure to be around.

Karp wouldn't have traded Harry, who'd become the head of the appeals bureau, for a dozen courtroom litigators. A lawyer's lawyer, Kipman had an almost total recall of the New York Penal Code, as well as the citations to major pivotal cases. He personally prepared the legal briefs and argued the People's case against the big-enchilada convicted murderers who sought their last legal refuge the system provided in the appellate process. His win-loss record was right up there with Ivory Snow's purity. He also insisted on "preemptive lawyering" by personally reviewing the high-profile or legally challenging cases before they went to trial. The idea was to advise the assistant district attorneys trying the case to create an error-free record.

However, it might have been Kipman's third role that Karp liked best. Harry was a sort of moral compass for the district attorney's office. He'd come to work for the legendary former DA Francis Garrahy about the same time Karp did and, like Karp, had adopted the old man's policy that the purpose of the district attorney's office was to seek justice, "not win at any cost."

If, in his running battle with evil, Karp was ever tempted to cut corners—and it wasn't often—Kipman was there to remind him, sometimes with nothing more than a look, that there was only one way to do things. The right way.

Kipman's black-and-white take on justice didn't make him a Goody Two-shoes, as some of the younger prosecutors sometimes thought of him. He could let loose a stream of profanity that would have made Dirty Warren blush, and there wasn't a defense or appellate attorney practicing in New York who went up against Hotspur Kipman without trepidation. They knew they had better come prepared and loaded for bear, or Kipman would tear them apart in front of a judge like an angry grizzly. But there was no one Karp trusted more.

"Got a call from the new mayor who said you'd be here, too, and that he wanted to talk to us both," Kipman said. He yawned nonchalantly. "There was nothing worth watching on the tube, sportswise anyway." Along with being a musical genius and legal god, Kipman was a sports fanatic. He collected sports memorabilia of all sorts and became a noted authenticator of baseball cards for devotees.

The pair was met at the elevator by a pretty, if officiously sincere and conservatively dressed, young woman who introduced herself as Mayor Denton's assistant press secretary, Alisa Mokler-Shreddre, and apparently took her duties and herself very seriously. "This way please," she said, and immediately turned on her heel and walked away with her well-formed butt twitching beneath a gray wool skirt.

Karp fastened on the retreating derriere for a moment before realizing he'd been caught. He scowled at Kipman, who was particularly adept at raising an eyebrow to imply guilt.

"Up yours, I got a daughter her age," Karp muttered under his breath. "And a wife who'd cut my nuts off if I ever so much as thought what you're thinking."

Kipman didn't reply. He just stared straight ahead with a half-smile on his lips and the eyebrow stuck at its zenith as Ms. Mokler-Shreddre escorted them to a door on which were the words *Mayor's Office,* where a clean-cut and equally serious young man was scraping the current officeholder's name off with a razor blade.

Michael Denton had won the election handily in November but wouldn't officially take office until January 1. However, the current mayor, who'd declined to run for a second term when he thought his opponent was going to be Andrew Kane, was in a hurry to vacate the premises and had invited his replacement to begin the transition process immediately after the election. He'd even allowed Denton to move into the main offices while he vacated to a smaller suite.

Therefore, Mayor-elect Michael Denton was sitting behind the big mahogany desk with the seal of New York City on the front when Karp and Kipman were shown in. Not for the first time, Karp noted that the man was the spitting image of one of his oldest friends in the city, NYPD Homicide Bureau Chief Bill Denton, the mayor-elect's brother. Bill had ten years on his sibling, but both men had large, square heads that looked as if they'd been chipped from blocks of stone, and wide, friendly Irish faces.

Like his brother, Michael had originally followed the family tradition of joining the thin blue line of the NYPD. But his career had been cut short by a shotgun blast from a robber—whom he'd killed in the gunfight—that forced the doctors to amputate what remained of his left leg. After he recovered, he didn't mope around feeling sorry for himself or climb inside a bottle but went back to school and earned his business degree, which in turn he'd used to buy, refurbish, and turn profitable a number of pubs in Irish neighborhoods throughout the five boroughs. Then he'd thrown himself into the other traditionally Irish business in New York: politics. First as a block organizer, then party leader, followed by several terms as a city councilman, and then—mostly because no one else wanted the job—as the soon-to-be mayor of Gotham.

Michael Denton was as surprised as anyone to now be sitting in the high-backed leather chair behind a desk festooned with the emblem of the City of New York, while his wife of thirty-plus years happily waited for the day the current first lady—who was somewhat more reluctant to give up the trappings of power than her husband—got the hell out of Gracie Mansion. He'd essentially been regarded as cannon fodder by his own party when Kane announced his candidacy and the incumbent decided against running. But then along came Butch Karp, and suddenly Denton stood alone in the field. The demoralized opposition party had hardly put up a fight, which Karp figured was the only way an essentially honest man was now in office.

Michael Denton's eyes were not quite as blue or intense as Kipman's, but they indicated a shrewdness that told Karp that very little escaped the man's attention.

He'd liked Denton's businesslike campaign, which had been devoid of flashy slogans and meaningless promises that couldn't have been kept.

Instead, the man had spoken with pride about how the people of New York had reacted following the devastating attacks of 9/11 and said he now wanted to harness that spirit to show the world that New York was "devastated by our losses but not defeated by hatred, nor daunted by cowards." It was as close to a slogan as he'd come, and he spent most of his time working the meeting halls and churches and going door to door, talking to people about the practical things he wanted to accomplish: more cops walking the streets, and schools that were safe for their children to attend.

Karp didn't mind that some of Michael Denton's speeches seemed to have been lifted directly from his own modest initial efforts at campaigning for the next year's district attorney's race. The message is a good one, he thought, and the more people who buy into it, the better off we'll all be.

Michael Denton rose from his chair and came from around the desk to shake their hands and point to chairs, inviting them to have a seat. When they were all sitting, he asked Karp how his campaign was going—"great, I guess"—and Denton said that he hoped that Karp would win "so that we get a chance to work together. In the meantime, whatever this office can do to help make the city safer, just ask."

Karp thanked him.

"Hate to be too cliché," Denton said, "but I suppose you're wondering why I asked you here today."

Harry chuckled but remained mute and stared at the fingernails on one hand as if he'd suddenly discovered a hangnail. Butch spread his hands and said, "I'm sure it wasn't to ask me about how my campaign was going, but I figured you'd get to it in good time."

Denton laughed, then leaned forward and pushed a button on the intercom. "Alisa, would you show our other visitor in, please." Mokler-Shreddre must have been waiting with her hand on the doorknob because Denton hadn't even settled back into his chair when the door opened.

Karp looked at the man who entered and this time it was his turn to raise an eyebrow and leave it there. It wasn't that he was displeased to see Richard Torrisi, another former cop he'd known since they were all wet-behind-the-ears crime fighters. But Torrisi had quit the force, gone to law school, and was now the attorney for the Police Benevolent Association, one of the most powerful unions in the city. And over the years, Karp had had his run-ins with the union, which tended to react like any organism when poked—by curling up in a defensive posture—such as on the few occasions he'd prosecuted dirty cops. But he had his union supporters, too, and had always liked Torrisi, even when circumstances put them at loggerheads.

"Hey, Butch, good to see you," Torrisi said, walking over to shake hands.

Karp stood, wincing when a shot of electricity went through his bum knee, and gladly took the hand. He noticed that the once coal-black and wavy hair was now mostly silver, but the brown eyes were just as sharp above the Roman nose. He pointed to Harry, who had also stood. "Dick, I don't know if you've met my appeals division head, Harry Kipman."

Torrisi held out his hand. "Only by reputation."

Karp, noticing that Harry actually blushed at the compliment, filed it away to tease him about later. He knew his colleague was supremely confident in his abilities, but he had always preferred to work in the background, pitting his mind and knowledge of the law against another like-minded attorney out of the public eye.

Denton cleared his throat and the other three men turned toward him, then took their seats. "Sorry about the secrecy, Butch—part of it's that I'm still not here in an official capacity, but there's more to it than that as you'll see in a few minutes." He paused but as there was no reaction, he went on. "I asked Mr. Torrisi to meet us here because of my concerns about how the so-called Coney Island Four case is being handled. Have you been following it in the press?"

Karp looked at Harry, who'd resumed studying his hangnail, then back at Denton and shrugged. "Somewhat, I suppose, like any other citizen who gets the newspaper and has a television."

"And your impression?" Denton asked.

Karp noticed that the mayor-elect and Torrisi seemed to move forward in their seats waiting for his answer. "Well, if I were to believe everything I read or hear— and I do not—it would appear that the NYPD and the Brooklyn DA fucked up, which means that the city is in trouble with this lawsuit."

Denton pursed his lips, then nodded. "Glad to hear you don't believe everything you read. In fact, whether it's the newspaper or television, neither you nor anyone else in this city is getting the truth, which is why I've asked Mr. Torrisi—"

"Dick is good enough, your honor," Torrisi interjected.

"Dick it is, and it's Michael to you, so quit with the 'your honor' shit." Denton continued, "Which is why I've asked Dick to give it to you straight this morning."

As Denton spoke, Torrisi rose and walked over to the

window as if he were preparing his speech. He looked out for a moment, then turned to face the other men. "I'll try to keep this fairly short though I feel I pretty much have to lay it all out chronologically so there are no mis-understandings. So I'm sorry if any of this is redundant. On the night of May 19, 1992, five young black men from Bedford-Stuyvesant—Jayshon Sykes, Desmond Davis, Packer Wilson, Kwasama Jones, and Kevin Little—took the bus from their neighborhood to Coney Island, where they consumed a large amount of beer and smoked marijuana to psych themselves up for a night of what they called 'wilding.'

"Over the next few hours, they harassed and assaulted a half-dozen people who had done nothing more than be in the right place at the wrong time, including an elderly Korean immigrant, Mr. Lee Kim, who was robbed and then beaten so badly his skull was fractured. We know all this because the so-called Coney Island Five—which became Four when Kevin Little was later shot and killed—admitted to these crimes at the time and haven't tried to recant. Plus, Mr. Kim lived and was able to iden- tify the suspects from live lineups, especially Jayshon Sykes, who he said was the man who hit him with a piece of steel bar. When the crowds finally went home, the sus- pects decided to wait for the dawn beneath the pier, where they continued to drink and get high.

"On the morning of May 20, a twenty-eight-year-old Brooklyn housewife and mother named Liz Tyler got out of bed, kissed her still-sleeping husband and her child, and went for her daily jog along the boardwalk and beach at Coney Island. It was a beautiful morning, unseasonably warm . . . low tide and a red sky in the east where the sun was just coming up. Her path took her to the pier, which she intended to pass beneath."

As Torrisi spoke, Karp could picture the scene. He could almost hear the sound of seagulls and the whispering rush of small waves over the sand. But his pleasant childhood memories were soon shattered by Torrisi's account of the attack on Liz Tyler.

"We don't know . . . because she doesn't remember . . . but Liz may have ignored, or didn't see, the danger when she approached the pier where these poor, innocent young men we've been watching on television were lurking."

Torrisi paused and seemed to find it difficult to go on. Man, he's tied up in this one, Karp thought, but before he could give it more reflection, Torrisi started talking again.

"We don't really know all of what happened next or in what sequence. As you may have read, this time accurately, Liz Tyler suffered head injuries during the attack and can't remember anything about it. However, several witnesses heard a woman screaming and men shouting from the direction of the pier about that time of the morning.

"These folks were mostly other joggers and a few beachcombers, but they weren't about to inquire, not even after they saw five young black men—and one non-black we were never able to identify—running away from the pier. I suppose we're lucky that one witness finally did call the cops, but by the time they arrived, a bloody, badly injured Liz Tyler was standing in waist-deep water trying to wash herself. That she was able to stand at all and simply hadn't fallen over and drowned was something of a miracle. Her skull had been fractured by a blow from a blunt object, another blow had crushed the orbital bone around one eye, permanently blinding her on the left side, her nose was broken, and several of her teeth had been knocked out. She'd been bitten, stomped, and raped both vaginally and anally."

"This blunt object happen to be a piece of steel bar?" Karp asked, his jaw starting to ache from setting it so hard as his anger simmered.

Torrisi held up a hand. "If I may, let me get to that in a moment. Sorry if this is going on too long, but I still feel it's necessary. Liz Tyler was taken to the hospital for a standard rape examination and to be treated for her injuries. The doctor who examined her reported that she exhibited the signs—the tearing and bruising—of forced sexual intercourse. Unfortunately, she'd done too good a job of washing herself with seawater, and DNA samples from her body weren't available. However, one sample— a mixture of semen, blood, and fecal material—was recovered from her sweatshirt, where apparently one of her attackers wiped himself afterward."

"The sixth man . . . Villa-something," Karp said.

Torrisi nodded. "Enrique Villalobos. But again, I'll get to him in order. If you've been reading the newspaper accounts and watching television, you've undoubtedly heard that brutish cops coerced and intimidated these Boy Scouts into confessing to the rape and attempted murder of Liz Tyler. Never mind that these same paragons of virtue also confessed to the assaults of the half-dozen others—of course, they've already served the sentences for those crimes."

Torrisi stuck his hands in his pants and rocked back on his heels. "I'm going to cut the story a little short now and leave it for Mayor Denton—Mike—to explain why I asked for his help and why he asked you here. But I want to finish by assuring you that the officers and detectives in this case followed procedure and kept to both the spirit and letter of the law."

Torrisi looked down at his feet for a moment before looking up. "I know that to be a fact because I was one of the detectives. And I know I did everything I could to make sure I didn't foul up this case by giving these guys some way out on a technicality or because I abused someone's rights. You would have been just as careful if you'd seen her like I did a couple days after the attack—her head swollen up like a basketball, her face all yellow and purple. . . . The docs were great; they fixed her up pretty good and the swelling went down, but doctors can't fix everything.

"As the lead detective in the case, I got to know her pretty good. The trial was real tough on her, she couldn't remember much of anything, but these fuckers would turn around and grin and leer at her whenever the jury was out of the room. She became more and more withdrawn until I don't think she cared what happened in the courtroom. Her husband, a real good guy, tried to stay by her, but she pushed him away and for a while wouldn't even see her kid.

"After the trial, I hoped she'd start to come around and for a while it looked like she might—she wouldn't go home, but she started seeing her daughter on weekends. That is until the day she took the kid, Rhiannon was her name, down by the pier, and while the kid was playing in the sand, Liz swallowed a bottle of Valium. Someone saw the little girl crying next to the woman who wasn't moving; otherwise Liz might have finished the job for the Coney Island Four. As it was, her husband divorced her and got full custody of the little girl. I hear he's living in Colorado or someplace like that now."

Torrisi looked up at Karp, who saw the tears glistening in the man's eyes. "Anyway, Butch, we got those guys fair and square and nailed their asses to the wall. Now they're going to get away with murder—maybe not in the traditional sense but they took Liz Tyler's life that morning as surely as if they'd killed her right then and there."

"What about Villalobos?" Kipman asked.

Torrisi nodded. "We always knew there was a sixth man. The DNA on the sweatshirt didn't match any of the five other guys. But we didn't try to keep it a secret. The ADAs—Robin Repass and Pam Russell—turned over the test results with all the rest of the exculpatory evidence to the defense. During the trial, the defense even tried to argue that the "missing man" did it all. Our argument was that just because we didn't have the sixth guy, it didn't mean the other five weren't guilty as sin. But thank God, we had the confessions videotaped. The jury only deliberated for less than two hours—a lot of it, from what I understand, taken up just filling out the paperwork on all the counts. Now, here we are only twelve years and change later and these guys have been set free based on a lie. And to pour salt on the wound, they may win a couple million dollars or so that could have been used for more cops and safer streets from the likes of these pieces of shit, excuse my French."

Karp waited a moment to make sure that Torrisi was done. "Okay. Sounds like the city has a defense . . . the best defense . . . the truth," he said. "But you didn't call me down here to hear what you already know. What else can I do for you?"

Torrisi looked at Denton, who picked up the thread of the conversation. "Actually, we'd like you to do a bit more than that. The reason I asked Dick to spell out the whole story was I was hoping it would persuade you to agree to a favor I'm asking. I'd like you to look over all the evidence, draw your own conclusions, and if you agree that Dick was straight with you regarding this case, I'd like you to represent the city in this lawsuit."

For a long moment the only sound in the office was the clanging of the old radiator that heated the room. Then Karp let out his breath and leaned forward. "Let's just suppose that even if there was nothing preventing the district attorney for Manhattan—whose responsibility it is to prosecute criminal cases, not represent the city in civil lawsuits—you have Corporation Counsel Sam Lindahl, who is paid to represent the city. He seems to be a competent attorney."

Denton shook his head. "He doesn't work for me yet, and I believe that Lindahl is going to recommend a settlement before I'm sworn in. What's more, I don't like him, I don't trust him, and I look forward to getting rid of him and appointing my own man as soon as I'm official. But that may be too late. I want to fight this case—not just to save taxpayers the money but in the interests of justice. I think I can pull some strings with the outgoing mayor to stall any attempts to have the city agree to a settlement, but the trial is set for late January, so we'll be under the gun to be ready after I toss Lindahl out on his ass."

Torrisi added, "Maybe he senses his time is about up, but it still doesn't explain why Lindahl has been in such a big hurry to move this toward a settlement. What's more—I'm, by the way, here without the knowledge or approval of my PBA bosses—for some reason the union and the NYPD brass, especially those in internal affairs, seem to have decided to let the officers and detectives involved in the case take the fall without a fight. The guys who are still on the force have been suspended, though officially they're calling it 'administrative leave.' And, of course, Robin and Pam are already being lined up for the firing squad."

Karp interrupted, "If you're planning on stalling for

your swearing-in anyway, why not have your own Corporation Counsel take the case?"

"Fair question," Denton said. "I have a great guy to step in as Corporation Counsel, Brad Bradberry, good ol' Georgia boy who came to the big city. Great civil attorney, but the way I see it, this is going to be a repeat of the criminal trial, so I want the best prosecutor I can find. You. And to be honest, we're taking a lot of hits in the public relations campaign from Hugh Louis—all the press has been one-sided—and if we're going to find a jury that isn't ready to open the city coffers and make millionaires out of rapists, we need to trot out our own big cannon . . . someone whose name will at least give us a chance of finding an open-minded jury."

"Well, it's all very interesting," Karp admitted. "And I appreciate the votes of confidence. If what you say is true, and I believe it is, it really burns me to think these pieces of crap are going to be paid for what they did. But even if I wanted to, I don't think I could legally take on a civil case while I'm the sitting district attorney."

Karp noticed how Denton and Torrisi turned to look at Kipman. Aha, he thought, *et tu Brute*, a plot!

Kipman looked at him and quickly up at the ceiling. "Ahem, well, Butch," he said, reaching up to adjust the half-moon reading glasses on his nose. "Apparently, you can. We . . . um, I, did a little research and, um, apparently the governor has the authority to appoint you as special counsel in this matter. It seems that because you were appointed by him to replace Keegan, rather than elected, he can also appoint you as special counsel on this case. Officially, as the interim DA, you are working at his pleasure, not the electorate's."

Karp couldn't help but be amused by Kipman's unusual discomfiture. "So Harry," he rubbed it in, "apparently you've been plotting behind my back? I thought you said you didn't know what this was about?"

Kipman swallowed hard, his Ichabod-like Adam's apple bobbing in his throat, but he nodded and adjusted his glasses again. "Well, um, technically what I said was that I got a call from the mayor who said you would be present and that he wanted to talk to us, which was the truth. But ah, yes, I've had a previous conversation or two with Mr. Denton and Mr. Torrisi and, um, it's a no-brainer that you are the best man for this job, and they enlisted me in their, um, well, I guess you could call it a plot."

Denton chuckled. "Don't blame him, Butch. I've known Harry for a long time and knew that if there was some legal way to do this, he'd know about it or could find it. I approached him and asked him to look into this possibility because I knew you might not believe me or Dick. But I also swore him to secrecy until you and I could get together without the press being around to wonder what the DA and mayor-elect were discussing with one of the former detectives involved in this case."

The room fell quiet again. Karp gazed up at the ceiling; Torrisi stood near the window looking at the gray day outside; Denton kept his eyes on Karp; Kipman stared at his fingernails again. At last Karp sat up, but he shook his head. "I'm sorry, gentlemen, but I don't think you need me, and my job is prosecuting criminals for the people of New York City."

Torrisi started to say something, but Denton held up a hand to silence him. "Look, do me a favor, read the evidence, then make up your mind. If you still feel you can walk away from this, then no hard feelings, we'll get someone else."

With the other three men looking at him like dogs

waiting for someone to throw a stick, Karp exhaled. "Okay, I'll take a look and let you know. I doubt I'll change my mind, but maybe I'll be able to help you or whoever you find with the strategy."

The meeting ended with a round of handshaking. A few minutes later, Karp was walking north on Centre Street when a Yellow Cab pulled up on the other side of the street and a tall, blond woman hopped out. She waved as she ran across the nearly deserted street toward him. "Hiya, Butch, imagine finding you here. Heard you just came from City Hall. Imagine that . . . and on a Sunday . . . and my sources tell me the mayor-to-be and a couple of other interesting folks were there, too."

If Karp could have run away with any chance of success, he might have started sprinting. But he knew Ariadne Stupenagel would just have followed him all the way home.

Loud, brassy, obnoxious, and persistent as lice, Stupenagel wasn't the worst journalist he'd ever met; in fact, if put on the rack or jabbed with a red-hot poker, he might even have admitted that she was pretty damn accurate and fair in her reporting. He also knew she was fearless and indefatigable in her pursuit of a story.

That past summer and fall, she'd done a series of four stories for the *Village Voice* based on what was supposed to be the rather ordinary life of a district attorney. While she did a good job on it, she was still *one of them*. The media. The ink-stained, hollow-eyed wretches who lied and misinformed depending on what was in it for them. She'd even managed to seduce his aide-de-camp, Gilbert Murrow, which made him nervous as all hell about their pillow talk.

"Hello, Stupe," he said with the least enthusiasm he could manage. He knew she wouldn't take the hint, but he wanted to let her know that he wasn't pleased about being spied on.

Ariadne fell into step beside him. "So want to tell me what's up between you and hizzoner-to-be?"

"Nope."

"Oh, then that was an admission that you met with Mr. Denton?"

"Nope."

"You're not going to tell me much of anything, are you?"

"Nope."

They'd reached the entranceway to 100 Centre Street, and Karp pulled up and faced the reporter. Stupenagel had her usual irritating "I know more than you think I know" smirk on her face, but he wasn't giving in.

"Sorry, Ariadne, you're going to have to go find some other mouse to torment today. This is where we part ways. I'm going inside."

Ariadne looked hurt. "That's cold, Karp. I thought we had a great working relationship and here you're not even going to invite a girl in to get warm."

"Nope," he replied, and walked up the steps where a security guard held open the door for him.

"You know I'll find out," she yelled before the door closed, but he didn't turn around.

Karp smiled. She probably will, he thought. Doesn't matter, I won't be getting involved in this. He took the elevator up to his eighth-floor office and let himself in. Flicking on the light, he pulled up short.

In the middle of the outer office was a mountain of boxes all marked in black Magic Marker "People v. Jayshon Sykes et al."

He sighed. Why is it everybody seems to know me better than I know myself? Well, I don't want to leave these here for the secretary to find in the morning. The newspapers and television stations would have a field day if word got out.

An hour later, he'd carried all the boxes into his inner office and stacked them in a corner with the telltale lettering against the wall where it couldn't be read easily. But he didn't open them. Instead, he put his coat back on, tugged the Cossack hat around his ears, and left the building. As he headed north toward home, the wind pushed him along, adding to the feeling that he was being swept along in a current he couldn't see or control.

4

MARLENE DABBED HALFHEARTEDLY WITH HER
paintbrush at the canvas on her easel. She couldn't quite
get the dark green–gray ocean around the pier right,
though she was reasonably satisfied with how she'd
roughed in the Coney Island Ferris wheel in the foreground of the painting.

The day had fortunately warmed up quite a bit since the
morning, but the sun was weakening and clouds were moving in; she was still starting to feel the cold seep beneath
her parka as she stood on the boardwalk. A little hot tea
would hit the spot, she thought, recalling the Russian teahouse she'd seen when she arrived in Brighton Beach a
quarter mile or so down the boardwalk from where she
had set up her easel.

She was working on her latest assignment in the
painting course that she was taking through New York
University. "A landscape," the professor had demanded,
"only I want you to work objects into the foreground to
get better acquainted with depth of field." Hence the
Ferris wheel . . . and she planned to insert a beach-

comber between it and the distant pier. It was really too cold to be painting; she kept the tubes of acrylic paints in a shirt pocket inside her parka but could put only a dab on her palette at a time or it would stiffen too much to use.

Marlene didn't really know why she'd chosen this location. Probably because of the discussion she'd had with her husband that morning about the rape case. But she'd also needed to take her mind off her visit to her parents' house that morning and she didn't want to go home.

Her parents still lived in the same house in Queens where she and her five siblings had been raised for most of their lives. It was a modest four-bedroom, three-story (including the basement) brick that epitomized the post-war era in which it was built—solid, family oriented, a celebration of middle-class values. There was a small backyard where her father had erected a metal swing set, taking inordinate pride in how he'd used Folger's coffee cans filled with cement to anchor the legs. It was still there—although rusted and unusable, her father had never been able to bring himself to take it down.

All of her life her parents had tended to their home and yard as proof of a good life well spent. But lately she'd noticed the signs of neglect: peeling paint inside and out that her father would never have allowed in bygone days; dirty windows; and little things that didn't work, like doorknobs. The gardens that her mother would have in the past carefully cleared of detritus and turned with fresh compost in preparation for the next spring were filled with the golden-brown husks of weeds, leaves, and bits of paper and other trash left by the passing wind.

When she entered the house, she found her father panicked as he trotted around, looking beneath couch cushions and under furniture. "My car keys," he said, his voice choking with tears, "I can't find them. Help me find them, Marlene."

"What's the rush, Pops? What's the matter?" Marlene asked, unsettled by the wild look in her father's eyes and the tears that rolled down his cheeks.

"Your mother, she's gone," he shouted. "I think she wandered off again . . . and in this cold she'll freeze to death." He overturned another cushion, and not finding his keys, began to sob.

Marlene moved quickly across the room and put her arms around him. "It's okay, Pops," she said. "When was the last time you saw her?"

Although she was determined to remain calm for her father's sake, there was some cause for alarm. Her mother suffered from Alzheimer's, and of late she'd taken to leaving the house—ostensibly to visit a neighbor or check on her gardens—but once outside she'd forget where she was going and then where she'd come from. She'd just wander off and was not always properly clad for the weather, which on a day like that one could be dangerous for an eighty-four-year-old woman.

"Maybe an hour ago," her father said. "I went back to our bedroom to take a little nap. . . . I'm so tired, so tired . . . she keeps me awake, you know, just gets up out of bed and wanders around the house. I just wanted a little nap. But when I woke up she was gone. Mary, Mother of God, please help me find my keys."

Marlene grabbed her father's hands and forced him to look into her eyes. "Pops, look at me . . . have you looked everywhere in the house?" Once they'd found her mother curled up in a ball in the linen closet; she said she'd just been looking for someplace safe from a mysterious "them" who were watching her.

Her father nodded. "I've looked everywhere . . . everywhere." But the pressure of Marlene's hands had the desired effect of helping him calm down. He brightened. "Except the basement," he said. "She hasn't gone down into the basement in years, but maybe . . . would you check the basement for me?"

Marlene gently guided her father to his favorite chair and told him to stay put. She then went to the doorway leading down into the basement. As a child she'd been afraid to go down into the musky, dark, damp basement, which was more of a root cellar. She was sure that if she walked down the wooden steps, something would reach through and grab her ankles . . . and that would be that, she'd disappear, never to be heard from again. The recollection sent a chill down her spine.

Get over it, Ciampi, she scolded herself. No monsters were down there, at least not the type that carried off little girls. A monster was carrying off her mother, but it was not dangerous to Marlene. She stood at the top of the stairs and, listening carefully, thought she heard some sort of furtive sounds coming from below. Putting aside childhood fears, she walked down the stairs.

A below-garden window allowed in a diffused light; there was no other illumination. But Marlene could see the back of a tiny, gray-haired woman facing a wooden workbench in the corner.

"Mom?"

The woman turned and when she saw Marlene, she smiled and asked in her slightly accented English, "Josephine? Is that you?"

Marlene moved closer, although she knew the misidentification had more to do with the Alzheimer's than the lighting. "No, Mom, it's Marlene, your youngest daughter. Josephine was your oldest."

The old woman's face took on a confused look. "Marlene? I don't have a daughter named Marlene . . . or do I?"

Marlene suddenly found herself struggling against tears. "Yes, Mom, me. Marlene. Your youngest. What are you doing down here? You had Dad worried. He thinks that you wandered off again."

"Nonsense," her mother said with a cheerful laugh. "I'm just down here canning peaches. Would you like to help?"

Marlene walked over to her mother and looked at the bench. In years gone by, she had happily assisted her mother in canning peaches and snap peas, as well as putting away jars of olives. All she saw now were dusty old mason jars and rusted lids, but no peaches or paraffin. Her mother's birdlike hands, however, fluttered away with invisible ingredients. "Remember when you were a little girl and we would can peaches, and you would sing to me the songs you'd learned in school?"

"Yes, Momma, I remember," Marlene said. She had seen a lot of cruelty in the world, but she had never known anything as cruel as Alzheimer's. Bit by bit it took the human being—the wife, the lover, the mother, and friend—who had occupied the body and left some replacement, like one of those body-snatcher science fiction movies.

As a result, a marriage that had been as solid as the rock beneath Manhattan and remained warm and loving through sixty-five years was crumbling before Marlene's horrified eyes.

She would never have thought it possible. Her father, Mariano Ciampi, and mother, Concetta Scoglio, met in the main hall on Ellis Island in 1936, both just off the ships that brought them from an Italy that was plunging headlong into fascism and war. He was twenty, she was seventeen, and it was love at first sight. However, her parents had hustled her away from the barbarian who hailed from Sicily, "that land of gangsters and sheepherders," pointing out to the protesting girl that she came from Florence, a civilized city. Oil and water, her parents said, but the young couple managed to stay in touch, and six months later—under threat of elopement—her parents gave them permission to wed.

Mariano had found work at a fruit and vegetable store in Washington Heights, delivering orders and eventually running the store for the owner. His benefits included getting to take home all the bruised fruit he and Concetta could eat, as well as free rent in the tiny flat above the store. They'd scrimped and saved and eventually he bought the store from the owner. Over the years he had purchased other fruit and vegetable markets from Washington Heights to Little Italy and the Village.

The only interruption in their upward mobility was when Mariano volunteered for the army, feeling it was his duty to fight for his adopted country. He'd been wounded at Anzio and honorably discharged, returning home quietly with a Purple Heart and a piece of a German grenade still in his shoulder, ready to resume building his fruit and vegetable empire, which Concetta had proved adept at running in his absence.

In the first four years of marriage, before he shipped out, he and Concetta had produced three babies—one of whom, Frankie, had died at age three of a childhood illness. The war had briefly interrupted the production line, but by the time Marlene was born in 1948 (something of a surprise to all involved) she was the sixth (living) child.

When they moved to the house in Queens, Mariano and

Concetta handled the prejudices of the predominantly Anglo population—the snide remarks about being "connected" to the Mafia, the wop jokes, and comments about "dirty Italians"—with grace and dignity that eventually won the respect of even their most acrimonious neighbors.

Naturalized as citizens, they'd emphasized the importance of good citizenship and education to all of their children. Instead of vacations, new cars, and a bigger house, they'd put their discretionary income toward sending their children to the best parochial schools and colleges.

Marlene thought her parents had the most perfect marriage of any she had ever encountered. Yes, Mariano and Concetta could fight like bantam roosters. Her mother was no wallflower or shy, mail-order bride from the old country. She wasn't afraid to speak her mind, and if Mariano stepped out of line, he was bound to hear about it. But their love was just as passionate, and the rhythmic squeaking of their old bed echoing throughout the house at night was as reassuring to Marlene and her siblings as family dinners.

She'd even caught them making out in their bedroom at their sixtieth anniversary party, having escaped the well-wishers and family members. "Your father, he still turns me on." Her mother had shrugged at Marlene's teasing. Just a few years later, that woman was disappearing like a lost ship into fog banks, and for the first time in Marlene's life, her father spoke of her mother in words other than adoration.

It was especially tough on Marlene as she was the only child in easy commuting distance. Two other siblings had died—Lieutenant Angelo Ciampi in Vietnam during the Tet offensive of 1968, and Josephine, a chain-smoker, of lung cancer in 1986. The others were scattered about the country, none closer than a day's drive. So it had been left to Marlene, the baby of the family, to shepherd their aging parents through what were supposed to be their golden years.

Standing at the workbench, Marlene's mother leaned toward her and spoke in a conspirator's low voice. "You know, the man upstairs, he isn't really your father. Your father was never bossy like that one. That one keeps telling me what I can and can't do." She sighed. "I don't know what they did with dear Mario, but that's not him."

"Who is 'they,' Mom?" Marlene asked. When there was no answer, she continued, "Mom, that really is Pops. He's just tired, and you really should let him know where you are. He worries when he can't find you." It's you who's lost, Mom, she thought. Come back, Mom, please. "Let's go upstairs and make Pop some breakfast."

"Good idea, we'll take him some peach preserves," Concetta said, grabbing a cracked and empty jar. "He always loved my peach preserves."

Marlene whipped up a breakfast of eggs and Italian sausage and tried just as hard to whip up a festive "everything's normal" conversation, talking about the twins and Lucy and Butch's campaign. But there was little if any response, and eventually she stopped trying and they ate in silence, until Concetta looked up and asked Mariano if he'd liked the peaches.

Mariano had stopped eating and stared at her for a moment, blinking his eyes rapidly. "I can't take much more of this," he finally replied and stood up from the table. He stalked off into the living room with Marlene running along behind him.

"She's crazy," he said as Marlene helped him into his coat. Part of her purpose in coming over was to give him a break so that he could spend a few hours down at the local VFW post.

"She's not crazy, Pops, she has Alzheimer's, it's a disease . . . like cancer. She can't help it," Marlene replied.

"If she just tried a little harder . . . ," he said, but his voice trailed off as the tears sprang to his eyes. He hugged Marlene and headed out the door.

Marlene returned to the kitchen, where she found her mother still sitting in her chair, staring at the half-finished meal. "I'm tired," she said. "Would you help me to bed, Josephine?"

Sighing, Marlene did as asked. She was grateful that her mother slept for the next few hours. She used the time to return to the basement, where she located the big cardboard box marked Christmas and brought it upstairs. Inside was the old, plastic, three-piece Christmas tree her parents purchased in the 1960s and had kept ever since as a "family tradition." She set it up, strung it with lights, and hung ornaments. All in all, it was a pretty sad excuse but better than nothing.

When Concetta woke and came into the living room where Marlene was reading a magazine, she clapped her hands at the sight of the tree. "Well, hello, Marlene. I didn't know you were visiting. Mario should have come and told me. But at least he finally set up our tree. Now, I'll have to get to my shopping to have something to put under it. Christmas trees just don't look right without presents."

Happy for any little sign of her mother, Marlene smiled back and patted the couch next to her. "Pops is off talking to his buddies at the VFW, and I figured you could use the rest," she said.

"How many times do they need to hear the same old lies," Concetta replied, and they both laughed.

They were still sitting on the couch laughing as they pored over the photographs in one of the family albums that Concetta had so carefully put together when Mariano returned home. "Hello, my darling," Concetta said when he walked in the door. "How dare you leave me for those boys at the club."

"You go on now," Mariano said, winking at Marlene. "We'll be all right. Come Concetta, my love, say good-bye to our beautiful daughter and we can sit on the couch and watch some golf on the television."

Concetta nodded. "I'll see her to the door, Poppa. You turn on your golf game."

Happy that at least for the moment her mother's ship appeared to have sailed back into the sunlight, Marlene hugged her mother at the door. But just as she was breaking the embrace, Concetta whispered in her ear.

"If I disappear, you'll know I was telling you the truth about *that man*," she said, then hurried back behind the door.

Marlene went home and was glad that her husband and the boys were still gone. She didn't want to talk to anyone or have any reminders that the picture of a stable family might, in the end, be an illusion. She gathered her painting supplies and headed out before anyone got home.

While in New Mexico, and much to her surprise, she'd discovered that she had a talent for painting, and she also found it meditative and relaxing, especially after a morning like the one she'd just had. But it wasn't until she was in a taxi that she decided to go to Brighton Beach, and from there walked down the boardwalk to Coney Island.

Still thinking about the conversation she'd had with her husband about the attack on Liz Tyler, she'd decided

to feature the pier and, off to the side and in the foreground, the Ferris wheel. It took a bit of artistic license
because the scene in her painting didn't exist, at least not
in the perspective she'd drawn it in. But if I wanted accu-
racy, she thought, I'd have taken up photography.

She didn't really have the heart for it, though, so when
the cold started to make it past her coat, she decided to
pack it in and go get a cup of tea at the tearoom she'd
passed. As she walked back up the boardwalk, she saw
several older couples who reminded her of her parents,
only these were speaking to each other in Russian.

For decades now, the Brighton Beach area had been
an enclave for the Jewish Russian émigré community.
The women and some of the men she saw were dressed
as they might have been in St. Petersburg—in furs and
leather. The antifur crowd wouldn't have lasted two minutes. There were probably a dozen fur shops along
Brighton Beach Avenue that boasted—in signs written in
both English and Russian—"Real Russian Furs from
Siberia . . . Best Price, Half-Off Sale."

Marlene had just about reached the teahouse when
she passed a bench on which sat a young woman with her
face buried in her hands. Then she noticed that the
woman was crying.

She started to walk on past—she'd had enough emotional turmoil for one day—but she'd never been good at
walking away from someone, especially a woman, in trouble. She turned back to the young woman. "Are you okay?"

When the woman looked up at her, Marlene was
struck by the exotic beauty created by the wide Slavic
cheekbones below jade eyes that gave her face a feline
quality. She was somewhat older—early forties—than
Marlene had first thought but was one of those women
whose looks would change but not diminish with age.

The woman started to nod her head yes to Marlene's question. But then shook it and began to sob. *"Nyet,"* she cried. "Is not okay for me."

Marlene leaned her easel against the wall behind the bench and sat down next to the other woman. "Can I help?" she asked.

The woman shook her head again. "I am sorry, my English is not so good," she replied. "This is not for your concern. But I thank you for asking . . . showing me . . . umm . . . compassionate. I do not have many friends here, so I thank you for kindness." She wiped at her tears with the sleeve of her coat and held out her gloved hand. "My name is Helena Michalik."

Marlene's mind was telling her to stand up and walk away, but her heart kept her seated and she shook Helena's hand. "Marlene Ciampi. It looked like you could use a friendly face." She glanced up and saw the sign for the St. Petersburg Tea Room. "How about we get out of the cold and have a cup of tea," she said, nodding toward the establishment.

Helena hesitated but then sighed and nodded. "Yes, perhaps, some tea to warm my body and my heart."

When they entered the tearoom, it took a moment for Marlene's eyes to adjust to the dark interior. It wasn't just the dimmed lights, either; everything in the place was dark—the woods, the heavy velvets, and the rich carpets. Even the otherwise colorful Russian Orthodox icons seemed dark in tone. The Russians are a moody people, Marlene thought.

The room was long and narrow, and as her eyes adjusted she noticed two large men in monochrome rumpled sweatsuits watching her and Helena from the back of the room on either side of a door marked Office. Bodyguard types. This place must do a hell of a business to need that much muscle, she thought. Otherwise, the tearoom was empty except for the waitstaff.

Marlene looked back at Helena, who was also watching the two men with a worried look on her face. They frighten her, she thought; then she looked down as Helena took off her coat. "Congratulations! You're going to have a baby."

Helena blushed and smiled as both of her hands went to her belly as if to support the small mound growing there. "Yes," she said. "Finally. We have been trying for years. Now we say it must have been the water in America. A child has sprouted."

After a few minutes, an unsmiling waiter emerged from a side door, which, Marlene assumed, led to the kitchen. "You would like tea, no?" Helena asked Marlene as he approached. He came to a standstill in front of the table and just stood looking at them through heavy-lidded eyes as Helena ordered in Russian.

The waiter still hadn't said a thing when he turned on his heel and headed back to the kitchen. A moment later, he emerged with a pot, which he set on the table, and he quietly retreated from whence he came.

"So, want a shoulder to cry on?" Marlene offered.

"I don't understand," Helena said. "You want me to cry?"

"No, it's a saying. I meant, would you like to talk about what was making you cry outside on the bench?"

Helena bit her lip. "I should not trouble you. But I am in a strange country, and I know small number of people . . . no friend to talk to." The woman hesitated as if weighing Marlene's trustworthiness and apparently decided that she would do. "It is about my husband, Alexis. . . ."

An hour and several pots of tea later, Marlene had

the whole story—at least what Helena knew of it. The long and short of it was that Alexis Michalik was a visiting professor of Russian poetry at New York University who'd been accused by one of his graduate students of drugging and raping her one night in his office on campus.

He'd admitted "flirting" with the woman but denied having sexual relations with her. Yes, he'd met her at his office that night but, he said, it was at her insistence and to discuss her master's thesis. However, the next morning, the graduate student had returned to his office and accused him of raping her. He said she'd threatened to go to the university administration and the police with her allegations unless he approved her master's thesis and sponsored her admittance as a doctoral student. He'd refused to be blackmailed, and that afternoon, she'd made good on her threats.

Helena didn't know exactly what they were, but apparently this student had "proofs" of her husband's transgressions. They were enough for the NYPD to have arrested him. He'd since been released on bail, but the university had immediately suspended him without a hearing. Meanwhile, the district attorney's office had not yet decided to bring charges, but the Michaliks feared it was just a matter of time.

Although hurt by the confession of flirting, Helena said she loved her husband and did not believe he would have raped a woman. But she was fearful of what would happen. If Alexis did not beat the charges, he would go to prison. And even if he won, it appeared he would be fired and lose his work visa.

"Then we will have to return to Russia," Helena said, "where the only peoples paid less than Jewish professors of Russian poetry are Russian poets." She laughed at her own joke, but her fear was evident in her eyes and shaking hands.

The Michaliks believed that the "mean bitch" who ran the New York District Attorney's Sex Crimes Bureau wanted to make an example of her husband and that the case had not been well investigated before the police and university jumped to the conclusion that Alexis was guilty. In the meantime, the press had got wind of the case—presumably from the accuser—and was having a field day with it.

As Helena talked, Marlene remained largely silent, not volunteering that her husband was the district attorney or that she knew the "bitch," Rachel Rachman; indeed, she'd been another of Marlene's protégées, though they'd since had a falling out. When Helena mentioned the press coverage, she remembered the *New York Post*'s headline Russian Casanova Rapes Student, though she had not read the story.

Marlene wasn't sure what to think. It wouldn't be the first time a college professor diddled a coed, who then thought better of the whole thing. She'd decided not to get involved when she heard herself tell Helena that she might know someone who could look into the case. And then that in fact she, Marlene, could still practice law in the state of New York and was willing to take on the case "on the condition that after I talk to Alexis, I believe him." She was so surprised at what she'd said that she forgot to be embarrassed when the other woman burst into tears, grabbed her hands across the table, and kissed them as she thanked her over and over again.

"Uh, look, Helena," Marlene said, taking her hands back. "I should warn you that I might not be able to do much more than represent your husband while he gets convicted of rape."

Helena dabbed at the tears in her eyes with a napkin and nodded her head. "Yes," she said, "I understand. But now I feel at least that we have . . . um, how do you Americans say it . . . a fighting chance? Thank you, Marlene. My Alexis . . . sometimes he is, um, filled with emotions and doesn't think straight, but he is a good man and I love him very much."

Marlene felt the tears in her own eyes welling up. Love was a great thing, she thought, even if something like Alzheimer's came along later and made you fight to hold on to it. All of a sudden, she wanted very much to be back in her loft, curled up on the lap of her husband, watching her twin sons tumbling around on the floor. She dug in her purse and plunked a twenty-dollar bill down on the table.

"I'm sorry, but I need to go. Here's my telephone number," she said and handed Helena an old business card she found at the bottom of the bag.

"Yes, of course, I have kept you too long," Helena said.

"No, it's just time to get home and I—" Marlene was interrupted when she was nearly trampled in the aisle by a thin, pale-looking young man who stumbled in through the door and ran to the back of the room. She noticed that he had only one arm and that the empty sleeve was pinned up near the shoulder.

The two big men in the back had jumped from their seats when the young man blew in through the door. She noted that they both had reached behind their backs—and not to scratch an itch—with one hand while holding up the other to intercept the intruder.

Seeing Marlene's appraising look of the situation at the back of the restaurant, Helena grabbed her by the elbow and steered her out the door. "Those are bad men . . . is best not to look too closely," she warned.

The younger woman walked her to the avenue and waited until Marlene could hail a cab. When Marlene got in, Helena leaned in the door. "If you change your mind about helping, I will understand. I am a stranger."

"Hey, didn't we just drink three pots of tea together?" Marlene asked.

"Yes?" Helena said, puzzled.

"And didn't I show you photographs of my children and husband . . . and didn't you show me photographs of your husband and parents?"

"Yes."

"Then we're not strangers anymore." Marlene turned toward the taxi driver. "Crosby and Grand," she said, "and make it snappy, please."

5

SEVERAL HOURS BEFORE HE NEARLY TRAMPLED
Marlene Ciampi and Helena Michalik, Igor Kaminsky
had hurried down the steps at Grand Central Station to
catch the number 4 subway train to the Bronx. His
brother was supposed to meet him on the platform and
together they planned to celebrate his release from prison.
First, they'd score some Ecstasy and then hook up with a
couple of sisters they knew who lived near Yankee Sta-
dium.

Igor could hardly wait for the sexual pleasure of the
drug and its impact on whatever morals the girls might
possess. He was barely five hours from his release from
Auburn State Prison, where he'd served two years of a
seven-year sentence for armed robbery, and was ready to
start enjoying life again.

However, at the moment he was on edge. Part of it
was the bus ride back to Brooklyn; he worried that at
any moment the bus would be pulled over by the cops
and he'd be taken into custody again. He thought he
was supposed to have been released to an agent with the

INS for deportation back to Russia, but God—or the Russian mob in Brighton Beach for which he'd done a few odd jobs—had smiled on him and he'd been given a bus ticket and set free.

Yet it wasn't just the specter of the INS that had him looking over his shoulder. Igor wasn't the most brilliant of thieves. He'd lost one arm as an adolescent trying to break into a butcher shop in the Moscow suburb where he'd been raised. The butcher was home and had let him have it with a cleaver when he stuck his arm through the broken pane of glass in the front door to let himself in.

However, thanks to a generous benefactor who owed his father a favor, Igor and his brother had been smuggled into the United States aboard a freighter. He'd promptly resumed his life of petty crime but again proved that he wasn't cut out for the job. One night he'd tried to rob a Korean grocer and decided that the man was moving too slowly, so he put his gun down on the counter to help empty the cash register.

The store's owner, Mr. Kim Tysu Jung, quickly grabbed the gun, pointed it, closed his eyes, and pulled the trigger. This time Igor got lucky; the bullet whizzed past his shocked face and blew out the window behind him. Igor fainted, which may have saved his life, as the store owner couldn't bring himself to shoot an unconscious man and instead called the police.

Igor might not have survived prison, either, except that his benefactor on the outside was able to arrange for his protection by the mob behind the walls. He made himself useful as a sort of courier, but he was definitely not part of the inner circle and was merely tolerated. His benefits did not include getting to choose his cellmate, and so it was that he found himself bunking that past spring with Enrique Villalobos.

Igor didn't like Villalobos. Just looking at Enrique's oily, pockmarked complexion and protruding yellow teeth made Igor queasy. And he hated that the man bragged about raping old women and young girls and was, in fact, serving a life sentence for raping and killing an eighty-seven-year-old grandmother.

About the only prisoner who seemed to like Villalobos was his "chicken," a twenty-three-year-old Puerto Rican transvestite named Roberto Flores, who called himself "Little Rosa." Flores could pass for a reasonably attractive girl when he wore his makeup, and normally his favors would have been claimed by someone bigger, tougher, and meaner than Villalobos. However, Flores was HIV positive and already had some of the telltale purple blotches of Kaposi's sarcoma—a type of skin cancer associated with AIDS. As a result, the rest of the prison population steered clear but Villalobos didn't care. He was HIV positive, too, and already facing life in prison.

Roberto became even less desirable that spring when he had a nasty accident in the prison laundry. Somehow his head got caught in the massive steam press used to iron prison uniforms and sheets. He was horribly burned on the sides of his face—his ears looked like puddles of melted wax with holes—and from that point forward, his formerly well-formed head had a sort of pressed look to it, accentuated by a bug-eyed stare.

Igor had seen Flores when he finally got out of the prison hospital and the bandages were removed. He'd barely been able to keep his lunch down when he got a glimpse of the deformed ears and protruding eyes, but Villalobos had just shrugged and said, "I don't screw his face so who cares? He can wear a bag over his head." Roberto had wept at the cruel words, but with no one else willing to protect him and buy him the little things he required—like lipsticks and rouge—he stayed with Villalobos. At least while Villalobos remained at Auburn, which wasn't much longer after the "accident."

Only a few days following Roberto's mishap, Villalobos, who'd acted real nervous whenever large, hard-faced black men walked past the cell, asked to see the warden. Soon, a rumor swept through the prison: Villalobos had "come to Jesus" and confessed to the rape of a woman twelve years earlier beneath the pier on Coney Island. If true, the information—according to all the jailhouse lawyers—would exonerate four black men, all members of the notorious Bloods gang, currently incarcerated in that very prison.

The news struck Igor in a way he hadn't expected. The pier at Coney Island was just about his favorite place in the world. The American dream to him was riding the amusement park roller coaster with his brother and a couple of girls, getting high on pot or Ecstasy, and wolfing down as many hot dogs at Nathan's as his stomach could hold. He didn't like the idea that such an ugly crime occurred where he'd once made love to a willing girl from Buffalo.

Igor noted that the four black men were among those who'd been walking past the cell, frightening Villalobos. But he figured it was none of his business. If Villalobos said he did the crime, who was he to say different? In fact, the situation in the cell grew much less stressful, as now Villalobos seemed to be on great terms with the young black men, as well as the other members of the Bloods gang in the prison.

One benefit to Villalobos's having new friends was that one night he came back to the cell with a quart milk carton filled with prison moonshine, made by the kitchen crew using rotten, fermented fruit and sugar. Villalobos didn't offer to share any and was soon bragging to Igor, who had no choice but to listen, about his sexual exploits. He eventually got around to raping the woman at Coney Island, but it wasn't quite the story he'd told the authorities. "Sure, I got me some of that white bitch's ass, but those niggers got there before me, them's the ones that messed her up. I just got the leftovers."

The next morning, Villalobos—his beady eyes more bloodshot than usual and nursing a savage headache from the moonshine—had regretted what he told Igor. "You forget that shit I told you," he warned. "If the wrong people hear you been talking out of turn, somebody's gonna put a blade in your stinkin' guts. And it ain't me you're gonna have to worry about, if you know who I mean."

Igor didn't necessarily have all his tools in the shed, but he understood who Villalobos referred to: Jayshon Sykes, the ringleader of the Coney Island Four, as the television newscasts were calling him and his buddies. Igor had no intention of crossing that man's path. The other three of the four were tough guys, even killers, but Sykes was something else again.

He reminded Igor of a large shark he'd seen in the New York Aquarium at Surf Avenue and West Eighth Street in Brooklyn shortly after his arrival in the United States. As the beast swam past, one of its large, featureless black eyes had fixed on him for a moment, and Igor knew that it was sizing him up as potential prey. There was no conscience in that gaze, only a desire to kill and consume. Sykes had once looked at him that way, and he didn't want any encores.

Several weeks after his "confession," Villalobos was

transferred out of Auburn. The prison rumor mill had it that he'd been rewarded with a cushy setup on one of the prison farms. Igor didn't care; he was just happy to be rid of the disgusting man and his dirty little secret. He was even happier when Sykes & Co. were exonerated and left the prison.

By October, he'd pretty much forgotten about the Coney Island case. His chief concern was that in two months he was due to be released from prison, but then he was going to be handed over to the INS for deportation to Russia. And that would have meant more prison time, as he was still wanted by the Moscow police for a few of his youthful transgressions. He definitely did not want to return to his native country, where the prison cells made even Attica look like Club Med.

He was worrying about his release one afternoon while in the prison exercise yard when he uncharacteristically allowed himself to wander away from the safety of the Russian mob bosses, who held court in one corner. Most of the prison gangs had staked out territory that the other gangs respected, except when warring. However, outside of these islands, there was a sort of no-man's-land where the loners and lunatics, and the predators who fed on them, walked or huddled.

Igor was considering what to do about his problem that afternoon when a large, dark menace stepped in front of him and poked him in the chest with a finger the size of a Robusto cigar. Rubbing his bruised chest, Igor looked up, and up . . . into the huge, scowling face of Lonnie "Monster" Lynd.

A six-foot-three, 250-pound member of the Bloods gang and a bona fide sociopath, Lynd was reputed to have killed three men in prison, but no one had ever been able to prove it so he remained in the general population. Two other black men, nearly as large, remained a couple of feet behind Lynd with their eyes fixed on Igor's trembling face.

While Igor did not feel the pervasive sense of evil he had when near Jayshon Sykes, he was terrified of Lynd, whose bulging, prison-built arms looked as if they could crush his skull like a grape. His fear grew when Lynd bent over to speak face-to-face with him. "Yo, mutha-fucka," Lynd said quietly. "You was in the cell wit' Villa-lobos, right?"

Igor was so frightened that all he could do was nod. He didn't dare turn or try to flee, but he noticed that the other prisoners were moving away from him. If this turned ugly, no one else wanted to be in the vicinity where they might be considered a witness.

"Whatever that piece of shit might have told you 'bout that rape out at Coney Island you best be forgettin'," Lynd snarled.

Igor nodded again. He had to remind himself to quit holding his breath and got a whiff of foul breath when Lynd spoke to him again. "Just remember what happened to that little faggot Flores," the man said. "Only I'll keep pressin' till your head pops like a fuckin' pimple. You understand me, muthafucka?"

Grape or pimple, either sounded bad. Igor tried to say, "Yes," but no sound would come out of his mouth except a sort of moaning. He thought that fainting might be a good way out and was about to start holding his breath again, when he felt a huge hand grab his shoulder from behind.

"Is there problem here, comrade?" a voice he assumed belonged with the hand said. With relief, he recognized the voice of Sergei Svetlov, the chief enforcer for the Russian mob at Auburn and probably the only man in the

prison who could have waded into the middle of three
large Bloods without fear.

If Lynd was huge, Svetlov was immense. He'd been
the Red Army heavyweight wrestling champion and had
been considered a sure Gold Medal at the upcoming
Olympic games. But he'd accidentally injured the son of
an important Politburo member at a demonstration
match, breaking the other man's neck, and instead of
Olympic glory, he'd been sent to Afghanistan to fight
fanatic Muslims. He was two inches taller than Lynd and
outweighed him by twenty pounds, all of it lean muscle.
He was also bald as a bowling ball; his forehead was
crisscrossed with spidery white scars due to his favorite
way of rendering opponents senseless, which was to butt
them into submission.

Svetlov had never been particularly nice to Igor, so if
he was there to help, it was because he'd been sent by
someone higher up. Someone looking out for your Mus-
covite ass, Igor thought happily as he watched Lynd take
two steps back.

Lynd wasn't afraid of many men, but neither was he
willing to tangle with Svetlov, even with his two big
friends to back him up. However, he couldn't afford to
come off like he was scared or he'd lose face with his
gang, which could turn on perceived weak members of
the pack like wolves.

"Ain't nothin' but a pleasant little chitchat with your
bitch," Lynd said, looking over his shoulder to make sure
his comrades hadn't deserted him.

"Vatch vat you say, shits head," growled Svetlov, whose
command of American epithets was limited. "Or I may
pay you a visit. Perhaps, you would like to wrestle, no?"

"No, I don' wanna wrestle yo' gay ass," Lynd said,
laughing with a bravado he did not feel. In truth, he was

desperately wondering how he was going to get out of this without appearing to back down. He decided walking away while trash-talking was the best choice. "See you two bitches, later. Igor, 'member what I said," he warned.

Igor watched the Bloods melt into the population of the prison yard. "Thank you, Comrade Svetlov," he said to the big man next to him.

Svetlov looked down at the young man and grunted. He'd known this one's father, a brave soldier. Apparently courage and strength sometimes skipped generations. Still, he was under orders to watch out for Igor Kaminsky, and it had been dangerous to let him stray off. "You should stick with your own kind, and not hang out with these crap-in-their-pants," he said. He would have preferred to speak Russian, in which he was a noted user of profanity, but his boss had ordered him to speak only English to facilitate his assimilation into American society—not that he was going to get a chance to assimilate anytime soon.

"Believe me, comrade," Igor replied in kind, falling back into the speech patterns of the old Soviet regime. "I want nothing to do with them." He turned to smile at his protector, but the big man was already moving back toward the Russian corner of the yard. He noted enviously how other men parted in front of Svetlov like jackals when the lion approaches its kill.

Igor would have been only too happy to leave Enrique Villalobos, the Coney Island rape, and the Bloods out of his mind and his life. But fate would have it that he was in the prison library, where he went to read newspapers as part of an English as a Second Language class, and picked up a copy of the *New York Times*. His attention was caught by a story about the woman who'd been raped beneath the pier. His baser instincts told him to find another story to read, but he kept reading about the woman, Liz Tyler, and how her life had been taken from her by the assault. Not only had she been raped and nearly killed, she'd lost her husband and child.

By the time he reached the end of the story, Igor was fighting to keep tears from rolling down his cheeks. Not so much for Liz Tyler—though he felt a hatred for Villalobos, Sykes, and the others for what they had done—but for the memories it had dredged up of his own sister.

Except for his addiction to petty crimes, Igor wasn't a bad sort. He'd adored his mother, who'd died when he and his brother were five, and worshipped his father, a hero from the war in Afghanistan. He'd been close to his twin, Ivan, an exact replica except for the missing arm, and to his oldest sister, Ludmilla.

Ludmilla had been an *otkaznik*, from *otkaz*, the Russian word for "refusal." The *otkazniks* were known in the West as "refuseniks"—Soviet citizens, especially Jews like Ludmilla Kaminsky, who had been refused permission to emigrate and were often jailed on trumped-up sedition allegations.

One night Ludmilla had been taken from her apartment by the KGB and charged with anti-Soviet agitation. Even their father's war record had not protected her, and she was kept a prisoner for nearly two years, during which time she was systematically tortured, including being raped repeatedly. The bright, cheerful, and optimistic young woman he'd known returned to her family a dull, frightened creature who would shriek and run if a strange man entered the room. Igor had hated rapists ever since.

So Igor became something he would never have imagined. A hero. When no one was watching, he wrote a short, but to the point, letter to Kristine Breman, the district attorney of Brooklyn, and told her what Villalobos had said about the confession being a hoax. He considered sending it without a signature but realized that unless the authorities were able to question him, it would probably be ignored. So he signed and mailed it before he could change his mind or the letter could be discovered.

Igor thought there'd be a quick response. After all, Sykes and his crew were all over the television blasting the prosecutors and cops. He thought they'd be eager to clear their names. But when there was no reply after two weeks, he shrugged and decided to forget about it. If the law wasn't interested in the truth, he wasn't going to stick his neck out to give it.

Ever since the run-in with Lynd, Igor had made it a point not to stray far from his protectors. But he thought it was okay one day to head down to the prison mail center when a friend told him that there was a package there from his brother. Hoping that his clever twin had discovered a new way to smuggle in drugs—a little marijuana or perhaps some Ecstasy—he wasn't paying attention when he arrived in the hallway outside the mail center. However, he knew something was wrong when the normally busy hall was empty except for Monster Lynd.

Igor tried to turn and flee, but he was suddenly grabbed from behind by two men he couldn't see. His eyes went to the blade that had appeared in Lynd's hand. He tried to yell for help but a large hand covered his mouth.

In a way he was thankful that it was over quickly. He felt three powerful punches, knocking the wind out of him. There really wasn't much pain, though when he looked down at his hands, which were holding his belly, he noted that they were covered with blood. Then he was lying on the floor.

Someone kicked him and then he saw feet quickly retreating. He gasped but couldn't quite seem to catch his breath, and wondered if that was how fish felt when hauled onto land. His mind wandered to a time when he was a child and his father took him and his brother fishing in the Volga River . . . a fish flopping on the deck of the boat, working its mouth . . . and passed out.

Svetlov may have thought that the toughness that made Igor's father a good soldier had skipped a generation, but maybe not entirely. Although it took the equivalent of six bodies' worth of blood transfusions, he held on, fortunate that the shiv had only nicked his liver and no major blood vessels. After a few days, when he began to feel up to looking around from his bed, he discovered that the big man in the hospital bed next to him was also Russian. The funny thing was that there didn't seem to be anything wrong with the man. And, in fact, when the orderlies left the ward at night and there was no one to see—or at least snitch—the man would get out of his bed and work out, doing push-ups and sit-ups. As soon as the man was done, he'd stand, wink at Igor, and get back into bed. It finally dawned on Igor that the man was his bodyguard, and he slept peacefully.

After Igor had for the most part recovered from his wounds, he was placed in administrative segregation for his own safety until parole. He'd been told by the parole board that he was going to be released to the INS and then deported. However, on the day of his release from the prison, he was given a cheap suit and a bus ticket back to Brooklyn. Waiting for his ride in the station, he'd called his brother, Ivan, on a pay phone and told him to meet him at Grand Central station and "be ready to party like is no tomorrow."

Ivan laughed and said he'd be there. He was sure that

his boss, Olav Radinskaya, the Brooklyn borough president and a middleman for the mob who used Ivan to pick up "insurance payments" from business owners, would let him off early.

As soon as he arrived at Grand Central Station, Igor had hurried to the number 4 train platform. He got to the bottom of the stairs and immediately spotted his brother standing at the other end of the platform. Ivan didn't see him, however, because he was bending over looking down the tunnel for the train.

Idiot, Igor thought. How many times do I have to tell him not to stand so close? Someday somebody is going to bump him onto the tracks. I'm going to have to talk to . . .

Igor's brotherly thoughts screeched to a halt when he noticed the four young black men who were closing rapidly on Ivan, just as the light from the train appeared in the tunnel. One of the men was Jayshon Sykes.

"IVAN!" he screamed but wasn't heard above the crowd noise and the approach of the train. He started for his brother, knowing he was already too late. "IVAN!" His brother finally heard him and turned with a smile. But his face melted to a look of concern and then fear as a tough-looking black man walked up to him and pushed him out onto the tracks just as the train arrived.

Ivan's scream was cut short but dozens of other people on the platform took it up as the conductor hit the brakes far too late to save him. Igor stopped and doubled over as if he'd been stabbed again.

He looked up just as Sykes turned toward him. The killer had a smile on his face, which changed to a puzzled look and then a mask of rage. His eyes darted to the empty sleeve of Igor's cheap jacket. He shouted something to his comrades and started to run toward Igor.

The anger in Sykes's face brought Igor to his senses—

his sense of self-preservation. His brother was dead, and he would soon be, too, if he didn't run. He escaped only because the screaming, yelling crowd rushed in a half-dozen panicked directions, hindering Sykes and his gang. It had taken nearly three hours of staying to alleys and side streets—as well as a terrifying jog across the Brooklyn Bridge thinking that every car driven by a black man contained his brother's killer—but at last he'd arrived in the relative safety of Brighton Beach.

As he made his way to the tearoom of his benefactor, his fear was gradually replaced by anger. He had loved his brother, who was all the family he had left. *And he was murdered because they thought he was me,* he thought miserably. He entered the tearoom to beg for safety, but he was also blinded by a desire for revenge and hardly noticed the two women who had to jump out of his way to avoid being trampled.

He stumbled to the back of the room, where he declared to the bodyguards, "Please, I am Igor Kaminsky. I need to see my Uncle Yvgeny."

The two large men looked at each other. They didn't know this wild-eyed nobody with one arm and were about to throw him out on the street when the intercom on the wall buzzed. One of the men picked up the receiver as the other kept his hand on his gun in case the crazy man tried to make a sudden move for the office door.

The man listening to the receiver grunted, *"Da."* He approached Igor and did a quick pat-down for weapons, then motioned him toward the door.

Inside, Igor was surprised to see two men in the room. He'd expected to see his "Uncle Yvgeny" Karchovski, the muscular middle-aged man with the pewter-colored crew cut and a black eye-patch who sat behind the desk. But he was surprised by the presence of the old man who was sitting on a couch off to the side. Vladimir Karchovski, he thought, the big boss himself.

A deep, commanding voice brought him back from his surprise. "Igor Kaminsky," Yvgeny said. "I'd heard you were out of prison. What is it that brings you to me?"

Igor didn't bother to ask how Yvgeny, the de facto head of the crime family now that his father, Vladimir, had supposedly retired, knew so quickly that he was out of prison. He'd suspected all along that Vladimir had had something to do with the apparent confusion about the INS, as well as the protection in prison.

Suddenly tears and rage boiled to the surface of his face. "My brother is murdered!"

There was no reaction on Yvgeny's face, though Igor thought he saw a flicker of something that could have been interpreted as sadness or anger in the man's one good eye. "Explain this. Who would murder your brother?"

6

AFTER IGOR KAMINSKY WAS SHOWN FROM THE office, Yvgeny Karchovski leaned back in his chair without speaking. He was tall and his face looked as much Eurasian, with its high cheekbones and curiously slanted eyes, as it did Slavic. He would have been movie-star handsome, except that the right side of his face was disfigured as though by a fire. The black patch covered a missing eye, but it did not hide the waxy, melted appearance of his skin.

Beneath the thick, blue wool sweater and the shirt he wore, the right side of his body was also scarred from his waist up. A soft, black leather glove covered his right hand.

When he looked in the mirror, he felt repulsed by his appearance. Yet, women still found themselves drawn to him when he entered a room. It was something about the way he carried himself, as well as the combination of intelligence, humor, and a romantic sadness stored in his remaining gray-and-gold-flecked eye. Instead of being repulsed, as he was, women seemed to want to touch his scars, as if they might be the one to heal old wounds. But he'd remained a bachelor, even after arriving in the United States some ten years earlier from Russia.

Yvgeny's thoughts were interrupted by the sound of his father, Vladimir, clearing his throat. He looked over at the old man, who, although bent with age and arthritis, was gazing at him with the same appraising frankness that seemed as much a part of the family's inherited features as the color of their eyes. That the look could in an instant turn into a glare so fierce that most men could not withstand it comfortably seemed appropriate for a family whose history had rarely been peaceful.

Although Yvgeny was now a vigorous sixty-two years, very little of that time had been spent in the company of his father. The old man had left Russia in 1942, first captured by the invading German army, then unable to return to his native country after the war because of the political climate. So he'd immigrated to America, leaving behind his wife and two-year-old son, Yvgeny.

Like many other Russian immigrants, his father had settled in the Brighton Beach area of Brooklyn. While much of the rest of the country enjoyed a postwar boom, refugees from war-ravaged Europe endured the prejudices that came with being on the bottom of the barrel. It had been impossible to make a living without paying off the cops, city officials, and the bureaucracy that could withhold business licenses or close a shop for any one of a number of minor infractions. He'd saved his money from working as a laborer at the Brooklyn Navy Yard and opened the St. Petersburg Tea Room to cater to the growing Russian population in Brighton Beach.

The cops, the officials, the bureaucrats—all got their hands greased but he finally had had enough when none of that protected him from being billed by the Russian

mob for "fire insurance" to protect his restaurant. He'd
not survived the fighting on the Eastern front, nor the
Russian winters, nor the German slave labor camp to be
robbed of every bit of profit. At the same time, he knew
that he couldn't simply say *nyet* to the mob and expect to
be left alone. He needed to make a statement.

Gathering other survivors from the killing grounds of
Leningrad and Moscow—tough, hard men who were so
acquainted with violent death that they no longer feared
it—he set in motion the rest of his life. Feigning obei-
sance, he'd invited three of the more important mob
bosses and their top lieutenants to a "Christmas party" at
the tearoom.

The liquor had flowed freely, especially for the bodyguards, who were feted in their own room. When the
guests were all good and drunk, and distracted by strip-
pers who'd suddenly disappeared as if given a sign,
Vladimir nodded for the climax of his plan to begin.

The waiters in both rooms suddenly produced baseball
bats and tire irons. The bodyguards were quickly beaten
to death. Then, while Vladimir held a gun on the bosses,
who pleaded and threatened, his men broke their legs
and arms with dozens of blows. Two he ordered be left
alive "as examples." The third he had thrown from the
pier at Coney Island during high tide, where, without the
use of his legs or arms, he drowned. The body had rolled
up on the shore the next morning, where it was discovered by beachcombers and photographed for the *Times*.

While the suddenness and viciousness of the attacks
were still fresh in the minds of the other crime bosses,
Vladimir sent his emissaries to deliver a message. They
were free to divide the territory now vacated by the
demise of their former competitors. He wanted no part of
the vice market, the protection racket, or the growing

drug trade. They had nothing to fear from him, so long as they left him alone.

However, he did want a little piece of the pie. Nothing much, he assured them. Just a little sideline smuggling illegal immigrants into the United States—specifically those from what was then the Soviet Union and its Eastern Bloc satellites—and on the other end, smuggling goods into the Russian black market. The gangsters shrugged and said he had a deal. He'd proved that he wasn't a man to take lightly, and they saw no reason to quibble over his little enterprise when there were many other things easier and more lucrative to smuggle into the United States than human beings.

Vladimir's reasons for wanting to occupy that particular criminal niche wasn't just good business sense to avoid confrontations with other gangs. His own experiences as a refugee desperately trying to reach America and begin a new life had a profound impact on his decision even as he plotted the murder of "evil" men. He regretted that it had proved too difficult for him to survive in his new country except as a criminal, but he liked to think that he dealt in freedom, which was certainly a lighter shade of gray than dealing in the burgeoning heroin trade.

Occasionally over the years, he'd been forced to resort to violence to protect his assets and his turf. It always came as a surprise and with a swiftness and brutality that was stunning, a lesson he'd learned from the German blitzkrieg tactics.

One of the last "lessons" had been administered shortly after Yvgeny arrived. It was the first time the two had seen each other since Yvgeny was two years old. They were strangers and yet had immediately felt a bond. The irony of Vladimir's business had been that for all the thousands of people he'd brought to America, he'd been unable to secure the freedom of his family. First, it had been more than ten years after the war ended that he learned his wife and son were even alive. She had given him up for dead and remarried a professor at the University of Moscow who'd fathered Yvgeny's half brother.

Yvgeny had never blamed his father for his absence. As a child, he'd been told that his father was missing in action and presumed dead, another one of the millions of heroes who'd died to defend Mother Russia. When as a teenager he learned that his father was alive and living in the United States, he found the idea of someday joining him exciting to contemplate. He'd hated his stepfather, a mean drunk who beat his mother and the two boys but fortunately died of alcohol poisoning from a batch of homemade vodka before he killed any of them.

When Vladimir heard about the death of his former wife's husband, he'd tried to have her smuggled out of the country along with the boys. But they'd been caught and the consequences had been harsh. She'd been sent to a gulag in Siberia, where she'd died of a combination of pneumonia and starvation. Her youngest son had been raised by her father, also a professor at the university, who, to his regret, had introduced her to her second husband.

Yvgeny had been raised by his paternal grandfather, Yacov Karchovski, a retired general who'd fought as a Bolshevik and then again at Stalingrad. Impressed by his grandfather's war stories, Yvgeny had joined the Soviet Army and followed in the old man's footsteps.

As a Jew, Yvgeny had experienced discrimination all of his life. It was no different at the military academy where he'd had to establish his toughness with his fists. But he'd also worked harder and shown more aptitude for military life than his classmates, and even the most prejudiced of his instructors had not been able to deny that he was a superior soldier and leader. He'd served with distinction in numerous far-off lands from Africa to North Vietnam.

He'd achieved the rank of colonel when he arrived in Afghanistan in 1990 in command of an armored division. Many of his peers used their rank to stay behind in the relative safety of the army base or Kabul to avoid becoming targets of the mujahideen, who went after officers. But Yvgeny was not the sort to ask his men to do what he would not, and they loved him for it.

On a blazing hot day in July of that year, he'd been standing in the turret of his tank, traveling in a column through yet another desolate valley, when the vehicle was hit by a rocket-propelled grenade. The blast had knocked him senseless and set the tank and his clothing on fire. He'd also suffered a broken leg and would have died along with the rest of his crew if a sergeant riding in the tank behind him had not jumped down and raced through the small-arms fire to haul him by his underarms from the turret. The sergeant was struck in the legs by machine gun bullets, and they'd both toppled to the ground.

The sergeant's name was Vasily Kaminsky, a grizzled campaigner who preferred the hardships of field life to living with a shrewish wife, though he enjoyed spending his leaves seeing his daughter, Ludmilla, and twin sons, Igor and Ivan.

Kaminsky's wounds left him crippled and unable to get around without canes. Yvgeny had not fared much better, even after his leg healed and his months of skin grafts in the burn unit of a Moscow hospital.

Both men had been pensioned off; Kaminsky to a life of poverty, his wife leaving him and their children for a better provider. Yvgeny was a little better off because his grandfather, who'd died during his tour in Afghanistan, had managed to put a little away. But it was a life without meaning, spent drinking vodka, often in the company of his old sergeant.

Vasily's life had gone from bad to worse. His daughter had fallen in with the refusenik crowd and suffered imprisonment and torture before she was released half insane. The ill treatment of Ludmilla had pushed the old sergeant into a constant state of drunkenness until the day Yvgeny found him lying on his threadbare couch, an empty bottle in one hand and the still-warm gun in the other. On the table next to him was a note with YVGENY printed in large Cyrillic letters on the outside; the note inside asked that he try to look out for his children.

Yvgeny had taken the request as a sacred duty. But he'd been unable to save Ludmilla. Shortly after her father's death, she'd been found dead of a heroin overdose in one of Moscow's seedier neighborhoods. Feeling that he'd already failed in his duty, Yvgeny tried to watch out for the twins, but they were already mixed up in petty crimes. Then Igor lost his arm to the butcher.

Yvgeny despaired of saving the twins from a life of crime and prison. But one night there'd been a knock on his apartment door. In the former Soviet Union, which had since collapsed, such a knock in the middle of the night might have conjured up fears of the KGB. But the times had changed, and standing on the landing when he answered was a well-dressed man. The stranger explained that he'd been sent by Vladimir Karchovski, "your father," who had made arrangements "should you wish to take advantage of them" for Yvgeny to leave Russia and emigrate to the United States, albeit illegally.

Yvgeny started to say yes. He was tired of the poverty, tired of the corruption that was as bad as it was in the days before glasnost. But, he explained to the man, he had responsibilities—the twins—and couldn't possibly leave without them. The man had simply nodded and gone back out into the night. But three days later, he'd appeared again; this time the offer was for Yvgeny and the boys.

For most of the trip, they'd had comfortable accommodations and even dined with the captain of the ship, who was apparently an old friend of Yvgeny's father. But on the day they were due to arrive in New York Harbor, Yvgeny and the boys had been secreted in a specially constructed wooden box hidden inside a shipment of Siberian lumber. The box was hot and cramped, but finally it was opened by an old man with a crowbar.

"My son!" Vladimir had shouted, tossing aside the tool and embracing him. A tough, battle-hardened soldier, Yvgeny was surprised that when the old man starting sobbing, he began to cry, too.

His father, Vladimir, had welcomed him into the "family business." He explained that his was not the biggest or most powerful of the Russian crime organizations—those that made the easy money from drugs and gun sales—and in recent years, some young hotheads who'd learned their trade in Moscow had been encroaching. But he'd lacked the energy to do much about it. "I'm getting old," he complained. "Running a business like this, with the police on one side and the young gangsters on the other, is not for an old man."

Yvgeny had used his military training to assess the situation and plan a course of action. When his father asked what he intended to do, he'd smiled and said, "There is a saying in the West that I heard once. It goes something like, 'Those who do not learn from history are doomed to repeat it.' "

Yvgeny knew that the young Turks from Moscow couldn't have cared less about the old guard they sought to replace. They'd never heard of—or if they had, paid attention to—the stories about how the Karchovski gang got its start. He planned his event with a delicious sense of irony.

As had their predecessors nearly thirty years earlier, the young Turks responded to invitations to a "conference" at the St. Petersburg Tea Room. Hints were dropped that the Karchovskis no longer had the stomach for defending their territory and were simply looking for a way out with their skin intact.

Once again the alcohol flowed like the Volga River. The bodyguards, who'd been treated to dinner, drinks, and half-naked women in the same room their counterparts of another generation had, suddenly found themselves staring down the barrels of 9-millimeter handguns outfitted with silencers. Their captors put fingers to their lips to indicate that the men should be silent if they wanted to live. Not one tried to be a hero and warn his employer.

Meanwhile, in the main dining area the young Turks were enjoying cigars and cognac when Yvgeny nodded his head to the immense waiter who stood behind the most violent and aggressive of them. Sergei Svetlov stepped forward and dropped a loop of piano wire around the man's neck, then placed a foot against the back of the chair and pulled with all his might. The gangster had grabbed at the wire but too late; it sliced deep into his neck, severing his windpipe as well as his carotid artery and jugular vein. Blood sprayed over the men on either side of the dying man. Then with a final yank, Svetlov took his head entirely off. It struck the table with a dull thud and lay there, the sightless eyes gazing down past trays of the finest Russian caviar, smoked herring, and loaves of black Russian rye.

The killing took all of twenty seconds, but those who witnessed it would remember it as seeming much longer for the rest of their lives. They were used to violence, but usually from guns or even a quick knife in the kidneys. None had ever seen a man have his head cut off with a piece of wire. Several vomited and one crapped in his pants.

Meanwhile, Yvgeny had used the distraction to pull a gun from his coat. "So, who would like to steal the house my father built? You, Boris?" he said, whirling to point his gun at a fat young man seated next to the headless body.

Svetlov stepped toward the indicated man, who screamed and dived beneath the table, where he could be heard gibbering as though insane. A tougher member of the crowd stood, drawing his own gun. "You will never get away with this . . ." His threat died with him as the waiter behind him thrust an ice pick through his skull and into his brain. He fell forward onto the table, where his body continued to twitch as Yvgeny offered the survivors a choice.

"You can die now, or in the days ahead," he said. "Or we can all be smart businessmen. There is plenty for everyone. As you know, my family has no interest in drugs or prostitution or gun smuggling or extortion. We want only to be left alone to pursue our own small enterprise."

Yvgeny paused and looked at the faces around the table. Some were white with shock and fear, but a few were hard and angry. "I know that some of you are thinking, 'When this is over, I will kill this man, and take what is his family's,'" he said. "And it's true. You could kill me, and my father. But let me assure you that my men in this room, and those holding your men in the next room, are sworn to kill you if any member of this family or the people under our protection is harmed.

"From this moment, there is a one-million-dollar bounty on each and every one of your heads, as well as one hundred thousand dollars for each member of your family they kill. An attack on one of us will be their signal to begin collecting. It will not matter which of you commits this offense; all of you will be hunted. As you have seen, these men know how to kill—most were with me in Afghanistan and have certainly known tougher men to kill than you. I would suggest that it is vital to your interests that no member of my family or friends suffers an 'accident' as you will all pay the price."

Yvgeny paused to let his threat sink in. "Now, you are all free to leave in peace," he said.

When they were gone, Yvgeny slumped down onto the couch while his father, who'd watched the affair with admiration, sat behind the desk.

"You did not enjoy that," Vladimir said.

Yvgeny shook his head. "I hated it," he replied. "I've never enjoyed killing, despite my former occupation. But I learned the hard lesson that sometimes the death of one or two at the critical moment can save the lives of many later. In Afghanistan, I learned that the only way to combat terrorists was with terror. But I did not enjoy it then, and did not enjoy it tonight."

Vladimir pursed his lips and nodded. "Good," he said. "It is good that such a thing troubles you. It shows that you still have a conscience. This is a hard business that sometimes requires hard decisions, but we should never make them lightly. Americans like to argue that violence never solves anything, but the history of the world demonstrates that sometimes violence is the only way to stop the violent."

Vladimir rose from his seat behind the desk. "Come here," he said.

Yvgeny got up from the couch and walked over to the old man, wondering what he was up to.

"Sit," Vladimir said, indicating his chair behind the desk.

Yvgeny shrugged and sat down. He watched, puzzled, as his father walked around the desk to the couch where he sat as well and then grinned at his son.

"What?" Yvgeny said, smiling in his confusion.

"It's your house now," Vladimir said.

"What do you mean?"

"As I said before, I'm tired and this is a business for a younger man."

"But I don't want to be the boss."

"Perhaps not. But you need to accept the responsibility anyway. There are a lot of people who depend on the house of Karchovski remaining strong, lest the wolves of the world, those young men you dealt with so decisively out there, devour them. When we bring people to this country, we charge them, yes, and they give us a percentage of their paychecks until they have redeemed what they owe us. But they are paying for a service for which they receive good value. These other men, they would not care—they'd enslave them, threaten them all the days of their lives with exposure to the authorities. And there are the people who work for us. All of these depend on the leader of the Karchovskis to be strong for them. I'm no longer strong enough. I'm asking you to take my place as you have now behind the desk."

Yvgeny had looked at his father and saw that this was more than an old man turning over his business to his son. It was a plea to continue his life's work.

In the short time he'd been in America, one thing had perplexed Yvgeny about his father's attitude. He was a criminal, had even committed murder—whatever the provocation. Yet, he professed to believe in the American justice system, as well as the U.S. Constitution, which he called "the single greatest document in the world."

When he'd finally asked the old man about the apparent contradiction, Vladimir shrugged. "I've done what I had to do to survive, though I would have preferred to be the simple owner of a teahouse. I've been lucky and smart and avoided the authorities. However, if I'd been caught and convicted, I would have accepted my punishment. I am like the sinner who nevertheless loves God; I am a criminal, but I am also a patriot."

More than ten years later, Yvgeny thought about that conversation as he sat in the chair behind the desk and looked at his father on the couch. The Kaminsky twins had been a constant headache almost since their arrival in the United States. They weren't bad as in evil, but they were lazy, and rather than pursue any legal means of making a living, they'd constantly pressured him to let them join the family business.

When he refused, Igor had decided to strike out on his own, robbing stores. But he'd proved extraordinarily inept and got sent to prison. Yvgeny had called in a lot of favors and paid a lot of money to keep him alive.

It was fortunate that Sergei Svetlov was in the same prison. The former wrestling champion had made a mistake transporting the body of a man who'd raped a woman in the Brighton Beach Russian enclave and paid the price when Svetlov tracked him down. Such things were not to be tolerated.

Unfortunately, Svetlov had had the bad luck of getting pulled over for a missing taillight as he drove toward a pig farm in New Jersey where the tenants would have made quick work of the body. As he talked to the officer who'd pulled him over, a rookie cop on his first patrol and trying to look as if he knew what he was doing, the cop tapped his flashlight absently on the lid of the trunk. Apparently, the locking mechanism was faulty, the lid sprang open, and the rookie found himself looking into the dead eyes of the pigs' dinner.

Yvgeny's team of lawyers managed to get the charges reduced from murder to manslaughter. (There was some evidence that the rapist was still alive—barely—when placed in the trunk, which, the defense attorney contended, meant that Svetlov had not necessarily intended to kill the deceased despite breaking nearly every bone in his body.) They'd also introduced at his sentencing that the man he killed was a serial rapist. However, the big man was going to spend the next seven to ten in prison, which had been fortunate for Igor.

Svetlov was nearly beside himself for having failed to protect the young man from Lynd when Yvgeny visited him in prison. "Such things happen in a place like this," he consoled Sergei. "You are not to blame yourself, my old friend."

The attack was going to require retribution—otherwise, the black hoodlums would take liberties—but he'd let it wait until he'd arranged for Igor to be freed, which had taken large payments to the INS and Department of Corrections officials but had not been difficult to arrange.

Yvgeny had wondered why the Bloods were so eager to kill Igor that they'd risk a war with the Russian mob, knowing he was under their protection. But this story about the confession by the piece of garbage Villalobos explained it. He kicked himself for not sending a car to pick Igor up outside the prison, but he'd thought that once the young man was outside the prison he'd be safe.

Now, Ivan was dead. Obviously a case of mistaken identity, which meant that Igor was still in danger. Which means that what he was told by Villalobos must be the truth, Yvgeny thought, and they're worried.

He remembered the trials of the so-called Coney Island Four. A woman raped beneath the pier on Coney Island. A horrible thing, Yvgeny thought, and if it had happened to one of my own, then perhaps I would take care of the animals myself . . . but this is not my business. The family didn't need to draw attention to itself by having an associate, Igor, going to the authorities, who might or might not believe him, but they would certainly deport him. And who knew what he might say when questioned. Igor wasn't the bravest or toughest soul on the planet.

Unlike his father, Yvgeny was no fan of justice systems whether they were Russian or American, and not just because he was a gangster. He believed they were all just as corrupt—from the cops to the judges—as any crime family. And in the case of the Americans, what wasn't corrupt had been so bastardized in a ridiculous effort to protect criminals that victims had fewer rights.

The woman raped beneath the pier wasn't his concern, but protecting Igor was. Once again, he'd failed to live up to his oath to Vasily. Now two of the old sergeant's children were gone and there was only one left.

Igor had finished his story by demanding that his brother be avenged. But Yvgeny had waved him to silence before pressing the buzzer on the intercom and asking one of the men outside the door to enter. He turned to Igor and told him that he was sending him to a safe house. "You're not to leave until I give you permission," he said. "If you do, I cannot protect you anymore."

Igor started to protest that he needed to seek out the killers of his brother, and if he had to, he'd go by himself. But again, Yvgeny interrupted. "All in time, nephew," he said. "In the meantime, you'll do nothing that might make the authorities look into our activities here, do I make myself clear?"

The young man had stopped complaining and nodded his head. He wiped at his eyes and nose with his hand.

"Leave us," Yvgeny said, his voice softening. He pointed to the bodyguard. "Stefan will take you somewhere for a nice dinner. Then to your new apartment, where you should mourn your brother and get some rest if you can. We'll talk later of these other things."

When Igor and the bodyguard had left, Yvgeny had settled back in his chair when his father cleared his throat and brought him out of his contemplation. "So what do you think?" Yvgeny asked.

"I think he should go to the authorities and tell them what he knows about these men who did that terrible thing to that woman," Vladimir said.

Yvgeny frowned. "We don't need the attention if they ask him questions and he makes a mistake," he replied. "Besides, you heard what happened after he wrote to the authorities. They betrayed him and it nearly got him killed . . . as it did his brother."

Vladimir sighed and looked up at the ceiling as if seeking inspiration. "We have family who might help . . . ," he started to say but was interrupted by a snort from his son.

"And why should he?" Yvgeny asked. "He is family in blood only. You haven't seen him in years, and he and I have never met. Not to mention our 'occupations' are not exactly compatible."

Yvgeny shook his head. "I cannot allow it. I am sorry for what happened to this woman, but it was a long time ago and I have responsibilities to our people that I cannot jeopardize. You taught me that."

The old man held up his hand. "It is your decision," he said. "I asked you to sit in that chair, and these decisions are yours to make. But you asked me my opinion, and I gave it to you."

Yvgeny smiled. "Actually, I was asking you what should be done with these blacks who killed Ivan."

Using a cane, Vladimir stood up with a grunt. He fixed his son with the family look and said, "You know what needs to be done. You don't need the advice of an old man anymore." He shouted for his bodyguard, who appeared in an instant, and then left without another word.

Yvgeny sat back in his chair and picked up a remote control and pointed it at the video player for the security camera that monitored the restaurant. He backed the video up to the point before Igor had rushed into the restaurant until he could see the two women who'd been sitting at the table near the door. He'd been surprised that he knew both of them but more surprised that they'd shown up together and wondered what that might mean.

7

LUCY KNEW SHE WAS DREAMING BY THE WAY SHE seemed to be floating above the cave floor, following along behind like a tethered helium balloon as four men and a young boy ran for their lives below. Yet, she could smell the dank rot of the air in the narrow space and felt its cloying chill in her bones. She heard the crunching of feet running on gravel and the panicked gasps. Gunfire echoed behind her . . . and something else . . . a scurrying sound from side passages they ran past. As if large rats ran there in the dark, just out of sight.

The light was dim, and she could not see the boy clearly, but she could the men. She noted the fear in their eyes whenever they turned to look at whatever pursued them.

The men were dressed in insulated mustard-brown jumpsuits of the sort road crews wear in the winter, but these were no laborers. Their faces were swarthy, bearded—Middle Eastern, she thought—and they carried AK-47 rifles. She sensed that they were not good men, but those who delighted in bloodshed and murder.

Terrorists. The word flashed in her dreaming mind like a cheap motel Vacancy sign.

Yet Lucy almost felt sorry for them as they stumbled ahead, crying out to each other in Arabic, one of nearly sixty languages she understood. "Hurry, he's coming," shouted the leader, a pockmarked man who pulled the boy along by his arm. The others picked up speed as they frantically muttered prayers, beseeching Allah to save them.

Then she sensed that whatever it was the men feared . . . *He* . . . was right behind her. There was a fury in the air, as palpable as her heartbeat, which drummed even louder in her ears as He passed beneath her. She felt that she should be afraid, but while a coldness enveloped her, there was no fear. Then He was ahead of her—a hooded shadow in the darkness that caught up to the slowest of the men. A large knife flashed, and then a headless body stumbled forward two more steps before collapsing into a pool of fetid water.

Horrified, she wanted to reach out and touch the darkness and ask Him to stop. But she knew she was powerless to halt the relentless, deadly pursuit. She could only follow and witness the carnage.

He overtook the second man. The man cried out, "Shai-tan." *Satan,* her mind translated. The darkness obscured her vision for a moment; then a round object flew through the air in slow motion—a bearded head, the mouth still gaping in a soundless plea—and landed with a splash.

Lucy tried desperately to wake, but the dream pulled her along. The third man stumbled and fell against the cave wall near one of the side openings. He shrieked as thin white hands, white as bone, reached out of the opening and grabbed at him like vines. "Help me, the *rajim* have me."

Rajim, *the outcasts, she thought. The cursed ones. Then he was pulled into the fissure, his screams mixing with strange, excited whispering voices, then dying off completely.*

The last man and the boy ran on, then stopped. Beyond them stood another dark figure of a man, and behind him were hundreds of barrels arranged neatly and in their center was a scaffolding on top of which was a . . . a menace; the dream was unclear about its nature but when she saw it she shuddered in her sleep.

The pockmarked man turned back to face his pursuer. "Stay where you are, Iblis," he shouted.

Iblis? Lucy wondered in her dream. Satan's Islamic name from before his fall from grace.

The muscles of the man's pitted face twitched with fear, his eyes as wide and luminous as twin full moons, almost insane with hatred and terror. He pulled the boy's head back, exposing his neck with one hand, and with the other pulled a long knife from his belt.

Lucy gasped. Only now did she recognize the boy, her brother Isaac. "Zak," she tried to scream. But he could not see or hear her.

The presence below her—Him—stepped slowly toward the man and the boy. Somewhere a dog—or a wolf, she thought with a shiver—howled. He threw back his hood and she recognized the thin, haunted face. "David," she whimpered in her sleep.

Then the pockmarked man shouted, "Allah Akbar" and placed the knife at her brother's throat. "Allah Akbar," Zak said and began to howl.

Lucy woke trembling, her body covered in sweat. "David," she whispered in the dark. As if in answer, there was a sudden howling that made her heart jump like a panicked rabbit's. *"Allah Akbar,"* she prayed in Arabic. "God is great."

It took her a moment to realize that she was lying on a bed at the Sagebrush Inn on the outskirts of Taos, New Mexico, and that the person sleeping next to her was her boyfriend, Ned Blanchet. The howling was provided by a choir of coyotes out in the desert singing in the moonlight, which streamed in through the window. She looked at the clock on the nightstand. Dawn in an hour, she thought. Recalling the dream, she shuddered, but then chided herself for being a baby, afraid of nightmares. The He in her dreams, the man with the gaunt face and burning eyes, David Grale, was dead. He wasn't chasing terrorists through a cave, slashing their throats in an apocalyptic fury.

She'd met Grale a half-dozen years earlier and developed a schoolgirl crush on the handsome young Catholic lay worker. The strange thing was, that crush had not entirely disappeared even when she discovered he was also a murderous psychopath who had slaughtered a number of evildoers he believed preyed upon homeless men.

Grale had tried to explain to her that the people he killed were possessed by demons and that he'd been charged by God with their execution. "We're at war, Lucy," he'd told her. "Like it or not, the forces of good and evil are marshaling for the big showdown. Armageddon. And there will be no watching from the sidelines, no spectators." He further explained that New York City was a sort of epicenter for this battle, drawing the minions of evil like a magnet attracts iron filings.

Given her own Catholic-bred experiences with the metaphysical—she believed that during times of stress a martyred sixteenth-century saint named Teresa de

Alhuma appeared to counsel her—Lucy had not entirely ruled out Grale's basic premise. She sensed that what he said was, in some fashion, the truth.

Lucy even bought into the notion that her family—especially her father, Roger "Butch" Karp, the district attorney of Manhattan, and mother, Marlene Ciampi—were unknowingly but inextricably playing out their roles in the great drama that was unfolding. But her church's philosophy, and her own personal belief, was that no human life was beyond redemption, and she couldn't countenance Grale's butchering of other people . . . even if they were possessed by demons.

Hunted by the police and increasingly consumed by his cause, Grale had disappeared into the city's massive labyrinth of tunnels and sewers—some of them dating back to the earliest days of the city and long forgotten. There he'd become a sort of spiritual leader to what he called the Mole People. Homeless outcasts—many of them also bordering on the insane—they lived in the shadow world beneath the teeming city, emerging occasionally to forage and beg, and to gather news.

At unpredictable moments, Grale would resurface into Lucy's life. Each appearance would leave her troubled by the dichotomy of a man who judged and condemned to death others without even the benefit of a trial, and the haunted, gentle social worker named David. Twice recently he had shown up in the nick of time to rescue her and a family member.

The most recent rescue by Grale had been that summer. The murderous Catholic priest Hans Lichner, an immense bear of a man, had been preparing to sacrifice one of Lucy's twin brothers, Zak, on the altar in St. Patrick's Cathedral. Lichner's predilection for sexually abusing and then murdering young boys had been sanctioned by Andrew Kane, who was using the killer for his own purposes—one of them to eventually bring down the Catholic Church in New York through scandal and corruption.

Grale would have won the ensuing knife fight and, in fact, was about to deliver the coup de grâce, except that Lucy, ever the humanitarian, screamed for him to stop. With Grale momentarily distracted, Lichner turned the tables and planted his knife in his opponent's stomach. Fortunately for Zak and Lucy, John Jojola, who had tracked the monster to the cathedral, was there to protect them. Lichner had proved no match for Jojola's speed and skill, though it was too late to help David Grale.

Lying in a pool of New Mexican moonlight that fell across her bed, Lucy recalled when Jojola stooped next to Grale and felt for signs of life. Then he'd looked at her and shaken his head. She'd burst into tears, but Jojola wouldn't let her remain with the body.

Later when other cops arrived, they found large pools of blood but no bodies. DNA tests showed that the blood came from two different people, but who they were remained a mystery to the authorities. The medical examiner told Lucy's father that neither man could have survived the loss of so much blood unless they received immediate medical attention, including massive transfusions.

Just a typical summer for the Karp/Ciampi clan, Lucy thought as she sat up. A summer in which she'd almost lost her life and would have except for the man who slept next to her.

While still in Taos, before the trail led them to Lichner, she and her mother had been the targets of the local sheriff, who'd been hired by Kane to keep an eye on his "clients" at a retreat. When Marlene and Jojola started getting too close, the sheriff had tried to kill them all. But then a young cowboy had ridden to her rescue.

Ned was snoring like a desert thunderstorm, it being one of the rare mornings when he didn't have to be out before dawn taking care of his boss's cattle. Lucy swung her legs over the edge of the bed, trying not to wake him. But Ned was a light sleeper, used to sacking out on the ground with an ear tuned for signs that his bovine charges or his horse were in trouble.

"What's wrong?" he asked sleepily.

Lucy leaned over and kissed him, lingering for a moment. She loved the scrubbed soapy smell of him, with just a hint of the leather and horses he worked with, that never quite seemed to leave him even after a shower. Except for Felix Tighe's assault, which Lucy chose not to count, they'd both been virgins when they met. His courting had been shy and slow; he hadn't even tried to kiss her until she demanded that he accept it as his reward after saving her life.

Still, it surprised Lucy that she'd taken him as her lover. A deeply religious young woman, she'd sworn that she'd remain chaste until her marriage. And to be honest, it hadn't been all that difficult to remain a virgin.

She was a brilliant student with a savant's gift for languages. But for most of her life, Lucy had done little to dispel the first impression men had of her, which was of a bookish prude whose intelligence was frightening to most males. Combined with a beaklike nose and a thin angular body, the image had not helped her attract a lot of suitors. Nor had she cared . . . much.

When she came to New Mexico, she did have a boyfriend back East, a nice young man named Dan Heeney, who'd certainly wanted to be the first. She'd thought that he probably would be, but up to that point she'd easily managed to put him off by saying she simply wasn't ready. Nor would she be until marriage.

Yet she felt no shame as she looked at Ned. His blue eyes were only half open but still startling in their clarity and brilliance. He wasn't especially handsome—his thin features a bit too irregular, his teeth never having been introduced to an orthodontist, and his ears standing out like satellite dishes. But a life spent outdoors in the Southwest sun gave his face a tanned, rugged quality that mirrored the land he worked and loved. And she loved how she could see his blue eyes sparkle even when his cowboy hat—worn low so that he had to look up from under the brim—shaded his face.

He wasn't even well educated, at least not in a book sense, not even a high school diploma. But he was smart, and maybe it was the wide-open spaces that also made him a deep thinker. His long silences weren't because he had nothing to say; he just liked to think before he spoke. And when he did speak, it was with a simple sort of eloquence that didn't contain a lot of fifty-cent words but was dense with meaning and perception. And while he might not have been a master of many languages, he spoke Spanish—having grown up in a largely Hispanic culture—as if he'd been born to it.

Lucy traced his form beneath the quilt. He wasn't a big guy, but he had the fine, lithe body of someone who'd earned his ropelike muscles through hard work, not in a gym.

No, she had not planned on becoming his lover, and in the glow after it happened, she was surprised at the lack of guilt she felt—not for the broken vow of chastity, nor, at the time, her "betrayal" of Dan. Making love to Ned had come as naturally as taking a warm shower. She wasn't sure if this relationship was forever, but there were times when it certainly felt like it, and she would contemplate what life would be like as a ranch hand's wife. But then she'd stop herself, doubting whether anything so normal would ever be hers.

"Nothing's wrong," she lied. "Just restless. I think I'll go for a morning hike."

Ned started to rise. "Want me to go?"

Lucy pushed him back down. "No, it's your day off, cowboy," she said, as always both amused and flattered by his Old West gallantry. "Roll over and go back to sleep. Maybe when I get back we'll see if you've recovered sufficiently from last night's labors."

Ned lifted the quilt and glanced underneath before looking back at her with a mischievous grin. "I think I'm recovered just fine, ma'am," he said, allowing his eyes to take in her naked body as she sat on the edge of the bed. He made a grab for her, but she darted away with a giggle.

Just to tease him, Lucy made a show of stretching and at the same time looked at herself in the mirror. New Mexico had been good for her. She'd gained twenty pounds, having discovered an addiction to tamales and blue-corn tortilla burritos smothered in green pork chili. Every pound of it had been needed and all of it seemed to have settled in just the right places to give her a more womanly figure. The East Coast pallor that she'd arrived with had turned to a tan from spending a lot of time outdoors with Ned. Her face had filled out, too, which made the nose less noticeable, and she was a handsome, even beautiful, young woman.

Now Ned made a groaning noise, and she decided that she had better stop teasing him if she wanted to go for her walk. She quickly stepped into long underwear and wool socks, then pulled on polar fleece outerwear followed by a ski jacket until she was covered in warm things from head to toe. "I'll be back in a couple of hours, and you'd best be ready, pard'ner," she drawled with a western twang, which, given her abilities with languages, was right on.

"Count on it, ma'am," he drawled back as she opened the door and went out.

Lucy paused for a moment outside the door to adjust to the shock of the brisk December air, then walked quickly to the new Chevy F-10 truck her mother had bought for her after she returned from New York in September. As she walked, her boots squeaked in two inches of new-fallen snow and her breath puffed like a steam locomotive. She turned the ignition and the truck protested with a high-pitched squeal until it turned over and began to purr like a big circus cat.

A few minutes later, she was driving west toward the Rio Grande Gorge. With few other cars on the road, it seemed as if she had the entire high plains desert to herself—a white-blanketed, almost dreamlike landscape punctuated by lonely buttes and sudden gashes in the ground called arroyos that appeared suddenly in what had looked flat as a still pond.

By the time she reached the Taos Gorge Bridge, the longest single-span steel bridge in the world, the sky was just beginning to grow a shade lighter in the east. Once across, Lucy turned right, heading north along a four-wheel-drive track that paralleled the eight-hundred-foot deep gorge. At one point the road drew near the edge of the gorge and she had to look away. That was the place she and her mother had gone over the edge when the sheriff shot out one of their tires. Only the presence of a tree that grew from the side of the cliff had saved them

from plunging to their deaths. Even then, the tree was
giving way when Ned, who'd heard the shot from a distance and rode up on his horse, threw his lariat around
her and pulled her to safety.

Of course, Grale would have said that she and her
mother had been saved by divine providence. He would
have pointed out that cowboys who rode their horses to
the rescue of damsels in distress were a metaphor for the
struggle between good and evil with the good cowboys—
God's angels—triumphing in the end.

Again with Grale, she thought. He's dead. With an
effort she turned her thoughts from the madman and the
cliff's edge and toward a steep granite hill that jutted up
and out over the gorge like a ship's prow.

A man stood on the edge, wrapped in a blanket, facing
the east toward Taos Mountain. But she wasn't surprised;
she'd expected to find him there.

John Jojola was another thread she suspected was part
of the tapestry that connected her family to people like
Grale. Even the Tighes and Lichners of the world, not to
mention her father's latest and most dangerous adversary,
Andrew Kane, were woven in and out, and without which
holes would have appeared.

Lucy parked at the bottom of the path that led up the
hill to the edge of the gorge. She walked up the path but
paused below the summit, not wanting to disturb his
reverie . . . or get too close to the edge.

"Good morning, Lucy," Jojola said after a minute.
"Couldn't sleep?"

"No. Bad dreams," she replied.

Jojola was silent, his eyes fixed on the east as if it were
somehow important to witness where the first ray of the
sun would appear over Taos Mountain. He's looking for
signs, she thought.

She knew from the times she'd spent with him, as well as conversations about him with her mother, that John Jojola was a man who believed that he could sometimes communicate with the spirit world. A trait, he said, that was not uncommon with his people, at least those who still practiced the old ways. It might be the appearance of an eagle where none had been a moment before, or a dream conversation with a coyote across a campfire. Sometimes it meant nothing, but other times the spirits, he said, would give him messages about the future—if he could discern what they meant—or guide him toward the answers to difficult questions.

Lucy was hoping he might impart some piece of ancient Native American wisdom, telling her not to worry about the dreams. But he just sighed and said, "Yeah, me too."

The resignation in his voice frightened Lucy. Outside her father, if there was a rock of a man in the world, he was John Jojola. As far as she could tell, he feared nothing, except maybe liquor. He'd returned from Vietnam a haunted man who'd lost his childhood friend, Charlie Many Horses, to a Vietcong leader he knew only by his Vietnamese nickname, *Cop,* the Tiger. He'd sworn to find and kill Cop, but the man had eluded him. Back in Taos, he'd turned to the bottle to quiet the ghosts of his friend, who was one of the spirits, as well as those of the many men he'd killed who haunted his dreams. Many Horses, however, had remained a friend and his advice was always helpful. Jojola's wife, herself an alcoholic, had left him and their son, Charlie, who'd been named for his friend. He'd sobered up and turned his life around for his son and immersed himself in the ancient ways of his people so that his son would know his heritage.

Jojola turned to face Lucy. Whenever she looked at

him she thought of the sepia-toned photogravures by turn-of-the-century photographer E. S. Curtis of the western American tribes—the dark, searching eyes above the wide cheekbones and a nose that was even more beaklike than her own, although she thought of his as strong. His chest was barrel-shaped, his arms long and muscular. His bowed legs seemed too short for his torso, but she also knew from hikes with him that neither she nor Ned, who was no slouch, could keep up with him. And while they would be puffing and panting, he'd move effortlessly, his eyes constantly searching the ground and sky around him.

"So these dreams," he said, "is your friend David Grale in them?"

Lucy blinked but nodded. "Yes," she said. "And other men."

"Bad men."

"Yes . . . and . . . and my brother Zak."

Jojola nodded solemnly. "This takes place in a cave."

"You've had the same dream." It was a statement, not a question.

"Yes," he replied, then shrugged. "I guess. All dreams are different."

A flicker of some quickly hidden emotion that she found even more disquieting than his tone flew across his eyes. She wasn't sure what it was, but suddenly she felt sorry for him. Then he smiled, his large white teeth showing like snow on a mountaintop against his bronze skin in the gathering light, and pointed east.

Lucy turned and at first saw nothing but the landscape, dominated by Taos Mountain, behind which the sun was preparing for a grand entrance. Then she saw it. "An eagle," she said. She knew that Jojola considered eagles to be his totem, an animal spirit guide.

As they watched, the eagle continued east toward the mountain. Then, just as the bird was about to climb into the sky above the peak, the first rays of the sun shot over the top and the eagle disappeared into the golden light.

"Wow," she said. "I guess that means something, eh?"

"Yeah," Jojola said and laughed. "I guess that I'll get to see what New York City looks like at Christmas."

Lucy laughed, too, but then noticed that the strange look had returned to his eyes. "What's wrong, John?"

Jojola didn't answer her right away but instead allowed the blanket to slip from his shoulders as he lifted his arms. He stood that way until the sun was fully over the top of the mountain, then slowly let his arms sink back to his sides.

"I don't want to go," he said at last. "In Vietnam, I had to crawl through tunnels hunting men. On several occasions I almost became the hunted, and it troubled me that I would die beneath the ground, my soul trapped by the earth to rot with my body. I don't want to die where the sun cannot find me and carry my spirit up with the eagles. I'm afraid, Lucy. Afraid that if I go to New York and these caves are more than in our dreams, I may never see this place again."

"Then don't go, John," Lucy said, afraid for him. "They're just dreams. You don't belong in New York City."

Jojola looked at her oddly, as though puzzled that she couldn't see what he saw. "Don't you feel it, the drawing together?" he said. "I have no more choice than a leaf has floating down a river."

Lucy reached out and took Jojola's hand. "I understand," she said.

LATER THAT SAME DAY, BUT FIFTEEN HUNDRED miles away in New York City, Lucy's twin brothers arrived at the outdoor basketball courts at the corner of Sixth Avenue and West Fourth Street. Giancarlo and Isaac, better known as Zak, had no sooner opened the gate when a tall, young black man with a basketball tucked under his arm yelled at them from the sidelines of one of the courts. "Hey, you two punks are invited to leave. Ain't nobody wants you here."

When Giancarlo and Zak didn't move—mostly because they weren't sure where to go or why they were being singled out—the young man walked over with a scowl on his face. "You hear me? Take your little white asses and walk back the way you came."

Another tall, young black man walked up behind the other and gently grabbed his elbow. "Come on, Rashad. They're not hurting anybody. They're just a couple of kids who want to play ball."

Rashad Salaam yanked his arm away from his friend. "Ain't these the kids of that muthafuckin' DA, Karp?"

"Yes, but . . . ," Khalif Mohammed replied.

"Then why you want to stick up for them?" Salaam asked without taking his angry dark eyes off the boys. "It's because of their daddy that our lives was messed up, dawg. Why you want to defend them?"

"Because they're kids," Mohammed said. "We let them play with us back before it all went down. They're not responsible for what happened. They're good kids. And who knows, their daddy may still do the right thing." He smiled at the boys, who smiled tentatively back.

Salaam snorted in disgust. "Yeah, right, like he did when that bitch assistant DA of his sent us to Attica? You remember that, homes? Remember what it was like? Well, I do, and now we don't have nothin' . . . no scholarship, no college, no future. If you want to play ball with his punk kids, that's your business. But I ain't going to have nothin' to do with no Karps, no way, nohow."

With that he stomped back to the court, where he started shooting at a basket with several other young men. Mohammed glanced at his friend and then back to the boys.

"That's okay, Khalif," Giancarlo said. "We'll just go shoot a little over on the other court. Thanks for sticking up for us."

Mohammed nodded and raised his hand and high-fived the twins. "Shalom, peace, brothers," he said and trotted back to where Salaam was waiting.

The twins walked over to an empty court and played a game of H-O-R-S-E. But their hearts just weren't in it. The courts at Sixth and Fourth were famous for attracting some of the best street-ball players in the city and were normally no place for a couple of seventh-grade boys. But when the weather was cold—as it was that day—fewer players showed up and they sometimes got invited to play. But not on this day.

"It's not fair," Zak muttered angrily, glancing over at where the older guys were laughing at something. "We didn't do nothin' to them."

"We didn't do anything to them, you mean," Giancarlo corrected him.

"Whatever," Zak said, rolling his eyes. "We're getting blamed because of Dad."

"Dad was just doing his job, or the assistant DA was just doing hers," Giancarlo said. He lifted the ball toward the hoop but it clanged off and into Zak's hands. The brain surgery he'd undergone that fall to remove a shot-gun pellet—courtesy of a murder attempt in West Virginia—had restored his eyesight to near normal, but he was still working on his depth perception.

"But that girl lied," Zak said. "They didn't rape her. That's why they're out of prison. Dad or that prosecutor screwed up." He banked a shot off the backboard and in.

"Maybe, maybe not," Giancarlo said after outracing his brother to the ball. "Dad's still trying to decide. Just because someone wins an appeal on a technicality doesn't mean they were innocent."

Zak stole the ball and laid it up for another basket. "Don't tell me you think they really did it," he said. "We've known them ever since they started coming over here during breaks from Columbia. You *know* they didn't do it."

Giancarlo drove the lane only to have his brother swat the ball from his hands. "Foul!"

"No way!" Zak replied. "I got all ball."

"You got all hand," Giancarlo complained. "Look, you can see the red mark on my hand."

"I don't see nothin'," Zak said.

"Anything."

"What?"

"You don't see anything," Giancarlo said.

"Whatever."

"Good answer. And no, I don't think they'd do it either. But that's why you have judges and juries. Dad doesn't go around prosecuting people for no reason."

"Dad is just one guy. He can't know everything that goes on in every courtroom."

"Well, I'll bet he knows all there is to know about this case. He doesn't like it when one of their cases gets over-turned."

The case the boys were talking about—The People vs. Salaam and Mohammed—had been tried that summer. The boys didn't know all the details, only what they'd picked up on the basketball court and heard their father talking about to their mother.

Apparently that past February, Salaam and Mohammed, both varsity players for the Columbia University basketball team, had been accused of raping a young woman in her apartment bedroom during a postgame party. They'd been convicted and sent to prison. However, a defense lawyer had won an appeal that got them out of prison because of something the prosecution had done wrong, and now they were waiting to see if the twins' dad was going to try the case again.

In the meantime, the twins had been told by friends of the pair that the university had stripped them of their scholarships and kicked them out of school without a fair hearing. Giancarlo and Zak knew that both of the young men came from poor families in East Harlem. Now no other school would offer them a scholarship or even admit them, for that matter. Even if the charges were dropped, their lives were—as Salaam had said—messed up.

The twins also knew from the newspapers that their dad had been taking a certain amount of heat from black activists because Salaam and Mohammed were Black Muslims. The charges, according to one newspaper op-ed opinion piece by some attorney named Hugh Louis, would never have been brought if the defendants had been "white and Christian." Louis had accused their dad of "giving in to the racist hysteria of post 9/11 where every dark face and every Muslim is considered a terrorist."

The boys had wanted to ask their dad what it all meant, especially because they had known Salaam and Mohammed for nearly two years and didn't believe that they would have done the crime. But Butch Karp didn't like to "bring the office home" (as they'd heard him tell their mother) and they'd avoided saying anything.

Zak frowned, something he did so often that his mother warned him someday his face was "going to stick like that"—a not totally disagreeable result because he thought it made him look tougher. Of the twins, he was the stockier and more athletic, prone to act first and consider, if he ever did, the ramifications later. He was a good-looking kid who had his share of female admirers in junior high.

On the other hand, Giancarlo was beautiful by anyone's standard. Artists he met on the street or through his parents remarked that he looked as if he could have posed as an angel for Renaissance painters. His dark wavy hair was growing back nicely after having been shaved for the surgery. He was more likely to think before he acted and often surprised adults with his perception, as well as his nearly savant talent as a musician who now played the violin, guitar, harmonica, and accordion.

"Well, I think it's fucked up that just because someone says something a person's life can be ruined," Zak said.

"You shouldn't use language like that," Giancarlo scolded. "It doesn't make you seem smarter; in fact, the opposite."

"Whatever, fucker."

When the twins got home an hour later, they grilled their dad about what was going to happen to Salaam and Mohammed. "Sorry, boys," he said. "I've been a little preoccupied lately, and I'm not up to speed on that one, though I expect I'll hear about it at tomorrow's staff meeting. Not that I'll be able to tell you much even then."

"Why not?" Zak complained.

"Why?" Karp replied raising an eyebrow. "Because it's top secret. Oh, I suppose I could tell you, but then I'd have to have you whacked, which your mother would probably never forgive me for."

"Actually," Marlene said, entering the living room and catching the tail end of the conversation, "I've considered having them whacked myself for the state they left their bedroom in today when I specifically told them to clean it up or no basketball."

Recognizing the danger of imminent chores, Giancarlo decided this wasn't the time to press on about their friends. "Come on, Zak." He sniffed. "I'm hungry and since the parental units would just as soon starve us out as look at us, I suggest we go look in the refrigerator before we pass out from hunger." Zak said nothing but followed his brother's cue and immediately turned and fled for the kitchen.

"Bedroom," Marlene yelled after them. "Clean. Or no Santa Claus at Christmas."

"We don't believe in Santa Claus," Zak retorted over his shoulder.

"And besides, we're half Jew, we only half believe in Christmas," Giancarlo added.

"I guess we'll remember that on Christmas morning then," Marlene said.

The twins paused and looked at each other. But there'd been similar threats over the years, and they decided this one wasn't worthy of talking back. They continued on.

With the twins out of the way, Marlene settled down on the couch next to where her husband was reading Walter Isaacson's book on Benjamin Franklin, *An American Life.* He pointed to a sentence and said, "His guiding principle was 'a dislike of everything that tended to debase the spirit of the common people.' I like that."

"Uh-huh," Marlene said as she snuggled closer and began playing with the zipper on the front of his sweatshirt.

Karp recognized the prelude to something more immediately interesting than old Ben and closed the book. "What's up?"

"Remember me telling you about meeting that interesting Russian girl yesterday?" she said.

"Yeah, but you didn't say much," he replied.

"Well, I was a little preoccupied with Mom and Dad," she said.

Karp put his arm around her shoulders. He'd felt so helpless when she told him about her visit with Concetta and Mariano. What was there to say about such a horrible disease? All he could do was hold her and listen . . . and wonder if the same sort of thing might happen someday to them.

"What can you tell me about the Michalik case?" Marlene asked suddenly.

Karp stiffened. Marlene didn't usually pry into his work. In fact, she usually steered well clear of it. He felt an odd twisting in his gut and hoped it wasn't a premonition that she was about to stick her nose where it didn't belong, again.

"This have to do with the Russian woman?" he asked.

Marlene fiddled a little more with the zipper and nodded. "Her name was Helena Michalik."

"The wife of Alexis Michalik?" he asked. She nodded again. He shrugged. "He's been accused of sexually assaulting one of his grad students. Seems to be a strong case. I think Rachel's going to discuss taking it to the grand jury for an indictment at tomorrow's meeting. Why?"

Marlene cringed at the mention of Rachel Rachman, one of her former protégées when Marlene had run the DA's sex crimes unit years ago. At one time she'd considered Rachman the best and most logical choice as her successor. But somewhere along the line, Rachman had become a zealot who seemed to view all men as potential rapists and all women as victims.

"I don't know, maybe just the boys' questions about their friends," she said. "Sometimes people make false accusations. I was just wondering if someone's looked into the 'victim's' history. Helena seems to think that this woman was the one who was coming on to her husband." She told him what the other woman had told her.

As his wife spoke, Karp felt himself getting irritated. There were times when it seemed everybody in his family was backseat-driving his cases. "Coeds flirt with their professors all the time," he said. "It doesn't mean they deserve to get raped."

Now it was Marlene who flared a little. "I didn't say that. I was just asking if anyone's looked into the possibility that this woman might be lying."

But Karp wasn't backing down. "I'm sure that between the regular detectives and our investigators, we've looked under all the rocks. Besides, since when have you advocated that a victim's sexual history is relevant to a rape case? Isn't that the sort of thing that the shield laws were created to prevent? You used to be a big advocate of the shield laws. Isn't it a little two-faced now to suggest that we look into the alleged victim's sexual past just because you've taken in another stray dog?"

He'd meant for the statement to sound lighter than it had come out of his mouth. A gentle teasing, maybe a little good-natured chiding, but he knew as soon as he said *dog* that Marlene wasn't going to take it that way.

Indeed, she froze beneath his arm and stopped playing with the zipper. She sat back up and away from him. She glared at him for a moment, then announced, "I have a headache. I'm going to bed."

"Marlene . . . ," he said, intending to apologize, but she was already up and off the couch, and quickly disappeared down the hallway toward their bedroom.

Karp swore. Married to the woman for nearly twenty-five years and he still kept hitting the wrong buttons when he didn't intend it. No sense going back there until she's asleep, he thought, I'd get frostbite.

At about the same time that Karp was wishing he could take back words, Rashad Salaam and Khalif Mohammed were finishing their evening prayers at a small storefront mosque in Harlem. They had been inseparable since childhood—whether that was on the neighborhood courts, the high school team, or signing their letters of intent to play at Columbia while sitting at the kitchen table in Khalif's house as his proud mother looked on, bawling like a baby because "my child is going to college."

Khalif was their leader in most things, coolheaded and

studious. He'd also been the better player coming out of high school and could have attended a larger Division 1 university on a scholarship, but Columbia had been the only school to offer Rashad a full ride, so he'd opted to remain home with his friend.

It was also Khalif, born Joseph White, who'd first met a Black Muslim who spoke at the high school and began studying the Quran. He'd liked the simplicity of placing his life in the hands of Allah's will, as well as Islam's tenets of peace and faith. He'd persuaded his best friend, Bobby Humphrey, to go with him to the mosque. They'd both converted to Islam and changed their names at the end of their senior year in high school—Khalif because he felt genuinely drawn to the teachings of the Prophet, Rashad because he felt it was more appropriate for African-American men than Christianity "which was the religion of our enslavers."

It was Rashad, however, who had recently introduced Khalif to the Arab man with the pockmarked face and intense glittering eyes. "He's from Saudi Arabia, dawg," Rashad said before the meeting, "here to raise money for Muslim charities overseas. But he's also got a lot to say about how African-Americans are still enslaved to the white man in this country."

"I don't know, Rashad," Khalif said. "Some of those 'charities' are just fronts for terrorists—"

"Freedom fighters, homes," Rashad responded before his friend could continue. "It's The Man who says they're terrorists. But what about the Israelis bulldozing homes and killing little Palestinian kids? And what about the U.S. military machine that is bombing our Muslim brothers in Iraq as we speak? Isn't those terrorist acts?"

Khalif scowled. "You forgetting my auntie was in the World Trade Center? She was just a poor cleaning lady. It wasn't no freedom fighters that done that. And puttin' bombs on kids to blow up innocent people is nothing but cold-blooded murder."

"I know, dawg, I know. I ain't saying all that shit is right," Rashad said. "But Mr. Mustafa ain't no terrorist or freedom fighter, he's just here to raise money for the Red Crescent, which is sort of like the Red Cross. He'd just like to meet us and some of the other guys."

Khalif reluctantly agreed and Rashad led the way to the back of the mosque—really a former grocery store that had been converted into the prayer room, several offices, and another meeting room in the back. As they entered they were greeted effusively by the imam of the mosque, Ahman Zakir, a roly-poly jovial sort whose understanding of the Quran was probably less than many of those who attended his mosque. But he kept the place open and provided clean prayer rugs and a decent enough call to prayer.

What the two younger men, as well as most of the others in the room, didn't know was that Zakir was more of a front man than an imam. He'd found it tough to get by on what his local followers offered in the way of financial support so when the Middle Eastern men arrived in the mid-1990s offering to "sponsor" his mosque, which included a nice stipend for his living expenses, he'd happily agreed.

There were just a few things they required in exchange. Their leader, Mr. Mustafa, the only name he ever had offered, asked him to have a back storage area converted into a sort of barracks "for pilgrims" with cots, a stocked refrigerator, and a hot plate for cooking. Before being allowed access to the room, the pilgrims were supposed to give him the current code word—taken from a different page of the Quran each week. He wasn't supposed to go into the room himself, which meant that he just had to once when none of the visitors were around. But he wished he'd resisted when he saw the assault rifles and other weapons neatly arranged on a rack.

Mr. Mustafa later told him that he knew he'd been in the room. "Please follow my instructions from now on or we will have to find someone who can," he said.

Noticing that Mustafa did not say they would find a new place, only a new host, Zakir took it for the threat it was intended to be. But he'd still managed to complain about the guns.

"They are for defensive purposes only," Mr. Mustafa assured him. "In case the climate in this country should someday—encouraged by the Zionist murderers—turn against Muslims. Then you will be glad that we were prepared."

At times there were no pilgrims staying in the back room. At others there were as many as a dozen men—some Arab, some African. They were always mysterious about their comings and goings, never together but always one at a time. It all made Zakir nervous, especially because there was a lot of activity again, as there had been before September 11, 2001.

One of the other conditions of his agreement with Mr. Mustafa was that he introduce him to the young men from the neighborhood who came to the mosque to pray. "I am recruiting missionaries from America to go to Muslim countries to see how their brothers and sisters are subjugated so that they can return to the United States and be a strong voice against Zionist propaganda," he said.

Zakir didn't really believe him, but he did like the three-thousand-dollar bonuses he received for every young man who signed up for Mustafa's missionary program. The money went a long way toward assuaging his conscience. He'd recently pointed out the two tall young basketball players and told Mustafa how they'd been wronged by the white man's judicial system. "They might make good . . . missionaries," he'd said.

Tonight's meeting was going to be fairly well attended. Besides the two basketball players, there were six other young men. Even if only four join Mustafa, he thought, that's an easy twelve thousand dollars.

He had to admit that Mr. Mustafa was clever and didn't start right in with a high-pressure sales pitch. Instead, he concentrated on talking about the plight of fellow Muslims and how the United States had been duped into helping the Jews establish their "One World Order, in which all true believers will be forced to kneel to their false God or die." He asked why the richest, most powerful nation in the world continued to oppress people of color both at home and abroad. "Because it is in the interests of the white man and the Jews to subjugate brown-skinned people. After all, why be the master of no one?"

Zakir noticed that of the two basketball players, the one called Rashad seemed the most agreeable to Mustafa's message. The other, Khalif, had stood in the back of the room with his arms crossed and a skeptical look on his face. He'd barely listened for five minutes before saying he needed to go home. He tried to get his friend to leave—"Come on, dawg, this joker's full of shit"—but Rashad had stayed.

When Khalif stalked out by himself, Zakir caught the appraising look on Mustafa's face as he watched the young man leave. But he'd turned his pockmarked face back to his audience and shook his head as though sorry to see Khalif go. "We must always be careful of those among us who are so desperate to be a part of the world

of whites and Jews—though they would never allow it—
that they would betray our holy cause."

An hour after the meeting was over, Mustafa, an Iraqi
whose real name before joining Al Qaeda was Anan Al-
Sistani, left the mosque with one of his bodyguards. He
didn't stay at the mosque—he had a luxurious suite in
midtown Manhattan from which he directed his operations—and didn't like being there. Too exposed. But he
needed recruits to pull off his "event" and the mosque was
the best place to find them.

Outside on the sidewalk, he'd looked around with irritation for a second bodyguard who was supposed to be
watching the front entrance in case the police or federal
agents showed up.

"Where is that fool Jabal?" he muttered to the other
bodyguard. "Go look in the alley and see if he is relieving
himself."

The bodyguard walked down the block to the entrance
of the alley. The space between the buildings was pitch-
black and he couldn't see beyond a Dumpster ten feet
from the entrance. "Jabal?" he said.

There was the sound of scurrying and something sent
a bottle skittering in the dark, making the bodyguard
jump and put his hand inside his coat for the comfort of
his gun. Rats, he thought when his nerves calmed down,
just rats.

"Jabal?" he said a little louder. But there were no more
sounds. He considered exploring the alley for his colleague. But when he took a step into the blackness a chill
seemed to freeze his muscles, and he could force himself
to go no farther. He returned to his leader who was waiting impatiently.

"Well?" Al-Sistani demanded.

The bodyguard shrugged. "He wasn't there. Perhaps

he thought he'd been noticed by a passing police car and left to avoid being questioned."

Al-Sistani thought about it. "Yes," he concluded. "He wouldn't want to draw attention to this place. He'll meet up with us later."

The two men left, walking past the alley where the bodyguard had heard the sounds. He'd been right about the rats. Dozens of them had smelled the blood and come running to feast on the headless body of the second bodyguard behind the Dumpster.

9

KINGS COUNTY DISTRICT ATTORNEY KRISTINE BRE-
man peered through the tinted window of her official
limousine at the two black men leaning against the brick
wall of a dark office building that occupied the corner of
Adam Clayton Powell Boulevard and 121st Street. The
bigger of the two—his girth so wide that his arms stuck
out to the side like an immensely fat penguin—rocked
forward from his angle of repose and waddled toward
them, his broad face wrinkled into a menacing scowl.

A small, childlike voice began to chime in Breman's
head. *I don't want to be here. I don't want to be here.
Why am I here?* If she had been behind the wheel, she
might have stepped on the gas pedal and roared out of
there like Mario Andretti at the Indy 500. But she had no
choice except to get out of the car when her driver
opened the door for her.

The whole mess had started that past spring when Hugh
Louis called and asked for an appointment. As he pretty
much told her black constituency how to vote, she had

willingly granted him an audience. In fact, she'd sent out for a tray of snacks from the local deli and several bottles of root beer, which he was known to love.

After trading meaningless compliments and bromides, Louis popped the top on one of the root beers, washed down a canapé, and got down to business. He told her that a prison inmate named Enrique Villalobos would soon contact her and confess that he alone was responsible for the 1992 rape of a woman named Liz Tyler under the pier at Coney Island. Louis said he was representing the four men who'd been "falsely imprisoned" and that he intended to sue New York City as the employer of the police officers and detectives who had carried out this "abominable injustice," as well as the Kings County District Attorney's Office, which had "conspired" through the two women prosecutors who'd acted in concert with the police to deprive his clients of their constitutional rights. He also intended to sue the cops and the prosecutors as individuals, though obviously it was the government entities that had the deeper pockets. Louis paused to make sure she understood what he was saying.

Breman understood. She also knew that she was staring at him with her mouth hanging open but couldn't quite bring herself to try a different expression. This is a nightmare, she thought. She barely remembered the Coney Island case—she'd still been working for the New York DA's office in 1992 and had been too busy trying to stave off being released for incompetence to worry about some rape case in someone else's jurisdiction. It was only by chance—in the form of partisan politics, a strong political machine, and a few favors called in and promised in return—that a half-dozen years later she'd won the election for the office of Kings County District Attorney, which was essentially Brooklyn.

The press is going to make my life miserable, she thought. Got to find a way out of this. She cleared her throat, smiled weakly at Louis, and said, "Yes, umm, go on."

Sweating profusely already, Louis grunted and thought, Got the bitch right where I want her. Taking his time, he finished off the root beer and pounded his chest lightly before emitting a long belch. "Pardon me," he said not very convincingly. "Anyway, as I was saying . . ."

Louis said he was convinced that he could prove a pattern of reckless misconduct on the part of the two prosecutors, as well as Breman's predecessor in office. "A pattern I believe the jury, as well as the African-American community, will recognize was based on an institutionalized racism."

At the mention of *African-American community* and *racism,* Breman sucked in her breath and held it. She wasn't comfortable around black people; they always seemed to be looking at her as if they secretly blamed her for everything bad that had happened since the days of slavery. But without the black vote, Breman knew she was finished as the district attorney. Her future flashed before her eyes. If she was kicked out of office as the racist DA of Kings County, no firm would hire her. She'd have to hang her shingle out in front of some little strip mall office in Brooklyn and hope to pick up the odd criminal case, plus the cheapie divorces and DUI infractions.

She wouldn't be able to count on her husband for support. The pencil-dicked asshole was a plastic surgeon who preferred screwing his nurses and patients to her. She'd been his ticket into party politics—he saw himself as potential governor material someday—but there'd be no reason to keep her around if she was a nobody.

The image faded and was replaced by the immensely fat Hugh Louis. Fortunately, the plastic smile had never left her face and she pointed out, "I wasn't in office at that time. I—"

Louis held up a big sweaty hand. "I know, I know," he said in his most "Hey, we're all in this together" voice. "I've always liked you, Krissy. May I call you Krissy? Good. Yes, always liked you, thought you was fair and reasonable."

This sounded like a good thing, so Breman brightened. In fact, she was so grateful that tears sprang to her eyes. "Well, you know, I try . . ." but her mouth snapped shut when Louis held up his hand again.

"Please, allow me to continue," he said. "I would hate for you to suffer the consequences for your predecessor's mistake. We might even have on our hands a Rodney King sort of backlash here. . . ." He was gratified to see Breman blanch. "So because of my respect and fondness for you, and hating the thought of how this community could come apart at the seams, I thought I would speak to you first and see if maybe we could work out an arrangement. Something mutually beneficial to both of us, as well as our community."

Breman was all ears. "Yes," she said, nodding like a bobble-head doll in a car going down the railroad tracks. "I'm sure that's true. Here, have another canapé and a root beer . . . shall I open it for you?"

Louis accepted the groveling with dignity, although inside he was smirking. "Thank you, thank you . . . excellent spiced meat. May I ask where you got it? Perhaps later you can call my secretary with the name of the deli."

Smiling broadly, Louis said he thought he might be able to convince the African-American community that "these heinous transgressions against my clients" were the work of another regime and that she, Kristine Breman, was not responsible. "However, there is going to have to be a show of good faith from your office." He paused for her reaction.

Breman shook herself as if she'd been daydreaming. "Yes, of course, good faith. Umm . . . such as?"

Louis pulled out a white hankerchief and mopped at his face before continuing. "Well, nothing more than what would be just and fair. The first is that you meet with Mr. Villalobos and when you find that his story is credible, you will order DNA testing to see if his is a match for the evidence found on the victim's clothes."

Breman, who'd been wondering just how much of her soul she was going to sell to the devil, perked up. "You think it will be a match?"

Louis nodded. "I *know* it will be a match," he said. "But that's not all."

This is where the other shoe drops, Breman thought. "Yes?" she said, trying not to let her voice quaver.

"If what I say is true, then in the interest of justice I will immediately file a motion to vacate the convictions of my clients and seek their immediate release from prison. . . . And you will not oppose it," he said, the jovial bonhomie gone from his fat face. "In fact, you will join with me in my motion."

"Well," Breman said, then paused as her mind frantically worked over the political implications, "it is irregular. But I suppose we could go through the normal procedures and put Mr. Villalobos on the stand, under oath, and hold a formal hearing. Then we could issue a joint statement . . ." She stopped talking because Louis was shaking his head.

"I don't think that's necessary," he said. "I think you can meet with Mr. Villalobos, who with my assistance—

just to make sure he doesn't backtrack on the truth—will give you a statement. I think that with the DNA tests, you will have more than enough to do what I ask."

Breman realized that while Louis said "ask," it was a demand. He was telling her how to proceed or, as he'd said earlier, she'd face the consequences. She had no intention of facing anything of the sort, and so simply nodded her head.

Louis seemed to have caught her mood and misgivings. "Now, now, Krissy," he said. "I know this might be a little irregular, but my clients have just spent the last ten years of their lives locked up where they did not belong. They went in as young men, teenagers really, and missed the best years of their young manhood, not to mention the pain and suffering they experienced in prison.

"The DNA will check out, have no fear. Your own assistant DAs—Robin Repass and Pam Russell—conceded in the original trial that there was an unidentified assailant . . . the only assailant whose DNA was found at the scene. Indeed, we contend, the only assailant there ever was. We have some concerns, however, about Mr. Villalobos's change of heart—he is a vile and despicable man who has committed numerous rapes upon innocent women. He could change his mind again . . . if he thought he could get something out of it from the authorities. My clients have suffered enough. We don't need to put them through a lengthy hearing process or raise their hopes that justice will at last be served, only to have Mr. Villalobos retract and dash those hopes again. I'm sure you understand."

Breman surrendered. "Yes, of course. If all you say is true, it's only right that this office act with all due haste to correct this miscarriage of justice."

Sighing as though he'd been laboring long and hard in the cause of justice, Louis leaned forward and patted

Breman on the knee of her pantsuit, leaving a damp spot. "Yes, all due haste. And mark my words, you will come out of this a hero in the African-American community, a veritable color-blind champion of the truth."

Breman almost burst into tears. That was the nicest thing anybody had said to her in what had turned out to be a very long day. She'd never wanted a drink so badly in her life. A double shot of scotch poured over a cube of ice. "Well, then I'll wait for Mr. . . . did you say Villalobos? . . . to call," she said and started to rise as if to bring the meeting to a close. But Louis didn't budge, so she sat back down.

"Uh, yes, but there is one other thing," he said. "The people who perpetrated this crime against my clients need to pay for those lost years. I intend to wring every last cent out of them now and in the future."

"Of course." Breman was willing to say anything just to get the fat, sweating man out of her office. She'd decided she would need to take a shower before that drink. Just watching the sweat pour off the man made her feel nauseated.

"That will be easier if the police officers, detectives, and prosecutors responsible are not supported by their respective administrations," Louis said. "I think it is in your best interest to put some distance between you and them so that any prospective jurors will understand where you stand in this matter."

"What do you want me to do?" Breman asked.

"I want you to put Repass and Russell on administrative leave pending an investigation into possible criminal malfeasance, as well as civil rights violations," Louis said.

Breman blinked several times as Louis leaned over and grabbed the last of the root beers out of the little bucket of ice she'd arranged between them. She didn't like Repass and Russell—a couple of hotshots who'd come in during her predecessor's tenure to create the sex assault unit.

"Okay," she'd said. "If the DNA checks out, we have an arrangement." This time she stood up before Louis could add any more caveats. But he seemed well pleased with her response and rose with her. He'd stuck out his hand and she shook it, trying not to look sickened by the feel of his warm, wet grip.

"You won't regret this," he said.

And at first she hadn't. As she'd been told, Villalobos had approached prison officials and reported that a "positive prison experience" had led him to become a born-again Christian. That in turn led him to confess to the Coney Island rape because his conscience would no longer allow him to stand by and see other men "suffer for my sins."

When the news broke in the *New York Times*—a story written by a weaselly fish-faced reporter named Marvin Aloysius Harriman—Repass and Russell had immediately come to Breman and demanded that they be allowed to put Villalobos on the stand and take his "confession" under oath and be cross-examined. That was, after all, how such matters were supposed to be handled. But Breman had told them that she would personally handle this case and had asked that Villalobos be transported to the Kings County jail, where she conducted the interview with Louis the only other person present.

Louis insisted that she use a tape recorder he'd brought rather than the jail's installed system. In fact, throughout the interview, he'd controlled what was actually recorded. If not satisfied with an answer given by Villalobos, he'd stopped the machine, discussed the matter with the ugly little man, and then rewound the tape. Then on his signal, Breman had repeated her question, and Villalobos answered in a "more appropriate" manner.

After the interview was over Breman had announced to the press that there was "reasonable cause" to order DNA testing. She'd felt somewhat better when the DNA results came back positive. At least that part of Villalobos's story was accurate.

By arrangement, she'd leaked the results first to Harriman, who seemed to have made his own deal with Louis, so that the *New York Times*—quoting "an anonymous source in the Kings County District Attorney's Office"— had the story a day before the rest of the media. Shortly afterward, Breman had held a press conference on the steps of the Brooklyn courthouse with Louis at her side, announcing that "in the interests of justice" her office would be joining Louis's motion to have the convictions overturned. "It is my opinion that the so-called Coney Island Four have been exonerated by these developments, and this office will not seek further action."

In the days that followed, Breman was even able to convince herself that she had done the right thing. It helped that she got a lot of encouragement from others. Activists in the African-American and civil rights communities lauded her "courage in the fight against institutionalized racism"; the Kings County defense bar issued a statement that read in part, "finally a district attorney who recognizes that justice, not conviction statistics, is the duty of the state when prosecuting crimes"; and the *Times* even wrote an editorial. The editorial noted that based on the "exclusive" reporting of award-winning writer Harriman, the newspaper's hierarchy agreed with Breman's decision and that "perhaps other local district attorneys should take note of the evenhanded administration of justice by the Kings County District Attorney and seek to emulate her to bring credibility and honor back into their own dealings."

The only downside had been putting up with the tirades of the assistant DAs Repass and Russell, who'd insisted that they'd presented evidence in the original trial that there was a sixth perpetrator but that did not mean that the teenage defendants had not "initiated and participated" in the crime. "The jury understood this to be the case and convicted Sykes, Davis, Wilson, and Jones in less than two hours of deliberations," Repass argued.

Breman was proud of how she stood up to the know-it-alls. She pointed out that there were no eyewitnesses to place the five black teens at the scene—not even the victim could substantiate that allegation—"but we have irrefutable scientific evidence that Villalobos committed the crime, as well as his confession."

"An uncorroborated confession. There's a legal precedent for this—hold a hearing, put him under oath, at worst retry the case," Russell countered.

"A waste of time in my opinion, which is the opinion that counts here," Breman said. "Villalobos's confession is corroborated by the DNA evidence. There was no physical evidence or eyewitness testimony tying the defendants to the attack on Liz Tyler."

"We had a witness testify that five black teenagers were seen leaving the general area," Russell countered.

"No one who could say it was these boys," Breman countered.

"These 'boys' were also convicted of several other assaults that night," Repass pointed out, "including nearly killing an elderly man with a piece of steel bar like the one found beneath the pier."

"We try people for one crime at a time here," Breman said. "As you point out, they were convicted of those other crimes and served their time for them. It is *this* crime for which there are very large questions of guilt—questions that in my opinion raise a serious ethical question of how we were ever in a position to, in good faith, ask a jury to find these young men guilty beyond a reasonable doubt. . . . And, I might add, there was no physical evidence—blood or hair—on the steel bar suggesting that it was the same one used that night in the other crimes."

"By the time it was found, the tide had washed it off," Russell said.

"It's nonsense anyway," Repass added. "These 'large questions' were looked at by the jury, and they found that we'd answered them beyond a reasonable doubt. And what about the confessions? Those animals corroborated the evidence—hell, they boasted about what they did."

Breman bristled at Repass. "I'll thank you not to refer to these young men as 'animals.' It merely serves to underline the accusations that this office has a problem with racist attitudes. As for the confessions, they *were* boys at that time—coerced, badgered, and intimidated by grown, gun-toting men who threatened them with every sort of punishment under the sun, including the possibility of the death penalty if Liz Tyler had died."

"Oh, Christ!" Repass exclaimed. "They were laughing about it in front of the cops. One of them talked about how much fun it was—that's not exactly the response of a frightened 'boy.' "

"Nerves," Breman shrugged. "Trying to put on a brave face."

"What about the defendant who took me to the scene and said he didn't realize there'd been so much blood?" Russell asked.

"That was Kevin Little, who, if I remember correctly, was given a pretty sweet deal for turning on his childhood friends," Breman said. "Hardly an unbiased witness."

Repass started to say something, but Breman sat up in the manner bosses do when they've given recalcitrant subordinates a "fair" hearing but are ready to move on. "This conversation is over," she said. At last, she thought, I can get rid of these two, and I'll even look like the hero as far as the public's concerned.

"I think it would go a long way toward reestablishing this office's credibility with the public if you two took it upon yourselves to sign off on the motion in support of vacating the convictions, as well as demanding that these four men be released immediately from custody."

Seeing the shocked looks on the other women's faces, Breman barely contained a giggle before adding, "It might mitigate some of the damages should they prevail in a lawsuit against this office."

"Fuck you," Repass said.

Smiling, Breman shook her head as if she didn't quite know what to do with such an unruly child. She cocked an eyebrow and looked at Russell, who nodded her head toward her colleague. "What she said."

"Well then," Breman said, clasping her hands as if they'd all reached some mutually satisfying agreement, "that leaves me no choice but to place the two of you on administrative leave." She leaned forward and pressed the button on her intercom. "Teddy, could you come in here, please."

A moment later, Theodore "Teddy" Chalk entered the room and glared at Repass and Russell. His boss had already told him what was up and that the women, especially the hotheaded Repass, might get violent.

Teddy wasn't the sharpest tool in the shed, but he was one good-looking, square-jawed, dark-eyed, dark-haired, olive-skinned, body-building hunk of former-cop-turned-bodyguard. He was also madly in love with Breman, and she'd occasionally allowed him to service her sexual needs, although that was more to ensure his absolute devotion than out of any genuine desire for him.

"Teddy, would you please escort Ms. Repass and Ms. Russell to their offices, where they are allowed to remove a single box containing their personal belongings. However, they are not to take any legal paperwork or files. Can you do that for me?" She gave him her most beguiling smile, which made him blush and then straighten as if he'd been given an order by a superior officer. He'd been a marine for a couple of years out of high school, and once in a moment of passion she'd told him that it turned her on every time he snapped to attention when she spoke, so he'd stepped it up ever since. "Yes, ma'am."

Teddy stepped forward as if to physically remove the women but stopped when Repass snarled, "Touch me and I'll kick your balls up around your shoulders." He looked confused, then glanced over at Breman, who rolled her eyes and nodded her head toward the door.

The bodyguard and two angry women were gone from her office for only a minute when Hugh Louis stepped from the small antechamber where he'd remained out of sight during the discussion. "Well done, Krissy, well done," he said. "You go, girl. Good to hear that someone in government still believes in the Constitution and the concept of reasonable doubt." He shook a fat finger and looked at the ceiling as he recited, ". . . 'better that a hundred guilty men'—not that my clients are guilty of these crimes—'than a single innocent man lose his freedom.' . . . I believe it was Jefferson or someone like him who said that."

That had been that past summer. Now, as Teddy stood back from the car door and extended a hand to help her out into the frigid December air, Breman recalled how Louis's praise that day had made her skin crawl. Again the little voice was asking her to leave so that she had to remind herself that she was doing this because Louis could practically guarantee her the black vote. This is just a little thing, she thought, we're accomplishing a lot in the office getting bums off the streets and arresting graffiti taggers to make cleaner, nicer neighborhoods. And you can't do that sort of good if you're not in office, can you.

Breman also had higher aspirations than the district attorney's office, and Louis could get her there, too. He'd hinted as much when inviting her to this late-night meeting in Harlem. "A person with your ability and charm could do a lot of good for this community as a district court judge," he said. "And I might be in a position to help a friend with those sorts of ambitions."

Breman was certainly aware that Louis pulled a lot of strings behind the scenes when it came to political appointments. He was also known to have important contacts in the nation's capital. A spot on the bench was a nice dream, one she felt she deserved, but on the ride over she also couldn't get over the feeling that Louis had whistled and she'd obeyed like a well-trained dog.

"Maybe I should go in with you, Kri . . . I mean, ma'am," Teddy said, glancing meaningfully at the big man standing on the sidewalk in front of the steps leading into the building. The skinny one had also come off the wall and moved onto the sidewalk.

Breman wished more than anything that she could say yes to Teddy's request, but Louis had told her to come alone. He promised that she had nothing to worry about, even though he mentioned that Jayshon Sykes and perhaps another of the Coney Island Four would be present. Mustn't show fear. "No. I'll be all right, Teddy. I won't be long."

As she walked over to the steps, the fat man turned and proceeded up the steps ahead of her. After she passed, the skinny man parked himself at the bottom of the steps and stared insolently at Teddy, who stood looking after Breman like a retriever waiting for its master to come home.

At the top of the steps, Breman paused long enough to read the simple plaque on the outside of the building: Louis & Associates, Attorneys at Law. The inside of the office was nondescript, by all signs a no-frills, hardworking, underfunded legal firm.

Beyond the outer reception area was another spartan office with a desk on which rested the nameplate for Hugh Louis, Esq. The chair behind the desk was functional but nothing special, as were the two chairs in front. What art there was in the room consisted of cheap African knockoffs of Zulu masks and Swahili spears and a fake lion's skin made of horsehide.

Breman figured that this office was probably where Louis met most of his clients. She was sure of it when she was led into the inner sanctum—a richly appointed den done in teak and leather. The walls were adorned with expensive-looking art pieces, including what she believed might have been an original Jackson Pollock. A black-and-white photograph of Louis with his arm around an uncomfortable-looking Joe Namath hung behind the desk, signed Best Wishes, Joe.

As she entered, Louis came out from around a bar where he'd been mixing "a root beer and rum . . . care to join me?"

Breman shook her head. "No, thank you. It's been a long day and it would probably just make me sleepy." She laughed, wondering if it sounded as false as it felt.

Louis mopped his forehead with the omnipresent handkerchief, which he then stuffed back into a pocket and held out his hand. "Good of you to make it, Krissy," he said. "Sorry to make you—I mean, ask you—to make the drive from Brooklyn, but I thought it would be good for us to meet away from prying eyes. There ain't many in this neighborhood, at least none who would say anything to anybody who might care." He released her hand and pointed behind and to her side. "I believe you know my clients here, Mr. Jayshon Sykes and Mr. Desmond Davis."

Breman fought to keep the smile on her face as she turned in the direction Louis was pointing. She had not seen the two men slouching on the black leather couch in front of the wall of books. She nodded. "Of course. Good to see you again."

Neither of the young men acknowledged her greeting. They both appeared to have found something infinitely more interesting on the wall and on the floor respectively. Louis pretended not to notice the slight and waved her toward the chair in front of his desk while he went around behind it and sat down. Establishing who's boss, Breman thought miserably as she noticed that her seat was several inches lower than Louis's, who appeared to tower over her.

As a matter of fact, Louis was immensely pleased with himself. He'd filed a $250 million lawsuit against the City of New York and its police department, which he estimated might settle at one hundred million. He was contractually entitled to one-third of the settlement and by the time he added in expenses, including an apartment for his mistress, Tawnee, and the baubles she required to keep her happy, he'd get about half. And that didn't include the book and film rights.

Over steaks and martinis at the Tribeca Grill, he'd cut a deal to do a book with the *New York Times* reporter Harriman, in exchange for half the royalties and favorable stories in the *Times*. So far, the reporter, who had never met a scene he couldn't create out of thin air or a quote he couldn't manufacture, had kept up his end of the bargain.

Louis and Harriman had a meeting set up the next week with three different publishing houses whose executive editors were already pissing all over themselves for the rights to *The Coney Island Four: An American Tale of Racism and Injustice*. As soon as they had a deal, Louis planned to fly to Hollywood and talk to a couple of producers he'd contacted about the film rights.

Life was good, but he thought it could get better yet. He'd called Breman and told her to meet him at the office for two reasons. The first was—as Breman had surmised—to make sure she understood who was in charge. He figured that if she was willing to drive to Harlem on a cold night in December to be given marching orders, she was his whore for the duration.

The second reason was that for all his meticulous planning, dangers remained dangers. The major difficulty was that for some inexplicable reason, Igor Kaminsky was still alive.

The idiot brute Lynd was supposed to have taken care of the problem but now he was worm meat. Then the brain-dead ghetto niggers sitting on his couch couldn't count to two—the number of arms the man they'd shoved in front of the train had—and so the one-armed Kaminsky lived to rat on them another day.

Otherwise, there was only one other loose end that he had to worry about—and he didn't think it was much of a concern. At the original trial, a teenage female named Hannah Little had testified that Kwasama Jones admitted to her over the telephone that Sykes and Davis had raped Liz Tyler. Hannah's brother, Kevin, had been one of the five originally charged for the attack on Liz Tyler, but he'd agreed to a plea deal and testified against the other four.

Sykes had used his gang affiliations to find Kevin in California and have him killed in a staged drive-by shooting. He'd planned to have Hannah killed, too, but she'd disappeared from Bedford-Stuyvesant shortly after her brother's death and hadn't been heard from since. She could present a problem if the investigators working for the city found her, but given the long silence, Louis believed that she was too intimidated to come forward at this late date.

Which brought him back to Breman. He knew she'd talked herself into believing that she was "doing the right thing" in the cause of justice; he'd pounded that notion at her enough. But what if the letter from Kaminsky made her think again about Villalobos's confession?

Louis knew his clients were guilty of the crime and that Villalobos was lying—he'd insisted on knowing and Sykes had filled him in with a smirk. But Louis didn't care; some middle-class white bitch getting raped wasn't worth the millions he stood to make by representing the Coney Island Four. But he was worried that Breman might grow a conscience because of the Kaminsky letter. Or, if the little shit came forward, that she would find it politically expedient to turn on him. Louis needed to make sure she was his.

Louis cleared his throat, took a sip of his drink, and asked, "Have you heard from that lying piece of shit Kaminsky fella who wrote you a while back?"

The question elicited a pang of guilt from Breman. She'd read the letter when it first arrived and sat on it for a couple of days. If what Kaminsky said was true, and it came out, she was going to have a lot of explaining to do. All sorts of questions might be raised about why she had capitulated so quickly and not followed procedures in dealing with Villalobos. So she took the letter to her mentor, District Judge Marci Klinger, who also happened to be presiding over the Coney Island Four lawsuit.

Klinger was another castoff from the New York District Attorney's Office. She'd come aboard in the waning days of Garrahy's reign, recommended by one of his colleagues who'd done it as a favor to a friend, her father. But the recommendation only went so far, and she'd proved to be a mediocre prosecutor at best. But, as she'd later taught her protégée Breman to emulate, Klinger had involved herself early and often in party politics and when a spot on the bench opened up as a result of the sudden and unexpected death of its owner, she'd inveigled the appointment with the help of her dad, a major contributor to the party.

Even then she wasn't satisfied. She had her eye on becoming nothing less than the U.S. Attorney General. She and Breman sometimes got together at a private spa she belonged to in Manhattan for a "girls' day out" and a giggle about their aspirations. "You look so stunning in basic black . . . like a judge's robe," she hinted to Breman, who'd blushed and rolled her eyes.

After looking the Kaminsky letter over, Klinger had dismissed it as just another inmate who thought he saw a way out of prison. "He probably thinks that you'd jump at the chance to impeach Villalobos and preserve the case against four black men. But there's no proof here—at best just a he said/he said." Both women knew that a copy of the letter should have been turned over to the defendant's lawyer, in this case the Corporation Counsel. But Klinger said, "I see no sense in letting a red herring like this stand in the way of the truth or cloud the issues. There's a trial coming up; let's let the jury decide whether to believe Villalobos based on his testimony." She offered to hold on to the letter "so that it isn't accidentally discovered in your files and raises questions."

Breman had been only too happy to let Klinger have the letter. She was determined not to even remember its existence, except that in a moment of trying to one-up Louis, she casually mentioned it. At first she'd been pleased to see that he was shaken; after all, he'd done it to her often enough, but then she'd regretted telling him. He got surly and demanded to know who had the letter. She was relieved when he seemed to accept that the letter was in safekeeping with Klinger.

She was happy to report to Louis that she had not heard from Kaminsky since the letter. She glanced over at the two young men. Desmond Davis, a brooding, dark-visaged throwback to mankind's primitive past, had his head on the back of the couch and was staring up at the ceiling. But Sykes was looking right at her with a smile. She smiled back—at least she could feel good about saving this one. He was so well spoken and polite, a shame that the police had ruined his potential.

"Yo, Des, check out the bitch," he said. "She's afraid the big bad wolf might eat her." He leaned forward and made smacking noises with his mouth.

"Jayshon!" Louis rebuked him. "It is important to remember who our friends are . . . and Ms. Breman is one of them." He turned to Breman, who refused to look anywhere except at Louis. She was in shock. Whatever happened to the nice young man?

Sykes apologized, "I didn't mean anything by that—just the old prison defense mechanism, you know." He didn't like being lectured by the fat lawyer, but he did want to be a rich man. If he had to play the fucking game and listen to this fucked-up talk about trying to reintegrate him and his homies, he could deal. Just so long as after he got the money, nobody tried to tell him what cars he could and couldn't buy, or how many bitches he could have running around the mansion he planned to buy. Then he'd get a little payback on the people who locked him up and, if they weren't careful, the people who tried to boss him around now. The fat lawyer and this skinny bitch will get theirs if they keep pushing, he thought. Thinking about the other woman had been one of Sykes's favorite pastimes in prison. Exhausted by the long night of "wilding," he and his homies had been chilling beneath the pier that morning, drinking the last of the forties of malt liquor they'd stolen from a liquor store and smoking weed. He thought it was funny how easy it was to fool his teachers and others with his clean-cut, valedictorian act. This was the real Jayshon—the other guy was just a fake to get what he wanted.

He was idly whacking at a piling with the piece of steel rebar he'd found the night before when Desmond spotted the woman running down the beach toward them. He'd ordered his comrades back into the shadows until she was just about upon them, then jumped out in front of her.

"Boo!" he yelled in her face.

The woman tried to get away but he jumped in front

of her. "Say, where you going, bitch? Me and the home-boys was partyin' and thought maybe you should join us."

The woman tried to move around him. "Leave me alone!" she said in what was apparently meant to appear forceful but only made him laugh and taunt her more. He grabbed her by the arm and spun her around. Then to his surprise and rage, she'd reached out and clawed his face.

Without thinking about it, his hand with the steel rebar came up and hit her on the side of her head. She'd looked stunned, as if just given bad news, and sank to her knees. "Fucking ho," he snarled and grabbed her by the hair and pulled her under the pier and out of sight from anyone strolling along the boardwalk.

The pain of being dragged by her hair seemed to bring the woman back to her senses. She lunged up from the sand, screaming and scratching for his eyes. He'd felt fear and might have backed off, except Desmond kicked the woman in the small of the back, which knocked the wind out of her and sent her sprawling in the sand. She rose to her hands and knees, then paused, trying to catch her breath. Enraged by his fear, Sykes walked up to her and hit her on the head with the steel rebar again, only harder. The blow knocked her over onto her back, where she lay moaning.

Sykes reached down and grabbed her running shorts and tore them off. Excited by the sight of her half-nude body, he shouted, "Hold her" as he dropped his pants and got down between her legs.

Kwasama Jones ended up at her head on his knees and leaned forward to pin her arms. Kevin Little and Packer Wilson each grabbed a leg.

However, after having penetrated her, Sykes found he could not maintain an erection and ejaculate. This only served to anger him more and he punched her twice in the face before jumping up. "Yo, Des, your turn," he shouted and then egged his comrade on.

After Davis was finished, Sykes ordered Wilson to rape her but the fifteen-year-old couldn't get an erection at all, which brought loud guffaws from Sykes. "Look at the little fucker, can't even get it up. Fuck her, homes, ain't you a man?"

Not knowing what else might qualify him for manhood in his leader's eyes, Packer pulled up the woman's shirt and then bit her on the breast hard enough to draw blood. The woman screamed, which made Sykes and Davis laugh; Wilson tried to smile as he wiped the blood from his mouth but he then stood back and did not participate in the rest of the event.

Sykes next ordered Kevin Little to assault the woman, but he turned and threw up in the sand. "Ah shit, the little faggot got sick. Kwasama, you get you some now." But Kwasama shook his head. He'd continued holding her arms down, but he was crying.

Sykes was wondering what to do now with the woman when he noticed the ugly pockmarked Puerto Rican man standing twenty feet away. The greasy fucker looked like a hungry rat and was licking his lips and rubbing his crotch. "Hey, ratface, you want some of this bitch?" he asked.

Villalobos had jumped at the invitation. "Show you boys how to treat these bitches," he said. "If you want to teach them a real lesson, you got to fuck them dirty." He'd then kicked the woman so hard in the side that it knocked her over and onto her stomach. Laughing at the look on the others' faces, he'd then sodomized her, and when he finished, stood and wiped himself on her sweatshirt.

They all stood looking down at the woman. She was

bleeding from both of her ears as well as the ragged wounds on the side of her head from the rebar. There were no more moans, just a sort of fluttery breathing. Sykes kicked her in the head but there was no response. Then he became aware of a high-pitched wailing, in the distance but growing louder.

"Jayshon!" Davis had yelled. "It's 5-0! We got to get the hell out of here."

"What about her?" Kwasama asked.

Jayshon shrugged. "She's dead," he said and took off running.

Sykes had no idea what had become of the rat man after that, except that he wasn't caught. But the others were not so lucky. The cops had picked up Kevin Little and Packer Wilson as they were walking home to Bedford-Stuyvesant; when Kwasama Jones heard about his friends, he'd gone down to the precinct station with his mother. Based on what they said, the cops had showed up the next day and arrested Sykes and Davis.

Little had testified against them, but Wilson and Jones got the hint and clammed up, and Davis he'd never had to worry about. He'd made his own mistakes, like bragging to that ho, Hannah Little, that he'd enjoyed raping the white bitch.

Next time, no bragging, 'cept to the homies, he thought. But that stupid muthafucka Villalobos had to brag to Kaminsky, and maybe fuck up the whole plan. Well, when this is over, I'll have some of the homies pay him a visit and cut his fuckin' heart out and stuff it down his mouth while it's still beating. He was also pissed off that Lynd had messed up a simple knife job.

The fat lawyer had gotten on his case about shoving the wrong Kaminsky brother beneath the train but it wasn't his fault. How was I to know he had a twin? Louis didn't tell him until later that he knew where to find Kaminsky because he'd received a call from Olav Radinskaya, the Brooklyn borough president, who employed *Ivan* Kaminsky. *Ivan* Kaminsky had asked for the afternoon off to go meet his brother at Grand Central Station on the number 4 train platform.

Louis should have told me there were two brothers, Sykes thought, frowning at the lawyer. Now he was going to have to wait for the remaining Kaminsky to surface again. He tuned back in to the conversation between Louis and Breman when he heard the name Kaminsky.

"I just hope that if he does surface, you'll contact me first," Louis was saying. "I want to ask him a few questions before the police nab him and get a chance to feed him a story to protect their colleagues."

"Well, again, that's a rather unusual request," Breman said. She realized, though it was a jolt to her conscience, that at the same time she was pleased because it gave her power over Louis that he was afraid of what Kaminsky had to say. However, the pleasure and illusion of power were short-lived.

"Forgive them, but my clients here were the ones who wanted to meet you and have me ask that if you hear from Kaminsky, you call me first," he said. "They wanted me to express how very unhappy they will be if this lying sack of shit Kaminsky is allowed to ruin our hard work."

The reference to the gangsters made Breman want to go to the bathroom. How did it ever get this far? she wondered as she squirmed a little trying to get comfortable. She hazarded a glance at Sykes. He was grinning like the Cheshire cat and had a hand on his crotch. "Maybe you'd like a taste of this now?" he offered.

The men were still laughing when she hopped up and fled through the office and reception area and out the door of the building, stumbling down the steps. Teddy Chalk ran across the sidewalk and caught her by her arm or she might have fallen.

"Did they harm you, ma'am?" he asked, his face a mask of concern and anger.

"Oh, quit with the fucking chivalry, you idiot, and drive," she snarled as she jumped into the backseat of the limo. As they made their way south and east through Harlem into East Harlem, she broke down and cried. She cried so hard she hardly noticed the two Arab-looking men standing outside the small mosque, one of them staring down an alley with his hand in his coat.

10

Monday, December 13

"GOOD MORNING, MR. KARP," MRS. DARLA MILQUE-
tost, his new receptionist, said in what was her perpetual
monotone when he walked into his office on the eighth
floor of the Criminal Courts building. He'd hoped that
she'd be away from her desk getting coffee or something,
as he'd had all the disapproving stares he wanted that
morning.

Mrs. Milquetost had informed him on her first day on
the job that she, too, found the name unfortunate but it
was the only one her husband had, and as a good Catholic
it had been her duty to assume her husband's family
name. "I'd appreciate it if you would avoid sniggering
when you say my name."

"Sniggering?"

"Yes," she replied. "Sniggering. Everyone always does
unless I put my foot down at the beginning."

"Well then, I assure you I will not snigger nor tolerate
sniggering in this office, Mrs. Milquetost," he'd said without sniggering . . . at least until he was in his office.

At first he'd wondered if Mrs. Milquetost, a temp from

the steno pool, might not be quite the right fit for the office. But she'd proved to be an efficient, hardworking, and, importantly, close-mouthed receptionist, even if she did dress like June Cleaver on the old television series *Leave It to Beaver.*

"Would you like me to have those boxes in your office removed, Mr. Karp," said Mrs. Milquetost, who refused to call him Butch and didn't like random piles of boxes showing up. "Do you need me to call someone to move them to filing?"

"No, Mrs. Milquetost, they're fine right where they are for now," he said, continuing through the door leading to his inner sanctum, where he hoped for a few contemplative minutes before the morning meetings began.

The day had not started off on a good note. Marlene was still ticked at him for the "stray dog" comment and refused to accept his apology. He even tried kissing her as she lay in bed, but she'd kept her lips as tight as possible and simply glared at him until he gave up.

Out in the kitchen, he'd cheered up some to find the twins, who, surprisingly, were already up and dressed in sweats, hoping they'd get a chance to play basketball with the big boys on the courts at Sixth and Fourth. Their lively banter had taken a little of the chill out of the air, until Zak was reminded that he and his brother had bar mitzvah class that night.

"Ah gee, during vacation?" Zak complained.

Zak's demeanor got worse when his brother then exclaimed, "Great! I can't wait." Zak then punched Giancarlo in the arm and called him a "butt kisser." A loud wrestling match ensued, which was broken up by Marlene, who'd stomped from the bedroom, separated the boys, then glared at Karp as if he'd put them up to it, before stomping back to the bedroom. The ice age had returned, so he dressed and left for work.

"Mr. Kipman is waiting for you," Mrs. Milquetost said just as he opened the door. He sighed; there went his few minutes alone, but at least Harry tended to calm his nerves, not rake them across the fiery coals of hell.

Kipman was sitting on the couch reading a book. Karp turned his head to look at the title: *The Dust-Covered Man: The Story of Ulysses S. Grant*.

"Good book?" Karp asked.

"Interesting," Kipman replied. "Funny how some of the famous people in history sort of come into the roles that will define their greatness by accident. Grant for instance. He was a West Point grad and a hero of the Mexican-American War for his actions during the storming of Mexico City. But he was out of the army, working as a clerk for his father-in-law's harness business, when the Civil War broke out. He went in as a captain. He ends up as the top general in the Union Army, and pretty much ends up winning the war for them. I doubt he gave greatness a second thought when he joined . . . in fact, he already had something of a drinking problem."

"Why the dust-covered man?" Karp asked.

"An allusion to the fact that he wasn't the sort of leader who hung back and expected his troops to do all the dangerous stuff," Kipman said. "Even at the end of a long day on horseback, he'd push ahead to get the lay of the land and scout the enemy's position. His troops would see him covered with dust and if they didn't love him the way Robert E. Lee's men loved him, they respected him and fought for him like they'd fought for none of the other Union generals. They came up with the nickname the Dust-Covered Man." The conversation was interrupted by a knock on the door, which only briefly preceded the appearance of V.T. Newbury, Ray Guma, and Gilbert Murrow.

Blond-haired and still boyish-looking, V.T. was the aristocrat of the bunch, a genuine descendant of the Pilgrims who landed at Plymouth Rock. His great grandfather—or maybe great-great, Karp couldn't remember—had started what was now one of the largest and most prestigious law firms in Manhattan. V.T. had shocked his father and set his illustrious ancestors rolling in their graves when, after graduating from Harvard Law School at the top of his class, he'd eschewed the family business and applied for a job at the New York District Attorney's Office, where he and another recent graduate, Butch Karp, became close friends.

Disenchanted when Francis Garrahy died in office and was replaced by a crook, Sanford Bloom, V.T. had gone to work for the U.S. Attorney General's Office. However, when Karp was appointed to complete the term of Bloom's successor, Jack X. Keegan, V.T. had been lured back to run the office's Special Investigations Unit, which was charged with rooting out and prosecuting corruption and malfeasance in city government, including its police department.

Bushy-browed and thick-featured, Ray Guma came from the other end of the social strata. Born and raised in an Italian neighborhood, he'd spent the first part of high school trying to decide whether to pursue a career in the mob or with the New York Yankees as the next great shortstop. Then "something snapped," he liked to say; he went to college on a baseball scholarship, even got scouted by the big leagues, but decided to go to law school. He surprised himself as well as his pals from the old neighborhood, several of whom were "made" men, by joining the New York District Attorney's Office, where he'd earned a reputation as a tough, no-holds-barred prosecutor not afraid to take on the mob, even his friends, if they messed up and got caught for something. He also had a reputation for cheap cigars, cheaper whiskey, and women cheap or not.

However, in recent years, a bout with colon cancer had forced him into retirement. The once-muscular, apelike body had aged almost overnight and his thick Sicilian hair had turned as white as bedsheets. But inside he was still the same old Guma—"minus a yard or so of my guts that the quacks hacked out of me"—and Karp had been only too happy to hire him to work part-time on special cases.

The last of the three new arrivals was also the youngest by twenty years. Gilbert Murrow was a short, slightly pudgy fellow who favored bow ties, plaid vests, and horn-rim glasses. He was a good lawyer—nothing flashy, just thorough—but had proved more valuable as Karp's aide-de-camp and office manager who kept the calendar and the staff in order.

Since that past spring, he'd also served as the de facto campaign manager for Karp's election bid. The party had recently made him accept a "professional" campaign manager in order to receive party funding, which had sent Murrow into a sulk for days. Only when Karp brought the new campaign manager into his office and told him that everything political needed to be run through "my chief political adviser, Gilbert Murrow" did the little man perk up. Ever since he'd happily filled his time by overseeing press releases and the efforts to reach out to the media and community.

Upon entering the office, V.T. gravitated over to Kipman. The two came from different backgrounds, but they shared a love for classical music and books, as well as the fine points and subtleties of the law. Guma plopped him-

self down in a big easy chair by the window and pulled
out a cigar to chew on while grousing about the doctors
who forbade him to smoke.

Murrow spotted the boxes that Karp had stacked in a
corner of the office and wandered over to spin one
around and read the filing label: "People vs. Sykes, Davis,
Wilson, and Jones," before turning to Karp with a question mark stamped on his face. But Karp held up his hand
and waved him to a chair next to Guma; his questions
were going to have to wait.

Karp sometimes thought of this crew in basketball
terms. Each man was a great player in his own way, and
none was afraid to accept a challenge and take the ball to
the hoop. But they all also understood that their main role
was to support the big man in the center as a team.

Monday mornings he met with his bureau chiefs. But
he liked to bring this particular group of friends and colleagues together an hour earlier to discuss the issues in a
setting where they could talk freely, without having to
worry about being politically correct, knowing that what
was said in the room would stay in the room.

"V.T., you ready?" Karp asked. The main topic he'd
wanted to address this morning was Newbury's continuing probe into allegations of police malfeasance.

Newbury quit thumbing through Kipman's book and
leaned forward in his seat. "As you all know, we've been
looking into years of allegations of police misconduct,
including acts that rise to the level of felonies, which
were reviewed either by Corporation Counsel or one of a
handful of large, private law firms hired for the purpose
of making recommendations on settling cases and
whether this office should pursue criminal charges
against the officers involved. We also all know that one of
these firms was that of our 'friend' Andrew Kane.

"So far, we've uncovered a pattern in which the Corporation Counsel and a handful of these firms almost automatically recommended that cases be settled with the complaining parties—for more than a hundred million dollars in taxpayer funds, I might add—and then marked the files No Prosecution. The files were then handed over to this office—although I hasten to point out not while our current *el jefe* was running the show. Anyway, at least two of Butch's predecessors apparently accepted the recommendations at face value and filed them away, never to be seen again, except that the files were subsequently rediscovered by this office.

"In some cases, we've concurred that the allegations were without merit or would now for reasons of the expiration on the statutes of limitations or other difficulties, such as witnesses who have passed, would be impossible to pursue. In those cases, I believe our recommendation will be to keep a close eye on certain officers who seem to have developed a habit of shooting, beating, coercing, or blackmailing the good citizens of this city. We've, however, devoted our primary attention to those cases in which criminal charges were warranted and can still be pursued. In point of fact, we're ready to file on some of these but have been holding off for now at the command of our fearless leader."

Newbury paused and looked meaningfully at Karp, who finished the thought for him. "I think there's more to all of this than lazy lawyers not deserving the high fees they charged for recommending that some of these cases be settled and forgotten." Newbury nodded and continued with his explanation. "We've noted that Corporation Counsel Sam Lindahl has, over the course of a dozen years, steered the big enchilada cases to several chosen law firms. Three caught our attention because of their high-profile senior partners and the fact that they all have a history of being anticop, yet here they were recommending that the New York District Attorney's Office turn a blind eye to obvious misconduct. Something didn't wash."

V.T., who occasionally delved into community theater and could ham up a role with the best of them, enjoyed watching Guma, who wasn't exactly known for his patience, squirm as he built toward the climactic scene. "The three notables are Hugh Louis, who I think we would all be familiar with even if he wasn't the current media darling due to the Coney Island rape case. . . ."

Without turning his head, Butch knew that Murrow had glanced toward him at the mention of the Coney Island case but he ignored the look.

". . . next is Olav Radinskaya, who also happens to be the borough president for Brooklyn and is said to have close ties to the Russian mob. Perhaps our resident authority on gangsters, Mr. Guma, can shed some light on that."

All eyes turned to Guma, who studied the chewed end of his cigar and shrugged. "Not my people. Do go on, Mr. Newbury."

There was a general chuckle from the audience, and Newbury moved to his last name, "Shakira Zulu." The name elicited a groan from everyone in the room. Born and raised as Sandra Bond, she had changed her name and joined the Black Panther Party in the late 1960s. Karp had personally prosecuted a case in which she was convicted for her role as the getaway driver for bank robbers who killed two off-duty police officers, working as security guards, in cold blood. After the jury came back with the guilty verdict for manslaughter, Zulu had been dragged from the courtroom kicking and screaming that she would someday "kill Karp and all his honky friends and family."

"I'm sure we all remember how seven years later, Zulu told the parole board that she didn't mean what she'd said about killing anybody," Newbury said. "She intended to 'work for change in this corrupt and racist society' through legal means."

After her release from prison, where she'd earned her GED and even took several college credit classes, Newbury noted, Zulu went to New York University and after graduation, to law school in Georgia. "The press was invited to her law school graduation ceremonies, where she consented to a dozen interviews, all of them some version on her mission in life being to 'take on The Man in his own backyard.' Ever since, she's been at the forefront of criticizing this office, as well as DAs throughout the five boroughs, and of course races to sign up any African-American family that feels wronged by the police . . . if Hugh Louis doesn't beat her to the punch. And she is, of course, at the forefront of any antipolice rallies, especially if she knows the television crews will be there. So it's pretty interesting that Shakira, not to mention these other firms who've made one side of their living by shafting the police and this office, were given these other cases."

Newbury paused for dramatic effect before wrapping up his presentation. "However, so far we haven't been able to make a case that these law firms have done anything illegal in recommending these settlements and recommending that this office not pursue criminal charges against the officers involved," he said. "After all, this office—and its previous tenants Mr. Bloom and Mr. Keegan—were not obligated to accept the recommendations."

Karp grimaced at the mention of his predecessor. It didn't surprise him that Bloom had been a crook from the beginning. In fact, Karp had helped put him in prison, where he remained. However, Jack X. Keegan had been one of his mentors, the head of the famous homicide bureau that he'd aspired to as a young prosecutor. When Keegan replaced Bloom, he'd chosen Karp to be his number two and then recommended that the governor promote him to the top spot when Keegan was appointed a federal judge.

Karp took over from Newbury. "Anyway, I've asked V.T. to hold off on pursuing the cases against the cops—at least where we're not worried about the statute of limitations running out—until we get a handle on how this relationship among the Corporation Counsel, these other law firms, and this office worked. To me, something smells worse than Guma's old gym socks."

"Hey, hey . . . cheap shot, *paisan*," Guma complained, though with a smile. "I haven't been to a gym since they gutted me like a trout."

As the others in the room chuckled, Murrow cleared his throat to speak. "I'm sorry to be the one who always has to mention the political considerations here, but I do think it's important to point out that Hugh Louis and Shakira Zulu pretty much control the black vote. Not to mention that Butch is already walking on thin ice with the NYPD because of what happened with Kane's little cadre of killer cops. Those guys in blue don't like anybody else cleaning their house. I'm not saying we ignore all this, but perhaps—since we're delaying things anyway to look at these law firms—if we took our time before we stirred up these hornets' nests it might help improve Butch's chances of remaining in this office. We're less than a year from the election and I think—"

Kipman interrupted Murrow. "And lose a few more of these cases to the passing of time?" he scoffed. "Or, take a chance that some of these people get wind of Newbury and his gang's line of questioning and skip town? Since when do we let political expediency dictate how this office prosecutes the bad guys?"

Murrow rolled his eyes. "Oh, since about the mid-1800s, if I remember my history of Manhattan," he said. "I know we'd all like to live in a world where Butch wouldn't have to walk on eggshells, but I think we all also agree that in the end, it's keeping him in office that will do the most good for the most people. Pursuing these cases—especially if we end up butting heads with several of the biggest, or at least most vociferous, law firms in the five boroughs—could take years. But if Butch gets tossed out on his ear next November, who's to say if they don't just go away again?"

"It's a matter of principle," Kipman replied.

"Principles don't do you any good if you're on the outside looking in," Murrow shot back.

Kipman started to retort but Karp interrupted him. "All right, all right, break it up, you two," he said. "I think we're getting a little ahead of ourselves. I want us to hold off on filing charges against these cops until we see if we can't find out how this whole thing worked and if there are others who deserve our attention—so long as we don't lose any of these cases to Father Time." He looked at Murrow. "We'll do our best to keep this all low-key, and we won't go forward against these law firms until we're sure, but I can't do my job if I'm hung up over the political ramifications."

Murrow started to protest, but Karp held up his hand. "Let's just let this be until we have to deal with it. Right now, we have a staff meeting to get to."

The others took that as a signal, rose from their seats, and wandered out the door. Murrow hung back until the others had left. He pointed to the boxes. "You want to tell me what those are doing here? A Brooklyn case?" But Karp just clapped him on the shoulder, and said, "All in good time, Gilbert. I appreciate your concern, I really do, but I have to do this my way, understand?" Murrow nodded but Karp knew it was more out of politeness than because he agreed.

The pair walked together into the meeting room, a long, wood-paneled space with paintings of previous New York district attorneys on the walls, an American flag and the flag of New York City in opposite corners, and a long, narrow table in the middle surrounded by black chairs. Karp took a seat at the head of the table with Kipman on one side and Murrow on the other.

The bureau chiefs and their assistants were quietly talking to one another or nervously shuffling their papers, preparing to present their cases for dissection by the others. Karp glanced toward the other end of the table, where Rachel Rachman, the chief of the Sex Crimes Bureau, sat staring glumly at the ceiling as she clenched and unclenched her hands. She'd always had a tendency to dress in neon-bright colors—today a pantsuit the color of a plastic Halloween pumpkin—that belied a personality as devoid of color and warmth as an ice cube. However, she was a tough courtroom litigator and neither asked for nor gave quarter when prosecuting rapists and child molesters.

"Okay, let's get started," Murrow said. He enjoyed the role of moderator while Karp sat back and listened. "Harry, you want to start by telling us the latest with the People vs. Salaam and Mohammed, otherwise known as the Columbia Basketball Players Rape Case."

Butch noticed that Rachman suddenly sat forward, her eyes narrowed and focused on Kipman, who didn't bother to look her way. Their mutual dislike was no secret.

Kipman adjusted his half-moon reading glasses on the end of his long nose, then looked up over the top of them at Karp. "I'll begin with a brief rundown of the case, which, as Gilbert has so colorfully quoted from the media, involves two now-former basketball players from Columbia University. As you know, one night last February a young man named Khalif Mohammed had consensual sex with the complainant, Rose Montgomery, in her bedroom during a party at an off-campus apartment she shared with two other women. Neither side disputed this during the trial, nor the fact that the young woman was intoxicated.

"The gist of our case was that after sexual intercourse, Mohammed left the room, which was dark, and then his friend and teammate, Rashad Salaam, entered and, pretending to be Mohammed, had nonconsensual sex with her. The complainant swore in both her statements to the police and on the witness stand that she did not even know Salaam, with the inference that she would not have had sex with a stranger.

"At trial, the defense argued that the young woman had sponsored a party at the apartment to which members of the basketball team had been invited. Evidence was presented that the complainant passed around a bowl full of condoms 'just in case'—"

From her end of the table, Rachman snorted. "Like that's some sort of crime." She stopped when Butch looked at her sharply and dropped her head and sat glaring at the tabletop.

"During pretrial motions, the defense tried to introduce evidence from the defendants that the complainant not only knew Salaam but had consensual sex with him several days prior to the incident in question," Kipman said. "However, we argued that there was no corroborating evidence of such a relationship, and we were able to prevent that information from being introduced at trial—"

Again Rachman interjected. "It didn't matter. Previous sexual history is not relevant under our shield laws," she said before again falling into a sulky silence due to another stern look from Karp.

"Apparently, the New York Court of Appeals disagrees with that contention, especially when there was corroborating testimony that not only were the defendants telling the truth, but that the complainant was using the allegations to get back at Salaam, who apparently had rejected her after their first sexual liaison," Harry said dryly. "Most damning, according to the justices, was that we did not hand over this corroborating evidence to the defense so that they could at least bring it to the judge at a motion hearing and have the judge rule on its admissibility. This evidence consisted of statements given to the police by the complainant's roommates that Salaam had spent the night in the complainant's bedroom several days prior to the incident."

Rachman made a sighing noise, but Kipman ignored her and instead read from a transcript of one of the roommates' interviews with a detective. "She told me that she was angry with Rashad because she felt he'd just used her for sex. He wouldn't return her calls. She said that if she ever got the chance to get even, she'd 'cut his balls off.'"

Kipman looked pointedly at Karp. "However, for some reason, this interview was never disclosed to the defense. In fact, it was 'lost' until a private investigator working for the appellate lawyer located the roommates and conducted his own interview. In the meantime, Salaam and Mohammed had been convicted of sexual assault and conspiracy to commit sexual assault, respectively, and sentenced to prison."

Kipman closed his file and looked around the table. "Upon review, the court of appeals held that the roommates' interviews were relevant in that they could have been brought to the witness stand to impeach the complainant, who testified at the trial and apparently lied under oath."

Rachman slapped the table with her hand and half rose from her seat. "It's bullshit," she said, "and just like a bunch of old men, which describes our court of appeals, to ignore twenty years of precedent that establishes under the shield laws that the previous sexual history of the victim is not relevant and cannot be brought up at trial."

Harry remained seated but his voice grew more heated. "The court of appeals, the highest appellate court in New York State," Kipman stated, glancing over at Rachman, "has ruled more than once that shield laws were not intended to protect someone who perjured herself on the witness stand when asked a direct question, such as 'Did you know Rashad Salaam prior to the night of the alleged assault?' The complainant told the jury that she'd never met him before that evening and, if I remember from her testimony, that she would never have consented to sex with a stranger."

"So what?" Rachman spat back. "How would you like to sit in front of a jury, not to mention half of the media in Manhattan, and let a defense attorney make you out to be a whore? Of course, only a woman is considered 'loose' and therefore not deserving of protection under the law if she has sex with more than one partner; a guy does it and he just gets to put another notch on the bedpost. The judge should not even have allowed the question of whether she had met Rashad before that night. The only relevant issue is whether a man entered the victim's bedroom under pretense of being someone else and while she was very intoxicated, and without so much as a 'May I?' proceeded to have sex with her. In fact, she did not discover that she'd been duped until Mohammed reentered the room and turned on the lights. It was just a big game to them."

"She lied on the witness stand," Kipman countered. "If she didn't tell the truth when asked that question about even knowing Rashad, what makes you believe that she was telling the truth about whether the sex was consensual? Why would you simply dismiss the statements of the two roommates, who in separate interviews stated that she'd told them that she was going to get back at him because he didn't want to be her boyfriend?"

"Typical male response!" Rachman shouted. "The woman's a whore so she doesn't deserve our protection." She turned to Karp. "I plan to refile the charges and this time put those two rapists in prison where they belong for ten to fifteen."

Kipman also looked at Karp. "I don't believe that best serves the interests of justice in this case. 'Full disclosure' has long been the policy of this office, even when doing so may make our job harder. We should have turned the police interviews over to the defense, and then argued their relevance in front of the trial judge at a hearing. But this was not done and instead, Ms. Rachman took it upon herself to rule on its relevance and then hide the existence of these interviews. In the meantime, the lives of these two young men have been irrevocably damaged—they were expelled from the university, even before the trial and without a hearing, lost their basketball scholarships, and I doubt will find any other takers out there, even if we don't pursue another trial. . . ."

"Poor babies," Rachman sneered. "They won't get paid to play a game while the victim—"

"Complainant; she's not a victim if the charges haven't been proved," Kipman interjected.

". . . the victim," Rachman continued, "has to defend herself from being called a whore by the people who are supposed to protect her."

"She's certainly a liar," Kipman retorted. "So if one follows the other . . ."

Rachman turned almost purple with rage. "See! See!" she shouted. "This office is a reflection of the same old Neanderthal thinking—"

"As I was saying," Kipman said, "lives have been ruined here on what may have been nothing more than a jilted woman's revenge. The coach of the team was placed on administrative leave, essentially labeled a pimp by the press because he was somehow supposed to monitor what his players were doing off-campus, and then, when the shit hit the fan, defended these two young men by telling the press that he believed them and not the complainant."

"Just more evidence of the good ol' boys' club, which as we all know has plenty of members in this room," Rachman added bitterly. "The only concern is whether two rapists have lost their scholarship and a coach his job because the university did the right thing and supported this young woman."

"We have an obligation to present the truth, and not grind our little personal axes," Kipman fired back. "It's my recommendation that we dismiss the charges. We have a witness who has shown that the complainant will perjure herself while under oath. I believe these young men have already suffered enormously for what appears to be nothing more than promiscuous behavior."

Rachman's eyes nearly bugged out of her head at the last remark and she looked as if she might rush down the length of the table to strike Kipman. Karp decided it was time to put an end to the rancor. "Enough!" he said in a voice loud enough to silence both attorneys. "I think it's time to cool off. Let's take a look again at ALL the evidence and, when we can discuss this without the personal invective, we'll decide whether to refile the charges."

Kipman nodded and Rachman took her seat. "So, Rachel," Karp said as if it was time to turn the channel on a television, "tell us about the Michalik case."

Rachman looked up at him with a frown and then quickly at Kipman as if she expected this to be a trick. Seeing no indication that Karp's query was anything more than it was, she shrugged and said, "Pretty straightforward case of sexual assault by a person in a position of trust . . . sort of like the priest cases.

"The victim"—Rachman glanced at Kipman, who seemed to be absorbed in reading through one of his files and did not challenge her use of the word—"Sarah Ryder, is a graduate student at the NYU school of Russian studies. The perp, Alexis Michalik, is a professor of Russian poetry and here on a work visa. Over a period of several weeks, he engaged in a pattern of flirtation clearly meant to seduce Ms. Ryder, until she finally asked him to stop. He seemed to get the message, so she felt comfortable calling to ask him to help her with her master's thesis. He told her that he could meet with her after hours at his office on the campus. Upon her arrival, he offered her a beer, which she recalls had a 'funny taste' but at the time made nothing of it. The next thing she remembers is that she's been bound over a couch, her wrists tied to the legs of the furniture, and Michalik is engaging in anal intercourse with her."

Rachman paused as though to calm herself. "When he was finished, he told her that he loved her, but that if she told anyone, he would deny it and make sure that she was drummed out of the department and the university—that all her hard work would go down the drain. The victim reported the incident to the university, which, as required by law, reported it to the New York Police Department. She was transported to a hospital, where she was examined by a doctor, who reported that she had 'lacerations and contusions to both her vagina and anal area consistent with forced sexual intercourse.' "

Rachman sifted through the papers in her file and held up one. "We've just received the results of DNA testing of a semen stain found on the victim's blouse; it's a match for Michalik. Also, fingerprints found on a half-empty glass of beer discovered by investigators match those of Michalik and Ms. Ryder. The beer was tested and shows traces of rohypnol, the so-called date rape drug."

Satisfied, Rachman stopped talking. Karp asked, "Questions?" It had been the practice since the days of Garrahy for those who attended that meeting to put their fellow prosecutors through an interrogation meant to discover any weaknesses in a case that a defense lawyer might later exploit. The practice had pretty much disappeared under Bloom, who couldn't have cared less, and had been at best desultory under Keegan, who was occupied with his own political aspirations. But the practice was renewed with vigor when Karp was appointed.

"Anything to place Michalik and Ms. Ryder in the building at the time in question?" one of the young assistant chiefs asked.

Rachman smiled like a student at a geography bee who just got asked her favorite question. "As a matter of fact, a witness—one Ted Vanders, a graduate student in the English department—came forward after the story appeared in the newspapers and told the police that he saw the victim as she was leaving the building that night." Rachman put on a show of again rifling through her papers before finding what she sought and began to read.

"Let's see . . . ah yes, here it is, 'He told the police that when he saw the victim about midnight, she appeared "disheveled and in tears" ' and that 'only after coaxing did the victim tell him she'd been raped.' "

"Did the witness know her previously?" asked another of the assistant district attorneys, probably to prove that he'd been paying attention to the previous discussion.

Rachman shook her head. "No, they're not even in the same department. And . . . ," she said, pausing to look at Kipman, "the police interviewed her friends and acquaintances, and none have ever seen or heard of Mr. Vanders. In fact, he's something of a geek, if I may use that term, with no known girlfriends. But if you saw Ms. Ryder, you'd realize that he's not remotely her type. A real beauty, in other words, and knows it."

"There's semen on the blouse?" another ADA asked and chuckled self-consciously. "Will he make a Bill Clinton defense and say he 'never had sex with that woman'?"

Rachman laughed just as falsely. "I guess there's a similarity. We believe this asshole wiped himself off on her blouse when he was finished."

"But no semen found in her?"

"The victim reported that the perp used a condom."

"What's the perp, this Michalik, say?"

Rachman looked disgusted. "Oh, the usual. It was her fault. She started the flirting—as if a twenty-five-year-old college coed has this irresistible power over an admittedly handsome, forty-five-year-old poetry professor with a nifty European accent.

"What is true is that this was a guy who could control what happened to the rest of her life. He not only was her adviser, with the power to accept or reject her master's thesis, he also sat on the board that approved which students would be accepted into the doctoral program. Of course, he claims that she only brought these charges after he refused to give her a free pass on the thesis and sponsor her for the doctoral program."

Rachman shook her head again. "It always amazes me how these guys expect us to believe these stories—like a woman would use rape charges to blackmail a college professor so that she wouldn't have to write her thesis paper." She looked around the table with a "can you believe this shit" smile on her face, but froze when she saw Kipman adjust his glasses and prepare to read from a document.

"It says in this report that the complainant did not go to university officials until nearly 3 PM the next day," he said. "Why is that?"

Rachman's eyes glittered with hate. "You want to tell me what you're doing with reports from my office?"

Kipman didn't blink. "I believe that you're aware that one of my functions is prior review of questionable cases before we make formal charges. In light of the recent reversal on the case we just discussed, I thought it might be a good idea to look over another alleged case of acquaintance rape."

"So you're checking up on me," Rachman hissed.

Karp cleared his throat. "Don't look at it that way, Rachel. It's just that sometimes two sets of eyes are better than one. This is not a reflection on your abilities as a prosecutor; we are all aware of your excellent work in the courtroom. However, if we are going to convict people in this office, I want to make sure we do it the right way so that they remain convicted. So what about Harry's question regarding the nearly seventeen hours between the alleged assault and the victim reporting it?"

"Well, I thought I'd covered that." Rachman sulked.

"Humor me," Karp responded.

"The victim was worried that reporting the rape would ruin her chances of getting her thesis accepted and moving on to the doctoral program—essentially all those years spent pursuing her education would be meaningless. Apparently this Michalik had a great deal of pull in the department—he's like the god of Russian poetry—which I probably don't need to point out is a very male-dominated gang. She was afraid that no one would believe her story. She didn't know that an investigator would find that glass of beer or the existence of the roofies. He could just claim the act was consensual and she'd be out of the department and out of a career."

"Then why did she come forward at all?" Kipman asked.

"She went to his office that afternoon to demand an apology. But he made it clear that he expected her to perform at his whim—essentially, she would be his sex slave for as long as she remained at the school. She was so repulsed by his behavior and the thought that he might be doing this to other female students that she felt she had a duty to report his behavior."

Kipman looked back down at the file. "I'm looking at her first interview with the police. It's pretty extensive, but nowhere does she say that she asked Michalik to stop what he was doing." He turned to another page. "And according to the doctor who examined Michalik following his arrest, there were no wounds as if she tried to fight him off."

Rachman rolled her eyes. "Again, I repeat myself here, but she was drugged, and when she woke up, she was tied to the couch. How was she supposed to fight him off?"

"What about the reports in the newspapers that the complainant may be mentally unstable?" Kipman asked.

They all knew that he was referring to a story in the *New York Post* that quoted a former roommate, who said that six months before the incident with Michalik, Ryder had been admitted to Bellevue Hospital after police decided that she was "a danger to herself and others," and that—according to another acquaintance—she had a few months later been taken to the hospital again following a drug overdose. "I believe the story said something about this being in reaction to splitting up with her boyfriend at the time, a member of the New York Rangers, if I remember correctly."

"Oh puhleeeze," Rachman said, rolling her eyes. "Since when are medical records not related to the case in question relevant? What's going on here? Have I suddenly been transported back into the Dark Ages of Jurisprudence when every slimy defense attorney got to paint the victim as a whore for wearing short skirts, or because she had consensual sex with one man before being raped by another?" She glared at Kipman. "Let's just go back to the days when anyone who wasn't a virgin wrapped in a burlap sack was a slut who got what she deserved. The shield laws were invented for just that sort of misogynist mindset."

"That's crap," Kipman retorted in his classic frustration-driven staccato.

Karp had to look down quickly so that Rachman wouldn't see the smile that had forced itself onto his face. He wasn't smiling about the case, but it always amused him when Kipman swore. It just didn't seem natural.

"Shield laws were developed for cases where strangers snatch the victims off the streets and rape them, and there is no doubt that crimes were committed," Kipman said. "Then a victim's sexual history or dress or mental state would not be relevant. They were not, however, created with acquaintance rape in mind, where there is a question not just of guilt but whether a crime even occurred. Which, by the way, is why *victim* is an inappropriate term for *complainant* at this stage of the game. Therefore, our first duty is to determine if there even was a crime—or whether the law is being used to further someone's agenda. In these instances, it is in the interest of justice that we weigh the complainant's sexual and mental history to see if it is relevant to establishing the truth. As much as sex has been used to control and debase women, it would not be the first time that a woman has used an accusation of rape to ruin the life and reputation of a man."

"Oh, my God," Rachman replied. "As if a woman would put herself through all the torment that a rape trial involves to get even. Studies show that less than 5 percent of rape allegations are manufactured, and most of those are dropped before charges are brought. In this case, we have a ton of physical and circumstantial evidence supporting the victim's story. And since you're reading the reports, you might note that Michalik first told police that—like Clinton—he didn't have sexual contact with the victim. If that's so, how did his semen get on her blouse?"

Kipman didn't answer right away, so Karp decided it was a good time to wind this discussion down. "Good point, Rachel," he said. "And good questions, Harry, the sort of thing your people will have to deal with, Rachel, when the defense gets a look at this stuff. But let's remember that it's Harry's job to make sure that we've crossed the *t*'s and dotted the *i*'s before we go forward. I'd like us to follow up on these reports in the newspapers, as well as the timing issue. Come back next week and we'll discuss filing charges."

"Bullshit!" Rachman exploded. The other attorneys around the table let their mouths hang open in embarrassed silence. "I was going to file this afternoon. I . . . well, I sort of alerted the press . . ."

"What!" Karp exclaimed, fighting a sudden urge to strangle Rachman. Unable to look at her for the moment without staring daggers, he looked instead at the others. "Now listen to me all of you, because I'm only going to say this once: This office will not go forward with charges unless we are 100 percent—no, make that 1,000 percent—certain that we can establish factual guilt and have legally admissible evidence to convict beyond a reasonable doubt to a moral certainty. A defense attorney's obligation is to zealously defend his client; ours is to establish the truth."

Finally Karp felt he could look at Rachman without spitting, but the famous Karp glare drained the color from her face nonetheless. "The complainant's sexual and mental history might not be relevant in the courtroom— that's for a judge to decide and a hearing is where you make your arguments that they're not—but they are damn relevant to her credibility with this office and whether we have established that moral certainty I just referred to before we go forward with a case. Furthermore, we do not try our cases in the media. Under no circumstances do we give them a heads-up on impending charges without clearing it through me, and I'll tell you right now that 99.9 percent of the time, my answer will be no. Do I make myself clear to all of you?"

There was a murmur of assents but he couldn't tell if Rachman's had been one of them, as she kept her face down, staring at the floor. He decided to deal with it later and said, "Okay, let's move on."

They got through the rest of the meeting with no further outbursts. There was the usual assortment of robberies, assaults, and murders, only one of which really stood out. A man of apparently Middle Eastern descent had been murdered in Central Park and his severed head placed on the spiked fence that ran around the Conservatory Gardens.

"I say apparently Middle Eastern," the head of homicide said, "because that's what our forensic people are guessing. The body hasn't been found, and we haven't been able to identify him. The police are treating it as a hate crime, possibly motivated by revenge tied to the execution murders of Americans in Iraq by Al Qaeda, because of the decapitation aspect. So far there isn't much else to go on either. Nobody saw anything, even though it's a fairly well-traveled area, even at night. Oh, there was one clue—Rev. 6:2."

"Revelations 6:2," Kipman said, "from the Bible . . . the riders of the Apocalypse prophecy that begins, 'And I looked, and behold, a white horse, and he who sat on it had a bow; and a crown was given to him, and he went out conquering and to conquer . . .'"

As Kipman recited the verse, Karp felt his stomach knot. One of the witnesses to the murder of a rap star that past summer was a former professor of English, Edward Treacher, who wandered the streets as a homeless bum quoting from the Bible. He'd also been connected to David Grale, which is what caused the pain in his gut. Grale's dead, he told himself, but he could not stop an involuntary shiver at the thought.

"Anyway, why I bring it up now is that the Muslim community is all over the cops to catch the killer," the head of homicide said. "And I got a call from them yesterday—the Muslims, not the cops—wanting to know why we were dragging our feet. I had to explain that we needed a suspect before we could press charges. What did they want us to do, prosecute a ghost?"

Again, Karp felt chilled. Get ahold of yourself, Butch old boy, he thought, you're starting to think like Lucy . . . ghosts and talking saints.

When the meeting was adjourned, Rachman slammed her briefcase shut and stormed out of the room before anyone else had even risen from the table. The other attorneys glanced quickly at Karp to see his reaction, but he kept his face neutral.

Out in the hall, Rachman swore, "Goddamn men." She felt like crying as she marched off toward her office. But that would give the bastards what they want, she thought. At heart they're all just a bunch of animals. Sticking together in their Brotherhood of the Penis.

11

"DID YOU GET A LOAD OF SOME OF THE LOOKS WE got when we came in?" Murrow said, peering back anxiously over his shoulder as if he expected an assassin to come running up from behind them. "You'd have thought we were attending a convention for the guys you've sent to Attica instead of a meet-and-greet at the Police Benevolent Association."

"Yeah, boss, you're not very popular with these guys right now," Clay Fulton said, only he was smiling. His boss had never been the sort who worried about his popularity; in fact, there were times when those closest to him wondered if he went out of his way to be unpopular. Fulton was handpicked by Karp to be chief of the NYPD detectives who were assigned to the DAO as investigators.

"Gots 'em right where I wants 'em," Karp said, returning the smile while clapping Murrow on the shoulder. The event had been set up months before as a "meet the candidate." The night before, however, Dick Torrisi had called and warned him to expect a cool, even hostile, reception.

"The word making the rounds is that you're letting the actions of a few bad apples slant the way you view the NYPD as a whole," Torrisi said. "It seems pretty orchestrated, but I'm not sure who's throwing the wood on the fire and it's pervasive from the union leadership on down."

Butch had thanked him for the heads-up but assured him that he was still planning on attending. The "few bad apples" was a reference to two fairly recent, but separate, cases against cops that he'd been directly involved in. The first had been the successful prosecution of two cops who'd gunned down a Jamaican immigrant they'd believed to be selling drugs. They'd tried to justify the shooting by claiming that the deceased grappled with them and seized one of their guns. But with the help of a forensic gunshot-wound expert, Karp proved that the killing couldn't have happened the way the cops had described it, and they'd been convicted of murder.

The second wasn't about one or two bad apples but a whole bushel—Andrew Kane's so-called Irish Gang. They were a half-dozen or so Irish-Catholic cops who'd been recruited by Kane to do some of his dirty work—such as killing a drug dealer—under the pretext that the orders came from the archbishop, who was using them to do "God's work." However, in reality, they were helping Kane expand and control his criminal empire through the coercion and murder of rivals.

Some of them were now dead, killed in a Central Park gunfight that still played out in Karp's head like a scene from one of the favorite movies of his Brooklyn childhood, *Gunfight at the O.K. Corral,* with Burt Lancaster and Kirk Douglas. In some ways, it didn't seem real, as if he'd been acting out a part in a play, except for the dead bodies and the fear that still haunted his sleep that Marlene had been killed.

Arriving at the PBA building, they'd walked into the main meeting room and all conversations had stopped. Eyes followed them to the corner where several minor union officials were conferring with the union president, Edward Ewen. They returned his handshake as perfunctorily as possible.

Personally, Karp had the utmost respect for the NYPD, especially after 9/11. They worked a hard, dangerous job, and he believed that it was the best big-city police force in the world. By and large, its members were fine, upstanding men who carried the torch of justice like latter-day knights. But it never ceased to amaze him the way they circled the wagons if one of their number was threatened, even if they personally thought the cop was a scumbag. It was always the NYPD on one side, everybody else on the other.

"Now remember," Murrow said a few minutes later as they stood in the wings offstage waiting for Karp to be introduced. "We're here to win their hearts and minds. You have your speech?"

Karp held up the set of notecards prepared for him by his assistant. It was what Murrow called his "law and order" speech, meant to appeal to any cop's heart. More support for the police. More officers. Better technology.

Ewen finally walked to the podium and with little in the way of an introduction asked Karp to take the stage. There was a smattering of applause but the boos and hisses were louder. He handed the notecards to a startled Murrow. "Here," he said, "I've changed my mind."

"Butch?" Murrow pleaded as Karp walked out onto the stage. "Butch, let's talk. What are you going to say, Butch?"

"I don't think he's listening," Fulton said, positioning himself where he could reach Karp if something went wrong. He had his own handpicked guys in the audience, even though it was unlikely that someone would go so far as to try to hurt his boss—at least in a public place. But he wasn't the sort to take chances, and heck, the PBA was probably the most heavily armed group Butch would talk to before the election.

"No." Murrow shook his head sadly. "He never does."

Out at the podium, Karp looked over the crowd—a lot of guys sitting with their arms crossed and slouched in their seats.

"Okay, let me propose a compromise," he began. "I left my notecards for the planned dog-and-pony show over there with my colleague, so you're not going to have to listen to political bullshit."

"We already are," came a voice with a thick Bronx accent from the back of the auditorium.

"Yeah, maybe," Karp agreed, "but in exchange for not throwing a bunch of campaign rhetoric at you—though I think some of the issues I was going to talk about are pretty important to you guys—I'm asking you to hear me out and make up your minds as men and women of integrity. The New York Police Department and the New York District Attorney's Office are like a married couple—"

"I want a divorce," a woman officer shouted, to general laughter.

Karp chuckled, too. "How about after the children are grown?" he replied. "Anyway, we need each other to achieve a common goal, which is to serve and protect the people of New York City. But it's obvious this relationship is not going to get better until we clear the air."

"The air will clear when you leave," the guy with the Bronx accent shouted. Some laughed, but a few also demanded that their fellow officers "pipe down, let him speak."

Karp used the break to launch into what Murrow called—and not always very happily—his "one bad apple only spoils the bunch if they let it" speech. Essentially, it boiled down to: It's not enough to be an honest cop if you know that the guy next to you is corrupt, not unless you do something about it.

"I believe that the New York City Police Department is the best in the world and that the press concentrates on the few bad apples."

"So do you, Karp." The Bronx guy again.

"But at the same time, those of you who hate that kind of press, if you tolerate the bad apples just because they wear the same badge, you're no better."

The last comment brought a fresh chorus of boos but he noticed there was also some applause. Karp looked over to the wings and saw Murrow with his hand clamped over his mouth as if he was about to throw up. "I KNOW most of you have never taken a bribe in your lives, not so much as a free coffee on a cold morning. I KNOW most of you have done your job day in and day out without stepping over the line. But that's not enough. . . ."

"Take a hike, Karp," the guy from the Bronx yelled again.

"Shaddup, Archie, I think he's talking about you," someone else shouted, which stirred more laughter.

"I don't care if you're pissed at me for convicting scumbags who happen to also wear that uniform," Karp said. "But who you should really be pissed at are the guys who sully their badges and yours with their greed or their laziness or their corruption. If you have a stain on your house, you're the ones who need to clean it up."

"Yeah, what about your house?" the female heckler said.

Karp knew what she was driving at. Everybody in the

law enforcement business in New York knew that Marlene had a reputation for working in some pretty gray areas of the law. In general, the cops liked her even better than him; they understood her vigilante sense of justice. But it certainly made it difficult to point fingers.

"What about the DA's office?" one of the union officials yelled from his seat in the front. "It seems to me that for all this talk about the so-called Irish Gang, which as an Irish-American I find personally offensive, there was some complicity in the DA's office. But I don't see anybody there in jail."

The audience liked that one and cheered. It took a minute before they quieted down enough for Karp to speak. The question was a good one, but not one he knew the answer to yet. He suspected that the No Prosecution files forwarded by Kane and others to the DA's office had been ignored because Bloom, and certainly Keegan, had trusted their opinion and because it was easier. So far there was no indication, as in evidence of bribes or kickbacks, that would establish that a crime of malfeasance had been committed.

"All I can say in that regard," Karp replied, "is that the investigation begun this past summer is continuing. We are following all leads, up to and including any that would point to wrongdoing by anyone in my office past or present."

"Yeah, whaddya bet only cops will take the heat on this," the union official grumbled.

"If a cop commits a crime that we can prove, he or she will be prosecuted," Karp said. "And if someone in my office commits a crime that we can prove, he or she will be prosecuted. You'll just have to take it—or not—on faith."

"Not," shouted several. Another added, "We have faith in our own."

Karp nodded. "Which is how it should be. I have always admired your loyalty to one another. But I think you have to ask yourself, what if a thief or rapist or murderer is one of your own, does he deserve to wear that uniform? I don't hire or fire anyone at the New York Police Department. My job is to prosecute criminals who commit crimes in New York County and that's what I do whether they're doctors or truck drivers or lawyers or police officers. Justice is blind, and justice can be slow. But anybody who tells you I'm anticop is not serving you, they're serving their own interests . . . you'll have to decide why that is."

The crowd was silent after that last comment. "Thank you for your time," Karp said. "I hope there's a next time when you and I can talk about the stuff that matters, like working together toward a common goal."

Karp turned to go and found himself almost face-to-face with Clay Fulton, who had walked out and stood with his hand extended. Fulton was well respected in the PBA, one of the guys who'd worked his way up through the ranks. Karp knew that his appearance onstage was his way of making a statement to the members.

"More of them heard you than you think," Fulton said as they shook hands. "It's just tough for them to break ranks."

Karp patted him on the shoulder. "Thanks. I understand."

At that moment, one of the union flunkies walked up to Karp. "Mr. Ewen would like to speak to you, if you have a minute."

Karp and his entourage followed the young man off the stage and through a door leading to a hallway. At the end of the hallway, Karp paused in front of a car-size photograph of the burning World Trade Center buildings in a frame, and around its edges were the names of the police officers who'd died that morning trying to save others.

"Quite a list, eh, Mr. Karp," said a voice from the office to the left.

Karp turned, and in the near dark of the room he saw the union president, Edward Ewen, a large, florid man, sitting behind a desk. With his bulging cheeks and bulging eyes, Ewen reminded him of a bullfrog. It would not have surprised him to see a long, pink tongue dart out from between the thin purple lips to snatch an insect, which was how he was looking at Karp.

Karp glanced again at the photograph and names. "Yes, quite a list," he said. "I can't imagine the courage it took to go back into those buildings."

"Ya know, Karp," Ewen said. "Sometimes ya sound like you was on our side. Then others, it's like ya got a hard-on for cops and think that the boys are a bunch of crooks."

"I don't think of it as taking sides," Karp said. "I get paid by the people to prosecute criminals; it doesn't matter if they're wearing blue jeans or blue uniforms. If the NYPD doesn't like the black eyes from these cases, maybe the membership and the union ought to work harder to ferret the bad ones out."

"None of the boys want to work with bad cops," Ewen said. "But it seems that every time one of you guys runs for office, you feel like you need to make a big splash in the newspapers by bustin' cops for ticky-tacky stuff."

"Murder, criminal conspiracy, extortion . . . a little more than ticky-tacky," Karp noted.

"No doubt. No doubt," Ewen agreed. "It's just that the boys don't see no one in the DA's office going down on this one, and you can't tell me . . . them . . . that Keegan and that other idiot, what was his name, Bloom, were squeaky clean and didn't know what was going on."

"As I told 'the boys,' this investigation isn't over," Karp said. "If crimes were committed by anyone in the district attorney's office, we will pursue those charges as vigorously as we do the others. Now, was there something in particular that you wanted to talk to me about?"

"I just wanted a little face time, Karp," Ewen said. "Personally, I think you're a good guy . . . heart in the right place and all that. I just thought that as one old campaigner to another I'd let you know that there's a perception out there that you're anticop. You need to do something about it, or even a supporter like me won't be able to persuade the membership to back you in the election."

Karp rankled at the implied threat: play ball with the union or jump to the back of the unemployment line. "I guess I'll just have to trust that most of the membership can think for themselves and don't need to be persuaded by someone else," he replied.

"Careful, Karp," the union boss said, narrowing his frog eyes into slits, "I'm not someone you want as an enemy."

"Neither am I, Ewen," Karp shot back.

Murrow, who'd started to feel nauseated as the situation deteriorated, jumped in. "Hey, hey, in the immortal words of Rodney King, 'Can't we all just get along?' "

Ewen looked at Murrow as if he were a fly he was about to snap up, but then he laughed. "Yeah, yeah, young man . . . sometimes a coupla bull-headed guys like your boss here and me, we gotta butt heads. But we all want the same thing, a safe city. Them guys out there, they pay me to look after 'em. I'm just trying to give your boss a friendly reminder that sometimes you get more with honey than a stick."

"And we certainly appreciate that, Mr. Ewen," Murrow said before Karp could reply. He looked at his watch.

"Oops, we got to go, Butch. You're supposed to pick up your sons in less than an hour."

Karp had locked eyes with Ewen, but neither of them flinched. A tough old bastard, he thought, been around since Garrahy's days. "Yes, I believe Mr. Ewen and I have said what needs to be said."

Most of the members had left by the time they were escorted back out to the auditorium. A few stragglers gave them dark looks, but there was one reasonably friendly face, that of Richard Torrisi.

"Hi, Butch, good speech," Torrisi said, holding out his hand.

"Yeah, I really wowed them," Karp replied, shaking it.

Torrisi laughed. "Yeah, well, tough crowd but they're not as sheeplike as some people might want you to believe. I think most of them are waiting and watching. They won't be afraid to break from the leadership if there's a good reason."

"Aren't you talking ill of your bosses?"

Torrisi grimaced. "I suppose I am, technically. But to be honest, I think of the rank and file as my real bosses. I was hired by the leadership but to represent the members' interests."

"I think a lot of us have been in the same boat," Karp said.

"Yeah . . . hey, if you have a minute, there's someone else I'd like you to meet," Torrisi said.

Murrow answered. "Sorry, but not really. He has to be somewhere in . . . ," he looked at his watch, "forty-seven-and-a-half minutes."

"That's okay," Karp said, "we've got time." He'd caught some sense of urgency in the union lawyer's voice and was curious as to what it might be about.

Torrisi led the way to the back of the auditorium and

an exit door that opened into yet another hallway. "This place has more secret passages than a Scottish castle," Murrow muttered. "If these walls could talk."

"Just an old building with lots of cheap remodeling," Torrisi replied. "But you're right about the walls." He reached a door and grabbed the knob, but before opening it he said, "I'm sorry but Clay and Mr. Murrow will have to stay here."

Clay started to protest. He was responsible for Karp's safety and his boss had a way of ending up in more jams than ants at a picnic, as his grandmother used to say. Murrow, worried about some unknown political ramification of all the secrecy, began to voice his concern, too. But Karp waved them both to silence.

"Clay, I'm sure I'm quite safe. Even if the PBA wanted to shoot me, I think they'd plan it better than to do it in their own building," he said. "If you guys wouldn't mind getting the car and pulling it up to the curb, I'll just be a few minutes."

Clay Fulton and Murrow stalked off, muttering under their collective breath. Torrisi turned the knob and led the way into a room. Again the lights were low, leading Karp to wonder, What's with these union types. Is it for mood or are they too cheap to buy more lightbulbs? It took a moment for his eyes to adjust; only then did he notice the dark figure of a woman sitting in a chair on the far side of the room. He glanced sideways at Torrisi, who spoke as the woman stood up.

"Butch Karp, I'd like you to meet Liz Tyler. Liz, this is the district attorney of Manhattan."

The woman said hello but, Karp noticed, made no attempt to shake his hand or approach too closely. It was Torrisi who spoke again. "Sorry about the surprise, Butch; I wasn't sure Liz wanted to do this until just before the meeting. But I think it would be good for you two to talk." He stepped back through the door and said, "I'll wait in the hallway."

When the door closed, Karp was thinking how he would have liked to shoot Torrisi. What was he supposed to say to a woman who'd been through what she'd been through? *No, I can't help you.* He'd met thousands of victims, seen all sorts of injustices perpetrated on them not just by the criminals but also the system. If what Torrisi had told him at the meeting a week ago with mayor-elect Denton was true, she had been raped by both and was still being assaulted.

"Sorry . . . about what happened," he said, immediately regretting it as insufficient. But she seemed to appreciate the sentiment.

"Thank you, Mr. Karp," she replied. "Would you mind if we sat? I'm not real steady on my feet and, well, to be honest, looking up at you hurts my neck." She tried a half-smile at the joke, and he smiled broadly back.

"Of course not," he said, taking a seat on the couch while she sat back down in the chair.

As she adjusted herself, Karp used the time to observe. He knew she was in her forties, but she looked haggard and much older because of the dull gray hair and dowdy clothing. However, when she looked up and fixed him with eyes as green as a cat's, even in the dark, he realized that she had once been a beautiful young woman. But there was a slightly crushed look to the right side of her face, and the eye on that side wandered in its orbit sightless. She quickly lowered her head so he couldn't see her face.

"So Mr. Torrisi tells me you might represent the city in the lawsuit," she said, "brought by those . . . those men," Tyler said, still looking down.

"I . . . well, I don't know," Karp replied. "Ms. Tyler, please, there's no need to be ashamed. My wife lost her eye in an accident, and I haven't believed for one day that it ever detracted from her beauty. Like you, she is still beautiful."

Liz Tyler looked up, her eyes wet with tears. She didn't say anything, but the way her lip was trembling in a smile, she didn't have to.

Karp pushed on so as not to embarrass her. "I'm not sure it's the right thing to do . . . the district attorney representing the city in a civil lawsuit. It does sound to me like the city has an excellent chance of winning without my help."

"Do you think so?" Tyler asked. Her voice held hope but fear ruled her face.

"Well, yes, the truth is a pretty powerful defense . . . um, forgive me, but is it still Mrs. Tyler?"

The question appeared to slam into the woman like a wrecking ball. She blinked several times and seemed to take several deep breaths before she could answer. "No. Just Miss Tyler, or better yet, Liz. I'm . . . I'm divorced."

Karp blasted himself for not thinking quickly enough to have maneuvered around the question. He smiled and said, "Liz it is. And I'd appreciate you calling me Butch. Mr. Karp was my dad." It was an old joke, but it did seem to take some of the embarrassment out of the air.

"Have you read the files?" Tyler asked.

Now it was Karp's turn to be embarrassed. The boxes remained sealed in his office. In fact, he'd about decided to call Denton and tell him to have them picked up . . . that he just didn't feel he should get involved. "No," he said. "I haven't. To be honest, Liz, my forte is not civil law. The city would be wise to use someone else."

Karp's answer seemed to deflate Tyler. "Oh."

"What would you recommend that I do in this situation, Liz?"

His question seemed to take her by surprise. She looked up and this time held his gaze. "Since we're being honest, I don't know. After the first trial, I tried to put it all behind me . . . and failed miserably. It cost me my family. But over the past four or five years, I've found a place where sometimes I can pretend that I don't even have a past. None of it. Not the good things, not the bad things. I have no memory of that . . . that day, except random snapshots in my head. . . ."

"You remember faces?" Karp asked.

Again, fear on Tyler's face. She shook her head. "No, no . . . not like that. I meant the beach. Waking up in the hospital. That sort of thing." She moved quickly on. "My point is that I don't know that I really want to go through all of this again."

Karp looked puzzled. "I don't understand," he said. "Why are you here then?"

"I guess because Mr. Torrisi asked me," she replied. "He and his partner were so good to me following my . . . my . . . problem. So were the two assistant district attorneys, Robin and Pam. I would never have gotten through the trial without them going above and beyond to protect and support me as best they could. Do you know that Robin let me sleep on her sofa when I couldn't go home? They took some of the defense attorney attacks on me personally . . . like friends would."

Tyler looked down at her hands and he saw the tears fall and splash on her fingers. "I wasn't a perfect person before my problem, Mr. Karp. I had an affair outside of my marriage. It was meaningless and short-lived; nonetheless, the defense attorneys found out about it and tried to introduce it at my trial. They tried to say that it showed that I was promiscuous and that explained why I was running by myself on a beach in the morning and maybe didn't try as hard as I could have to avoid being gang-raped."

Karp noted the flash of anger. Good, he thought, she isn't completely beaten and will make a good witness . . . for somebody else.

"Pam and Robin stopped them with the shield laws, so at least I didn't have to put my husband through that twice, a second time in front of a jury and a full courtroom. But, of course, the motion hearing where the defense lawyers brought it up was open, and so the press had all sorts of fun with it anyway. Between the defense lawyers and the press, they wouldn't let the wounds close and heal. They just kept tearing and tearing until I didn't want to go forward with it. I wanted to drop the charges so that I could run away—find some hole, crawl in it, and pull the dirt back in over the top of me. But Robin and Pam wouldn't let me give up. I needed them to be strong for me. Now they need me."

Karp decided to play a little devil's advocate. "You told me that you don't remember the attack. What if the wrong men were convicted? What if the only one involved was Enrique Villalobos? Wouldn't you want those other men exonerated?"

Tyler leaned forward so that her face moved back into the light. She touched the side that had been crushed. "There was no mistake, Mr. Karp," she said. "The men who did this have now made a mockery of everything those police officers and detectives, and Robin and Pam, stand for. If you knew these people like I came to know them, you'd know that I'm telling you the truth. Mr. Villalobos might have been there, too, I truly do not know. But the right men were sent to prison."

Tyler stood up and walked over to where a small mirror hung on the wall. "I'm not asking you to do this so that I can have my life back or so I can 'move on.' That's not going to happen. I'm asking you to do this, Mr. Karp, because those other good people, who still have lives, need you."

Karp felt the wall crumbling. You can't do this, he told himself. "I'm sorry, Liz. . . ."

Tyler turned away from the mirror and faced him. "Please, just read the files. Maybe you can just advise whoever takes the case. Please?"

"But there are other lawyers. . . ."

"Yes, but it's your integrity that matters." As if someone had taken control of his body, Karp heard himself agreeing to read the files. Then he was shaking Liz Tyler's hand as she thanked him. Then he was out in the Lincoln sitting next to Murrow, who started peppering him with questions.

"What? What was that all about?" Murrow asked. "What did I miss? You didn't agree to do anything . . . dumb . . . I mean politically sensitive, did you? What's going on?"

Karp looked into the genuinely worried face of his aide-de-camp. "All in good time, Gilbert," he said.

"You've been saying that a lot lately," Murrow groused. "It's not nice to keep secrets from your adviser."

"Just for the moment," Karp replied. "I need to do something, but nothing to worry about. Now, let's move. We've got to run if I'm going to pick up the boys and get to class on time."

A half hour later, Fulton pulled the Lincoln up to the curb at Crosby outside the loft. Karp was disappointed to see Marlene emerge from the building, obviously headed for the Yellow Cab that was waiting across the street. He'd hoped to have a minute alone to talk to her before he had to leave with the twins, but now she was leaving first.

Karp felt drained by the long day and would just as soon have "left the office" back at 100 Centre Street and forgot about it for a few pleasant hours with his family. But he also felt compelled to warn his wife about getting involved in the Michalik case. The evidence looked pretty damning, and Rachman seemed pretty sure of winning a conviction despite Kipman's questions.

Of course, what he said wouldn't really matter; Marlene would make up her own mind. It was just that life around the loft had been so much better since she'd returned from New Mexico. Regardless of the little spat earlier, the uncomfortable, brooding feeling that had wedged itself between them over the past few years as their philosophies about the administration of justice took divergent paths had lifted. She seemed so much more at peace with herself than she had in ages. Even the near-death experience at the hands of Kane's men in Central Park, as well as Hans Lichner's attempted murder of their son, had not sent her spiraling back down. Still, he worried that some perceived injustice would set her off again as the avenging angel of the downtrodden. He liked the new Marlene and didn't want to let her go.

"Going out?" he asked as he got out of the Lincoln.

"Yeah, sorry, but there's spaghetti on the stove and a nice surprise waiting for you," she said. "The boys are already eating and ready to go to class."

"Where's the fire?" he said as he walked up to her.

"Ariadne called and asked me over for dinner," she said a little nervously. She was never quite sure how he would take hearing the reporter's name. "Apparently there's something very mysterious and very important she wants to talk about."

Karp's heart skipped a beat. As Marlene suspected, the mere mention of Ariadne Stupenagel was enough to make him tense. The two women had been friends since their days as college roommates at Smith, but Ariadne was trouble even when she was asleep. Attaching words to her name like *mysterious* and *important* was like throwing gasoline and dynamite on a fire. He happily accepted Marlene's good-bye kiss (pleased that she had initiated it after the chill of the morning). "Be careful," he said, opening the door of the cab for her.

Marlene sat down and looked up. "I will," she said. "My new middle name is Careful. Careful Ciampi, that's me."

Yeah, he thought as he closed the door and watched the cab pull away from the curb. The only problem is your old first name is Notvery.

"I'll be right out," he called to Fulton, who'd offered to drive him and the twins to the synagogue before he headed for home. Karp and the boys would catch a cab back later.

Karp hurried up to the loft where a surprise was, indeed, waiting for him. "Daddy!" Lucy squealed, springing off the couch where she'd been petting Gilgamesh, who bounded around like a 150-pound puppy at the unexpected party atmosphere. The saucemouthed twins jumped up from their plates of spaghetti and joined in the family hug.

With his arms around his daughter, Karp could feel that she'd gained weight and muscle. He held her away so that he could see her better. He'd always loved her and couldn't have cared less what she looked like, but this was the first time that he could recall thinking that Lucy had become a beautiful young woman. "Wow!" he said. "You're looking good, baby."

Lucy blushed and hugged him again. "It's all the tortillas and beans," she said with her head against his chest. At last she pushed off and said, "Come on, sit down and have a plate of spaghetti. You and Mom must have had a fight because she rushed to whip this up before leaving."

Karp looked longingly at the pot containing Marlene's famous spaghetti marinara, a recipe she'd learned from her mother, who'd learned from her mother and so on back through the generations apparently to the founding of Rome. But then he glanced at his watch and remembered Fulton was waiting.

"It will have to wait," he sighed. "We're going to be late to class."

"Ah, Dad, do we have to," Zak complained. "Lucy just got home and John's here. . . ."

Karp looked puzzled. "John?" He about jumped out of his skin when a man spoke behind him. "Hi, there, chief. Remember me?"

Karp's look of surprise turned to one of delight as he spun to face the voice's owner. "John Jojola! You nearly gave me a heart attack."

"We Indians are sneaky like that," Jojola said, smiling. "Hey, sounds like you need to get going, I'll be here when you get back . . . if you don't mind."

"Ah, jeez," Zak whined. "It's just a stupid bar mitzvah class."

"Hey," Jojola said to him with a half-serious scowl. "Don't neglect your spiritual side or when you need it most the spirits may not be there for you."

"Is that an Indian saying?" Giancarlo asked.

"Um, no, not that I know of . . . I just made it up, but I believe it," Jojola said. "Now get going or I won't tell you that story later of how Brother Bear lost his tail."

When the twins had grumbled their way out the door,

Karp looked back. "So what brings you to New York?" he asked, not sure that he wanted to hear the answer.

"A dream," Jojola said. He laughed when he saw the confused look on Karp's face. "Go on. It's no big deal. We'll talk when you get back."

Why are these things always no big deal, Karp thought as he headed down the stairs, until they are a big deal.

That past spring, the twins had suddenly expressed an interest in going through their bar mitzvah. The request had taken him somewhat by surprise as the boys had been brought up in the Catholic heritage of their mother. However, the more he thought about it, the more pleased he was that his sons were so open to exploring their other half. Then that summer he'd been approached by the rabbi at the synagogue where the twins were taking classes. The rabbi was asking prominent Jewish men to teach classes, which would also contain girls who were studying for their bat mitzvah. Karp had agreed, in large part because of the lure of spending more time with his sons.

The meeting with Liz Tyler and the lesson about integrity were on his mind when he began that night's lesson by setting up a slide show and then turning to the class. "I'm going to talk to you today about a Jew who changed the world. Can anybody guess who?"

"Solomon!" Giancarlo shouted. "Our legal system is based on his court."

"Bob Dylan!" Zak shouted louder. "He rocks!" He didn't really like Dylan—that was more his mother's music—but it was the only Jewish rock musician he could think of quickly and it got the desired laugh from the class. All except Rachel Levine, the thorn in the side of his twelve-year-old maledom and the class know-it-all.

"Try not to be so silly if you can possibly help it, Zak," Rachel said and turned her attention back to Karp. "I believe Mr. Karp must be speaking of Abraham, the father of three great religions—the oldest, Judaism; Christianity; and Islam, which calls him Ibrahim." A look of concern crossed the girl's face. "Of course, the answer depends, Mr. Karp, on whether you're speaking about actual people. As I'm sure you know, Abraham may have been more myth than man."

"What makes you think he wasn't real?" Karp asked. "Isn't he buried with his wife, Sarah, in the Cave of Machpelah near Hebron?"

Rachel rolled her eyes. "Yes, there was probably a historical figure named Abraham, hard to prove scientifically, but really, Mr. Karp, I was talking about the man who spoke to God and all that nonsense."

"My sister talks to a saint who's been dead for five hundred years," Giancarlo said matter-of-factly.

"Yeah, some dudes shot her full of arrows—the saint, not my sister," said Zak, always one to dig into the bloodier side of any story.

"My mother says your sister is crazy," Rachel retorted. "I guess talking to dead saints proves it."

"My sister is not crazy—at least not legally," Giancarlo replied thoughtfully. "She definitely knows the difference between right and wrong. Besides, it could just be the manifestation of post-traumatic stress syndrome after nearly being slaughtered by a homicidal maniac and then almost murdered by a sheriff in New Mexico. Other than that, she's as normal as you are."

Zak, having run out of anything clever to say himself, backed up his brother. "Yeah, and take that back or I'll—"

"You'll what? Physically assault me? I'd call the cops

and you'd be locked up and then your dad would have to prosecute you and send you off to prison," Rachel said and stuck her tongue out.

"And she speaks about sixty or something languages," Giancarlo continued in the defense of his sister.

"Speaking in tongues is demonic," said Ira, a timid boy but acknowledged by all but Rachel as the class's religious scholar.

"She doesn't speak in tongues, you idiot, she knows other languages—French, Chinese, Samoan," Zak shouted and then stuck his tongue out at the girl.

While this was going on, Karp had looked on with slack-jawed amazement at how quickly things had deteriorated. Just like my staff meeting, he thought. "Okay, okay, enough, this debate has veered off into the spectacularly ridiculous," he said. "I wasn't talking about Solomon or Abraham or even Bob Dylan, although they were all good answers and great Jews. Did you know that *Positively 4th Street* was written just a few blocks from my home? Never mind." He turned on the slide projector. "The Jew I was talking about was . . ."

The first slide appeared on the screen. It was El Greco's painting of Jesus upsetting the tables of the money changers in front of the temple in Jerusalem. ". . . Jesus of Nazareth," he said.

"Jesus!" Ira exclaimed in something near to a panic.

"Isn't he a Christian?" Zak asked.

"He was a Jew first . . . everyone knows that," Rachel said. "Mr. Karp, are you sure this is appropriate for this class?"

"Sure, why not?" Karp replied. "He never stopped being a Jew. He was born a Jew and died a Jew and somewhere in between being born and dying, he delivered a powerful enough message that a lot of Jews, as well as a lot of other folks, came to believe that he was the Messiah. But as Jews, we considered him a rabbi—like Rabbi Yakowitz—and a great scholar of the Torah. That's all he is in this painting by El Greco called *Purification of the Temple*, a Jewish carpenter and rabbi."

"What's he doing?" Zak asked, hoping for a good riot story.

"Well, this is during Pesach, or Passover—which, as we know from our studies, is the eight days in the spring when we celebrate the freedom and exodus of the Israelites from Egypt—and Jesus was upset that the money changers were conducting business in the Temple of Herod, which was supposed to be a place to go to pray. He was also upset that sacrificial animals were being sold there—'the blood of innocents,' he said—and the money changers were part of that business.

"The point is that this attack on the establishment was one in a series of acts of civil disobedience by Jesus that would put him in conflict with the people in charge," Karp said.

"The Romans," Zak said helpfully.

"Yes, but almost more so the Jewish leaders—the old rabbis and holy men," Karp said. "These acts frightened them because they knew he was morally right."

"Bet he wouldn't have done it if he knew he was going to get nailed to a cross," Zak said.

"Really, Zak?" Karp asked. "It's an interesting question. Christians say that Jesus knew what lay ahead of him and chose his path anyway. But let's say for the sake of argument that he didn't know. He was a carpenter, he could have settled down, married, had children, and lived happily ever after. But there was something inside of him— some say it was God—that made him do the things that would get him crucified. Whether it came from God or was just part of who he was, what it amounted to was that he had integrity."

Karp paused. He hadn't intended to use that word, but now that it was out, it seemed right. Jesus had integrity. He pressed the button on the slide projector and the next image appeared on the screen, El Greco's painting *The Crucifixion*.

"Sometimes having integrity can cost you everything you have, even your life."

The class sat in silence, until Giancarlo asked, "What does INRI mean?"

Pleased that his son noticed, Karp pointed for everyone else to the inscription on the top of the cross. "It's short for the Latin *Iesvs Nazarenvs Rex Ivdaeorvm*, which is the title a guy named Pontius Pilate, who was sort of the Roman judge for that region, gave Jesus."

"What's it mean?" Rachel asked, now as intrigued as the others.

"Jesus of Nazareth, King of the Jews. The Romans lacked the letter *J* and used *I* instead. They also used *V* instead of *U*. It's an interesting part of the story. Pilate had the inscription placed on the cross after he allowed the rabble—a Jewish rabble I might add—to take Jesus to be crucified. One of the Jewish leaders asked Pilate to change the inscription to 'He said, "I am King of the Jews." ' But Pilate replied, 'What I have written, I have written,' which was a way of him saying that he believed it to be true."

"But why did the Jewish leaders want to kill Jesus," Ira said; he seemed about to cry.

"Because they were afraid, Ira," he said. "Afraid of how a man of integrity made them examine their own conduct."

"What about Pontius Pilate?" Giancarlo said. "In the

Bible, he didn't think Jesus had committed any crimes. He told them that, but in the end he let them have him.''

Good point, Karp thought, but old PP was just the most famous judge who gave into popular sentiment rather than doing the right thing. There would be many others.

"You're right," Karp replied. "Pontius Pilate wasn't a good fellow. He was supposed to keep the peace and watch out for rebels who popped up from time to time, like the Maccabees, whose rebellion we just finished celebrating at Hanukkah. His job would have been easier if Jesus had just preached against Roman law, but Jesus didn't. All he talked about was living in peace and people loving their neighbors and praising God for all the good things in life.''

"Then why'd he do it?" Ira wailed.

Ira's emotional outburst got the rest of the class tittering until Karp brought up his hand to silence them. "Actually, Ira, that's the best question of the night—and the answer is the whole point of tonight's lesson," he said. "Pontius Pilate gave in to the mob and the Jewish leaders because he lacked integrity. Jesus, on the other hand . . . ," he said, turning toward the painting on the screen, "in those times, just a Jewish carpenter and scholar, had integrity."

"Look where it got him," Zak pointed out.

"Ah, yes, but look how he's remembered today by an awful lot of people," Karp replied. "To some, he's the Son of God. And even others, including Jews and Muslims, see him as a great man. But how is Pontius Pilate remembered? As a corrupt coward who wouldn't stand up for justice, a man who washed his hands of a murder.''

The class was silent for a minute until Giancarlo quietly said, "It must have hurt.''

Karp looked up at the painting, letting his eyes wander to the nails that protruded from the hands and feet. "Yes, it hurt," he said. "Whether he was just a Jewish carpenter with a different way of looking at the world, or the Son of God, he had to go through the pain and suffering. He could have backed out at the last minute, you know. Pontius Pilate gave him the opportunity to renounce his claims to being the Messiah. But he told them, 'I am what I am,' and sealed his fate."

Hitting the lights and turning off the projector, Karp added, "My dad used to put it another way, sometimes, quoting William Shakespeare. It's from the play *Hamlet* and is basically the advice of a father, Polonius, to his son, Laertes, when he tells him, 'This above all: to thine own self be true.' I think if you follow that one piece of wisdom, you will find that you are people of integrity, too."

"And end up like Jesus?" Zak asked.

Karp looked at his son. Sometimes he wondered what would become of this boy. Like Marlene, he sometimes seemed to have a foot on one path that led to trouble, and other times one foot on a path that led away from trouble. "Maybe," he said. "But there are worse ways to end up. You could end up as a heroin junkie. Or people may know you as a liar and a cheat and want nothing to do with you. Or you could be a judge who sends an innocent man to the gallows, all because you lacked integrity. You could be the next Pontius Pilate. Or you can choose to live your life with integrity, like Jesus, and make a real difference in this world."

The class was quieter than normal when they filed out a few minutes later. Karp was certain he'd hear from their parents about his choice of topics. But he thought that, as Christmas approached, it didn't hurt for Jewish kids to learn that all the fuss was being made about one of their own.

12

ABOUT THE TIME KARP AND THE BOYS HAD BEEN arriving at the synagogue, Marlene's cab pulled up to the curb outside Ariadne Stupenagel's walk-up loft, which occupied a corner of the fifth floor of a turn-of-the-century brick warehouse between Avenues A and B on East Thirteenth Street in the East Village. Lucy and John had arrived only ten minutes before she'd had to leave—much of that time spent chattering with and holding her daughter, so there hadn't been much time to grill Jojola.

The Indian police chief had given her the same "no big deal" dream answer when she asked what brought him to town. But unlike her husband, she knew that dreams were taken seriously by Jojola. And if this dream was enough to get him away from his beloved home in the desert, it was because he deemed it serious indeed. But he'd also told her they'd talk later about it "when there's more time and the kids aren't around."

"Madam, we are here." The cabdriver was half turned in his seat, obviously anxious to get on to his next fare.

Marlene glanced at the New York City cab driver's permit hanging from the dash. Hassan Ahmed. She wondered if he was sympathetic to Islamic terrorists and immediately felt ashamed at the thought. That's what fear does to you, she thought as she handed her money through the partition. Divides and conquers. "Keep the change," she said and hoped he wouldn't know the extra-large tip was paying off a guilty conscience.

"Thank you, madam," Ahmed replied with a smile. "God bless you."

"And you," she said, exiting the cab.

As Ahmed sped off, she stood for a moment looking up at Stupenagel's building. It wasn't much on the outside; its dingy mustard-colored bricks had been surrendered to the neighborhood's graffiti artists, and the rusty metal fire escapes looked more ornamental than practical. But otherwise the building and the surrounding buildings had that look of the newly gentrified, as the upper middle class moved into yet another run-down ethnic neighborhood and caused the rents to skyrocket. There were no weeds in the repaired sidewalks and staircases; the small cement basketball court across the street had a fresh coat of paint, and the playing area was swept clean of the broken bottles, beer cans, and syringes she'd seen there in years past. Many of the windows had flower boxes, now dormant in winter but indicating a certain pride of ownership; in a window of the building across the street, she could see the black fin of a baby grand piano cruising above the sill.

Stupenagel, who'd moved into the neighborhood years before it was safe to do so, complained that it had been a lot more entertaining before the junkies got chased out and the Dominicans couldn't afford to live there and blast salsa from their car stereos. True, there were many fewer reports of robberies, rapes, burglaries, and domestic violence, as well as an increased police presence due to the income level of the new owners, "but it's all been sort of . . . I don't know . . . sterilized," her friend had said sadly.

The journalist was proud of the fact that she had been living there before Beat poet Allen Ginsberg bought the corner loft opposite from hers. She was there when he died in April 1997. "I got invited to the party when he was dying in the back bedroom; it was all very Buddhist," Stupenagel told her whenever she got the chance. "All sorts of important literary and arts people were there, like Phil Glass, Gregory Corso, Lucien Carr; Bill Burroughs showed up the next day. Did I ever tell you about the day Allen came over with Bob Dylan? They were working on a collaboration putting Allen's poetry to music and wanted my opinion. I've seen his ghost, you know . . . Allen's, that is, wandering around in the hallway, reciting 'Howl' . . . 'I saw the best minds of my generation destroyed by madness . . .'"

A large black-and-white poster of Ginsberg sitting naked in the lotus position greeted Marlene when Stupenagel opened the door. Catching her glance, the reporter said, "It's a self-portrait, one of only fifty original prints from his private collection. I got it for a steal after helping his secretary, Peter Hale, catalog some of his recordings. Come in, come in, some old friends have joined us."

Marlene followed Stupenagel down the hallway, wondering what sort of mischief her old roommate had in store. A moment later, she knew, as she entered the living room and saw Robin Repass and Pam Russell drinking wine and chatting.

"I think you know Robin and Pam," Stupenagel said in her best hostess voice.

Marlene shot her a dirty look but smiled with genuine affection at the two younger women when they stood up and moved quickly over to her. She embraced each of them, then stood back and asked, "So how are you two holding up?"

Their smiles faded. "You've heard about what happened with our Coney Island case and the lawsuit?" Russell asked.

"How could she not unless she's been living in a cave," Repass said.

She was always the brash one, Marlene thought, Pam the polite counterpart. Together they'd been a dynamic team.

"I'm holding up about as well as can be expected after being labeled a lying racist pig, losing my job, and being sued for every cent I've ever made and ever will make," Repass said.

"And then being told to bend over and take it," Russell added, the unexpected sexual reference causing them all to burst out laughing.

The laughter stopped abruptly at the sound of the front door opening and a man's voice calling out, "Honey Buns, I'm home."

Ariadne jumped up to intercept the visitor but not before Gilbert Murrow entered the room with an armful of flowers and a handful of videos, which he promptly dropped when he saw that he and Honey Buns were not alone.

Marlene bent over and picked up one of the videotapes. "Hmmm, a classic . . . *Last Tango in Paris*," she said with an amused look on her face. "Should we remove the butter before we leave tonight?"

Stupenagel plucked the video out of Marlene's hands and gave it back to her boyfriend along with the other two she'd picked up. "Murry, sweetie, don't you remember," she said, relieving him of the flowers. "This was supposed to be boys' night out. You're supposed to go out with your guy friends, get drunk, go to strip bars and place folded dollar bills in G-strings, get all horny, and THEN come home. Remember? I was going to spend a quiet evening at home with my girlfriends, and then after I kicked them out, wait up for you."

"Oh . . . yeah," Murrow said. "Sorry, thought I remembered this was movie night." Only then did he get a good look at the women beyond Marlene and his girlfriend. His mouth and eyes opened wider. He quickly covered both with his hands. "See no evil. Hear no evil. Speak no evil. I don't even want to know what's going on here." He spun on his heel and made for the front door.

Stupenagel smiled at the other women. "I'll be right back," she said and rushed after Murrow. There was the sound of urgent whispers from the hall, a period of quiet, and then the door opened and closed. Stupenagel reappeared with her lipstick smeared, tucking her shirttail back into the waist of her skirt. "He's such a sweetheart," she said, her voice somewhat husky, "if a little forgetful. Now, where were we?"

"Well, I for one was wondering about all the secrecy," Marlene said.

"I wasn't sure you'd come," Stupenagel replied.

"Why? Because I might not want to be part of whatever story you're working on?"

Stupenagel looked hurt. "Sure, I like having the inside track on a juicy story. But believe it or not, I arranged this because I'd like to stop what I think is a huge injustice. I don't know if you remember this, but I was the first reporter to write about what really happened to Liz Tyler on that beach. That was back when I was working for the

Times. And I covered the trial from gavel to gavel. I guess you could say this is one of those stories that really stuck with me. I don't know about this Villalobos guy—maybe he was there from the beginning, or came along during or after—but those other guys are guilty as sin."

"So what's this have to do with me?" Marlene asked. When the other three women were silent, she shook her head. "Oh, no, I'm retired. No more private investigator, no more lawyer, no more vigilante shit. I'm a painter, a mother, and a housewife. Besides, aren't you two being represented by Corporation Counsel?"

"The office is, and by all appearances, Corporation Counsel is about to offer a large settlement to the plaintiffs," Repass said dryly. "But we're on our own as private individuals. The law allows such suits if we were 'acting outside the constraints of our official duties.' Apparently, the plaintiffs are alleging—and Corporation Counsel isn't doing anything to say different—that our actions were so horrible that we can be sued for violating their civil rights."

"You need a good civil attorney," Marlene advised.

"Oh, come on, Marlene, there's something going on here that requires more than a good civil attorney," Stupenagel jumped in. "Robin and Pam, as well as a few good police officers and detectives, are being offered up as sacrificial lambs when the city, the NYPD, and the Kings County DA ought to be fighting this tooth and nail. I was thinking you might be willing to poke around a little. I'm working on some angles—a little bird told me something interesting I can't divulge at this moment—but I don't always have your . . . imagination . . . when it comes to getting to the bottom of things like this."

Marlene glowered at Stupenagel. "You know Butch

would blow a gasket if he thought I was trying to 'get to the bottom of things like this.' "

Russell reached out and touched her arm. "That's okay, Marlene. You're right, we need to find a lawyer who'll represent us and fight this thing ourselves."

"Let's forget about it," Repass added, "and just have dinner and a little conversation between friends. Stupe says she's been sweating over a hot stove, but we think she ordered out—"

"Lies!" Stupenagel complained. "I've been wronged!"

"And the wine is probably homemade."

Stupenagel laughed and agreed. "Yep, squashed the grapes in the bathtub with my own size-ten feet."

Marlene looked at the three women who were grinning at her. "Shit," she swore. "I suppose it can't hurt to drink a little wine with old friends, can it?"

Somewhere into the third bottle, Marlene decided that letting her two former protégées run through their case also wouldn't hurt.

One of the most pernicious aspects was the position taken by DA Breman in what Marlene viewed as an improper vacatur of the convictions, based on purely hearsay revelations by Villalobos, which were unsworn and suspiciously documented by Breman.

"The fact that Villalobos was one of the assailants does not answer whether the other five, including Kevin Little, who would testify for the People, weren't also participants," Russell said. "We always conceded in the trial that there was a sixth assailant."

"And nothing he said warranted an outright dismissal of the convictions," Repass added. "In fact, it's prohibited under relevant New York legal precedent—Section 440.10 of the Criminal Procedure Law. The law does not permit an otherwise valid conviction to be set aside merely on the basis of a third party's claim of guilt for a crime for which other defendants were convicted."

"At best," Russell said, "such a claim mandates only that the court conduct a full evidentiary hearing—complete with sworn testimony and the right to cross-examine him—to test Villalobos's allegations that he, and he alone, was responsible for the assault on Liz Tyler."

"And the court should have decided at such a hearing if Villalobos's account was trustworthy enough to justify a new trial—not whether the convictions should be set aside," Repass said.

"Yet, Breman ignored legal precedent and set up you, the NYPD, and the city to take a fall," Marlene mused as she swirled a red cabernet around in her glass. "But why?"

"Ah, that's what we'd all like to know," Stupenagel said.

The women sipped their wine silently for a minute before Repass, who was opening the fourth bottle, spoke. "The thing that really bothers me is that we would have won at trial again, using the defendants' own words. We went through an exhaustive month-long Huntley Hearing before the trial to determine the voluntariness and admissibility of their confessions, took testimony from over twenty prosecution witnesses, and heard from the defendants and their families and friends. The court concluded that the statements were properly and legally obtained and that no improper methods were employed to secure them."

There were tears in Repass's eyes when she looked at Marlene and, slurring somewhat from the wine and emotion, added, "You trained us well, Marlene. We won those convictions fair and square. The only thing that would have changed at a new trial would have been that we'd be able to tell the jury who the sixth man was—

although, of course, Villalobos waited until the statute of limitations had run out so he couldn't be prosecuted for it."

Stupenagel tossed in her two cents. "From what I understand, there's no trick that Hugh Louis or any other scumbag defense lawyer could have pulled to simply have those confessions thrown out. The Huntley decision had already been tested at the appellate level and sustained. He had to get Breman to vacate the convictions."

The reporter, with the two prosecutors' concurrence, said she suspected that Villalobos had "confessed" as a favor to the Bloods or under threat. "What we can't figure out is why Breman capitulated so easily—"

"Except that she would do anything to appease the minority population," Repass said. "But even then there's got to be more to this."

Corporation Counsel had set them adrift. As soon as Sam Lindahl settled, they and the individual police officers would be sitting ducks.

"At stake, of course, are our reputations and future job prospects," Russell said. "But I know Robin agrees with me that the most important issue here is justice for what those pigs did to Liz Tyler."

Marlene was quiet for a moment and then she asked, "But what do you want me to do?"

Repass brightened. "Maybe you could sign on as our private investigator for the time being. You could back out later, but you could do some of the poking around that Lindahl won't do," she said. "We got a tip from an anonymous caller with some sort of Euro accent that there may have been an inmate who heard something that would discredit Villalobos."

"Maybe you can get that big shot husband of yours to

weigh in," Stupenagel added. "Part of the problem now is that no one is speaking out for the other side and there's a perception in the public—from which the jury will come—that it's a slam dunk case against these guys."

Marlene shook her head. "I'm willing to do a little, as you say, poking around," she said. "But I wouldn't hold out much hope that Butch will weigh in through the media. As you know, if the media was a snake, he'd get a stick and beat it to death."

At about the same time, the man in question was back home, talking to John Jojola, who'd been resting on the couch when they walked in.

"Off to bed," Karp had ordered the twins, who were tired enough that they didn't complain, although Giancarlo stopped at the entrance to the hall and said, "Thanks, Dad, I really liked class tonight."

"Butt kisser." A voice, Zak's, had come from farther down the hall. Giancarlo disappeared in that direction and the sound of a brief scuffle ensued.

"To bed!" Karp yelled, but smiled and winked at Jojola, who was shaking his head.

"Hey, I think it's great they have each other," Jojola said. "My boy, he's got me and the extended family of the tribe, but there are things you can only tell a brother."

"Where's Charlie?" Karp asked.

"Staying with his Auntie Maria," Jojola said. "She's not really his auntie, just a nice neighbor woman who sometimes comes around a lot."

"Comes around a lot?" Karp said, wiggling an eyebrow.

"Never mind, just a friend," Jojola said.

"I believe you're blushing," Karp said.

"Indians don't blush," Jojola said, trying to scowl but

not doing a very good job of it. "This is our natural color, remember? Anyhow, this time of year, my tribe sort of pulls into itself. The Taos Reservation is closed to all but our people, and families—most of whom live in modern houses the rest of the year—take up living in the old pueblo. Sort of a way to touch base, tell stories, and remember who we are. I don't like taking Charlie away from the res during this time, I want him learning the ways of his people."

"Sounds like something the rest of us have lost," Karp said a little sadly.

"Oh, you have it, only it's shorter and the reasons for it sometimes get lost in the other stuff . . . Christmas and Hanukkah . . . a time to come together and celebrate the past, and remember who you are as a people. When it gets cold outside, ancient peoples from all lands have always seen winter as a time for gathering together—if for no other reason than body heat and to keep from going stir crazy when the snow gets too deep for going outside. They have also always seen it as a time for intro-spection and deep thoughts."

Jojola stopped talking and smiled. "Sorry, didn't mean to pull the Indian medicine man out on you."

"No, not at all," Karp said, sitting down in his favorite chair and kicking back with his feet up on the coffee table. "I just came from telling a bunch of Jewish kids about Jesus . . . you don't get more controversial than that. I confess that I'm more interested in some of these matters now than I ever was back in the day."

"It can take an entire lifetime to find out what you really believe in," Jojola said. "As for the lecture on comparative religions, I find it fascinating that we all have such similar ways of thinking and so much of it is tied to the seasons. In winter, we all seem to have traditions of family gatherings and touching base with our spirituality, if you will. In spring, my people celebrate with the New Corn Festival, which is based around the renewal of the earth and its plants and animals; Christians have Easter, the rebirth of Jesus, following the emptiness of winter. They both represent hope for the future in either culture. Then in fall, we dance in celebration of the harvest that will get us through the winter, and feast; European Americans feast after the harvest, too, at Thanksgiving.

"Yet, for all we have in common, religion is so often at the root of war. But why? Jews, Christians, Muslims all call the same man, Abraham, the father of their religion, and yet they have slaughtered each other for centuries. Hindus slaughter Sikhs. Chinese Buddhists kill Nepalese Buddhists."

Jojola laughed again and slapped his knees. "There I go again, running off at the mouth," he said. "Must still be jumpy from the plane flight. Anyway, that was the long answer to your short question asking me about my son."

Karp laughed too. He felt comfortable around Jojola. It wasn't just that what you see is what you get with the man—he was certainly deeper than might be expected of the police chief of a small Indian reservation. Karp wondered if the other members of his tribe were as introspective and insightful. Probably no more than the other members of my tribe are all wise as Solomon, he thought.

"Where have you been, my friend?" Jojola said when he saw that Karp was back from his reflection.

Karp chuckled. "Sorry, was just reliving tonight's bar mitzvah class . . . all this talk about spirituality. Let me ask you something."

"Shoot."

"So I take it you don't like leaving the res either," Karp said.

"Nope."

"Then why are you here?"

Jojola pursed his lips and looked at the ceiling. When he looked back down, his dark eyes were glittering like black opals. "Are you ready for another long answer to a short question?"

An hour later, Karp was still sitting in his chair in the dark with only a little light from the streetlamps illuminating the living room. Jojola had gone off to bed in the boys' room; they'd insisted he take the bottom bunk while they shared the top.

Then Lucy had come bouncing in from whatever adventure she'd been on. He would have liked to remind her that this wasn't Taos, New Mexico, it was Gotham City, and young women did not flit around its streets unaccompanied at night. But she'd kissed him and said, "I'm going to bed. We can talk in the morning."

He was thinking about going off to bed himself when he heard a key being inserted in the dead bolt of the front door. Gilgamesh picked up his head and whined. The door swung open, revealing a small, dark figure silhouetted against the light in the entryway.

"Aren't you getting home a little past your curfew, young lady?" he asked. He looked at the clock in the kitchen; it was ten minutes after midnight.

"You waiting up for me, Pops?" Marlene giggled.

"Yeah, come over here, I want to see if I can smell alcohol on your breath," he replied, patting his lap.

Marlene kicked off her shoes and in a few quick steps had crossed the room and was straddling him on the chair. She planted a long, warm kiss full of promises on his lips. "What do you think?" she asked.

"Merlot . . . perhaps masking an earlier cabernet," he said as she snuggled against his chest. "Glad you weren't driving. So, what was the very important mystery . . . or do I dare ask?"

Marlene sat up and put her arms around his neck. "Well, it was kind of a sneaky way to get me together with Robin Repass and Pam Russell," she said and waited for the reaction. She was almost disappointed that all she got was an arched brow.

"Anyway, they wanted to ask if I would do a little digging around," she said.

"And?"

Marlene searched his eyes as best she could to see if he was angry. She decided that now was the time to fit as many words as she could into as small a space as possible.

"I think there's a big injustice coming down on a lot of people, including Robin, Pam, the cops, and the victim," she said quickly. "I told them that I would consider their request, but I wanted to run it by you first."

The last was sort of a lie. She'd pretty much agreed to their request. When her husband didn't answer, she finally asked, "Well?"

"Well what? Since when have you listened to me?" He'd meant it as a teasing remark and immediately regretted it when she tensed up.

"That's not true," she complained. "Yes, I do what I feel is right, and we all know that it nearly destroyed me, and nearly destroyed us. But I've always listened to you, and even when I didn't follow your advice, I knew that you were usually right. It's not fair; after all, I'm not the only one in this family who does what he thinks is right, even if it gets him in trouble."

Karp raised his hands in mock surrender. "Hey, it's

okay, I didn't mean it in a bad way," he said. "I agree it sounds like Robin and Pam are getting a bum rap."

Marlene was surprised. He almost sounded as if he wasn't bothered by the thought of her "poking around." She decided to press her advantage. "You know, Stupe thought that maybe if you made a public statement, maybe wrote an op-ed piece for the *New York Times*, it might counteract all the negative publicity stirred up by Hugh Louis."

"It's not the business of the New York district attorney to be critiquing the decisions made by the Kings County district attorney," he said to see how she'd react.

It was with anger. "What's the matter, afraid it might hurt you politically?"

"No," he said, refusing to take the bait. "But it would be highly irregular."

Marlene caught the tone of pseudo-pomposity. She cocked her head to see him better with her good eye. "Okay, Butch, what's up?"

"Nothing," he said. Delighted, he received her kiss, but then she bit into his tongue and held on. "Ow . . . 'at 'urts," he complained. "O'ay, o'ay, I'll 'ell 'ou."

Marlene released his tongue. "Give it up, buster."

He told her about the real reason for his meeting with the mayor and then his talk that day with Liz Tyler. "I think I'm going to take the case, but I wanted to run it past you first. You mad?"

Marlene smiled and kissed him again. This time there were no painful bites, but he became aware of the increased pressure she was exerting from her groin to his. She reached down and began fumbling with his belt.

"What about the twins? Lucy? John?" he asked huskily.

"Whatsa matter Big—and I do mean BIG—Boy," she said as she unzipped his pants. "Afraid of getting caught?"

As an answer, his hands dived beneath her sweater and turtleneck shirt and in one motion removed them all.

"I guess not," she murmured.

Later as they lay in bed, having decided that prudence was the better part of valor for the second round, Marlene sleepily asked if he'd found out the reason behind Jojola's unexpected visit.

"Hmmm?" Karp mumbled. "Uh, yeah, a dream."

"I know that," she said, nibbling on an earlobe. "What dream? Come on, tell me, I'll give you a reward."

"Thought you already did," he said and pulled her over and onto his chest. But he started to breathe deeply, his prelude to snoring.

"Dream," she said. "What about the dream?"

"Noth . . . nothing," he said. "Impossible."

"What's impossible? Karp, don't you go to sleep and leave me wondering all night."

"Grale."

Marlene tensed. Was Butch the one dreaming? "What about Grale?"

Karp patted her on the back in the way he did when it was time for her to leave him alone and go to sleep. "John thinks he's alive."

"What!"

"His dream . . . he needs to find him, or we're all going to die. Now . . . time to sleep."

"Karp?" Marlene said. "Karp, dammit." But all she got back was a deep, rumbling snore.

13

IN ANOTHER PART OF THE CITY THAT NIGHT,
Ahman Zakir caught up to "Mr. Mustafa" in the hall outside the meeting room of the mosque. "It was a warning. Someone knows your plans," he said. "I think we better call this off . . . tonight's event, anyway."

"Nonsense," Al-Sistani said. "It was nothing more than stupid American racists getting even for our brothers' righteous execution of the Crusaders and their lackeys in Iraq. As if this is some tit-for-tat game of revenge. Their inability to see the, as they say, 'big picture,' is why we will win."

Al-Sistani spoke the words with conviction. His Oxford-educated English was clipped and cultivated, his manners in polite company impeccable—on the outside, just another spoiled oil prince, perfect for a mujahideen cell leader. True, he'd initially been shocked and momentarily unnerved when he heard that his bodyguard who'd disappeared that night outside the mosque had been butchered and his head stuck on a spike in Central Park. For that one moment, he felt panic start to rise in his throat like bile, wondering if he'd been betrayed and his plan ruined.

However, the more he thought about it, the more he was sure that he and his men were safe. The American police and even their intelligence agencies were too weak willed, too emasculated by their politicians and civil libertarians, to make such a dramatic statement as killing a wanted terrorist and displaying his head for all to see. Maybe in Saudi Arabia but not here in America with its silly rules against torture and "cruel and unusual punishment." How could they expect to win?

As the days passed and there were no arrests of his people and "the supplies" remained in place, he was further convinced that the bodyguard's death was not even the work of some rogue element of the New York Police Department or any agency of the American government, including the laughable Homeland Security Department.

"Their culture of fair play dooms them," he lectured his closest aides. "They want to arrest us and put us on trial, then place us in prison, where we become the new symbols of the jihad. They do not have the testicles it will take to win this fight. In the meantime, we will slaughter them by the thousands in their homes, their stadiums, and their office buildings."

Al-Sistani was not, therefore, surprised when someone claiming to represent "the American Aryan Jihadi" called a popular radio talk-show host and claimed responsibility. As expected, the infidel had said the killing was in retaliation "for killing white men in Iraq. So all of you fuckin' little towel heads out there, consider yourselves warned. Get the fuck out of white man's country and go back to your little piles of shit sandboxes."

The police and district attorney's office had released a joint press statement saying they had no prior intelligence on any hate group called American Aryan Jihadi. The statement assured Muslim-Americans and Muslim visitors that every effort was being made to bring the murderer to justice. The statement also urged other citizens to "refrain from escalating tensions and unfairly singling out any one group based on events in Iraq and the Middle East."

The American Civil Liberties Union, the Anti-Defamation League, and the Muslim-American Anti-Defamation League of New York had immediately joined in condemning the police and district attorney's office for not taking a more proactive stance. "One cannot help but think that if this had been a Christian white man," Imam Abdul Ibn Barr, head of one of the largest Muslim congregations, wrote in a *New York Times* op-ed piece, "or a Jew, the police response would have been much more forceful and all-encompassing. Yet, they don't even know who this poor immigrant is, or anything about him, except that he died horribly and his head was left in plain sight of where police officers supposedly walk their beats. In all likelihood, he left behind a family in some far-off land who now waits to hear from their breadwinner—a call that will never come. And all the DA and police can do is promise some future justice."

Police chief Bill Denton, the mayor-elect's brother, got himself into hot water by angrily going on television to demand that the complaining organizations "point out the guilty man, and I'll arrest him personally." Which only resulted in another op-ed piece labeling him as "apparently too lazy to do his own work . . . trying to shift the blame back on the people who are trying to demand accountability from their police department."

District Attorney Karp, a man Al-Sistani knew was an enemy to be reckoned with from his past run-ins with

Islam's holy warriors, had been more circumspect. "As in all homicide cases, we are working with all due diligence to bring any and all perpetrators of this heinous crime to justice. Whatever the cause or justification, murder is murder in New York County. All perceptions to the contrary are disingenuous and without merit."

It was almost laughable how the Americans had started backbiting. The fat lawyer Hugh Louis had taken a break from his television appearances talking about his case against the city—a case Al-Sistani had followed closely because it promised to yield more angry young black men who might become recruits—to denounce "the attack on our brown Arab brothers." Of course, Louis had used the extra television time to plug the Coney Island case, too. "The same institutionalized racism that imprisoned four innocent African-American men based on Gestapo-like police interrogation techniques is also responsible for the fact that racist murderers are roaming free, victimizing people of color."

The city councilwoman Shakira Zulu had joined in the fray by calling a press conference to raise the ante. "Until the black man and the brown man arm themselves, they will be preyed upon by the power structure of white America. Let us not forget, the black man suffering in the ghettos of America has more in common with his Palestinian brother, who daily faces the tanks and bullets of Zionist oppression with nothing more than rocks and his blood, than he does with the white man."

Although Al-Sistani regretted the death of the bodyguard, a well-trained man he'd known for years, the murder only played into his cause by distracting federal agents from the real danger. He wasn't worried about his man being identified, if for no other reason than after his rat-chewed body was discovered in the alley next to the mosque by a believer assigned to take out the trash, both the body and that of the believer had been taken to a landfill operated by a sympathizer and buried.

If the Americans wanted to play tit-for-tat, well, then, he'd see how they felt after New Year's Eve. As for the others, the lawyers and the whiny activists, he cared no more for any of them than any other infidel who did not accept the Prophet as the representative of Allah and the one true faith. Even these Nation of Islam blacks would have to learn the errors of their misguided interpretations of the Quran or have their heresy cured by the sword.

Soon they would all be trembling with fear and awe when he struck at the very heart of their loathsome city. But he would be long gone to California, where he would lie low and plan his next triumph in the name of Allah. In his dreams, he saw the Golden Gate Bridge crashing into the sea loaded with early-morning commuter traffic, and airliners falling from the sky on fire, or crashing into sky-scrapers in Chicago, Seattle, and L.A.

The stupid Americans would lash out at the next tinpot dictator, like that secular idiot Hussein, crush his army, and find itself in another quagmire where the holy war-riors of Al Qaeda would flock to sow the seeds of insur-rection and martyrdom. Soon enough the Americans would be abandoned by the timid Europeans, cowed like the Spanish into submission, their rail systems in sham-bles and their hospitals overflowing with the dead and maimed. Until at last, the United States would stand alone, ostracized by its former friends who feared retri-bution from their huge Muslim immigrant populations and the martyrs of Islam.

Then, with no other country willing to be a trading part-ner, the economy of the United States would be crippled and its population living in terror of the next World Trade

Center or, he laughed, New Year's Eve in Times Square. Thus, the most powerful nation in the world would have to sue for mercy and give itself over to Islamic law.

Despite having spent many years among them in his youth, Al-Sistani was amazed and delighted that the Americans could not see what needed to be done to save themselves. Worried about political correctness, they allowed him and others like him to travel freely. Instead of paying close attention to young men, even women, of Arab extraction or those coming from Muslim countries, they wasted their time and resources at airports checking the bags of their grandmothers and patting down small children. It was all for show, anyway, a farcical allegory right out of their stupid children's book *The Emperor Who Had No Clothes*. It was all for an illusion of security when their government was too hamstrung by partisan politics to react effectively. If ever there was a plum that was ripe for the plucking, it was the God-accursed and decadent United States of America.

When he lay in his apartment at night, this was the pleasant dream of the future he saw unfolding before him like the desert sands of Arabia. Even now, it took an effort to bring himself back into focus outside the door of the meeting room. The Islamic States of America would not be accomplished merely by dreaming. It would take hard action.

His plan needed volunteers to make sure that all his preparations and energy weren't wasted. There were always too few trained men for these operations, and most of those he had with him were too valuable for martyrdom. Of the dozen, now minus one, he'd had slip into the U.S. and meet up with him in New York, he planned to leave half to carry out his glorious blow against the infidels; the rest would go with him to California for the next plan. But he wanted a half-dozen more volunteers to help set up "the supplies," a dangerous job in itself, and then guard them until the moment of martyrdom was at hand.

Ever since the destruction of the World Trade Center, Al Qaeda had redoubled its efforts to recruit American Muslims to its cause, especially from within the ranks of the more militant offshoots of groups like the Nation of Islam and the Black Muslims. Al Qaeda operatives such as himself, as well as those from affiliated organizations like Hamas, had for years been establishing contacts in sympathetic community mosques all over the United States. Not all, or even most, were welcoming—some had even betrayed the cause by reporting their activities to the police; someday they would pay a price for their treason to God. But here and there the recruiters had made inroads, especially in poor neighborhoods like this one in East Harlem, where poverty created fertile ground for spreading anti-American seeds of destruction. Waiting for the young men in the meeting room to come in and take their seats, he looked at Zakir and smiled.

Zakir smiled back, but he was not happy. He knew that Mr. Mustafa wasn't working for any charitable organization. He didn't know precisely what the pockmarked zealot was planning, but he knew it was big and that it was going to happen on New Year's Eve. He suspected a bomb set in Times Square. Maybe, he thought with a mixture of fear and excitement, a plane out of JFK International will be hijacked to dive into the crowd. More than a hundred thousand people would be crowded into the area. The hijackers will want a plane still loaded with fuel to burn as many as possible . . . there'd be no escape; they'd be caught between the buildings.

Zakir tried not to think about the burned bodies—the

innocent people. This was the evolution of the race war he'd advocated in his youthful days as a Black Panther. But Times Square will be filled with black as well as white, his conscience told him. *Some of them Muslim.* He pushed the thought away and concentrated on the money he had in the bank, plus the money he'd been promised when the deed was done. There was going to be another large payment after tonight's ugly business, a business he'd objected to until Mr. Mustafa told him he'd be paid twenty-five thousand dollars.

"We have a traitor in our midst who endangers you as much as the rest of us," Mr. Mustafa had told him. "We must make a bold statement if Allah's will is to be accomplished."

"Have you heard from Basir and Moammar?" Zakir asked, more for something to say than because he cared about the answer. He didn't ask a lot of questions about the men who used the back rooms of his mosque, nor was much information ever volunteered.

Al-Sistani furrowed his brow. Basir and Moammar were two of his best men, handpicked from the training camp on the Afghanistan-Pakistan border. They had been due to arrive from their shift guarding the supplies a half hour ago. Then again, they'd all been ordered to be careful going to and from the mosque and might have taken a circuitous route; something might have made them nervous—a cop walking his beat or patrol car moving slowly in close proximity to the mosque—and they were taking their time just to be safe.

"No," he replied, "but they'll be here. Come, let's do this."

While Al-Sistani trusted his own men with his life, he did not trust these recruits. He'd done his best to weed out the weak and those whose commitment to Allah was not as great as it needed to be. Those who remained had been told that they would be taking part in a plan to humble the United States and the white men and Jews who oppressed them.

Of course, they would never be told the real plot. But there were ways of rooting out traitors, which, after his bodyguard's death, he'd decided to implement. He'd told the recruits at the last meeting that he was going to give them a taste of what was to come for infidels in America. He told them to pay attention to the news two days hence coming out of Union Square and involving a UPS delivery truck.

On the morning of that day, he'd called UPS from a pay phone and asked that a package be picked up from a law firm across from Union Square. He then went into a nearby Starbucks, ordered a venti caffe latte, and sat at the window to watch what happened. When the delivery truck arrived, it was immediately swarmed by SWAT team officers, who yanked the driver from his seat before he knew they were there.

Of course, the truck was just a truck, there to pick up a package. The driver, one Benjamin Hamm of South Queens, was taken away to be questioned but released a short time later when the police decided he'd played no role in the "hoax."

Al-Sistani left the Starbucks wearing a grim smile, which had returned to his face as he and Zakir and two of his men entered the meeting room. He had a traitor to deal with and there was only one way to do it.

Worried that the mosque was no longer secure, he'd withdrawn his men from the barracks the night before he called UPS and had them disperse to safe houses throughout the city. He'd then had the mosque watched for several days to see what happened. But when no teams of federal agents swept down on Zakir and his congregation, he decided that the traitor had not told them everything and probably intended to sell information bit by bit for the money.

Unfortunately, it did mean that the mosque was no longer completely safe. Even coming back this night was taking a chance, but he'd also wanted to make a dramatic statement the recruits would not soon forget. If the federal agents were watching him, he would know by how the recruits responded to tonight's event. But if they came looking for him, either here or at his midtown apartment, they would not find him. And soon it would not matter.

Al-Sistani entered the room and looked at the upturned and expectant faces of the young black men sitting in rows on folding chairs. Someday we will have to recruit their women as well; they are easier to get past security, he thought. "A *salaam alaikum,*" he greeted the audience.

"Peace be unto you," Zakir translated for the non–Arabic speakers. He listened proudly as some of his more adept students replied: "*Wa alaikum salaam.* And unto you, peace."

"I would like to read to you from the Quran," Al-Sistani said, opening his copy. "O you who believe, let Me inform you of a trade that will save you from painful retribution. Believe in GOD and His messenger and strive in the cause of GOD with your money and your lives. In return, He forgives your sins, and admits you into gardens with flowing streams, with beautiful mansions in the gardens of Eden. This is the greatest triumph. Additionally, you get something you truly love: support from GOD and guaranteed victory. Give good news to the believers!"

Al-Sistani closed the Quran and looked up. "I come to you tonight, my brothers, at a monumental time in history . . . when the shackles of Christian and Jewish oppression shall be cut from the legs and arms of true believers. In the days ahead, a few of you will be chosen to take part in an event that will shatter their world. You should be proud, as you will be freeing your people and other peoples around the world from the oppression of centuries."

As he spoke, Al-Sistani began to pace in front of the recruits, watching their eyes, searching for a doubter. "In the days ahead, the chosen few will take part in this glorious undertaking that will mark the beginning of a new world, a world dedicated to the one true faith and the worship of Allah. For security's sake, I cannot yet divulge the entire plan, nor can I meet you here again, though we will be in contact." He paused and wagged his head sadly. "One reason for that is tonight, sadly, there sits among us . . . a traitor."

Al-Sistani stopped in front of Rashad. He wondered about this one. He seemed to hate the "system" that he viewed as having ruined his life and had sworn fealty to jihad. But he had the friend Khalif, who'd made his distaste for Al-Sistani and his men no secret. Could he have influenced his friend to betray them? He'd half expected, when he set his trap for traitors, that his spies who'd followed Rashad and had his home telephone bugged would return and point the finger at him. But instead, the spies told him that the traitor was a small, yellow-skinned man named Robert, who was sitting next to Rashad. He'd been seen talking to a man who was obviously a plainclothes detective the night before the UPS ruse, and received an envelope.

Meanwhile, Robert sat quietly wondering what was going to happen to the basketball player, who was obviously the traitor. Serves the motherfucker right, he thought, *Mr. Big-Time Basketball.* Robert was still feeling flush from the two hundred dollars the detective had given him for snitching on that crack house in East Harlem. He'd been a snitch most of his adult life; it was how he made his living, though he was hoping that the "reward" Mr. Mustafa kept talking about would soon be forthcoming. He was happily fantasizing about how much money it might entail when Mr. Mustafa suddenly yelled and turned to him.

"Those who betray us, betray Allah!" Al-Sistani shouted. "In the name of Islamic jihad, I condemn this traitor and send his soul to hell."

Robert's mouth dropped open. He was going to protest that they had the wrong man—he was just a snitch—when the big bodyguard who'd been standing to the side suddenly pulled a handgun with a silencer out of his coat and pointed it at his head.

"Wha . . . ," Robert said just before the .22-caliber slug struck him dead center between the eyes. His head flopped back as blood spurted from the little hole like a geyser, causing a general scramble by the men behind him to get out of the way. The bodyguard placed the gun on the dying man's chest and pumped several more rounds into his heart.

"Oh, God," Rashad screamed, jumping up and away. "Oh, God." He'd panicked when Mr. Mustafa started talking about traitors. After he told everyone at the meeting to watch what happened at Union Square with a UPS truck, Rashad had boasted to Khalif that "things are about to change; you can either get with the program and be part of a new Islamic state, or you can go down with the rest of the muthafuckas."

As far as Rashad was concerned, his life had been ruined. Ever since childhood, he and Khalif had talked about how they'd use their basketball skills to get out of the ghetto. They'd go to college on scholarships and then play in the NBA. They even joked about who'd have the upper hand when their respective teams played each other, or if they were really lucky, maybe they'd get to play together for the Knicks or the Nets. They'd have money and all the things it bought; they'd buy nice homes for their moms and their siblings, too. Their kids would grow up happy and prosperous. Such would be the will of Allah.

Then it all came tumbling down. He'd had sex with the bitch, just like everybody else, if what he'd heard was right. Then when she kept calling, he'd told her he wanted no part of her. Then there was the party. The bitch got drunk and lured Khalif into her room and they'd had sex. When Khalif came out, he looked troubled. "It was a sin to lie with a whore," he said. "I'm going to go get my coat and leave. You coming?"

"Yeah, just a minute," Rashad said, and went into the bedroom. There were candles burning, and the bitch had known who he was. "I knew you'd come back, Rashad, if you thought I was going to be with your friend. Now come here."

A lay was a lay and Rashad had not minded sloppy seconds. But then Khalif returned to the room and flicked on the lights. He looked disgusted but only said, "I'm going," and turned away. Rashad had laughed and jumped up, pulling up his pants.

"Come on, baby, stay here tonight," the woman pouted.

Rashad had laughed again. "Fuck no, bitch. I ain't spending the night with a whore. There's another five guys out in the living room, but you can get one or two of them to keep you company." Then he left, thinking it was the last time he'd see her.

Then the bitch lied and went to the university and said she'd been raped by a man she didn't know. But worse than that, the district attorney's office had believed her, and then compounded it by hiding evidence that would have demonstrated it was a lie. That's the way it was when a white woman accused a black man.

Nightmare followed nightmare. First, the university kicked them out and withdrew their scholarships. Then there was the trial, where he'd had to sit quietly in his seat and listen to the bitch lie and the prosecutor lie worse. After that the jury came back, and as he listened in disbelief, he and his best friend were found guilty. But nothing, nothing could compare to the terror of arriving at Attica, trying to look tough while real criminals leered and taunted. Except for the night he was gang raped when the Bloods caught him alone in the prison laundry. He'd been too ashamed even to tell Khalif, but Mr. Mustafa had understood his hatred.

Mr. Mustafa had put it all in perspective. The district attorney was a Jew. The prosecutor, Rachel Rachman, was supposedly a Catholic, "but look at her name . . . she's just another Jew," Mustafa said. The jury had contained some blacks "but the Jews on the jury swayed them with their lies and deceits." He'd lost his dream and been defiled "because of the Jews." That's when he'd sworn to join the jihad.

Then Mr. Mustafa started talking about a traitor, and he wondered if they thought it was Khalif. He hadn't told his friend any of the details, having taken Mr. Mustafa's warning to keep secrets or be considered a traitor to heart, but he'd gone to Union Square that morning just to see what would happen. When the UPS truck was swarmed by cops, he figured Khalif must have somehow figured it out and snitched. He'd been about to jump up and explain that his friend was just misguided and not a traitor when Mr. Mustafa turned on the little man next to him.

"Thus, it is written, will be the fate of all traitors who have sworn to Allah to carry out jihad," Mr. Mustafa said.

Al-Sistani looked over the frightened faces. Good, he thought, there will be no more traitors. Still, as one of his men dragged the body out of the room for its final journey to the New Jersey landfill, he wanted to try one more test.

"Tonight, I am going to tell you our plan and your role," he said. "But first, I want to ask you to search your hearts, and if you do not have the will for jihad, leave us now in peace."

No one moved but a lot of eyes went to the man with the gun.

"Do not worry," Al-Sistani said. "I do not consider it an act of treason to leave, so long as you make no attempt to contact our enemies, which we would surely know and take our revenge for. But until I have divulged the plan, you are free to leave, the blessings of Allah upon you." It was a lie, of course; anyone who stood up was going to receive a bullet in the head, but no one stood.

"Please," Al-Sistani said, motioning those who were still standing back to their chairs. "It is time to reveal the great blow you will help us strike for Allah."

Of course, he wasn't going to reveal the real plan. These martyrs would have no role except as laborers, and then would defend the supplies up until the moment they, along with thousands of others, were sent to meet the Creator. He didn't want them thinking, however, that this was a suicidal mission. Even the brainwashed children of Palestine sometimes balked at that; no, they would be told that they would live to fight another day.

"We have discovered an old, abandoned tunnel that the

infidels have forgotten," he said. "This tunnel happens to run beneath the New York Stock Exchange, the financial heart of the oppressors. On New Year's Eve, we plan—with your help—to break into the building from below, set explosive charges, and bring the entire building crashing to the ground, and with it, the financial stability of the United States and its loathsome puppetmaster, Israel."

It was a good plan, he thought, one that did not seem to involve a lot of deaths to innocent civilians and would therefore be·more palatable to these new warriors of the jihad. They could strike a blow for freedom without a lot of killing, which might have weighed on their consciences.

"Of course," he said, "there is some risk. You will be asked to help with final preparations and then to guard my men as they prepare the bomb. You will be given weapons for this task. But you will also be compensated so that you can live decently while continuing your efforts on behalf of the jihad. You may not know this, but the infidels keep quite a bit of currency in the building; my men will retrieve this and distribute it among you."

"How much, dawg?" asked Mahmoud Rauf, a hardened gang member who'd been among the first to swear fealty.

"About one hundred thousand dollars each . . . dawg," Al-Sistani replied, smiling at the different inflection he'd given *dawg* so that it came out as an insult.

"Damn," Rauf declared. "I'm in."

Al-Sistani smiled. "Great, Mahmoud. Now, the rest of you, are you in?" All the heads nodded. "This is good, here are your instructions."

Two hours later, Zakir prepared to turn in for the night. He lived in a small room upstairs in the back of the building. Mr. Mustafa and his men had quickly left, followed by the recruits. The killing had frightened him and he just wanted everyone to leave so he could forget about the whole thing in his slumber. He was just about to turn out the lights when there was a pounding on the front door of the mosque.

Sighing, he rose from his bed and walked down the stairs. Someone had probably forgotten something, though why they couldn't wait for the morning peeved him. He took out the .45-caliber Colt he kept in a box at the door—an imam couldn't be too careful in such a high-crime area, not with all the cash he had stuffed under his mattress.

Zakir looked out of the peephole and saw shadows moving away from the door. He could just make out a bag that had been left on the doorstep, and he smiled. Sometimes the members of his congregation left food and other items for him because they lacked cash; these had probably been too embarrassed by their pitiful donation.

He opened the door and saw a large, plastic shopping bag from Macy's. Picking it up, he was surprised by its weight. He looked inside . . . then started to scream and dropped the bag, which fell over on its side. Two round objects rolled out, one of them bouncing all the way down the three steps to the sidewalk, where it came to a stop.

The bearded head of Rajid Basir, a former member of the Taliban in Afghanistan, stared back at Zakir from the stoop. He assumed the round object on the sidewalk had belonged to Akmed Moammar, a Libyan who'd fought in Chechnya, Iraq, and Afghanistan. He didn't really care to go find out and instead just continued screaming as lights came on in the buildings near the mosque.

In the alley across the street, two hooded shadows stepped farther back into the darker recesses. "That went even better than I'd hoped, Father," the shorter of the two shadows whispered. "He screams like a woman. Shall I go slit his throat before the police arrive?"

The taller of the shadows placed his hand on the other's shoulder. "No, my son," he said quietly. "We need this one to tell the others. Let his fear infect them."

A police siren wailed in the distance. "Come, let us depart," the taller shadow said. He took a step, then bent over as a gasp of pain escaped his lips.

"Father!" the shorter man whispered. "Are you all right?"

"Fine," his comrade said, straightening with an effort. "I am fine enough for these last days. But come, we've stayed too long."

As the screams of the siren began to drown out those of Zakir, the two shadows slipped from the alley and, unnoticed by the small group of people who'd gathered around the head on the sidewalk, moved away.

Reaching their destination several blocks away, the shadow men pulled the cover off a manhole and climbed down the ladder, pulling the cover shut just as a taxi came around the corner and nearly caught them in its headlights. Standing in several inches of filthy water at the bottom, the taller of the two mussed the hair of his comrade and sniffed.

"Ah," he said, "home sweet home."

14

TED VANDERS REACHED FOR THE BREAST OF THE naked woman in the bed lying next to him, only to have a finger bent back nearly to his wrist. "Jesus Christ!" he cried out. "What did you do that for?"

"Because I didn't want you to touch me," the woman replied. "When I want you to touch me, I'll tell you. Until then, keep your fucking hands to yourself."

Sarah Ryder stretched like a cat and then rose quickly from the bed and stood in front of the full-length mirror, turning this way and that. By and large, she was pleased with the response from men she got to the breast augmentation surgery she'd had a year earlier, changing her from a 34C to a 36DD. However, of late she'd been wondering if more was better and she should revisit her plastic surgeon and pump up the volume, so to speak. The bigger the bait, the richer the tiger, she thought.

"What do you think, Ted," she said, turning sideways. "Should I get bigger tits?"

"I think they're perfect just the way they are, my love,"

Vanders said with a pout. "That's why I wanted to touch them . . . at least until you almost broke my finger."

Ryder rolled her eyes. "Fuck, why would I ask you," she sneered. "You'd think an old water balloon was a turn-on. And if I'd wanted to break your finger, I would have. Now quit with the fucking 'my love' shit, it makes me want to throw up."

Having just screwed Ted Vanders didn't mean she liked Ted Vanders. In fact, she pretty much detested Ted Vanders—from his skinny, sunken white chest and muscleless arms to his crooked teeth and myopic eyes. However, it was his imperfection that made him perfect for her plan. After all, who would believe that a hottie like Sarah Lynn Ryder, who had a body and face that real men fought over, would have anything to do with a faggy little English major like Ted?

Ted, on the other hand, was hopelessly in love with her. He actually thought that she was attracted to his stupid poetry and romanticism. My love, blech. Oh yes, she'd giggled like a virginal schoolgirl when she picked him out at the student union on the NYU campus, but she'd nearly regretted it the first time she let him have sex with her. He was so excited that it hardly lasted thirty seconds and that was if you included his amateurish attempts at foreplay. It was all she could do to keep from gagging when she told him it was all right and that "a few minutes of perfection is better than hours with another man."

After that he was hooked, and she treated him pretty much like dirt. He would do anything to have sex with her, which she kept to a minimum both because it sickened her and because she wanted him desperate. As she figured, he became so enraptured that he'd even agreed to go along with her plan to exact revenge on her professor of Russian poetry, Alexis Michalik. Of course, she'd framed it in a way—the man had used her and cast her aside—to appeal to both his jealousy and romantic nature . . . the bull (albeit a skinny, nearsighted bull) who sees another bull in the paddock with the heifer in heat.

Twenty-five-year-old Sarah Ryder had known for more than half her life that men found her attractive—especially when, as her spinster aunt back home in Iowa said, she'd "blossomed early." The first such man was a friend of her parents who'd come over with his wife every Friday night for a friendly game of canasta and insisted on tucking "little Sarah" into bed. He'd gone from fondling her "naughty places" to more painful exercises, all the time warning her not to tell her parents or she'd be punished. Two years later, after she figured out that he was the one who should be worried, she told him that she didn't mind the sex, but if he didn't do what she wanted him to do—including giving her a rather large allowance—she'd not only tell her parents, she'd tell the cops.

Sex was a means to an end. She soon learned that she didn't even have to have sex to use it as a weapon. When she was fifteen, her parents divorced, and her mother remarried a year later. Her stepfather was a good man who would never have touched her, but when he tried to lay down the law on her curfew, she called the police and said he'd raped her. She was smart enough to know that the police wouldn't just take her word for it, so she'd had sex with one of the neighborhood boys before calling the police.

Based on her report and the initial examination at the hospital, her stepfather was arrested, a fact that was reported in the hometown newspaper. However, she'd been naïve and hadn't thought to make the boy wear a condom, so when the DNA tests came back negative for her stepfather six weeks later, she'd been confronted and she confessed. The Department of Social Services had sent her to a counselor, who'd lectured her about the harmful aspects of lying, pointing out that her stepfather's reputation in the town had been badly damaged.

Ryder had been so contrite, promising with many tears that she'd learned her lesson, that the counselor considered her a triumph of modern talk-therapy and recommended that she be allowed to go back to her family. However, her stepfather, who'd received dozens of pieces of hate mail and had even been accosted on the street, moved out and shortly thereafter left town.

"Good riddance," she told her mom when the divorce papers arrived a month later. "Even if he didn't, he wanted to and would have sooner or later." Her mother had just looked at her funny, then fled into her bedroom, where she sobbed all day. Sarah had rolled her eyes then, too. Ryder had moved to New York hoping to become a Broadway star. When leading roles, or any roles for that matter, weren't immediately forthcoming, she enrolled at NYU as a theater major, while hostessing at a Steak Sizzler on Times Square.

Life got better when she started dating a member of the New York Rangers hockey club. Dmitri Federov was stunningly good-looking, rich, and had a great accent. He was also generous—putting her up in a small flat in the Village and even buying her a five-carat diamond ring for Christmas. He didn't exactly call it an engagement ring or ask her to marry him, but she took it as a fait accompli. She thought they made the perfect couple and even took Russian lessons throughout that year so that she'd be able to converse with his family someday.

After a year of seeing him when he felt like it, she suggested that they get married. But he just laughed and said, "But what would I tell my wife in Moscow?"

Ryder reacted first by threatening to tell his wife and/or the police. However, he'd pointed to a small camera hidden in a corner of the ceiling of his bedroom where they were talking—a camera he admitted he'd used to film their lovemaking. "It's still on." He smiled. "Now, shall I take that to the police and tell them you are trying to blackmail me?"

"Ha ha, just teasing," she'd said. "I don't want to get married."

"Get out," he replied. "I don't want to ever see you again. And by the way, your breasts are too small."

With her face burning, Ryder stormed off to the bathroom—"to get my things"—where she promptly swallowed a bottle of Ambien sleeping pills. She figured she'd either almost die and make him see how much she loved him and then he'd take her back, or cause him enough embarrassment in the press to flee the country. Maybe he'll even lose his work visa, she thought as she drifted off to sleep.

However, Federov soon discovered her and called an ambulance. His agent then paid off the right people to keep it out of the newspapers and have Ryder committed to Bellevue for observation "as a danger to herself and others." By the time she got out, Dmitri's lawyers had obtained a restraining order preventing her from calling, writing, or coming within one hundred yards of their client. She also discovered that he must have removed the diamond ring from her finger while waiting for the ambulance and cleaned out and closed the bank account he'd set up for her "expenses."

Ryder had returned to her classes at NYU much poorer but also wiser. She was determined that the next time some guy fucked with her, he'd pay one way or the other. She was still trying to figure out her best option—turn her charms on one of the rich old men who hung out in TriBeCa looking for trophy wives ("But with my luck, they'd live to be a hundred and be as horny as a goat," she complained to one of her few friends), or try for a rich young man "except they're all married, gay, or allergic to commitment."

In the meantime, there were bills to pay and things she wanted. A brief affair with a married plastic surgeon got her the new boobs; another with the married owner of a BMW car dealership in New Jersey the new 320i; and yet another with a married real estate developer entitled her to a small but tasteful flat in the East Village in exchange for the occasional dalliance when his wife was out of town. She knew the score with those men and wanted nothing more from them than she got; they were simply her means to an end.

She was in her last semester at NYU and had decided to go on and get her master's—mostly because she didn't know what else to do, and a horny married banker was willing to pay tuition—when she took a class in Russian poetry from newly arrived Alexis Michalik. He was maybe just a shade or two less handsome but his maturity made him more distinguished than Dmitri, with that same killer accent, and he was certainly more intelligent.

Ryder began hanging around after class and volunteering to help him with such things as making copies of poetry for the rest of the class and fetching him coffee, then lunch. Then she asked if she could work as a sort of unofficial intern, assisting him with his efforts to translate his work into English. She'd continued her Russian language studies—she figured that somewhere, somehow they would come in handy.

After graduation, with Michalik's help, she entered the master's program in Russian literature with an emphasis on poetry. She'd also convinced herself that she was in love with him and that they were meant to be together. She figured he probably made six figures, maybe more, because he was a popular speaker at poetry events around the country, and she could imagine herself the good wife, playing hostess for all the intellectuals who would visit their home, and helping promote his career.

There were only two problems: he was married, and he wasn't in love with her. While it was obvious that Alexis enjoyed her company and even a little harmless flirting, he made no attempt to take it any further. She'd all but spread-eagled herself on his desk, but he treated her like a schoolgirl with a crush, telling her, "You need to find a young man and not waste all that energy and beauty on what cannot be."

At home, Ryder fumed over the rejection. But her history had taught her to have a Plan B ready. So if she couldn't have him as her husband willingly, she would blackmail him into becoming her husband unwillingly, though he would of course learn to love her. Plan C was simply to blackmail him into letting her get away without having to write her "stupid" master's thesis and then getting her into the doctoral program. She was pretty sure that once she had her doctorate and, with his help, got onto the faculty at NYU, he'd realize that she really was the best life partner for him.

When her plans had been laid, she'd called him and asked to see him in his office that evening. "I'd like to talk to you about my thesis when there're not so many interruptions like there are during the day," she said. She then pretended there was a problem with her telephone and couldn't hear his response. "Would you call me back, please?"

A few seconds later, her telephone rang. "Thanks," she said. "I don't know what the problem was. Anyway, could you spare your poor, dedicated, infatuated student a few minutes this evening?" She detected a sigh—he was way behind on the translation—but he was also too dedicated a teacher to turn her down. "Sure, come on over, Sarah."

She loved the way he said *Sarah*. It sounded so exotic. She then called Ted Vanders. "Okay, Ted. Tonight's the night. I'll be over about twelve." She couldn't help but compare Michalik's unenthusiastic response to Ted's, who'd been without her favors for nearly three weeks and sounded like he'd wet his pants when she called.

Ryder dressed quickly. She'd already spent some time thinking about what to wear and had chosen a baby-pink thong but decided against a bra. These puppies don't give an inch when I walk, she thought, as she pulled an almost see-through silk shirt over her surgically enhanced chest. It only came down to just above her belly, which she thought was one of her best (natural) assets, especially when emphasized by a pair of skintight, low-rider jeans that only just covered . . . my naughty parts, she thought, and giggled.

Flouncing her hair into what she called her "just fucked look," she then checked her mascara and applied a shade of lipstick to match her thong. She stepped back with a skeptical look. Hmmm, maybe it's time for a little collagen in the lips. She pouted, then used the tip of her tongue to trace her upper lip seductively. Nah, you've still got it, baby.

Satisfied with the look, she opened the medicine cabinet, took out a pill bottle, and glanced at the label to make sure it was the correct one. Hello, roofies. She opened the bottle and took out three, then closed it and put it in her purse. As she was closing the purse, she saw the steel glint of the surgical scissors in the bottom. She thought about removing them but let them remain where they were. A girl can't be too careful these days, she thought with a smile.

It's a use-me, use-you world, she thought as she closed her purse to go to Michalik's office that night. She put the three pills on a plate and smashed them with a spoon until they were powder; she wondered if three was too many, then figured she'd lost some in the crushing and poured it into a small piece of folded paper. She then walked out to the kitchen, took a small cooler from the refrigerator, and left her apartment.

When she arrived at Michalik's office, she waltzed in, plopped the cooler on his desk, and took out two bottles of beer and two glasses.

"Not me," he said, waving them off. "Beer will put me to sleep."

"Come on, professor, all work and no play will make Alexis Michalik a dull boy," she teased. "Besides, I'd just like to have a beer with my favorite professor, relax, and talk him into approving my master's thesis."

"You have to turn in a thesis to have it approved," he said, shaking his finger at her. "And no work and even a little play for Alexis Michalik, and he will lose his book contract." He laughed as he spoke, and she was happy to see that his eyes kept straying to the twin points that protruded from her shirt. She poked her bare tummy toward him, knowing the effect that usually had on men whose eyes measured the distance between the top of her jeans and her belly button, then did the math.

Ryder cajoled and flirted until he relented. She

opened one of the beers and was opening the second when her hand slipped and knocked the beer over just enough to splash some on his papers before righting it. He jumped up and ran to the bathroom to get a paper towel to wipe it up.

When his back was turned, Ryder quickly dumped the contents of the folded piece of paper in one of the glasses and then poured a beer in on top. He returned and mopped up the spill, then accepted the glass she handed to him.

"Mazdorovya," she said raising her glass.

"Mazdorovya," he replied, taking a sip. "You are a bad influence, Sarah Ryder."

They sat back down and for the next ten minutes talked about her master's thesis, or lack thereof. She couldn't have cared less about the conversation; she didn't plan on writing a thesis. She was just watching and waiting for the drugs to kick in.

"Whoa," he said suddenly, placing his hand on his desk as if to steady himself. "That's some beer to get a Russian drunk on just one."

"You're just tired, darling," she said, rising from her seat and walking around the desk until she was standing in front of him with her hips inches from his face.

Michalik fastened his eyes on her crotch, then shook his head and smiled weakly. "Yes. I am tired. I . . ." He suddenly stopped talking as she knelt in front of him and started fumbling at his belt. He tried pushing her away. "Sarah, please, you must not." But she just laughed and kept at it until she had his pants unzipped and his manhood in her hands.

"Sarah, you are very beautiful and any man would want you, but I must insist." His protestations stopped when she took him in her mouth. Under her expertise, it didn't take long. "Oh, God," he groaned in both pleasure and remorse.

Ryder spit in her hand, then wiped it on her shirt.

"I am so . . . so sorry," he said. "I am ashamed."

"Don't be silly, Alexis," she said. "I love you. You needed the relief, and it was my pleasure to . . . to please you. I'd like to do more if you'd let me."

"No, you don't understand," he said. "I am sorry for my wife. . . ."

Ryder froze. She'd just given him the best blow job of his life, then offered her perfect body, and he was feeling guilty about his wife? *Bastard. You need to stick with the plan. Plan A isn't going to work; obviously the clown's in love with his wife. So it's on to Plan B, and if necessary, Plan C.* She figured that where she'd gone wrong in the past was a lack of options.

Alexis's head flopped forward and he began snoring. She left him there with his pants to his knees and picked up his nearly empty beer glass. She made sure to leave her fingerprints clearly on the glass and gently placed her lips at several places around the rim, leaving little pink smudges. Satisfied, she placed the glass on the bookcase, slightly behind a trophy he'd been awarded at some international poetry event, where it wouldn't be noticed . . . at least not right away.

With regret for the loss of perfection, Ryder looked in the bathroom mirror and mussed up her hair, then wiped the back of a hand across her lips, leaving a pink smear on her right cheek. She ripped the top button from her shirt and adjusted it as if she'd been in a struggle. She sighed, regarding the mess she'd created, but she wanted to look the part if she ran into the janitor, another student, or a professor. Pausing at the door to the office, she worked up a few tears and sniffles . . . just in case.

Ryder was a little disappointed that she didn't see anybody on her way out of the building. But, she reminded herself, it doesn't matter, because I have an alternate plan. She stepped out into the night and, seeing no one, practically skipped to the bottom of the stairs and even allowed herself a pirouette and a giggle at the bottom, before composing herself in case she ran into anybody.

Ryder drove immediately to Vanders's apartment, where she rushed past him when he opened the door and ordered him to "undress and get in bed, you little idiot. I'm about to make you a very happy little worm." He'd almost squeaked with excitement and ran into his bedroom and promptly fell flat on his face while trying to remove his pants and socks at the same time.

In the meantime, Ryder walked to the bathroom where she took the pill bottle out of her purse, removed another roofie, and swallowed it. Gonna need that puppy in the ol' bloodstream tomorrow, she thought. And it might be the only way I can stomach having sex with Ted.

Waiting for the drug to kick in, she placed the bottle back in Vanders's medicine cabinet. Can't have the cops finding that in my place. She didn't know if they'd search, but her plan was foolproof as long as she stayed true to the details.

Reluctantly, Ryder walked into Vanders's bedroom, only to be grossed out at the sight of him lying on the silk sheets he bought "for us." He was stretched out in what he must have thought was a seductive pose. He patted the place next to him, but she ignored him.

Instead, she took a piece of clothesline out of a bag she'd left in the closet, placed a loop around her wrist, and then violently sawed it back and forth to give herself a rope burn. "Christ, that hurts," she said, mostly to herself.

"Want me to kiss it and make it better, my love?" Vanders said, making kissing expressions.

"Shut the fuck up, you idiot," she snarled and placed a loop of rope over her other wrist and sawed it back and forth, although not quite as enthusiastically. She also avoided swearing so she wouldn't have to hear Vanders's sympathy.

When she was done, she undressed, placing each piece of clothing she'd been wearing in a plastic bag, taking extra care with the moist spot on her blouse. Then she got down on her elbows and knees.

"I want you to fuck me as hard as you can," she told Vanders, who could hardly believe what he had just heard and hopped off the bed. This was the stuff other guys wrote letters to *Penthouse* magazine about. But when he attempted foreplay, she angrily shoved his hand away. "You idiot, I told you I need this to look like I was raped," she said. "Are you wearing a condom?"

"Yes."

"Then tear me a new one . . . both holes, you faggot, and if you stop before I tell you, I'll rip your dick off and shove it up your ass."

Vanders did as he was told, but fortunately the roofie kicked in full speed about then, and she hardly felt him hammering away. Just a faraway burning that reminded her of her childhood, accompanied by the sound of Vanders grunting and trying to talk dirty. The more things change, she thought idly, the more things stay the same.

Seven hours later, the morning arrived with her brain throbbing against the interior of her skull. It was sort of how her feet felt after a night of wearing that five-hundred-dollar pair of Manolo slingbacks she bought a half-size too small out of conceit.

She was in Vanders's bed but didn't know how she got

there and was suspicious of a dream she'd had of him "doing it" again that morning while she was still out of it. He was still sleeping next to her but woke with a start when she sat up. He smiled and attempted to stroke her arm. She hissed and clawed at his face, drawing blood, which made him cry out. "What did you do that for?" he complained.

"Unauthorized fucking," she replied. "Did you use a condom every time you had sex with me?"

"I think so," he said, playing dumb. She raised her hand to claw his eyes out. "Yes! Yes!" he shrieked. "Jeez, no sense of humor."

Ryder got out of bed and looked at her wrists, happy to see the ugly red marks looked worse than they had the night before. No pain, no gain. She shrugged.

Vanders rubbed at his wounded cheek and sniffled on the bed, hoping she'd come back and make up for hurting him. But she didn't even look his way as she strode over to the closet and dressed in the outfit she'd picked out for that day and left there. She'd chosen a knee-length beige skirt and a high-necked white blouse, both of which showed off her figure but in a modest way.

Part of her still hoped that Michalik would come to his senses—Plan B—and this whole thing could be handled much more easily and pleasantly. They'd begin their affair, he'd leave his wife, she'd get her doctorate, they'd get married, maybe even have babies. So long as we have enough money to have a nanny, she thought. And there'll be no nursing on these tits. It was all she could do to look troubled as she walked through the building, past students and professors, and the protesting secretary outside of Michalik's office.

The fantasy lasted until she walked in and shut the door behind her. She'd hoped that he'd look up from his papers, his eyes teary with love. Instead, he looked up from where he'd been holding his head in his hands, bleary- not teary-eyed . . . and angry. "What did you put in my beer?" he demanded.

"What do you mean?" Ryder replied. She saw that he was wearing the same clothes and hadn't shaved. Good, she thought, he'll have a hard time explaining that to the little woman. Her eyes had already drifted over to the bookcase and she saw that the lipstick-smudged beer glass was still in place. "You know very well that I came to you last night for help on my thesis and you raped me." She raised her voice a little at the end and hoped the secretary at least caught the word *rape*.

"I did no such thing," he said. "You, you . . . put something in my drink and then did *that* . . . like a cheap whore."

"Oh, please, Alexis, it was you who put what's commonly called a roofie in my drink and then had your way with me," she said. "I am still sore, you animal you. At least, that's what I'll be telling the administration and, I dare say, the cops before the day is over, unless you do what I say."

"You are a liar," he said and started to rise from his seat but the pain in his head forced him back down. "I did none of these things."

"Maybe you don't remember," she said and shrugged. "But believe me, dear Alexis, I can prove that you did." She pulled up the sleeve of her shirt and showed him the rope burn. "See how you tied me up, Alexis, so I could not resist you."

He stared at her wrist dumbfounded. "Proves nothing," he scowled, but a worried look occupied his face.

"Ah, yes, wondering how your wife is going to react to all of this?" she said. "I guess she's used to you not coming home at night. Or is she? And how is she regarding young women claiming you raped them on nights when you didn't make it home? Hmmm?"

With a supreme effort, Alexis rose out of his chair. "You lie! I will tell the truth and you will be exposed!"

"Fine," Ryder said. "We'll both tell our sides of the story, but believe me, I'll win. However, there is a way out of this for both of us."

"Out of this? How? Is it money you want?"

What she wanted at the moment was to laugh. Such a look of hope had briefly crossed his face. He thinks he might buy his way out of this. It was clear Plan B wasn't an option; the idiot really did love his wife. So on to Plan C. "No, not money. But you'll, of course, give me exceedingly high marks on my thesis paper that I gave you last night," she said.

"Paper? You didn't give me a paper."

"Alexis, listen, don't be dense if you can possibly help it," she said. "You will give me high marks for my thesis. Then you will sponsor me before the doctoral committee which, with you putting in a good word, will make my appointment a done deal."

Michalik looked at her so long and hard without saying anything that she wondered if the drugs were still affecting him. But then he shook his head. "I will not," he said, "give in to your blackmail. I could never live with myself."

The anger went out of Michalik's eyes, and he hung his head. "Please, I ask you not to do this thing. My wife does not deserve this pain, but I cannot do as you say, my honor will not allow it."

"Fuck the honor, Alexis," Ryder sneered. "You're going to lose poor little Helena, and your baby, if I remember correctly, and lose your job. Hell, after they let you out of prison in a dozen years or so, they'll probably kick your pathetic poetic ass back to Moscow."

She sighed as if he was forcing her to make a difficult decision. But she'd pretty much expected the reaction—all part of the plan—from having listened to his lectures for the past two years and knowing what a romantic fool he was. He was bound to make his choice based on his self-image rather than practical consideration.

"Well, if that's how you feel," she said. "You know, it's really too bad, Alexis. You could have had it all. Me. Your life. But now it's all going to go away."

Sarah smiled. It was good to have a plan. Initially, there wouldn't be much in it for her except the publicity, and it never hurt an aspiring actress to have her photograph and résumé in the newspapers and on television. But as soon as the criminal trial was over, she planned a civil suit to wipe him out.

Most of all, she'd have her revenge. Revenge on every man who had ever taken liberties with her since childhood. They'd all told her they loved her, fucked her, then left her. She was going to get even for every man who had required sex for her to get the things she wanted—*no, deserved*—in life. And for every man who had ever stood between her and those things Alexis Michalik would pay the price.

"I would never want to be with a woman like you," he said quietly, looking up. "A whore. An evil person. If I gave an evil person what they wanted, I would be evil myself . . . so no matter what the cost, you can go to hell."

Ryder listened to the statement with a smile on her face. "Oh, Alex, that really hurts," she said, then sniffed. "But thanks, I'll use it to get into character." She promptly burst into tears and ran over to the door, which she flung open, nearly scaring the secretary out of her seat.

"Miss, are you all right?" the secretary asked.

Ryder wiped a tear from her eye and swiped at her nose. "Ask him," she wailed and pointed back into the inner office. "Ask your boss, Mr. Michalik." She sobbed once more and then ran from the office.

A few minutes later, Ryder appeared in the office of the university vice president of student affairs where she promptly burst into tears. "I . . . I . . . was raped," she gasped. "Alexis Michalik. I asked for his help on my master's thesis . . . but he raped me." The male vice president of student affairs listened to her story and immediately sent a campus security officer to escort Michalik from his office.

"Tell him to go home and remain there until he is contacted by this administration or the New York Police Department," the vice president said. He was rewarded for his swift, decisive action with a smile from Sarah's beautiful, trembling lips.

A female police detective arrived and took her initial statement. Sarah had gone to Michalik's office to get help with her thesis. He'd been coming on to her a lot lately, but she thought it was just harmless flirting. Saying she needed to relax, he'd given her a beer. "Suddenly I couldn't think straight," she said. "It was as if I was in one of those dreams where you want to wake up, but you can't." The next thing she knew, her jeans and panties had been removed and her wrists were tied to the office couch.

Ryder paused, as if gathering herself for the stretch run. She burst into tears. "And then he raped me," she cried. "I think he was wearing a condom. But when he was finished, he still wiped himself on my blouse."

The detective reached for her hand. "That's okay," she consoled. "It wasn't your fault. These things aren't about sex; it's about power and control. These guys are predators."

Ryder grew impatient waiting for the detective to ask the right questions. "You know," she volunteered, "there was this guy . . . I was coming out of the building after . . . after . . . I was attacked. I was still groggy so I don't remember everything, but I think I told him that I'd been raped. He seemed concerned, but I don't remember what happened from there."

The detective scribbled furiously in her notebook. "A witness, that's great," she said. "Did you know this guy? Ever seen him before or know how we can contact him?"

Ryder shook her head. "No, I'm certain about that," she said. "I didn't know him from Adam."

"That's okay, he may still come forward," the detective said. In the meantime, they needed to go to the hospital for a rape examination.

"Oh, that reminds me," Ryder said. "I have all of my clothes from last night in this bag." She handed the bag to the detective. "I read a story in *Cosmo* once that rape victims shouldn't bathe or wash the clothes in case there is some DNA evidence."

"Well done, young lady," the detective said, patting her on the back. "That's using your head. A tough thing to do under these circumstances."

At the hospital, everything went as planned, except that she had to remind the crime lab photographer to take pictures of the marks on her wrists. Sloppy police work, she thought, no wonder criminals own the streets. She also felt she shouldn't have had to mention for a second time that shortly after she drank the beer, she felt drugged.

"Well then, we'll certainly need to take a blood sample," the examining physician said. "He may have slipped something in your drink."

No shit, Sherlock, she thought but said, "Do you really think so? I wondered about that but I just couldn't imagine someone famous like him doing something like that to one of his students."

A few minutes later, the doctor who examined Ryder came out and talked privately to the detective, who then walked over and relayed the information. "He said the preliminary examination shows trauma to your vaginal area as well as your anus consistent with sexual assault. Apparently you were torn up pretty good. They're going to send the vaginal and anal swabs to a lab for DNA testing—"

"I told you he wore a condom," Ryder reminded her.

"Yes, I know, but they check anyway so that the defense attorneys don't come up with some surprise attack. Don't sweat it." The detective hesitated as if embarrassed to ask the next question. "You said that you haven't had sex with anyone else within the past twenty-four hours?"

"What do you mean by that?" Ryder snapped.

"Nothing, we'd just have to explain evidence of other sexual activity, that's all," the detective said. "Sometimes these things come up and we want to be prepared."

Ryder thought about Vanders and the condoms. It would be just like him to forget, she thought. But she'd checked his bathroom trash can before leaving and there were two used rubbers lying on top of the tissue.

"No, I wasn't having sex with anyone else," she told the detective, willing a few more tears for sympathy's sake. "I know this sounds weird in this day and age, but I'm not into casual sex; I'm pretty celibate unless I'm in a strong, committed relationship. And, well, you know, I just haven't found the right guy."

"That's okay, sweetie," the detective said, handing her a tissue and taking one herself. "I know what you mean. Hell, I'm forty-five and I still haven't found Mr. Right, though I've met more than my share of Mr. Wrongs. I'm just sorry this happened to a nice girl like you. But I think we have enough to get a warrant for Michalik's arrest. Would you like me to drop you off at your apartment on my way back to the precinct house?"

Ryder agreed. "You will call and tell me when he's been arrested," she said when the detective pulled up in front of her building. "I'm afraid . . . afraid of him. He's awfully clever."

"Well, he wasn't smart enough to keep his pants zipped, now was he?" the detective replied. "Just try to get some rest. I'll call when we get him."

A few hours later, Ryder thanked the detective profusely when she called to announce the arrest of Alexis Michalik. "He'll probably make bail, but we'll let him know that under no circumstance is he to make contact with you or I'll be on him like white on rice," the detective said. "And we're still looking for your mystery witness. He'll pretty much drive a nail in this one."

Later, Ryder met with an assistant district attorney and a victim's advocate. The ADA interviewed her and seemed satisfied with her responses. "Before I leave, I want to explain a little about how this works," the young female attorney said. "Just because the police arrested Mr. Michalik doesn't mean the district attorney's office will charge him right away. We want to do this right, so that when we do go after him—and I think that I can say between me, you, and the wall, that we will be going after this creep—we nail his ass to the wall. The process can take a little while, but just stay patient and justice will prevail here."

That evening, Ryder reluctantly but graciously accepted telephone calls from reporters with the *New York Post* and the *New York Times*. It seemed that some anonymous caller had tipped them off to Michalik's arrest. "I've been told not to say anything at this time," she said. "But thank you for your concern."

"I understand you can't talk about the case, Miss Ryder," both reporters had said, using virtually the same language, "but can you tell my readers a little about yourself."

"Well . . . I suppose that's all right," she said. "I'm from Iowa and like every little girl from Iowa, I came to New York hoping to make it on Broadway. . . ."

The next day, the news hit the stands. RUSSIAN CASANOVA RAPES ACTRESS, screamed the headline on the front of the *Post*. The *Times* was somewhat more reserved, putting the story below the fold under the headline Internationally Acclaimed Poet Accused of Raping Student Actress.

She was reasonably happy with both stories, although she thought more could have been done with the small list of acting credits she'd provided—several television spots, a Card Girl appearance at a boxing match in the Garden, and as the dead nude woman in the off-off-Broadway production of *Son of Sam, I Am*, which had required her to remain absolutely still for ten minutes while the antihero gave his longest monologue as a knock-off of a Dr. Seuss poem. But the newspaper coverage was a start.

Stamping her feet with glee, she read and reread the part about the university suspending Michalik "pending further investigation" and the outcome of the criminal case. "We want to make it clear that NYU will not in any way tolerate any behavior from its faculty and staff that compromises the physical safety and emotional well-being of our students," President Helen Coffman was quoted. "We point out that Mr. Michalik is innocent until proven guilty and will receive due process under the American justice system; however, we feel that there is sufficient grounds to warrant taking this measure to protect our students."

The *Post* had even dredged up a file photograph of Michalik reading at one of his poetry presentations shortly after his arrival in the United States. Ryder was pleased to see they'd chosen one in which he looked just like a wild-eyed Russian of the sort who'd rape innocent young American girls. Ryder had declined to allow herself to be photographed. "Not at this time. Please understand, I don't want to jeopardize the work of the police department." But she'd handed out black-and-white prints of a glamour shot she'd had made a year earlier for her portfolio.

All day she'd fielded calls. Some from her former lovers, several of whom seemed to find the whole thing about her being raped sort of sexually exciting; of course, they didn't say that flat out, but they wanted to see her "when you feel up to it." She was disappointed that Dmitri wasn't among the callers, but the plastic surgeon had been so titillated by the whole thing—"The newspaper story said he tied you up?"—that she was sure she could get a lip job out of him. The few friends she had—other would-be actresses and models, none of them the sort you'd trust with your life—also called, trying to be associated with the girl in the papers.

There was even a call from the producer of *Son of*

Sam, I Am, who wanted to know her availability in February for a new play he was considering called *The Sky Is Falling,* "based on a fictional account of people trapped in the World Trade Center on 9/11; they all die." She was polite and said she'd definitely be interested in reading for a part, just in case, but she was hoping for bigger offers than that.

The best call was from Harvey Schmellmann, a lawyer. "You need representation, my girl," he'd said. "And Schmellmann, Fiorino and Campbell is the best in the business. We'd protect your interests in the criminal proceedings—I'm sure you're aware of what happened to the victim in the Kobe Bryant case—as well as any civil litigation we might consider. Not to be insensitive to the trauma inflicted upon you by that monster, but I dare say that a woman of your obvious beauty and strength of character will soon be receiving a lot of calls—if you haven't already. Have you?—from a lot of shysters in the entertainment business trying to lock up your options . . . I'm talking books, movies, television, and speaking engagements, which can be very lucrative. You don't want to wander into that quagmire without effective counsel, and my partner Gino Fiorino is the very best there is at protecting those rights."

Schmellmann even sent a limousine to pick her up and deliver her to his office "for a first consultation, absolutely free and no strings attached." By the time she left, she'd signed the necessary papers to be his client—"one-third of any profits from lawsuits, plus expenses; 15 percent of any artistic or literary recompense . . . but don't worry, sister, there'll be plenty to go around by the time we get through with these schmucks. You know, I think we have a good case against that freakin' university for not monitoring this perverted Russkie."

Then the limo whisked her back home in time to meet the first of three television crews, whose producers had called her after reading the morning newspapers. "Should have called us first," they'd said. But they'd all sent over crews and eager reporters who breathlessly told their stories.

Ryder was proud of the performances she'd given: understated yet powerful, the serious student of Russian literature who'd been preyed upon by a man she'd trusted. "But I really can't go into the details," she said. The only reason she'd agreed to the interviews was "to empower other young women who find themselves in my position." If this had been the stage, I'd win a Tony, she thought. Oh, well, next year.

The story only picked up speed the day after it broke, when Ted Vanders went to the police and said he'd entered the building that night and nearly bumped into a disheveled young woman. "She was crying," he'd said in his statement. "Said she'd been attacked by some professor. But she didn't want to call the police and then took off."

The detective read Sarah the transcript of the interview with Vanders. "He came forward after he saw you on television. So I guess the media did its job. Anyway, he said he'd never met you before that night, didn't even know your name. He'll make a great witness. Pretty much a slam dunk case. You just relax and keep your head up, kid."

The detective hung up feeling good about her job. She hadn't bothered to tell Ryder that this character Vanders—a funny little guy, artsy-fartsy type—had a couple of scratches on his cheek she found interesting. She'd worked in the sex assault division for ten years and had seen a lot of fingernail marks on the faces of perps.

"What happened to your face?" the detective had asked him.

Vanders's hand had gone up to his cheek and his face turned red. "My cat scratched me."

Mighty big cat, the detective thought.

Later that evening, Ryder went over to Vanders's apartment and gave him a mercy screw. "You were a good boy today, Ted," she said. "Keep it up, and I'll keep you up . . . get it?" Vanders reacted like a puppy who'd been praised by its owner; in fact, she wondered if he was going to pee on himself.

But that was weeks ago, and Michalik still hadn't been charged. At first she'd been happy when the top dog in the district attorney's rape bureau, Rachel Rachman, personally took over the case. The woman had paced back and forth behind her desk when they first met, giving a little speech about how men in positions of authority had used sexual violence against women from the beginning of time. She'd also noted that the police had found plenty of corroborating evidence, "including a beer glass on a bookshelf that he apparently didn't see, with your fingerprints and lipstick on it and traces of rohypnol."

"What's that?" Ryder asked innocently.

"Sometimes called roofies, or the date rape drug . . . essentially takes away your ability to resist," Rachman said, flashing in anger. "It's the latest thing. Drop it in a drink at the bar, offer to give her a ride home, and then rape her when she's defenseless. Happens to a lot more women than we know about."

Rachman had called Monday saying she was going into some meeting with the district attorney, Karp, and expected to file charges later that day. She was excited because the lab reports were back. "There are traces of rohypnol in your blood," she said. "Even better, your blouse tested positive for semen, and it's a match for

Michalik. In other words, he's toast. . . . Um, I was thinking about calling a press conference today to announce the charges—the media has been hounding me about this one. Okay with you?"

"Whatever you think is best, Rachel," she'd replied.

But instead of calling later with the happy news that Alexis was about to be charged, Rachman said there was going to be a slight delay. Karp and some troll of an assistant DA named Kipman apparently had some sort of problem with the case. "They want me to cross a few more *t*'s and dot some *i*'s. It's no big deal. We'll file next week."

"I don't understand," Ryder complained, trying not to sound hysterical. This wasn't the way the plan was supposed to go. "You promised."

"Don't worry," Rachman assured her. "We have him by the balls. Karp and Kipman are like all men; they just don't want to believe that sexual assault is at epidemic levels in this country, much of it acquaintance rape, such as in your case. So I have to go twice as far just to get them to budge. But I'll get them there."

"What if Alexis . . . I mean Michalik, comes after me?" Ryder said. "You know he said he was going to hurt me."

"He contacted you?" Rachman asked.

"Yes . . . no . . . I mean, this was after he did it. He said if I went to the police, he was going to find me and hurt me," Ryder said.

"Was that in the police report?" Rachman said. "I don't remember the threat, although I suppose the nature of the crime implies that there is a threat of retaliation later."

Ryder cursed herself. She didn't want to make Rachman suspicious. "I thought I told the first officers. Maybe I forgot to tell the detective. I still don't remember everything clearly or who I told what. . . . I think there's some lingering effect of the drugs."

"Sure, sure, completely understandable," Rachman said. "We just are going to have to be patient. Maybe conduct, or reconduct, a few interviews to make sure there are no holes for a defense attorney to exploit."

Ryder had said she understood and hung up. On Friday night, when there was still no word from Rachman, she'd decided to go see Vanders and make sure he got his story straight. After he'd repeated it verbatim a half-dozen times without a glitch, she'd gone to bed with him after taking another roofie, which had made the experience bearable.

In the morning, however, she woke up in a foul mood. She felt fat, bloated, and got out of bed to look at herself in the mirror. Not seeing the imperfections she had imagined, she smiled . . . until Vanders came up from behind and wrapped his arms around her while he pressed his groin against her backside.

"Ted, what did I just tell you about taking liberties," she said, looking at him in the mirror. She expected him to back off.

However, Ted's lust had emboldened him. He figured she owed him big and that it was time he had a little more say in their relationship. After all, he'd done everything she'd said, to the letter—well, except the part about screwing her again in the morning while she was still passed out. He'd had to reuse one of the rubbers, but it had been worth it. And it didn't matter; he could expose her plans.

"Maybe you should be a little more cooperative if you want me to keep being a good boy. Sometimes you aren't very nice to me," he said, pouting.

Ryder, who'd tensed when he touched her, relaxed and

let his hands continue to roam over her body. She reached behind and started to fondle him. He groaned . . . and then screamed when she pulled his balls as hard as she could. She'd whirled around with her scissors in her hand and placed them as if she intended to turn him into a eunuch.

Vanders cried again when he felt the pinch of the blades as they cut into his skin. "I didn't mean it. I didn't mean it. You're nice. Please, don't," he begged. He felt like passing out but was afraid of what she'd do if he did.

"You little piece of shit," she snarled. "You ever threaten me again and I'll cut your fucking balls off and cram them down your throat." She squeezed the scissors a bit more. "We clear?"

"Yes, yes, yes, yes," he yipped, nodding his head rapidly. "Please, let go."

"Well, okay then, Teddy," she said, smiling sweetly as she eased up on the scissors. "Just remember, not only would I find a way to get to you and your little nuts if you went to the police, but do you think they're not going to care that you lied to them just so you could get laid? They'll put you in prison where you'll get laid every night by some big, hairy hillbilly."

Ryder withdrew the scissors, which she waved in front of one of his weepy eyeballs. She had a sudden urge to plunge it in but figured that might be tough to explain.

"There, there, Teddy," she said, lifting his trembling chin with the point of the scissors. "Just be a good boy . . . no more threats . . . and I might even throw you a bone from time to time."

Five minutes later, she walked out of the apartment. Stopping to fix her makeup, she noticed a shadow move away from behind the door across the hall. Nosy neighbors, she thought. I'm going to have to be more careful and disguise my face when I visit Ted the Idiot.

Just thinking about him and his threat as she walked out to her car pissed her off. Just another guy trying to fuck her over. Well, someday Ted Vanders and his balls might have a fatal meeting with a certain pair of scissors. She laughed at the thought of Ted's face as she dangled his nut sack in front of his eyes. Now that would be funny.

Ted wasn't laughing, however, as he inspected his wounded nut sack with a mirror in the bathroom. Jeez, he thought, I better never tell her about the condom breaking or she really will cut them off.

15

One of the great things about jogging down a New York sidewalk accompanied by a 150-pound dog, Marlene thought, is that the crowd scatters like a school of herring when a barracuda shows up. Some of the fish did the New York shuffle, which was to look straight ahead at nothing and everything while skirting dog and owner without breaking stride. Others darted to the side and stood there staring at the dog as if it were some strange creature from another planet.

For his part, Gilgamesh cruised along indifferent to the people—except that his enormous brown eyes seemed to click on each for a moment, assess the danger to his owner, and then move on to the next. He was happy just letting his teacup-size nose take in all the wonderful, to a dog, smells and being on a walk with Marlene. Occasionally a brave soul would stretch out a hand to give him a scratch, which he accepted without reaction, although on a word from Marlene he would have removed the appendage about up to the elbow.

Marlene's route took her to an apartment building on

the East Side, actually not far from Ariadne Stupenagel's loft. She was on her way to the Michaliks'. She'd called that morning and told Helena that she wanted to drop by and talk to her and Alexis.

"I want to take my dog for a run; then I'll drop him off and be over," Marlene said.

"Oh, bring your puppy, too," Helena replied. "I love dogs and had to leave my schnauzer at home when I came to the United States."

"Well, he's considerably bigger than any puppy or schnauzer you've probably met."

"Doesn't matter. Please, I insist. I would like to meet your dog."

Marlene agreed. She was proud of her dog and knew that Gilgamesh would enjoy the longer outing. She regretted forgetting to ask Helena if she owned a cat. As well trained as Gilgamesh was—he'd hold his ground if a bomb was going off next to him—there was one small flaw in his nature and it was that he loved cats. For breakfast, lunch, and dinner.

"Nice doggy," said a voice behind her.

Marlene and Gilgamesh turned, the latter emitting a deep, low rumble that was not quite a growl but a warning to stay back. Caught us both by surprise and that takes some doing, Marlene thought, as she sized up the stranger she saw.

The man was obviously no threat. He was dressed sort of like a monk in a cowled brown robe that hung to mid-calf, revealing that he was wearing a worn pair of running shoes but no socks despite the cold and damp. It was hard to get a good look at his face because he kept most of it inside the hood and looked up at her sideways. But she saw he had the sunken cheeks and protruding eyes of someone who didn't eat well or regularly. His legs and arms, what she could see of them, were filthy, and the fingernails on the hand he stretched out to her were long, yellow, and dirt-caked. He smiled, revealing that most of his teeth were also gone. "Can you spare a buck?" he asked.

Marlene reached for her fanny pack. She was worth millions—exactly how much she didn't know because she let others handle the details of her investments and disbursements, including generous donations to a variety of charities and nonprofit agencies—and could afford to be generous to the beggars who roamed New York's streets. Some people said giving them money just encouraged more begging and contributed to whatever addictions they had, but she didn't see the harm. If a buck toward a bottle of cheap gin could get some old guy through the day, then who was she to deny what little pleasure he had. She unzipped the pack she was wearing and pulled out a five.

The little man skipped forward and snatched the bill, apparently not worried that he had to pass so close to the Hound of the Baskervilles. Marlene had been ready to command Gilgamesh to sit tight, but still she was surprised that he appeared no more concerned than he would have been if one of the twins had run up to her.

"Thank you, thank you, have a Merry Christmas, Marlene Ciampi," the man yelled over his shoulder as he trotted off down the street.

"Wait! How'd you know my name?" Marlene shouted. She wasn't sure she liked strangers in monk's costumes knowing who she was.

The "monk" pulled up and looked back, most of his face still hidden in the cowl. "Why, everyone knows Marlene Ciampi," he said and cackled. "I seen you in a newspaper once."

"Then can I know your name?" Marlene said, relieved

by the simple explanation though she couldn't remember the last time her photograph had been published.

"Roger," the man said. "Thank you for asking. It's been a long time since one of you up-world people cared what my name was. . . . I was beginning to think it was 'Fuck Off, Bum.' " The man cackled again and resumed his retreat.

"Well then, have a Merry Christmas, Roger," she called after him. Too late, she wondered what he meant by *up-world*.

Marlene shook her head. Sometimes living in Manhattan was like living in the old *Twilight Zone* television show. She rang the buzzer across from the name tag that said *Michalik*.

"Da?" answered a female voice.

"Helena. It's Marlene."

There was a buzz at the door and a click. Marlene pushed the door open and climbed up to the second floor, where Helena was standing out in the hallway.

"Oh, my goodness," the woman said, laughing. "You're right . . . that is some puppy." She bent over and patted her thighs. "Come, puppy, say hello."

Gilgamesh wagged his tail and looked up at Marlene with a question on his broad face. "Sure," she answered, releasing his leash. "Go say hi."

The hound bounded down the hallway and nearly bowled Helena over. She grabbed him by the scruff on either side of his face as he licked hers.

"Umm, I should have asked," Marlene said, looking at the open door to the Michalik apartment. "But do you have cats?"

Helena stopped playing with the dog and looked at her. "No. I am not a cat person," she said. "Should I have a cat?"

"Not if you want Gilgamesh to visit. How are you?"

The smile dropped from Helena's face. She shrugged. "As well as can be expected, I guess. Please, I'm forgetting my manners, welcome," she said, stepping forward and giving Marlene a kiss on each cheek.

Helena led the way into the small but comfortable and well-appointed apartment. Several Russian icon paintings hung on the wall in the entryway; vases of fresh flowers seemed to occupy most flat surfaces. Marlene noticed that the crib in the living room was already occupied by a half-dozen stuffed animals.

"When are you due?" Marlene asked.

"In June," Helena said, brightening. She looked happily at the crib, but then her face fell again.

The bedroom door in the back of the apartment opened and Alexis Michalik stepped out. Wow, Marlene thought, no wonder college coeds wanted a piece of this guy. The dark, wavy hair had just enough gray in it to qualify as highlights, and he had the deep, soulful brown eyes that qualified him as a poet whether he could write or not. He smiled and held out his hand though with one eye on the dog.

"Alexis Michalik," he said. "Helena told me about how you have offered to help us. I cannot thank you enough." He looked at Gilgamesh and laughed. "I did not know that they allowed you to keep bears as pets in New York City."

Marlene liked Alexis immediately, just as she'd liked Helena. But she felt compelled to set the record straight. Butch had warned her that the Michalik case might not be winnable. In the time she'd spent protecting women from the men who abused them, she'd met plenty who seemed like Prince Charming on the outside, only to find they were monsters inside. "As I told Helena," she said, "I'm willing to look into your situation. If I don't take the case as your lawyer, I might be able to recommend someone who will. But we need to talk and I'm going to have to ask you to be absolutely honest with me . . . and Helena."

"What do you mean?" Helena said.

"We'll get to it," she said. "But first tell me how you two met." This part wasn't necessary for what she needed, but she'd found through long experience that when she had to ask difficult questions, it was good to throw a few softballs first to loosen up.

"I was a student at the university in Moscow," Helena said, drifting into the tiny kitchen and reemerging with a pot of tea and three cups. "I was an architecture major—to draw buildings, you know—but my roommate was a poetry student and deeply infatuated with Alexis. To be honest, I was not much a fan of poetry—especially Russian poetry, which is always so dark and moody—"

"Unfair," Alexis complained. "This first poem I wrote to you compared you to spring on the steppes—'a rush of flowers on heaven's stairs.'"

"Yes," Helena said, but then rolled her eyes, "with the obligatory ending that if I would not be his, winter would come to the steppes and freeze his heart for all eternity."

Marlene laughed.

"Anyway, I would much rather go dancing . . . to the Rolling Stones, preferably," Helena said. "But he was so cute and earnest with his poems—"

"And she was the most beautiful woman I had ever seen," he finished her sentence. "I knew as soon as I spoke to her after the reading that she and I were meant for each other."

"What about your roommate?" Marlene asked.

"When she learned that, Alexis had asked me out, and I'd said yes, she threw all of my clothes out the window of our apartment."

"Which was good for me because she had nowhere else to go but my place," Alexis said.

They'd married soon afterward, but life was a struggle in Moscow for a poetry professor. Even though Alexis had won several prestigious international poetry awards, and several of his books had been published in Europe, his salary barely kept them above the poverty line. Helena had to quit school to work as a secretary, but even then they could not make ends meet.

The offer to teach as an endowed chair at New York University where he would be paid nearly four times the amount they made from both their salaries combined had seemed like a miracle. They had both fallen in love with America and hoped to be allowed to remain.

"I am a Russian in my soul," Alexis said. "I love my native land. But the end of the Soviet Union did not bring the economic boom everyone hoped for; it brought even more corruption and gangsters. If you wanted justice, you had to pay for it. There was no hope that things would get better. Here it is better. You can dream, and while Americans may not speak as highly of their artists, they pay them better. So, I am Russian in my soul, but becoming an American in my heart."

If only we all felt as strongly, Marlene thought but cautioned herself against letting this poetic man sway her with words when his actions might not have been so noble.

"So," Helena said, changing the subject, "you said you wanted to talk to us about Alexis's case."

Marlene looked at the younger woman and saw the fear in her eyes. She didn't want to hurt her but this had to be done. She turned to Alexis. "Like I said, I need to ask you some questions before I'll take this case. And let me warn you, you have to be completely honest with me, no matter how painful the answers, or I'm out of here. Understand?"

Alexis hung his head and sighed. "Yes, I will be honest," he said. "Ask."

"Then tell me the truth about your relationship with Sarah Ryder—from the beginning and right through to when you last spoke with her," Marlene said. Rather than ask specific questions at the moment, she wanted to see if he would try to downplay certain aspects or lie. But he didn't.

He spoke about how he'd met his accuser, the helpful student and friend. "She was—how do you say this, flirting—yes, flirting. I know now that I should have . . . um . . . nip this in the bud, but I admit I found it to be flattering and I thought harmless."

"Was there any physical contact?" Marlene asked.

"None. Well, except that she liked to hug and seems to be infatuated with the European custom of kissing on the cheeks. But nothing else, not until just before the incident when she kissed me on the mouth and told me that she was in love with me."

"How come you did not tell me this?" Helena interrupted angrily.

Alexis shrugged. "I did not think it was a big deal. I told her that I enjoyed her friendship, but that I did not feel the same . . . that I was already married to the woman that I loved."

"I don't suppose you made any sort of dated notation about this incident with Ms. Ryder?" Marlene asked. "A memo in a file or an email?"

"No. It was a kiss. I told her that it could not happen again, and she seemed to accept that . . . she said we could be just friends."

"What happened after that?"

Alexis leaned back in his chair and looked at the ceiling with his hands clasped in front of his stomach. "Nothing. She was just the nice, helpful student struggling to complete her master's thesis, which is why I agreed to see her that evening in my office. I was feeling somewhat guilty as her adviser because I had been so focused on trying to complete the translation of my book. I felt I owed her the time."

Alexis reached the point where Sarah arrived and brought out the beer, which she then spilled. "That is when she must have put something in my drink," he said.

"Something in your drink?" Marlene said. "The toxicology report indicates that she had rohypnol in her bloodstream. Are you saying that *you* were drugged?"

"I did not see her do this," he said, explaining how he'd left to fetch a paper towel. "But I'm Russian and no stranger to stronger drink than a weak American beer. Yet, after we talked for some minutes, I felt . . . well, actually, I felt good, relaxed, but my mind was like . . . you would say mush. The next day, I confronted her with this, but she says I drugged her."

"Did you tell the police detective who interviewed you that you thought you'd been drugged?" Marlene asked.

"No. It did not come up. He did not seem too interested in what I say, except the part where . . ." Alexis stopped talking and looked at his wife and then back to Marlene. "Helena has not heard most of this next part. Only that this woman claims I raped her."

"I'm afraid she's going to have to know the whole truth now," Marlene said. "If this goes to trial, she will learn anyway, and it's best if she doesn't look surprised and hurt in front of the jury."

Alexis nodded and looked at the ground so it was at first difficult to hear him. "She gave me oral sex."

"What?" Helena asked, her voice barely audible.

"When I was in my chair and feeling woozy, she gave me oral sex."

Helena looked stunned and then angry. But Marlene pressed on. "Did you ejaculate?"

"Yes," he said, nodding. "She would not stop."

Helena set her teacup down with a crash. "She would not stop? Poor Alexis, you could not push her away? She excited you enough that much? Perhaps you did nothing to resist?"

Alexis said nothing.

"Well, the legal question is, did you force yourself upon her at any time?" Marlene asked.

"No."

"You didn't tie her up?"

"What!" Helena exclaimed.

"No."

"You did not rape her vaginally or anally?"

"I never did these things," he said, starting to seethe himself.

"She says he did this?" Helena asked Marlene.

"Yes."

"Does she have proofs?"

"There is evidence that she had sex in this manner. There are also traces of Alexis's semen found on her blouse."

"This is not possible!" Alexis cried. "I did not . . . have sex in this manner or do this on her blouse."

"Then how do you explain these proofs," Helena demanded.

"I cannot," he admitted.

"There is also a question of a beer glass found in your

office with Ms. Ryder's fingerprints—as well as yours—and lipstick stains," Marlene continued. "It contained traces of the drug."

"Aha!" Alexis shouted. "There is proofs that I am telling these truths. I never touched her beer glass, only the one she handed me."

"There's no way to prove that, Alexis," Marlene said. "Only one beer glass was located, and it had both of your fingerprints on it. Her version of the story checks out, including a witness who has come forward to say he saw Ms. Ryder on the night in question and that she claimed to have been raped by her professor."

"But her story is lies," he complained.

"Except that you accepted this oral sex from this woman . . . and her kisses," Helena cried and began to sob.

Alexis stood and went over to his wife. "It was not like that," he said and touched her shoulder but she angrily pulled away from him.

Marlene watched the couple and felt like a heel. But she also believed Alexis. If he'd tried to lie about the blow job or had tried to introduce some silly explanation, she'd made up her mind to walk away and leave him to his fate. But while he was defensive about his actions, which was normal under the circumstances, he'd answered truthfully with his wife sitting across from him.

"Helena," she said, "if Alexis is telling the truth—and I have to say I believe him—there are other explanations for these proofs, as you call them. But it's going to be tough to convince a judge and jury so we're going to have to decide if you want me to help and if you want to be part of this."

Alexis looked at her gratefully, but Helena just nodded as tears spilled down her face. Marlene was about to tell them that she'd decided to accept the case as their lawyer when Gilgamesh lifted his head and looked at the front door while letting go a low rumble that sounded like a diesel truck trying to start on a cold day.

A moment later, there was a knock on the door. Helena stood, wiping at her eyes with her sleeve, and went to answer.

Marlene noticed that Helena didn't look out the peephole before reaching for the doorknob. Definitely not a New Yorker, she thought, as Helena opened the door.

A large man—approximately the same size as an NFL linebacker *with* his pads on—pushed through the door with his right hand inside his suit coat. However, Gilgamesh had risen to his feet from next to Marlene and was already within closing distance before the man realized that the dog would be on him before he could get the gun out.

So, bud, now you know how a gazelle feels in that moment when it finally sees the lion in mid-pounce, Marlene thought.

The man froze, his jaw twitching and his eyes on the dog. Another man stepped in behind him and then moved to the side, speaking to the dog. "Hello, friend," he said. "There is nothing to worry about here."

As tall as her own husband, the second man had none of the fear in his voice that was playing over the first man's face. Nor was he threatening, which Gilgamesh seemed to recognize, and to Marlene's complete shock, he sat down wagging his tail and gave what she thought of as his happy bark.

"May I," the second man said to Marlene, indicating that he wanted to approach the dog.

"Sure," she said. "You two seem to be old friends."

When the second man approached Gilgamesh and knelt to scratch beneath his collar and accept the obligatory lick, Marlene had a chance to study the scarring she'd noticed on his face; her eyes were drawn, of course, to the black patch he wore over his right socket. He'd obviously been burned. She glanced down at his right hand, which did not flex or change positions as he tickled the dog. Extensively. But he's still a hunk, she thought as he stood up and faced her so that she could see what he must have looked like before the accident.

"A magnificent animal," he said. "I may need to visit your farm someday on Long Island and find myself a similar companion."

"We could probably work something out," she said, wondering why it was that every stranger in town today seemed to know her and her business but deciding not to give him the satisfaction of asking. "But this one's been acting strange all day. He wouldn't have attacked you or your friend over there—who, by the way, can pull his hand out of his coat—without the command from me, but he acts like you two came from the same litter."

The man laughed and motioned the other man to take his hand off his gun, which he did but couldn't stop looking at the dog. The laugh was a pleasant one, not forced, but at the same time she got the impression that he didn't laugh often.

"Dogs are just so much better than we are at instantly knowing who is a friend and who is a foe," he said. "If he thought I was a danger to his lovely mistress, he would have torn my throat out when I came in the door. Although, getting older, I sometimes think there is something to reincarnation, so perhaps we were once brothers in arms. Yes, yes, I believe I see in his eyes an old sergeant who served with me in Afghanistan. The one who saved me so that I could spend the rest of my life half blinded and looking like this."

As he said that his crippled right hand went up to his face. "But then I see that we share a similar fate regarding our right eyes." He turned back to the dog. "May I know his name?"

"Gilgamesh," Marlene replied, thinking that if this man was this attractive after he had been burned, he must have been a god before.

The man arched his eyebrows. "Ah, the ancient Sumerian warrior," he said. "Very appropriate." He looked over his shoulder at the first man. "It's okay, Milan, the big puppy dog won't bite you so long as you are well behaved." The man nodded but still kept his eyes on Gilgamesh.

"Now do we get to know your name?" Marlene asked. But the answer came from behind her.

"His name is Yvgeny Karchovski," Alexis said without enthusiasm. "He is a . . . what is the word, a gangster, a criminal. Unfortunately, he is also my half brother, though it has been many years since we've seen each other, which has been fine with me."

Looking at Yvgeny, Marlene thought she saw something akin to pain cross his face at Alexis's words. But he inclined his head to her and said, "I would argue with some of the semantics—I consider myself a businessman who operates within certain gray areas of law—but generally what he says is true."

"Yvgeny," Alexis continued, "this is Marlene—"

"Ciampi," Yvgeny finished. "The beautiful, adventurous wife of the district attorney of New York, Butch Karp. I know of your husband."

"Yeah? Not in a professional capacity, I hope," Marlene said.

Yvgeny smiled. "No, I know better than to conduct my business in Manhattan and thus have never had to worry about your husband. No, let us say we have some history and people in common, but is best that I leave this discussion for another day."

Yvgeny turned to Helena, who had backed up against a wall in fear when the first man came through the door, then remained there looking befuddled by the conversation that followed. "And this must be the lovely Helena, my sister-in-law," he said, embracing her and kissing her on both cheeks. "Is it the name that creates such a face as to launch a thousand ships?"

Helena smiled shyly. "You are kind, sir."

"You've never met?" Marlene asked.

Yvgeny exchanged a look with Alexis, then shook his head. "Regrettably, my brother and I were raised in separate households and we've, um, lost touch over the years. I was already living here in the United States when they became engaged, and apparently my invitation to the wedding was lost in the mail."

"It was so far to travel, brother," Alexis said. "And I would not have wanted to distract you from your business."

Yvgeny gave Marlene an apologetic look. "My brother does not approve of the family business—"

"Not my family," Alexis retorted.

"Yes, yes . . . he wants nothing to do with me," Yvgeny said. "But come, brother, there is no need to burden these lovely women with our estrangement." He turned and gave a little bow to Helena and Marlene. "However, I was wondering if I might speak privately to my brother for a few minutes."

"I have no desire to listen to what you say," Alexis said.

"No, but I will say it to you anyway if . . ."

Marlene decided to intercede. The appearance of Yvgeny had not, of course, healed the rift between Alexis and Helena. But she wanted to talk to Helena privately herself and said to the younger woman, "Why don't you and I and Gilgamesh go for a walk and give these two a chance to chat?"

"I don't need a chat with him," Alexis said.

"No, Alexis," Helena replied. "But I need the fresh air . . . and time. So you talk to your brother and Marlene and I will walk the dog."

Defeated, Alexis nodded. "Do you also wish for me to be gone before you come back?"

The tears rushed back into Helena's eyes, but she shook her head. "*Nyet.* I may wish it later, but I am thinking now that we need to have our own little chat after I've had time to consider this."

After the women left with the dog, Alexis angrily faced his brother. "How dare you come to my home uninvited," he said. "I have told you that I want nothing to do with you. I had hoped that you did not even know I was in this country."

Yvgeny motioned for Milan to leave the room. "Even if I did not know before, I could hardly have missed it in the newspapers of late—the Russian Casanova case, I believe they call it," he said. "But I've come to offer my help."

"I don't want it," Alexis said.

"No, no, of course not," Yvgeny said. "It would be like accepting tainted money. But tainted by what? Do you even know what I do for a living?"

"Other than break the law, including murder?"

"Your definition of murder in this case might be called self-defense by others," Yvgeny said. "It's a hard world, populated by evil men who we have sometimes had to defend ourselves against. But I ask again, do you know what I do for a living? I do not make a living killing, that is just an unfortunate and regrettable part of doing business."

Alexis shrugged. "Not that I care, but smuggling . . . black market."

"All right," Yvgeny said, "that is partly true. But what do we smuggle?"

Again the question met with a shrug. "What does it matter? It is illegal. You are a common criminal."

Yvgeny surprised him with his next question. "Do you and Helena wish to remain in the United States . . . perhaps become citizens?"

Alexis scowled but nodded. "*Da* . . . yes."

"Why?"

"Not that it's any of your business but I would say because I wish for opportunity to pursue my dreams, my work, and still eat."

Yvgeny pursed his lips. "Then it would not surprise you that many other peoples wish this same opportunity. But you are big, important professor of poetry, an artist, so they welcome you with open arms, give you a nice, well-paid job. Someday they let you become a citizen . . . lots of stories in the newspapers and on television about the great Russian poet who wanted to be an American. But is not like that for everybody who wants to come to this country, who wants this same opportunity. So my family business is to smuggle them here, find them work, give them hope . . . and for this you look down your nose at me and call me a gangster."

"I'm sure you don't do this out of the goodness of your heart," Alexis said.

Yvgeny chuckled. "No, you are right. We, I, am well compensated. Sometimes they pay in advance, or sometimes we take a little from their paychecks at a time."

"And the black market in Russia?" Alexis asked. "Aren't you a wanted criminal in Russia? How can our country push through proper economic reform so that poor people can hope for better times when crime bosses and smugglers own the politicians, the police, and even the military?"

"Yes," he said. "We smuggle goods into our country. But isn't that the American way? The law of supply and demand. People who make money should be able to purchase these things without passing through the gauntlet of politicians and bureaucrats, not to mention those police and military officials you speak of, all with their hands out."

"Oh, it is fine for you to talk about corruption," Alexis said. "But you just exploit people like any of them so that you can live in a fine house and drive fancy cars."

Yvgeny spread his hands. "Put it like that and I am guilty as charged. I prefer to think of myself as a businessman who provides a service and has a right to recompense. Is that not also the American way?"

"I think that's the same argument drug dealers use," Alexis sneered. "Addicted children demand their products and they are merely supplying that demand."

Yvgeny's eye flashed with anger. "Do not, brother, compare me with drug dealers. I do nothing to harm people unless they attack me or people I am responsible for. I do not deal in drugs or prostitution or force people to pay me so they can have a business. It is easy for you because you are desirable to look down your nose at people who would not be allowed to pursue these same dreams because they did not have your advantages."

"What about the American people, don't they have a right to control immigration?" Alexis asked.

Yvgeny shrugged. "Yes, and they do. Many more try to

come to this country than arrive. If a boat or truck carrying my customers is caught, they are turned away. But they will continue to try to come. Some, like my grandfather, arrived at Ellis Island and were given papers that allowed them to live freely. Others come and are forced to live in the shadows as second-class citizens who do all the dirty jobs no one wants and are mistreated by employers who refuse to pay and threaten to call the immigration authorities. This country needs these people, they are the fresh blood and fresh ideas. At least I provide them with the documents to allow them to live openly, pay taxes, and know that their children born here are Americans."

Finally, both men seemed to have run out of steam. Yvgeny broke the silence first. "Come, let us discuss this some other day; perhaps you and Helena will join me for dinner at my house in the near future. But I did not come here to argue immigration policy. I came to offer my help as a brother. You are in trouble because of this woman's accusations, no?"

"That's my own problem. I'm taking care of it."

"It is your wife's problem, too. Perhaps you should think about what happens to her—three months' pregnant—if you go to prison or are deported."

"Leave my wife out of this."

"It is not up to me to leave her out of this. The difficulty will be getting you out of this. I may be able to help."

"What are you going to do, have the woman killed?" Alexis sneered.

Yvgeny laughed, but this time it was not as pleasant. "You watch too many American gangster movies, Alexis. I was thinking more along the lines of helping you disappear. You could start over again."

It was Alexis's time to laugh. "And what, work as a cab-driver or a day laborer?"

"There are worse things to be, Alexis," Yvgeny said. "One of them is a prison inmate. But if you insist on remaining yourself, perhaps you could go to a country where they would not extradite you to the United States."

"Yes, I hear Cuba is a wonderful place for Russian poets."

"They have nice beaches, a university . . . and I could help you with funds so that you and Helena and the child, my niece or nephew, by the way, could live in style."

"No, thank you," he said. "I have done nothing wrong. I will trust to the American justice system."

"The American justice system," Yvgeny scoffed. "There are many things to like about this country, but that is not one of them. I seem to keep having this conversation with my family, but the American justice system is as corrupt as anything in Russia. At least there, you know what prosecutors, defense lawyers, and judges are on the take because they all are. Here you roll the dice, or, if you have the money, you simply buy your way out of trouble. So if you will not accept my help to escape, how about my financial help to buy your American justice. And there are some things I have learned that might be of interest."

"There is nothing you could know that would interest me," Alexis said. "Quit trying to play the older brother that you never were."

"You know that is not fair, Alexis. We were separated as boys. I did not even know what happened to you until I was older. Then I tried to write to you but my letters went unanswered."

Alexis turned his back. "We are not brothers except that we share some blood. I didn't need you when I was growing up. And I don't need you now. In fact, I have a lawyer; you just met her, Marlene Ciampi."

"Well, I suppose you could do worse," Yvgeny replied. "She is as tough as an Afghani, and it doesn't hurt that her husband is the district attorney who must share the same bed with her."

"Glad you approve," Alexis said. "Now, I'd like you to leave, please."

"As you wish, brother," Yvgeny said. "If I can help, you know where to find me."

A minute later, Yvgeny Karchovski was back in his Mercedes. He leaned forward and pressed the intercom.

"*Da,* comrade," Milan Svetlov replied.

"Has the problem been taken care of?"

"Tonight."

"Good. Your brother?"

Milan looked at him in the rearview mirror. "*Da.* He sends his affection."

"A good man, your brother. As are you, Milan."

"Thank you, sir. So are you, sir."

That night was the weekly intramural "gangsters" basketball game at Auburn State Prison. The games were the brainchild of one of the counselors, who felt that the various gangs in the prison might be persuaded to work out their differences in a less-than-lethal way in the pursuit of athletics.

"A healthy way for them to take out their aggression and establish their pecking orders," he'd explained to the warden, who'd rolled his eyes. However, the counselor had been awarded a substantial grant—not all of which would find its way to the prison athletic fund—from some dumb bleeding-heart prisoners' organization in Washington, D.C.

The last game of the night was supposed to be between the Bloods and the Aryan Knights, but at the last minute the Knights bowed out, claiming that they were all suffering from food poisoning after eating the Turkey Surprise ("What's the surprise?" "That ain't no turkey, unless turkeys got tails and teeth") for lunch. They were replaced by a team composed of Russian gangsters.

As the game began, Lonnie "Monster" Lynd found himself pitted against the hulking Sergei Svetlov. Once he got over his nervousness, it didn't take long for Lynd to realize that Svetlov was no basketball player, and he used the opportunity to make up for the humiliation in the exercise yard. He grew so bold as to start talking smack.

"Come on, you Russian cracker, show me something," Lynd said, dribbling the ball outside the three-point line. "You can't touch this." With that Lynd drove and dunked the ball while Svetlov looked on helplessly.

Running back down the court, Lynd wagged his finger at Svetlov. "This my house, baby. Come on, Moby Dick, you big dumb white whale, come get you some of this."

The Russians turned the ball over and one of the Bloods fed the ball long to Lynd, who again slammed it home and then ran back down the court wagging his finger. However, the next time Lynd drove the lane, Svetlov fouled him hard, raising a red welt on his back. "Damn muthafuckin' cracker," Lynd said. He missed both of his free throws.

The same thing happened the next time. In fact, it seemed that Svetlov was purposely letting Lynd see an open lane to the hoop only to hack him as he went by.

"What the fuck, peckerwood. Keep that shit off the court," Lynd yelled, but the Russian just smiled and wagged his finger.

The third time Svetlov fouled him, Lynd was knocked

to the ground. He got up and pushed Svetlov, which was about as successful as pushing against one of the prison's walls. Svetlov grinned but then spat on Lynd.

In a rage, Lynd swung at him and connected with Svetlov's nose. The Russian put his hand to his face and looked unconcerned at his bloody fingers. He took two steps toward Lynd, ignoring another hard right as he waded in, and shoved Lynd so hard the black man was launched into the spectators. The gym erupted into pandemonium. Both teams came off the bench, and the inmates who'd been watching poured onto the floor, where a dozen fights and scuffles ensued. In the meantime, the guards stood back to wait for the prison's riot team to show.

In the center of the action, Lynd and Svetlov squared off. A Bloods gang member handed a piece of razor-sharp sheet metal to Lynd, who slashed at the Russian, but Svetlov easily avoided the attacks as he crouched in a wrestler's stance.

All around the two men, the other fights began to subside as the combatants realized that something big was going down center stage. One of the guards yelled, "Lynd, put the weapon down."

But Lynd wasn't listening. Connecting with the two punches had given him the confidence that Svetlov wasn't fast enough to deal with him. He smelled blood and felt like slashing the giant's throat open in front of the homeboys.

Lynd lunged, trying to cut Svetlov across the stomach. But Svetlov deftly turned to the side, and the blade missed eviscerating him by half an inch. His left hand slid along Lynd's knife hand until it reached the heel, where he gripped as tight as he could and then turned the hand back, reinforcing the move with his own right hand. There was a popping noise as the jujitsu technique called *katate tori ichi* snapped Lynd's wrist like a dry stick.

Lynd screamed and the knife went flying. Svetlov wheeled around behind his opponent and quickly put him in a figure-four headlock with Lynd's throat in the crook of his right arm and his left arm behind the black man's neck. He then squeezed his massive biceps and applied pressure to the side and back of Lynd's neck.

Lynd struggled, trying to break the grip with his remaining hand. He was losing consciousness from the pressure on his carotid artery. He looked beseechingly at his fellow gang members, but they had turned their backs and were walking toward the bleachers. He caught the eye of the man who'd handed him the shiv; the man shook his head and then he too turned away.

Muthafucka. It was a setup, he thought, a moment before he went limp. When his muscles relaxed, there was another cracking sound, more subtle than the wrist yet at the same time more final. Lynd's head flopped to the side, his eyes wide and staring but no longer capable of sight.

As the riot team came rushing up, Svetlov let go of his victim and the body crumpled to the floor. He placed his hands behind his back to allow the guards to cuff him.

"Vas self-defense," Svetlov protested. He spat again on Lynd and laughed. "He vas a bad sport, *da?*"

16

"STOP IT! THE WAITRESS IS COMING," MURROW
whispered, pushing Stupenagel's hand away from where
it was groping at him beneath the table in a dark corner
of Mr. Brown's Pub at the Sagamore Hotel.

"She's not the only one, lover," said Stupenagel, who
for the moment stopped her assault but left her hand
within striking distance.

Stupenagel had suggested a romantic weekend at the
grand old hotel set on Lake George in the eastern
Adirondacks. When he protested that he couldn't possibly
get away, she mentioned certain physically challenging
sexual positions that she'd been fantasizing about and
he'd quickly wilted under the pressure.

Ariadne was a woman of her word. They'd no sooner
checked in, tipped the bellhop, and closed the door than
she proceeded to make good on her promises. Sometime
after the fourth or fifth round—he'd lost count and was
feeling somewhat like a dazed boxer just before the knock-
out punch—she suggested they disengage and go grab a

drink and dinner. "And give my tiger a chance to recover his claws," she purred.

"Mmmph," Murrow said into the pillow before turning his head to the side so he could be understood. "Couldn't we just order room service. I don't think I can stand up. . . . Ow!"

Ariadne had slapped him hard on the butt. "Nonsense. That last effort was nice but hardly up to your peak performances. We need to get the blood flowing, and there's nothing like a Last of the Mohicans Martini to bring the color back to your cheeks and get you primed for the main event."

"Main event?" he asked, half in terror and half out of curiosity. "I thought we just did the main event."

"Oh, my, no, that was just to limber up," she said. "Next we're going to . . ." She leaned over and whispered in his ear.

"Really?" he said, his face a picture of concern. "Are you sure that's possible?"

"Absolutely," Stupenagel purred, "I saw a picture of it in the *Illustrated Guide to the Kama Sutra*, volume 10, with foreword by the Maharishi Bhagwan Yodi."

"Bhagwan Yodi? You're pulling my leg."

"If this is your leg, I hope you have another one just like it. Anyway, his real name is Mark Cook and he used to jockey a cab in Boston until he had this transformation and decided to go to India to become a holy man."

"They have schools for that?"

"Apparently, and he knows what he's talking about with the *Kama Sutra*. Legend has it he's deflowered more than three hundred vestal virgins—I guess they don't count nonvirgins—and set them on the path of enlightenment."

"Sounds like a sexual predator to me."

"Probably, but you're missing the point."

"No, I'm getting the point. I'm just trying to catch my breath."

"Exactly, my little big man. Which is why you're going to get that cute little tush up and escort me down to Mr. Brown's Pub, or I'll go on my own and maybe be abducted by a gang of bikers."

"Those poor bikers, if they only knew that they'll be spent and worthless men before you get done with them," Murrow teased. "Ow!"

She'd slapped his butt again. "Just my luck there aren't any gangs of outlaw bikers at the Sagamore. A bit highbrow for their tastes. But if you don't come along, I'll find someone who's willing to explore the *Kama Sutra* volumes 1 through 100 with me."

"All right, all right," he said. "Man, the things I do for science."

Stupenagel kissed him on the back. "Art, dear boy, it's an art, and you are my Picasso."

Ten minutes later they left their room, which had been tastefully decorated in Georgian Colonial, and headed for the lobby. As they passed, other people turned to stare and sometimes giggle at the odd couple. To start with, Ariadne was a good six inches taller, and she added to the difference with her affection for stiletto heels, the higher the better. She also dressed as if she'd bought her wardrobe off an avant-garde runway in Paris, preferring bright, splashy colors regardless of the season or time of day, and had a lipstick to match every variance of color.

As for Gilbert Murrow, she'd made no attempt to change his de rigueur business attire of bow ties, vests, and cardigan sweaters. "I fell for the geek in you and wouldn't change a thing," she'd told him. "At least, not at work." She did, however, have "suggestions" on how she wanted him to dress when they went out as a couple—a lot of Land's End khakis and polo shirts for casual, and knockoff Armani suits that she got from some mysterious connection in the Garment District. He only hoped it wasn't a couple of wiseguys knocking off trucks.

Murrow rarely complained about her treating him like her own life-size Ken doll. Ariadne always made it seem as if he'd made the selections, and she believed in rewards for good behavior. Nor had she ever insulted him by suggesting that he wear lifts or even a bigger heel. "In fact, I like the idea that every time you face me your mouth is so close to these babies," she said, waving the babies in his face.

Yet, their relationship wasn't all about sex. For all of her tough-girl bluster and locker-room talk, Ariadne was well read and could intelligently discuss a wide variety of philosophers and writers from Plato to Dan Brown. She'd traveled the world as a working journalist and had interviewed many of the most famous people of her day, as well as covered the usual assortment of wars, scandals, and disasters. Although mostly a reader of nonfiction, she confessed to the "occasional romance novel." She told him they made her hot and so he had not teased her when he came to bed one night and found her reading a paperback titled *Heathen Sins* with a picture of a bare-chested Indian warrior who looked amazingly like Fabio with dark hair, holding a helpless, buxom white woman. A half hour later, she turned out the lights and rolled over on top of him. "Come here, my noble savage. I need to be ravished with lots of heavy panting and a few threats if I don't comply with your wishes fast enough."

She loved to talk about serious matters, too, and loved that he was a good listener. But she knew when to be quiet and let him hold forth on the topics that mattered to him. He'd a real affection for political strategies and running Butch's race, and she encouraged him to try out his ideas and some of Butch's speeches on her. "No one has a better bullshit detector than Big Mama," she told him. "If they sound good to me, the public will eat 'em up."

No one had ever listened to him as she did, not even Karp, whom he worshipped. Once when he'd been belaboring the value of public-opinion polling, he looked over at the couch where Ariadne was lying down and saw that her eyes were closed. He stopped talking, hurt that she'd been so bored that she fell asleep. But then she opened her eyes and asked him why he quit.

"I thought I'd put you to sleep," he said, pouting.

"I wasn't sleeping, baby," she said. "I was just concentrating on what you were saying. I love listening to you talk, Gilbert. I love the way your mind works."

That might have been the day, even the moment, when he realized he was in love with this big brash woman. It terrified him. He knew she was much more worldly than he was and, until he'd finally objected, due to the seeming endlessness of the list, she'd had no compunctions about discussing former lovers. It was usually in some fun anecdotal sense, but still it made him wonder if he was just the next former lover. The thought broke his heart, and he sometimes cried when alone in the shower, thinking about how dull life would be if she ever left him. But they'd been lovers for four months and she showed no signs of wanting to split, so he did his best to go with the flow.

When they got to the lobby of the hotel, Murrow wanted to go straight to the Trillium, a five-star restaurant that he'd been salivating about since they got on the road. But she'd insisted that they start with a drink in Mr. Brown's Pub. Once inside, she chose a booth in the darkest corner. He figured it was to try out another one of her kinky ideas when she almost immediately began toying with the zipper of his Dockers.

Then the hand that had been temporarily at ease started inching its way up his leg again. "Don't you ever stop thinking about sex?" he asked, though for the moment he let her hand wander.

"Not when I'm near you," she replied and gave him a squeeze.

Murrow yelped, which at least served the purpose of getting the waitress's attention. She hurried over to the table. "I'm sorry, I didn't see you two," said the girl, obviously a local kid home from college for Christmas break and trying to make a little money. "What can I get you?"

"The lady and I will each try one of your Last of the Mohicans Mar-TEEN-ies," Murrow said, squeaking out the last word when Ariadne gave him another squeeze.

"Shaken not stirred," Ariadne added innocently. "Just like Bond . . . James Bond."

The waitress gave them an amused look and left for the bar to put in their order. Stupenagel turned to watch her go but suddenly tensed and turned back around to face Murrow. "Look who just walked in," she said in a low voice. "But don't be obvious."

Murrow stole a peek around her head. "Hey, Hugh Louis! I didn't think he wandered this far from the 'hood."

"Do you think he'd recognize you?"

"Nah. I've seen him at a couple of functions that Butch has attended. But I was in the background both times and never even got introduced. Will he recognize you?"

"Maybe," she said. "I interviewed him about fifteen years ago when he was representing that girl who claimed she'd been abducted by white supremacists. I was the one who broke the story that it was all a big hoax. He wasn't real happy with me, so he might have my face memorized. What's he doing?"

"He's bellying up to the bar. Now he's ordering . . . a beer. He's drinking the beer and . . . uh-oh . . ."

Stupenagel started to look but he whispered urgently, "Don't turn around. Olav Radinskaya and Shakira Zulu just walked in."

Forty feet away, Zulu looked around the dark bar and sniffed. Honkytown, she thought, only people of color in this hotel are the bellboys and the waitstaff. She didn't like being this far from her constituency, nor did she like the amused looks she got from the local crackers for her Angela Davis afro. Maybe I'll just come up here during the revolution and burn this bastion of whiteness to the ground. Burn, baby, burn.

Unfortunately, revolutions cost money, so sometimes she had to make compromises with her ideals—such as the stock portfolio and real estate investments that she mothered like the children she'd never had. Zulu meant to continue amassing her personal fortune, even if it meant dealing with white devils like Olav Radinskaya, a repulsive man with an egg-shaped head and thinning blond hair. He favored blousy silk shirts from which tufts of wiry, gray chest hair poked out, and thick gold chains. He apparently didn't believe in bathing and reeked of acrid nervous sweat and onions. Radinskaya looked dumb as a stick, but she knew he was clever and ruthless, a middleman for the Russian mob but with his fingers in his own dirty pies as well.

Radinskaya noticed Zulu looking at him and smiled. Ugh, he thought. He didn't like women in the first place. But this is a particularly ugly one, dark as a piece of coal, almost makes that pig, Louis, look white. Ugh, hardly more than animals, these niggers, but necessary that I deal with them as if friends for now.

He lifted his Stoli on the rocks and clinked glasses with Louis. "To our new venture," he said. Although neither man could stand the other, and both detested Zulu, who hated them in return, they'd all managed at various times in the past to forget their personal distaste and cooperate for their mutual benefit. A favor done here. A string pulled there. They were all richer for it. "I'll drink to that," Zulu chuckled as she sipped her black (naturally) Russian.

Meanwhile, back in a corner of the pub, Murrow had been excitedly giving the color commentary of the meeting when his eyes got big and he slumped down in his seat so that he was hidden by his girlfriend's large head of hair.. "What's the matter?" she whispered, trying to look over her shoulder without having to completely turn around.

"Christ!" he exclaimed. "You'll never guess who just walked in. No! Don't turn! . . . I just met one of them, PBA union boss Ed Ewen. There's some other middle-aged guy with him . . . dude's a cop if I've ever seen one but in a suit . . . wait a second, that's Tim Carney, the captain in charge of Internal Affairs!"

"I know Ewen and Carney, but odd that the head of the union and the guy whose job it is to bust dirty members of the union are hanging together at a swanky hotel in the Adirondacks," Stupenagel said. "Hmmm . . . as Alice once said, 'This gets curiouser and curiouser.' Have the other three seen them?"

"Had to but you'd never know it. They're standing maybe six feet apart and acting like they're complete strangers, but you and I know that Ewen and Carney know who every member of the city council is—not to mention that Louis and Shakira made a career out of suing the police department. Something doesn't smell right."

"Now what are they doing?" Stupenagel asked.

"Nothing much." Murrow noticed the glint in his girlfriend's eyes. "Hey, wait a minute. This is why you wanted to come up here. You knew these guys were going to be here."

"Nonsense," Stupenagel lied.

The truth was, she'd received a telephone tip that there was going to be a meeting "between some folks you'll find very interesting bedfellows . . . and once you figure out who they are, you might want to check into some of the real estate transactions in Bolton Landing, which should lead you—if you're as good as they say—to the story of the year." The caller then hung up before she could ask any questions or get a good handle on the voice, which seemed familiar but she couldn't quite place it. Whoever he was, the tipster certainly had the goods. In the morning, she'd have to head over to Bolton Landing, the town on the other end of the bridge that crossed Lake George to Green Island, on which the Sagamore was built, and find someone who could tell her about real estate in town. Maybe the tax assessor's office, if there was one way up here.

"No way," Murrow hissed. "I can see the 'hot scoop' look in your eyes. You used me."

Stupenagel was prepared to launch into a rehearsed spiel that would at least give her plausible deniability when she noticed the hurt look in his eyes. She didn't know what it was about this funny little man—she'd been the confidante and lover of pro athletes, world leaders, artists, and movie stars—but she'd found love in an intelligent, gentle bureaucrat (though she would never have called him one to his face). She resolved that she would never lie to him again . . . unless she had to.

"Okay, you're right, but only partly," she said. "I got a tip that there was going to be a meeting of some kind up here and that when I saw who was involved, I'd know what to do. But I could have come up alone and done my job. I just thought that this way, I'd get some time with you away from work and the city. And if this tip didn't pan out, we'd have even more time to ourselves."

Murrow allowed himself to look a little mollified. He had to admit that life with this woman was a hell of a lot more exciting than his usual fare. "Wait a second," he said, throwing himself into the spy game and stealing a glimpse over her shoulder. "Something just happened . . . some sort of signal between Louis and Ewen. Everybody's finishing their drinks and leaving . . . mmmph!"

Ariadne had stopped him from finishing his sentence by putting a hand behind his head and pulling him to her. Then she kissed him ferociously. When she let him go, he blushed. "What was that for?"

"Because I think I'm in love," Ariadne said. She wasn't surprised that she'd said it—she'd said a lot of things to a lot of men to get what she wanted—she was only surprised that she meant it.

Murrow was surprised to see the tears in her eyes. While very much a woman in most respects, she wasn't given to girlish emotions. "I love you, too, Ariadne. What do you say we skip dinner and go back to the room for the main event."

Instantly, the tears in her eyes were gone and she looked shocked. "Are you kidding me? We've got to find out what the hell's going on here." She slapped a twenty on the table, stood up, and practically yanked him out of the booth by the hand. They ran to the pub entrance and peered carefully around the corner. They got a glimpse of the backsides of Ewen and Carney just before the men reached the end of a hall and turned right.

Tugging Murrow along, Stupenagel crept down the hall. He wondered if someone might cue the music for *Mission: Impossible*. They went around the corner where the others had disappeared just in time to see a large man closing the door of the Algonquin meeting room and positioning himself in front of it. He looked up and saw them.

At the same time, Ariadne pinned Murrow against the wall and began kissing him passionately as she fumbled at his trousers.

"Hey, hey, you two, go find a room why don't ya," said the man, who looked as if he were made of rectangular parts—a rectangular, crew cut head sat on top of a rectangular torso that was supported by two rectangular legs.

"Up yours," Stupenagel snarled. "It's a free country."

Rectangle Man reached inside his coat and pulled out a wallet, which he flipped open to reveal the gold shield of a New York City police detective. "Beat it," he ordered.

"All right, all right," Stupenagel said. "Aren't you a little out of your jurisdiction? I swear, you can't get away from the pigs anymore."

"Oink. Oink," the detective said. "Take your midget boyfriend and go for a hike."

"He's more man than you'll ever be," Ariadne replied. "Especially now that the steroids have shrunk your balls into peanuts."

Rectangle Man furrowed his Cro-Magnon brow. How'd she know I'm juicing, he wondered. But before he could think of a snappy comeback, the couple beat a hasty retreat.

Stupenagel and Murrow scampered to the front desk, where they summoned a bored clerk. "Hi, we're trying to find out if some friends of ours have checked in yet," Stupenagel said. "Hugh Louis and Olav Radinskaya and Shakira Zulu?"

The clerk looked at them, wondering if they were teasing her with the odd names. But when they didn't crack up, she looked at the guest registry. "No, no one with those names is registered, and they'd be pretty hard to miss." She flipped forward in the book. "I don't see any reservations under those names in the next few days either. You sure they're supposed to be here?"

"How about Tim Carney or Ed Ewen?" Murrow asked.

The clerk brightened. "I just saw Mr. Ewen and he was with another man. Mr. Ewen doesn't stay here—he's got that nice house over in Bolton Landing at The Landings—but he and his . . . I think she's his wife, although she looks more like his daughter . . . sometimes come in for a drink or dinner. He's with another man tonight." The clerk picked up the telephone. "Shall I try to page him for you?"

"No!" Stupenagel and Murrow said at the same time.

"They don't know that we decided to make the drive from Manhattan," Stupenagel explained. "And we'd just as soon spend the night together, alone, if you catch my drift." She winked at the clerk, who giggled and nodded. "We'll surprise him at his home tomorrow, so just keep it a secret, okay?"

"My lips are sealed," the clerk said, making the appropriate motion across her mouth. "You two lovebirds go enjoy yourselves."

Murrow was perfectly willing to do as the clerk suggested, but Ariadne led him through the hotel to a back exit and was soon tugging him across the snowy landscape in the direction of the Algonquin Room.

"I didn't wear the right shoes for this," Murrow complained.

"Don't be such a baby, baby," she replied. "This is an adventure. And you know how hot I am after a good adventure."

With that for encouragement, Murrow stopped complaining and even took the lead, creeping through the shadows just outside the reach of the light thrown from the hotel windows, until they were opposite the large bay window of the Algonquin Room. They could see clearly the people in the room, all except one who was sitting with his back to the window, engaged in conversation with Louis.

A moment later, they both stood stunned, their mouths hanging open in disbelief, when the man Louis had been talking to stood and approached the window. He peered out into the dark, obviously saw nothing of interest, and closed the drapes.

"You see who I saw?" Stupenagel whispered.

"Corporation Counsel Sam Lindahl!"

"In the flesh. Come on, we need to figure out a plan."

"A plan?" Murrow said, trotting after her on his tiptoes, trying unsuccessfully to keep more snow out of his loafers. "A plan for what? Ariadne? Hey, wait up!"

They hurried to their room, where Stupenagel began to dress in more appropriate clothes for traipsing about in the woods on a winter night. As he followed suit, she told him more about the anonymous call. "Somebody wanted me to see these folks together and look into local real estate dealings. The clerk told us that Ewen has a house over in Bolton Landing. The Landings sounds pretty upscale to me, especially for a union boss. Something's going on here and it ain't a fishing trip. I'm going to follow Ewen and Carney and see for myself."

"I'm coming with you," Murrow said.

Stupenagel patted his cheek. "I don't want to tell you what to do, but if this group splits up, I'm going to need you to stay with whoever remains at the hotel."

"You going to take the car?"

"No, the hotel has a twenty-four-hour taxi over to Bolton Landing. I'll leave the car with you in case you need to ride to my rescue." She slipped into her parka and turned to look at Murrow. She laughed. He was dressed entirely in plaid from his waist up—a black-and-green plaid deerstalker complete with earflaps, a plaid scarf, a plaid shirt, and over it, a plaid coat. He rustled when he walked, due to the bulky ski pants he'd pulled on—the only piece of apparel that wasn't plaid as, looking down, she saw that he was even wearing plaid wool socks.

"What?" he asked.

"Nothing; you look prepared for a meeting of the wild Scots tribes from the Highlands," she said. "I didn't buy all that for you, did I?"

"No," he grinned. "I ordered it from the Land's End catalog. Cool, huh?"

"Cool," she said, making a note to herself to burn it all when he wasn't looking.

A half hour later, they were sitting in their rental car in the hotel lot when Lindahl, Ewen, and Carney emerged from the hotel and walked briskly to a car, got in, and left. Stupenagel kissed Murrow, then jumped out and trotted to a taxi she'd asked to wait for her "until our friends get done yakking inside."

Murrow walked back inside the hotel as if he'd been out for an evening stroll. He continued to the back of the hotel and exited, making his way to the spot where he could see inside the Algonquin Room. The drapes were pulled apart again and he could see that Louis, Radinskaya, and Zulu were still there, engaged in conversation with a lot of smiles and laughter. Unsure of what else to do, he stationed himself in the woods, jumping when some bird suddenly screeched as it flew above him. Probably an owl, he thought. Then there was a loud crackling in the bushes off to his right. Raccoon, he guessed. Bears would be hibernating this time of year . . . I think.

The crackling noise got louder. Murrow decided he'd seen enough and could go in now. He made for the door, sure that he was being followed by a man-eater who'd awakened from his nap in a grumpy mood. He sighed with relief when he got inside the door and looked out. He couldn't see anything but felt sure he was being watched by a pair of beady, ravenous eyes.

Actually, the eyes were large and brown. Having hoped for a handout, which hotel guests sometimes gave in the form of crackers and carrots, the doe gave her tail a disappointed flick and disappeared back into the trees.

Murrow arrived in the lobby and nearly panicked. The three targets were standing near the elevators talking. He pulled his hat down until he could barely see out from under the bill. They hardly gave him a second glance as he wandered off to the pub. He peeked out a minute later in time to see them get in the elevator and the door shut.

Flipping open his cell phone, Murrow was suddenly aware that he was sweating profusely beneath all those layers of plaid, which included plaid long underwear that Ariadne had not seen. He hit the preset number for her cell.

"Hi, Honey Buns," Stupenagel answered.

"Hi, Big Mama," he replied in his best secret agent voice. "The chickens have gone to bed. I repeat, the chickens have gone to bed."

"Oooh, you sound so clandestine and sexy," Stupenagel purred. "If I was there I might be tempted to forget this whole thing and let you have your way with me."

"I'll take the rain check, sweetheart," he said, using his best Humphrey Bogart voice. "This is kind of fun." He was feeling quite bold and dashing. "Where are you, doll? I want to come pick you up."

"That'll work, Agent Murrow," she replied. "Here, I'm going to let you talk to Jimy Murphy. He's my handsome young taxi driver; he'll give you directions."

"What? How cute?" Murrow asked, trotting out the front door to the car. "Agent Murrow? Where in the hell did that come from?"

"Just listen to Jimy for now, Agent Murrow, I'll explain the scenario when I see you," she said. "These lines are not secure. I repeat, these lines are not secure."

After leaving Murrow, Stupenagel had jumped in the waiting taxi and shouted, "Follow that car."

The teenage driver—whose taxi driver photograph hanging from the rearview mirror identified him as James D. Murphy—turned around and said, "Really? I've always wanted to have someone say that. Course, this won't be too hard as everybody around these parts knows Mr. Ewen. Heck, his nephew works as a mechanic down at the taxi barn. They're probably going to his house in The Landings."

"Well, then, James," Stupenagel said, "this will be easy. Just hang back a little."

"Jimy, just call me Jimy . . . with only one *m*. . . . I used to use two *m*'s but I wanted to do something different."

"Well, then," Stupenagel said, "pleased to meet you Jimy with one *m;* it's good to be different."

They drove in silence over the bridge and had almost reached Bolton Landing when Jimy cleared his throat. "Uh, I was just thinkin'," he said. "You're not a private detective or something, maybe working for his wife in New York City? I don't want to get him in trouble. He sometimes calls me for a ride, and he's a good tipper."

Uh-oh, Stupenagel thought, kid's worried about losing his date money. Interesting about "Mrs. Ewen in New York City." The hotel clerk seemed to think that Mrs. Ewen lived at The Landings. She leaned forward conspiratorially. "Okay, Jimy, I'm going to have to trust you here. But actually, I'm working undercover to protect Mr. Ewen. As you know, he's an important man, the head of the police union, right?"

"Yeah," he said cautiously.

"Well, then, you can understand that he's the sort of high-profile target terrorists are looking for, right?"

Jimy nodded and swallowed hard, his jutting Adam's apple bobbing rapidly.

"So you know about his wife?" she asked.

He started to turn around to answer but she stopped him. "Don't turn around; better that you can't identify me if the enemies of this country try to connect you to me. Now I need you to answer me truthfully, so that I know you're on the up-and-up. What do you know about his wife here in Bolton Landing?"

"Well, not much . . . but everybody knows that Inge isn't the real Mrs. Ewen," he said, then got a sly smile on his face. "Not unless his kids—he's got two sons who come up here to fish sometimes—are older than their mother."

"Yes," Stupenagel said, trying to keep the glee out of

her voice. Curiouser and curiouser. "This Inge talks with a foreign accent, right?"

Jimy looked at her in the rearview mirror as if she'd divulged a state secret. He nodded. "Yeah, I think she told me she's from Sweden."

Stupenagel snorted. "Sweden? That's what she's telling people? I'm sure you recognized the accent, and it wasn't Swedish."

"Sure," Jimy said, stealing another glance.

"Any idiot would peg it for at least Russian."

"She's Russian?"

"Chechen."

"A terrorist?"

"We think so," Stupenagel said. "Let's just say we're watching her. Mr. Ewen's going along for the ride, if you get what I mean?" She looked in the mirror and winked.

"Oh, yeah." Jimy grinned. "Nice work if you can get it. She's hot."

"She may also be a killer known in agency circles as the Lioness."

Jimy gulped audibly. "The Lioness?"

"Yes, sort of like the Jackal, who I'm sure you've heard of."

"Oh sure, I saw the movie."

"Then Mr. Ewen, the agency, and I can count on your discretion until the moment we're ready to move? At some point, you'll be free to tell anyone you want about tonight. Might even be a book in it, who knows? But right now, we don't even want Mr. Ewen to know when we're watching and when we're not so that he doesn't accidentally give it away that we're watching her. I'm sorry, Jimy. . . ."

"Sorry? What for?"

Stupenagel bowed her head to hide a smile and let

her voice become choked up. "Sorry that I may have put your life in danger. These people we're watching don't play nice."

The Adam's apple was working double time and the voice quavered, but Jimy managed to reply bravely, "That's okay. I was an Eagle Scout. I know how to keep a secret. And don't you worry about me. I've been taking tae kwon do with Master Kim Soo. I'll be a brown belt this summer."

"I'm so relieved," Stupenagel said. God, are you milking this one, Ari, but where are you going to find an audience like this guy again. "You looked like someone who could take care of himself. I just . . . well, never mind."

Jimy nodded. Some things are understood between a man and a woman. He maintained his silence manfully for the rest of the drive. On the wooded outskirts of Bolton Landing, he slowed the car down.

Looking ahead, Stupenagel saw the headlights of Ewen's car as it turned and began to wind its way back toward the lake and a huge log house. "Pull over and turn the lights off, I want to make sure we're not followed," Stupenagel ordered.

About the same time, her cell phone buzzed its special code for Murrow. "Hi, Honey Buns," she answered. She looked up and saw a quizzical look on Jimy's face. "Code name for Agent Murrow," she whispered.

She covered the telephone and said to Jimy, "Our cover is that we're a married couple, so a little of the mushy stuff is necessary just in case someone's listening. If you saw Agent Murrow, you'd understand we're not exactly a match made in heaven." Jimy gave a small tilt of his head to indicate he understood and slumped down in his seat to keep watch on the house. She spoke into the telephone again, "That'll work, Agent Murrow. Here, I'm going to let you talk to Jimy Murphy. He's my handsome young taxi driver; he'll give you directions."

She paused, then spoke again. "Just listen to Jimy for now, Agent Murrow, I'll explain the scenario when I see you. These lines are not secure. I repeat, these lines are not secure."

Stupenagel passed her telephone forward. "Would you please tell Agent Murrow how to find us?"

When Jimy finished giving instructions, he handed the telephone back without looking. "What next?"

"I'm going to get out and stand guard until Agent Murrow can back me up," she said.

"You want me to wait?" Jimy asked. He could tell she liked him, and despite the code names, he doubted two agents who worked together would also be shacking up.

"Only until Agent Murrow arrives, so you can tell him the direction I went," she said. She saw the disappointed look and knew what it meant. "Please, don't try to follow me. I couldn't live with myself if something happened to you, Jimy. Murrow, well, he's not much to look at, but he's a trained assassin."

Jimy nodded but said nothing. She heard him sniffle and wondered if he was crying.

"There is one last thing you can do for me," she said. "But I can't order you to do this, it's too dangerous. . . ."

"No, please, ask."

"After I get out, I need you to get somewhere public . . . like a bar or a restaurant, as far away as you can get, but you have to get there quickly—ten minutes max. And make sure you're seen by people and that they know the time."

Jimy looked confused. "Why?"

"Your alibi, silly," she said, getting out. She leaned in

the window and gave Jimy a quick kiss on the cheek. "And thank you . . . for everything."

There were definitely tears in his eyes now. "I'll never forget you," he croaked. "No matter what happens to me."

"*Au revoir, mon ami,*" Stupenagel said, stepping back from the taxi.

"Goo . . . good-bye. But wait . . . I don't even know your name."

"Lauren," she said. Sheesh, straight out of *Casablanca.* "Now wait until Agent Murrow arrives, point him in the right direction, then drive like the wind. But keep your lights off until you're out of sight of the house."

Stupenagel ran across the street, hopped the rail fence, and, sticking to the tree line on the outside of the property, made her way to the back of the house. She ran the last few yards from the trees until she was standing in the shadows beneath a back deck that overlooked the lake. Nice pad, she thought, looking out at the dock in the backyard to which a brand-new thirty-five-foot sailboat was tied. Cool million at least. Not bad for a union boss; wonder what the rank and file would think.

The deck lights came on, nearly giving Stupenagel, who thought she'd been discovered, a heart attack. But it was just Ewen, Lindahl, and Carney stepping out for a cigar.

"Sorry to make you fellas light up out here but the little woman insists."

"I sure wouldn't want to piss her off on a cold night," Carney said. "That's some little doxie you got stashed up here away from the missus."

"Yeah, she ain't half bad." Ewen chuckled. "Met her on a flight to Stockholm. She was a stewardess . . . wouldn't have nothin' to do with my ugly mug until I started flashing hundreds. That's when there was a definite attitude adjustment and it's been 'Harry, hold your horses' ever since. Dumb as a stick and barely speaks the language but she likes the bump and grind as long as I keep the presents coming. Don't bother me. I got money, she's got what I want; it's a nice arrangement."

The men puffed on their cigars for a minute, sending a blue cloud into the starry night. Carney again broke the silence. "Nice little fishing lodge."

"I like it. I hear your place in the Keys ain't half bad either," Ewen replied.

The two laughed and turned to Lindahl. "Hey, Sam, what are you doing with your share? Got yourself a little young thing stashed away in a 'fishing lodge'?"

Lindahl ignored the chuckles. "I don't like this. I don't trust those two niggers or that Russian faggot. If somebody saw us all together we'd be dancing pretty damn quick to explain it."

Ewen rolled his froggy eyes. "Nobody likes working with them three," he said. "But we're hundreds of miles away from the city. We needed to sit them down and make sure we're all on the same page with that fucker in the DA's office, Newbury, and his little Goody Two-shoe investigators poking their nose in old business where they don't belong. Then that bitch Marlene Ciampi calls you and that fat fuck Louis and says she's been 'retained' as a private investigator by Repass and Russell and wants to see the files. Couldn't you have told her 'thanks, but no thanks'?"

"And what?" Lindahl said. "My clients went to her on their own and now say they want her to help with the case, and I'm supposed to say, 'No thanks. I have no intention of even looking like I'm trying to protect the city's interests'? If you think Newbury's breathing down our necks on some of this 'old business' now, just let him get wind of that. At least if she's working, ostensibly, for me, I'll know what she knows."

"If she tells you," Carney said. "But I'm more worried about what she tells that fuckin' husband of hers. We don't want him taking an interest."

"I'm not worried about him," Lindahl said. "His jurisdiction begins and ends on the island of Manhattan. This is a Brooklyn case as far as the assistant district attorneys go, and a city matter with the police department. He's not in the picture."

Stupenagel couldn't hear the muffled replies as the men put out their cigars and moved inside. The lights went out but she waited to make sure anyone looking out the window wouldn't see her. She was ready to go when a large hand came down hard on her shoulder and turned her around. She found herself face-to-face with the big police detective who'd guarded the meeting room at the Sagamore.

"Hey, you're the bitch from the hotel, what the fuck are you doing here?" he snarled.

Obviously wasn't at the top of his class at the academy, Stupenagel thought. She smiled sweetly. "I was driving by when my car ran out of gas. I saw the light was on and came to ask for help. But I can go ask someone else if this is a bad time." She tried to walk past the cop but he grabbed her by the arm. "Yeah, well I think you need to come in and talk to the boss."

"Hey, asshole," said a voice behind him.

The cop whirled and got a face full of pepper spray. "Goddamn mother fucking *gaaaaaah*," the man bellowed and began groping inside his coat for his gun.

Stupenagel saw her opportunity and kicked up as hard as she could between his legs. "Oh fuck," the cop groaned and passed out face-first in the snow.

"Big baby," Stupenagel said. She looked up and saw her frightened boyfriend still holding the pepper spray. "Hey, you better put that away before you hurt someone, Honey Buns."

Murrow dropped his arm. "You okay, Sugar Lips?"

"Great, thanks to my hero, Agent Murrow."

"Please, call me Bond . . . James Bond."

The cop groaned and appeared to be coming to. Stupenagel leaned over and took his gun out of his coat. "Come on, Bob, Mrs. Ewen is going to love hearing about this place."

They ran back along the tree line, where Stupenagel tossed the gun into the woods. Driving back to the hotel as fast as they could, they hurried to their room, packed their bags, and were back in the lobby in ten minutes. "We're going to check out now," Stupenagel told the sleepy clerk. "And I'd like to pay with cash. Would you please give me any credit card imprints you have. Sorry, a little paranoid about identity theft."

"I understand," the clerk said. "It's a big problem these days."

"Oh, and would you be a sweetie and get me the manager's business card," Stupenagel said. "I'd like to write and congratulate him on the service."

When the clerk trotted to the back office to get the card, Stupenagel reached over the desk, flipped to the page in the hotel registry where they'd signed in, and tore the sheet out. The clerk returned but there was no one to give the business card to.

A big sedan came barreling toward them as they crossed the bridge. "Duck," Murrow said, slapping his deerstalker onto his head. He looked away when the car bearing an angry New York police detective, as well as Ewen and Carney, passed.

"Drive like the wind, baby," Stupenagel said, sitting back up.

"What was that 'Mrs. Ewen is going to love this' comment?" Murrow asked.

"Just something to throw them off our tail, maybe panic them a bit. I want them to think that we're private investigators working for the real Mrs. Ewen."

"Wow, nice work," Murrow said with genuine admiration.

"Experience, lover. I've been talking my way in and out of trouble for more years than I care to admit," she said.

On the way back to Manhattan, they argued about what to do next. Murrow wanted to go to Karp with what they'd seen and heard.

"Not yet, baby, not until I've had a chance to get to the bottom of this," Stupenagel pleaded. "I want to figure out how this all adds up. I mean, what do we really have? A bunch of people who normally wouldn't be caught within a mile of each other have a secret meeting. Ewen has a house he can't afford, but I'll bet you he's not stupid enough to have it in his name. Not to mention we just committed trespass and then aggravated assault on a New York City police detective."

Stupenagel leaned over and nibbled on his ear. "Please, baby? Just a few days, then I promise we tell Butch everything."

"Well, a few days, but that's it," Murrow agreed.

"Cross my heart, hope to die. Oh my! Look what I found."

"Stop it. I'm driving."

"That's okay, baby, just don't take your hands off the wheel or your eyes off the road."

17

Monday, December 20

KARP WALKED INTO THE MORNING MEETING LIKE A
man crossing an open meadow during a lightning storm.
There was something in the air that made his hair stand
on end and his skin crawl waiting for a bolt out of the
blue.

The apprehension began at the premeeting conference when he noticed that Murrow seemed more than a
little preoccupied. "What's up, Gilbert?" he'd asked after
the others left, and Murrow hesitated at the door as if he
intended to say something. But he just mumbled, "Nothing," and wandered off.

The premonition increased as Karp entered the meeting room. Harry Kipman, who'd begged off the earlier
conference, looked up, said, "Good morning," and went
back to reading his book on Ulysses Grant.

At the other end of the table, Rachel Rachman
hunched over her files like a junkyard dog guarding its
supper and rapidly drummed the fingers of both hands
on the table. She was staring at Kipman and it was not a
friendly look.

The other bureau chiefs and assistant DAs seemed subdued, as if they were reluctant to be the one to set off the spark. Well, let's get this over with, he thought as he took his seat, then nodded to Murrow, who mumbled, "Harry, you're up."

Kipman closed his book with a definitive snap and opened the file in front of him. "In the case of People v. Salaam and Mohammed, I'm afraid I have to concur with the appellate court that this conviction was wrongfully obtained. We withheld exculpatory evidence that the complainant knew one of the defendants, whom she claimed, both to the investigating officers and, even more damning, under oath on the witness stand, she did not know. In fact, she had sexual relations with this defendant several days prior to the incident from which the charges arose."

"Nonsense," Rachman hissed, half rising. "The shield laws were created to protect sexual assault victims from defense attorneys—and I guess some prosecutors—making an issue of their past sexual history when the ONLY issue is one of consent."

"Rachel, please," Karp said calmly but firmly. Rachman didn't look at him and continued to glare at Kipman but she shut up.

"The rape shield laws, which I fully support, were created for cases in which a perpetrator sexually assaults a stranger—say someone abducted off the street—and it's clear a crime was committed," Kipman said, his voice level but tight. "In those instances, the past sexual history of the victim is irrelevant. However, at the time of the creation of the shield laws, little attention was being paid to date or acquaintance rape. These are often he said/she said cases—difficult to prosecute, as we all know, in part because there is a legitimate question as to whether a crime was even committed. In these instances, a complainant's sexual history, especially if it is a history involving the accused, is certainly relevant for both this office to consider when deciding whether to prosecute and the defense to argue before a judge in pretrial motions."

Kipman stopped and returned Rachman's stare until she looked down at her clenched fists. "It would have been proper to argue that the complainant's sexual history was not relevant in this case and to have invoked the shield laws in front of a judge. However, we did not do that, nor did we discuss it in this meeting. We simply took it upon ourselves to hide a police report containing information that we did not like."

Rachman started to speak but Kipman raised his voice. "And yet that is not the most egregious of our errors. That would be that we knew the complainant was lying on the witness stand, and yet we allowed it—in fact, we encouraged it in our line of questioning—which is a serious breach of the law and accepted attorney conduct. It is therefore my recommendation that we concede error and drop the charges. Let's face it, we'll be lucky if we're not sued, and if the New York Bar Association doesn't censure the attorney involved."

Rachman jumped to her feet and shouted, "Since when do we let fear of a lawsuit dictate what crimes we prosecute?"

"You weren't listening," Kipman replied. "I am not making my recommendation because I'm worried about being sued. I'm recommending that we concede error because it was just plain wrong to allow a witness to get on the stand and lie. And it was simply dumb not to hand over that material to the defense."

"You're the one who's not listening," Rachman countered. "All that matters is whether the victim gave her consent to have sex with him that night."

"That is indeed the pertinent question," Kipman agreed. "However, as I said, this is a he said/she said case. There are no other witnesses, except the other defendant who claims that the sex was consensual. You might recall that he was prevented from testifying that his codefendant knew the victim and had previously had sex with her. So if there is a question whether a crime was even committed based on anything other than the complainant's word— which by the way is why it is more appropriate to use *complainant* rather than *victim*—is it relevant that she would lie to the police and under oath?"

Rachman sneered. "Just like a man. I guess maybe you need to actually try a few thousand of these cases yourself to know when the *victim* is telling the truth and when she's not. There are a lot of reasons that a woman wouldn't want to delve into her sexual history in front of a judge and jury, starting with the fact that if a man has sex with multiple partners over the course of a week, he's Casanova, but if a woman does, she's a slut. Who wants to admit that in front of a room full of strangers, especially after going through the most frightening, humiliating, and degrading experience a woman can have?"

"Then you should have turned it over to the defense and argued it in a closed motions hearing," Kipman retorted. "If the judge had agreed with you that it was not relevant, then the defense attorney would not have been allowed to question the complainant about it on the witness stand and there would have been no reason for her to perjure herself. But to simply try to sweep it under the rug and hope nobody would notice is woefully bad judgment."

"Are you questioning my competence as a lawyer?" Rachman demanded. "You wouldn't do this if I was a man."

"Bullshit!" Kipman shouted back. "This has nothing to do with your gender and you know it. Nor does it reflect on your abilities as a prosecutor. However, it is my opinion that in this particular case, you made a mistake . . . a bad one."

Rachman started to say something, but Karp had had enough. "I think this conversation has reached an end," he said. "I concur with Harry's judgment in this matter. We will concede error and drop the charges—"

"NO!" Rachman screamed. "I cannot allow this . . . this . . . this travesty to happen. Those two spoiled athletes took advantage of an intoxicated young woman who did not give her consent. We can't let them off."

The room was shocked into silence as Rachman finished raving and stood with her knuckles pressed into the tabletop and sobbing. "I won't—" she started to say but was brought up short by Karp.

"Ms. Rachman, that's enough. You will remove yourself from this room and return to your office, where I expect you to pull yourself together. We'll talk about this later this afternoon.'"

Rachman stifled her sobs and narrowed her eyes as she looked from Karp to Kipman. "I see," she said, scooping her files together. "I see."

"If those are files from other cases, please leave them and have your assistant deliver your report," Karp said.

Rachman froze and appeared ready to say something really scathing, then thought better of it. She dropped the files on the table with a thud, then walked around the table, her eyes straight ahead, and out the door. The door slammed shut and a voice at the other end of the table exclaimed, "Holy shit. The Ice Princess had a meltdown!"

There were a few chuckles around the table and a full-fledged guffaw from Guma, but Karp wasn't in the mood.

"Now, if we can proceed with the matters at hand, I know we all have a busy day ahead of us. Anything else?"

"Well, the morning's newspaper," Murrow said.

Karp winced. "I'm sure you are all aware that Murrow is referring to the appearance of two more heads . . . without their bodies . . . in East Harlem," he said. "What can you tell us, Clay?"

"I'm getting updates from the PD but they don't have much more than the newspapers reported," Detective Clay Fulton responded. "Apparently some nutcase with a thing for cutting the heads off Middle Eastern men is running amok in the city. This time the heads were dropped off at the front door of a small mosque. The imam—that's the preacher—was turning in for the night when he heard a knock on the door. No one was there when he answered, but someone left two heads in a bag for him. The police are apparently having a tough time identifying the victims—they obviously aren't carrying wallets and their fingerprints are . . . uh . . . unavailable. There are no claims of responsibility reported by the media, so far. NYPD has stepped up patrols in tradition-ally Muslim areas and is warning people in that commu-nity not to go out at night alone."

"Any description of a suspect or suspects?" Karp asked. He'd arrived that morning with messages on his answering machine from the Arab-American Protection League and the Muslim Society of New York, who demanded a meeting. He'd put off returning the calls until he actually knew something about what was going on.

"Not really," Fulton said. "A taxi driver swears he saw two men—at least he thinks they were men—one tall and one short, jumping down a manhole about three blocks from the mosque after the heads were delivered."

"I take it the police don't put a lot of credence in the report."

Fulton shook his head. "They checked it out but didn't take it much further from there. According to our witness, not only did the suspects fly several inches off the ground, they flew down the manhole and then the cover replaced itself magically. Turns out the cabdriver is taking psychotropic medication prescribed for hallucinations. The office pool in our bureau is that he forgot to take his pill that day."

The rest of the meeting was, by comparison, uneventful. As the others stood to leave, Murrow asked, "We still on?"

"Yep, my office in, say, fifteen minutes?" Karp replied, looking at his watch.

Ten minutes later, Murrow and Kipman walked in on Karp, who was already deep in conversation with Clay Fulton, Ray Guma, and Richard Torrisi. As Karp was making introductions, Mrs. Milquetost buzzed and said, "Robin Repass and Pam Russell are here to see you."

When the two women entered there were more introductions, and then Karp asked them to all be seated as he walked over to an easel that had been set up behind his desk. "All right, we have quite a bit to get through and because this isn't entirely Manhattan DA business, I don't want to use up any more of the taxpayers' crime-fighting dime than I have to. A few of you—Harry, Ray, and Richard—are already aware of this, but I've been asked by Mayor-elect Denton to take on the case of Jayshon Sykes et al. v. City of New York . . . the civil lawsuit involving what is otherwise known as the Coney Island Rape Case."

"What?" Murrow said, showing the first spark of political sensitivity all morning. "How can you do that? How come I wasn't told?"

Karp held up his hand. "Please, Gilbert, if you'd let me get through this, it should answer your questions. But it was not my intention to keep any of you in the dark as an indication of a lack of confidence in your counsel. Most of you I've known for many years and I would trust with my life, including you, Mr. Murrow. The truth is that initially I was reluctant to choose this course and only recently reached this decision."

Murrow didn't look any happier, but he sat back in his chair and waited.

"The answer to your first question is that after Mr. Denton is sworn in, the current Corporation Counsel, Sam Lindahl, will be replaced"—Karp paused for the applause to die down, although he noticed Murrow suddenly sat up again in his chair—"and at the same time, the governor will announce that I have been appointed as special counsel for the case on behalf of the new Corporation Counsel. Harry has checked the statutes, and apparently the governor can do it as I'm not really an elected official."

"Yet," Murrow muttered.

Karp smiled at the effort his younger colleague was making to get himself back in the game. He noticed that Repass and Russell, who had not been told the purpose of the meeting, had exchanged surprised glances and were now smiling broadly at him.

"Thanks for the vote of confidence, Gilbert. . . . Anyway, over the past couple of days, I've had the chance to review a good bit of the case files with the assistance of the inestimable Mr. Guma and Mr. Kipman." After the Friday meeting with Liz Tyler, he'd spent the weekend with Ray and Harry poring over more than sixty large, three-ring binders filled with police notes, affidavits, statements—sworn and unsworn—lab reports, and trial testimony, as well as more than two dozen videotapes.

Karp flipped over the blank front of the chart on the easel. "Those of you more familiar with this case than I, please bear with me and feel free to point out any grievous errors or omissions, but I'll try to lay this out as best I can for everyone here."

After a night of wilding that had ended with the rape and near murder of Liz Tyler on May 19 and 20, 1992, Karp explained, the gang split up. Kevin Little and Kwasama Jones had been picked up that morning by the police as they tried to make their way out of the Brighton Beach area and they almost immediately confessed to having "hurt a woman" near Coney Island. "Hearing that his friends had been taken in by the police, Packer Wilson turned himself in voluntarily in the company of his mother. Based on the statements given by the others, Sykes and Davis were contacted the next day by police. They attempted to run but were apprehended."

Karp flipped to another page with two items on it. "Essentially the case against the city is twofold. It begins with the premise that the confessions of the defendants were coerced by the jack-booted police and that the evil prosecutors Ms. Repass and Ms. Russell—"

"Boo, hiss," Guma said, and was promptly given the bird by both women.

"—condoned and encouraged these actions, and then used these illegitimate confessions to convict and imprison the innocent defendants. The second issue is that during the trial, the prosecution also brushed over the evidence of a sixth unknown attacker."

Karp paused to make sure everyone was up to speed. "Any questions so far? No? Moving on, I think the allegation of prosecutorial misconduct regarding the sixth attacker is laughable. Not only did Robin spend nearly ten minutes discussing the existence of this sixth man in her opening remarks, it was the prosecution, not the defense, that presented expert witnesses to go over the DNA evidence, which pointed to another perpetrator who was not among the five defendants. Pam again spent considerable time in her closing arguments acknowledging that there was a sixth, unknown attacker—even referring to him, I believe, as 'the one monster who still roams our streets.' I have no doubt that we will quickly dispose of that question."

Karp flipped to another page headlined by the bold capital letters CONFESSIONS and beneath which began a list of the defendants with numbered statements. "The issue of the confessions having been coerced is equally laughable," he said. "To begin with, prior to the last trial, there was a thorough and lengthy Huntley Hearing to determine the voluntariness and admissibility of the defendants' confessions and other evidence. The court took testimony from over twenty prosecution witnesses, including defendant-turned-witness for the prosecution Kevin Little, and heard from the defendants Sykes, Davis, Wilson, and Jones, as well as their families and friends who were present or involved in the initial encounters with the police. In the end, the court ruled that the statements were properly and legally obtained."

Karp took a sip of water. When he and the other two finished with their first pass through the files late Sunday night, he'd been so incensed that he didn't even remember the walk from 100 Centre Street back to the loft. It wasn't just the bestiality and complete lack of human compassion the defendants had shown Liz Tyler. If anything, he was angrier that Brooklyn DA Breman had rolled over so easily. She'd ignored time-honored legal procedure. Most egregiously, Breman never demanded a full evidentiary hearing before

accepting Villalobos's word as reason enough to exonerate the four men. And, from everything he could tell
looking at the motions that had been filed in the civil
trial, Lindahl had made very little effort to defend the
case and let Louis get away with every demand without
fighting any of it. Karp smelled a rat and maybe more
than one.

"Of significant importance with respect to the admissibility of the statements and the fairness of the process used
to obtain them," he continued, "no defendant under age
sixteen was questioned without a parent, relative, or
guardian present, all of whom gave consent. Of the four
convicted, only Sykes was over sixteen."

Flipping his chart, Karp gave his audience a rundown
of some of the "highlights or lowlights, if you will" from
the statements of the defendants.

"For instance, defendant Desmond Davis gave a written statement and a videotaped interview. His grandmother was present at the former, his father at the latter,"
Karp said. "He was contrite and sorry with his relatives
present, but quite another character while waiting for
them to arrive at the precinct so that questioning could
begin. In fact, he and defendant Jayshon Sykes had a
grand time sitting in the holding area with police and
other detainees present, laughing about what a good time
they'd had that night. At one point, in front of other
police officers, if you can believe this crap, Desmond
called out to a female police officer and asked her if she
'wanted some of what that other bitch' got. Not to be outdone, Sykes said to the same officer that he wanted to
lick her 'pussy.' Hardly the behavior characteristic of
frightened, vulnerable boys that Hugh Louis is now trying to make these punks out to be."

As Karp spoke and pointed to his charts, the others in

the room remained quiet. They could be an irreverent bunch, even when discussing the most heinous crimes. So-called dark humor was a way of getting past the horror. But no one was in the mood for joking this time. They just sat patiently as Karp next introduced what he had labeled "incriminating admissions to investigators and third parties as corroboration of the defendants' guilt."

"That next afternoon, shortly before he turned himself in, Packer Wilson was walking on the sidewalk when he saw two school chums and warned them to stay away from him because 'the cops will be after me.' When they asked him why, he responded, 'You heard about that woman that was beat up and raped at Coney Island last night. I'm in it.'

"Feeling that Kevin Little seemed to show the most remorse for the crime," Karp said, "and might want to help us out, our Ms. Repass and Detective Torrisi escorted him to the pier at Coney Island. Although some of the evidence had already been washed away by the tide, there was still a large pool of blood beneath the pier. According to the affidavits of our two friends here, Mr. Little was heard to mutter, and I quote, 'Damn, damn, that's a lot of blood. I knew she was bleeding, but I didn't know how bad she was. It was pretty dark under the pier. I couldn't see how much blood there was.'"

Shortly after that, he said, Kevin Little had agreed to testify against the others. "I should note that he did not ask for a deal." A few days later, however, Kwasama Jones called the home of codefendant Kevin Little from Rikers Island and talked to Little's sister, fourteen-year-old Hannah. "He was passing on a message from Sykes, who was in solitary for assaulting another inmate, that there'd be dire consequences for Kevin if he didn't keep his mouth shut. During the conversation, Hannah asked Jones how he could have committed such a vicious crime and, she would later testify, he denied raping Ms. Tyler and said, 'I only held her shoulders. It was Jayshon and Desmond, and some other dude, who fucked her.'

"Detective Torrisi escorted Desmond Davis to the pier," Karp said while Torrisi looked out the window. "And according to the detective's report, Mr. Davis laughed as they walked beneath the pier and said, 'Yes, yes, this is where we got her. This is where we fucked the bitch. Man, she was tight.'"

"I wanted to kill him," Torrisi said.

"When I read that, I did, too," Karp said. "But we can hope that what goes around comes around for these guys."

When he read through the files, Karp had wished that he was not defending the city and the three defendants in the room, trying to prevent paying the cretins who stole Liz Tyler's life, but that he was prosecuting them instead. Repass and Russell had done as good a job as anyone could have. They and the police had gone by the book, and, as they'd told his wife, won a fair and just conviction. But he would have liked to have struck a blow himself in this case.

Karp paused and looked into the eyes of each person in the room. "Lest anyone doubt the assailants' character and cruelty on that night at Coney Island, I want to read to you from Detective Torrisi's memo book an entry of a statement given to him by Jayshon Sykes. 'I hit her with that piece of steel. She went down and I hit her again. Then I fucked her. Then Desmond fucked her. To me it was just something to do. It was fun.'"

The silence in the room was broken by sniffling. Russell looked up through teary eyes and wiped at her nose with a tissue. "I'm sorry," she said. "I've never really gotten over this one. And to hear it all again, to remember their faces—those bastards laughed and giggled throughout the trial, too—brought it all back. Then to have them walk out and demand money . . . I don't sleep too well these days."

Repass reached over and patted the arm of her friend. The others murmured their support. "I think we all feel the same," Karp said gently. "My job now is to make sure these pieces of crap don't profit from what they did to Liz Tyler. But we've still got a lot to do and not much time to do it."

"Are you going to ask for a continuance after your official appointment to the case?" Newbury asked.

"Haven't completely decided," Karp replied, "but I'm leaning toward going ahead with the late-January trial date. Louis thinks Lindahl is going to settle this one—at least that's what Denton believes. So I'm betting that he's not doing much to prepare, at least if the lack of action in the file is any indication. They're definitely not girding for war. So I'm thinking maybe we keep the date, only we get out ahead of the game before my appointment is officially announced and Louis realizes he's got a fight on his hands."

Karp handed out the assignments. He asked Fulton to assign a team of detectives from the DA's team to find Hannah Little. To Repass, Russell, and Guma he gave the task of going through the remaining boxes looking at "every slip of paper, every video. I don't want any surprises, unless they're on Louis. . . . And, ladies, I'm sure I don't have to tell you this as you used to work in this office and know full well that Mr. Guma is not to be trusted around good-looking women."

"Hey, hey, that was a cheap shot out of left field,"

Guma complained but leered at the two women who stuck out their tongues.

"Keep those in your mouths unless you intend to use them," he warned.

"On that note, I believe we can go on about our other business," Karp said.

"Oh, wait, speaking of notes," Guma said, refocusing on the subject at hand. "I wanted to mention a note—on one of those sticky pad pages—I found in one box. It had evidently fallen off of some other envelope or sheet. It doesn't say much, just 'Kaminsky letter . . . To Breman . . . re: Villalobos . . . FWD: Klinger.' I don't know what it means and a cursory search of all the boxes didn't turn up a letter from anyone named Kaminsky to Breman, so I'm assuming FWD means it got forwarded to Klinger. But if so, why wasn't a copy left in the file and why hasn't the Corporation Counsel been given a copy as the rules of evidence demand?"

"Have you called Breman or Klinger and inquired about it?" Russell asked.

Guma shook his head. "Nope. Of course that would be the logical step at some point, but at this point neither knows that Butch is involved with this case."

"And right now I'd rather keep it that way," Karp interjected.

"Are you suggesting some sort of hanky-panky between Breman and the judge?" Karp asked.

Guma shrugged. "Can't say. However, I also can't think of a reason why a letter from someone to the Brooklyn DA regarding Villalobos would be sent to the judge and then no one hears about it again. It would seem to be exculpatory."

"Well, as I said, we have a lot of work ahead of us," Karp said. "Let's get busy."

After everyone else had left, Kipman and Murrow remained seated. "Yes?" Karp asked.

It was Murrow who took the floor first. "I know I'll come off as the insensitive lout here, but I wouldn't be doing my job—at least not the part of my job that has to do with getting you elected—if I didn't voice my concerns about the ramifications of getting involved in this case." He took a quick glance at Kipman, who was studying his fingernails, before continuing. "I know you hate hearing this stuff but it's a political reality that race is going to be a hot button if you pursue this. I can hear Louis, and all the other race baiters, now whining about how the white establishment is defending a grave injustice by calling in its heavy hitter—in a role that's not even his to take—to persecute young black men. And the press will gladly go along with that ride for the fiery quotes if nothing else."

Kipman knitted his brow and appeared about to speak, so Murrow quickly went on. "I'm also sure your political opponent, whoever he turns out to be, will make a big deal about the Manhattan district attorney, who instead of getting criminals off the streets of Gotham apparently had enough time on his hands to take on a civil case in another jurisdiction."

"What about the police vote and the law and order types?" Kipman asked.

"He might pick something up there," Murrow conceded. "But the rank and file will be influenced by what the union bosses say, and I think it's pretty obvious to everyone here that the bosses are willing to let a few cops swing in the wind."

"Doesn't make it right," Kipman said.

"Look, it's not that I think this case shouldn't be fought tooth and nail," Murrow said, facing Karp. "And if you ask me, it seems like a slam dunk for the city defendants and all once Lindahl is out of there. All I'm asking is does it have to be you? The new mayor is going to have to pick a new Corporation Counsel, and he'll have a lot of qualified lawyers to choose from including—and I mean no disrespect here—some better qualified to take on a civil case than you."

"I don't take any offense, Gilbert," Karp said. "I've said and thought many of the same things and you deserve to hear the reason that tipped the scales for me when I was considering whether to accept this job. I was saving this speech for the trial, but I'll run it by you first."

Karp stuck his hands in his pockets and gathered himself as if giving the jury his trial summation. "This isn't just about Liz Tyler, though she deserves our protection and justice," he said. "Nor is it just about trying to keep these animals from winning millions from the city.

"What truly troubles me is that by acting as she has, the Brooklyn DA has destabilized and delegitimized the credibility of our justice system. She's placed in jeopardy law enforcement practices, methods, procedures, and techniques utilized in solving crime. To wit, she's exonerated guilty, puny, punk predators who committed vicious, unimaginable outrages against several innocent individuals, including Ms. Tyler. She's fractured the moral high ground and credibility of key and essential crime-solving methods. And she's enabled the guilty to turn the justice system upside down by illegitimately providing these assholes and their asshole lawyer the grounds to sue the city, my city, and those sworn to uphold the law for substantial money damages. Someone has got to stand up for the system, Gilbert, or we're all lost."

Karp looked at Murrow as if he were the last juror he knew he needed to convince. "They said it was fun, Gil.

They laughed about it. And now they want to be paid for it."

When he stopped talking the room was so quiet that Mrs. Milquetost, who had been standing at the office threshold, made the most dominant sound when she crossed herself and whispered, "May God have mercy."

It stayed that way until at last Murrow sighed and nodded his head. "Okay. How can I help?"

18

Tuesday, December 21

"SAY, IF IT AIN'T ZAK THE HACK AND G-DAWG. YOU
boys up for a little balling?" Khalif Mohammed arced a
fifteen-foot jumper at the basket—nothing but net—then
picked up his ball and walked over to the twins, who'd
just arrived at the courts.

Exchanging high fives and homeboy handshakes,
Giancarlo looked up at the tall, young black man. "We
heard the good news from our dad. You guys don't have
to worry about prison anymore."

"Yeah." Mohammed smiled. "Now I can get on with
it."

Zak furrowed his dark eyebrows. "Aren't you mad?
Like Rashad? I'd be mad if someone lied about something I'd done and I had to go to prison."

"And got kicked out of college and lost my scholarship," Giancarlo added.

Mohammed reflected for a moment. Sometimes these
kids seemed a lot older to him than twelve-year-olds.
Maybe old souls, he thought. "I won't kid you," he said.
"I've been plenty mad over this. When I was lying on my

bed in that prison staring up at a steel ceiling, listening to all the crazy bullshit you hear at night on a cellblock, I wanted to kill somebody. Kill that woman who lied. Kill the prosecutor. Kill just anybody to take the anger out of me."

As he spoke, the boys were surprised to see that he had tears in his eyes. "But I placed myself in the hands of Allah and said 'His will be done,' and then I wasn't so mad anymore. I believe that Allah has it all planned out and that I just had to accept it, and try to be a better man than the people who wronged me. It helped me realize that I lost that part of my life, but I didn't lose my life . . . and for a young black man coming from my neighborhood that's saying something. I still got my health, I got my faith, and I can still play ball."

He dribbled rapid-fire, then once between his legs and back in front of the twins and laughed. "You two Jethros think you can hang with Black Magic?"

The twins laughed back and tried to get the ball, which he kept easily out of their reach. Zak pulled up and asked, "Where's Rashad?"

The question broke Mohammed's concentration, which allowed Giancarlo to steal the ball and take off for the basket. Mohammed bit his lip and looked down the street. "He'll be along here in just a minute. To be honest, he and I haven't been hangin' quite as tight lately."

"Are you guys still friends?" Giancarlo asked, dribbling back after missing a layup.

"Sure. Sure. He's just been spending a lot of time with some people I don't particularly care for . . . but we're brothers, have been since we were both in diapers, and always will be."

"What are you going to do now?" Zak asked. "With your life, I mean."

Mohammed shrugged his broad shoulders. "Not

entirely sure. There's still some legal things to clear up, but I want to go back to school. Maybe find someplace where I can still play ball and get my degree."

A nondescript sedan pulled up to the curb in front of the gate and Rashad Salaam got out of the passenger side. He scowled when he saw the twins, leaned back into the car, and said something to the driver, who sped away. Salaam entered the gate and pointed at Zak and Giancarlo. "Shit, K, why are you talking to them little muthafuckas?"

"Watch your mouth, Rashad," Mohammed replied. "They're just kids. They had nothing to do with what happened to us. You might remember, our lawyer said it was their daddy who signed the papers to drop the charges."

"Well, ain't that nice since we didn't do the crime, but we already did the time. You might remember that it was their daddy whose bitch brought the charges against us in the first place," Salaam replied. "And their daddy's bitch who put us in prison even when she knew that other ho had lied."

"It still wasn't the kids' fault. It's over, brother, time to move on."

Salaam turned and spit at the fence. "It ain't never going to be over. Our lives are ruined; all part of the white man's master plan to keep the brothers, especially Muslim brothers, down. Nits make lice, man. Those two may be innocent little kids now, but they'll grow up to be just like their daddy and all the rest of the white muthafuckas—especially Jews like these two here and their daddy—that live off the sweat and blood of brown people all over the world. Unless we put a stop to it."

Mohammed scoffed. "We put a stop to it? You've been hanging out too much with the Arab brothers at the mosque, man. Everything's a Jewish conspiracy to them with Americans just following along like dumb sheep.

They never bother to ask Arab leaders where'd all that oil money go besides them fancy palaces and fine cars. How come 'we' ain't helping all them Palestinians in the refugee camps with that oil money?"

"Man, you starting to sound like The Man," Salaam said. "Or maybe you just his nigger."

Mohammed dropped the ball and started to walk toward his friend. "Who you calling a nigger, niggah?"

Giancarlo tugged on Mohammed's arm. "That's okay. Zak and I will just go shoot on the other court." He turned and started to walk away.

"No, you hold on, G-man." Mohammed looked back at his friend. "Come on, Rashad. I'm going to shoot hoops with these kids. Let's play a little hoop."

"Hell, no," Salaam said and turned to leave the way he'd come.

"See you tonight?" Mohammed called after his friend, who just kept walking without turning to indicate he'd heard.

Mohammed watched him go, and the twins could see he was hurt. But then he stopped watching and dribbled toward the basket, pulling up to shoot a ten-foot brick that bounced off the rim. Retrieving the ball, he looked back at the twins. "Hey, we going to play or what?"

After an hour, a dark Lincoln town car pulled up at the curb and the boys' father got out from the rear seat. He waved them over. The twins high-fived Mohammed and sauntered off the court to show that they were going, but on their own terms.

"Hi, Dad," they said. Then bending over to look at the driver, they added, "Hi, Clay."

Zak pointed back at the court. "That's Khalif Mohammed, one of the basketball players who went to prison."

Karp glanced over at the young man who stood with his ball tucked under his arm. "I know," he said. "I remember seeing him in a couple of games. He sure knows how to play ball."

"Want to meet him?"

"Maybe some other day," Karp replied. He didn't want to get into how Mohammed and his codefendant might very well sue the city because of Rachman's foul-up and that it wasn't appropriate to make contact with him now. "Let's go grab some hot dogs at Nathan's; I've got to meet someone near there briefly." Surprised but delighted, the boys hopped in the car for the ride across the Brooklyn Bridge.

The Karp family males debarked from the car at the corner of Stillwell and Surf Avenues, looking up at the Nathan's Famous Frankfurters sign like pilgrims at a shrine. They ordered two dogs each, three orders of fries, and three sodas, which cost in the neighborhood of twenty-five bucks. Then the twins listened patiently as their dad groused—as he did every time they went to Nathan's—about how things had changed since he used to come there as a boy. "Back then, my mom would give me a dollar bill, which would get me three dogs, fries, and a soda, and I'd still have change left over. Back then, they cooked them on a grill outside during the summer and you could smell them sizzling and popping with just a trace of garlic as soon as you got off the Stillwell Avenue subway station. Back then . . ."

As soon as they'd wolfed their dogs and washed the remains down with their soft drinks, the twins clamored to go to the boardwalk at the end of Stillwell. "Can we go over to the water?" Zak asked.

Karp looked at his watch. "Sure, just stay in sight," he said.

The twins jumped out of their shoes and were scampering across the sand before he could come up with any other rules. Karp watched them go, then turned to look down the boardwalk toward Brighton Beach. His eyes were drawn to the amusement park and the Ferris wheel.

After a moment Karp turned his eyes from the Ferris wheel and looked in the opposite direction. Two hundred yards away was the pier, a dark, forbidding structure. He'd never thought of it that way when he was a boy and liked to go stand out on the end and watch the fishermen. But it had been tainted by what Jayshon Sykes and his gang had done to Liz Tyler in its shadows. Part of the reason he'd asked the boys if they wanted to visit Nathan's was so that he could fix in his mind the scene of the crime as he prepared for trial.

There was, however, another reason for the trip to Coney Island. That reason, he saw as he looked back toward Brighton Beach, was walking slowly down the boardwalk toward him.

Karp was surprised at how old the man seemed. He walked bent over with a cane and seemed frail. When he was a boy and would sometimes see the man at his grandfather's house, he'd seemed huge. The man would pick him up and hold him level with his eyes. "Have you been a good boy?" he would always ask, his English heavily accented.

When Butch nodded his head, the man would put him back down. Then he'd reach in his pocket and pull out a piece of saltwater taffy wrapped in wax paper. The man—whom he called Uncle, although the relationship was never quite clear back then—never remained long after they arrived. When Butch got older, he sensed that his father wasn't comfortable around him, and the two men treated each other with a sort of stiff politeness.

Over the years, Karp had seen the man only rarely. He'd sent him an announcement when he married Marlene, and two weeks later a wedding gift had arrived—an expensive set of Russian nesting dolls, ornately trimmed in gold leaf—but his wife had never met him. There were good reasons for this—reasons that explained his father's coolness—but Karp was delighted to see the man now.

"Uncle," he said, smiling as he walked up to the old man and hugged him, aware of the large younger man who hovered discreetly in the background.

"Good to see you, nephew," the old man responded. "It has been too long."

After giving the old man a brief rundown of the family's health and happiness, pointing out the twins who were chasing each other at the water's edge, he asked the old man why he'd called and asked for this meeting.

"Well, I know you are running for the office of district attorney," the old man began, "and I just wanted to express my concern that if some person in the newspapers or television should make some connection between you, me, and my family's . . . enterprises . . . it might not be a good thing."

Karp patted the old man on his shoulder. "They never have before," he replied. "I don't know why they would now. And if they do, I can tell them the truth. We are family but distant, unfortunately, and I really don't know anything about these enterprises. Nor do I want to . . . as we've always said, 'That's in Brooklyn.' "

The old man laughed. "Good, good. Yes, I have kept our family matters out of Manhattan—at least since you returned from law school and began to make a nuisance of yourself to my good friends the Italians and other 'businessmen,' not to mention the other foul and evil men you have dealt with."

"And I appreciate that," Karp said and smiled in return.

The old man looked out toward the twins, who'd noticed their father talking to someone and had started to walk toward them. "They are fine-looking boys," he said. "They've had a . . . shall we say, exciting life so far. And Lucy, she is well?"

"Yes, she's doing great," Karp replied. "She's in New York at the moment."

"I've heard. Seeing a cowboy, I believe."

"How did you . . . ," Karp started to say, but stopped himself. He knew there was no threat to his family from this man, and how he gathered his information was his own business.

The old man's face grew serious. "Before the boys arrive, I want to get to the main reason I asked you to meet me. My sources tell me that your wife has agreed to help the women who prosecuted those pigs who raped that woman over there," the old man said, nodding toward the pier.

Karp saw no point in lying, although he was not going to volunteer any information about his own involvement. "Yes, she's working for the city attorney defending the case."

"Ah, yes. She is a tough one, and would have made a good addition to the 'family business' if her husband was not such a . . . what is the word I want . . . ah, a Goody Two-shoes," he said laughing again.

Karp laughed, too, and waited for the other shoe to drop.

"Anyway, I have some information that might help her."

"What's that?"

"Tell her that she should find the man who was in the prison cell with this lying bastard, Villalobos. Tell her that the man's name is Igor . . . Igor Kaminsky."

Karp couldn't keep the surprise off his face. "Kaminsky?"

"Yes, and I can see that it is a name you have heard," the old man replied. "Good, then perhaps this information is old news."

"Can you tell me any more about him or where to find him?" Karp asked. "Is he still in prison?"

The old man shook his head. "No, he is free. But I cannot tell you more than this. I am already breaking a confidence. Anyway, your boys arrive."

The twins ran up and stopped a few yards shy. "Giancarlo and Isaac, this is . . . an old friend of your great-grandfather," Karp said.

"Where do you live?" Zak asked.

"Brighton Beach," the old man said, pointing back over his shoulder. "Have you been good boys?"

The twins nodded their heads. "Most of the time," Giancarlo added for honesty's sake.

The old man looked at Karp with his hand in his pocket and a twinkle in his eye. "May I?" he asked, pulling two wax-wrapped pieces of saltwater taffy from his pocket.

Karp nodded although he couldn't speak because of the lump in his throat. The old man handed the candy to the twins, who barely had time to say thanks before popping the taffy into their mouths.

"You're welcome," he said. "Now, we say good-bye. But do me this favor."

"What?" the twins asked.

"Grow up to be good men like your father."

19

Tuesday, December 21

MARLENE WAS LOOKING FORWARD TO AN AFTER-
noon alone. The twins had run out of the house, headed
for the basketball court; they'd be going on from there to
bar mitzvah class with Butch so she'd probably have the
evening, too.

Lucy and John Jojola were still staying at the loft, but
they'd been spending a lot of time out at night on some
mysterious mission they wouldn't talk about. She figured
that it had something to do with Jojola's notion that David
Grale was still alive, although the evidence indicated that
it wasn't very likely. John, who'd offered to stay in a hotel
but Marlene wouldn't hear of it, said he wasn't sure
either. He seemed almost embarrassed to admit that the
only thing he was going on was a recurring dream.

"My old friend Charlie Many Horses came to me
and said I needed to find David Grale," he told her.
"When I told him Grale was dead, he turned his back
and walked away. I could be misinterpreting—sometimes the spirits are not very clear about what they're
trying to say—but I thought I should come and at least

try to do what Charlie asked. It can be a mistake to
ignore the spirits, too."

Marlene had not dismissed Jojola's dream as metaphysical nonsense. She knew that he was a deeply spiritual man—a member of the Gray Coyote, a spiritual
clan—and that he believed that the spirits talked to those
who listened.

Then again, when you're the mother of Lucy Karp,
who regularly claimed to converse with a martyred saint,
you get used to the people around you having strange
invisible companions. And Lucy said she'd been having a
dream similar to Jojola's. Neither would go into any detail
about what the dream entailed, but Marlene could sense
that it greatly disturbed them both, and if she hadn't
known Jojola's courageous spirit, she would have thought
he was afraid.

Whatever their reasons were, ever since their arrival
Lucy and Jojola left in the morning and often did not
return until late at night, long after the "old folks" had
gone to bed. So Marlene had found a good book and was
looking forward to her first concentrated and quiet hours
of pure reading in months, when the telephone rang.

"Marlene!" said the nearly hysterical voice of her
father. "Your mother is missing again!" He started sobbing.

"Calm down, Dad, I'm sure everything's all right," she
said, seeing her dream of an evening alone with a book
pop like a soap bubble. "Have you looked everywhere?
Remember, she was in the basement the last time."

"Everywhere, everywhere," he cried. "She even left a
note on the refrigerator. 'Gone to walk Barney.' She's
crazy, Marlene."

Marlene sighed. Barney was the family beagle, dead
for more than forty years. Her mother had been his

favorite person in the family, and she'd returned the love, letting him sit on her lap while she watched television and sleep on the bed. "She's not crazy, Pops, she has Alzheimer's . . . it's a disease," she said, trying to sound convincing.

"Marlene . . . she left her clothes at the front door."

"I'll be right over."

Marlene drove as quickly as she could to her parents' home. So quickly that she nearly missed seeing the elderly naked woman strolling along the sidewalk four blocks from her house, dragging an old dog leash. Her mother appeared to be looking for something but apparently couldn't see or didn't care about the two young boys who danced around her, pointing and laughing.

Screeching to a stop at the curb, Marlene jumped out of her car. "Get the hell out of here, you little bastards," she yelled. The boys took one look at her face and ran off, yelling "crazy old bag lady" over their shoulder.

Marlene flipped the boys off, then turned to her mother. "Mom, Mom, what are you doing?" she said, whipping off her coat to cover her mother.

The old woman was shivering from the cold but brightened when she looked up and recognized her daughter. "Marlene," she said. "How nice of you to come help me look for Barney. That rascal got out, and I'm afraid he's going to dig up Mrs. Johansen's rose garden again."

Mrs. Johansen, like Barney, had departed the earth decades earlier, but Marlene took it as a hopeful sign that her mother had called her by name.

"But what are you doing home, dear?" her mother said, a look of concern crossing her face. "Is something wrong? Why are you out of school already?"

Marlene put her arm around her mother's shoulders

and guided her to the car. "Come on, Mom, let's go home," she said. "Pops is worried."

"Oh, that man," her mother said. "He's impossible. 'Do this. Do that.' Who does he think he is, my husband?"

When Marlene arrived home with her mother, her father was standing at the door. He tromped out of the house, and before Marlene, who was coming around from the driver's side, could intervene, grabbed her mother by the shoulders and shook her. "Where the hell have you been, Concetta?" he shouted. "Walking around the neighborhood without your clothes. I'm ashamed of you."

"Help me," her mother screamed.

"Pops!" Marlene shouted, jumping between her parents. "What are you doing?"

Her father backed off, panting, with a wild look in his eyes. He pointed at his wife. "She's just doing this to torment me," he said. "There's nothing wrong with her. She just wants to give me a heart attack." He turned and fled into the house.

"I don't know that man," her mother said. "That's not Mariano. I don't know what they did with my poor husband but that's not him." She started to cry. "Oh, I just want to die."

"Don't talk like that, Mom," Marlene said.

"I don't care. I don't care," the old woman yelled and fled upstairs to her bedroom, where she closed and locked the door. Marlene followed and knocked but her mother responded, "Go away. Just go away."

Marlene left and went downstairs, where she found her father kneeling in front of the small family shrine to the Virgin Mary. He'd lit a candle and was praying fervently but so low that she couldn't hear him. When he finished, he looked up at his daughter.

"I'm sorry, Marlene . . . I . . . I don't know what came over me," he said. "I'm just tired. And ashamed. Ashamed that I go to confession and have to tell the priest that I sometimes wish that the woman I love was dead. But I don't, you know . . . I don't want her to die, I just want her back."

Marlene knelt beside her father. "I know, Dad," she said. "But you heard the doctor when we took her in for her checkup the last time. She's not going to get better. In fact, she's going to get worse, until she doesn't know anyone . . . not you . . . not even herself. It's the disease, Dad, and no amount of praying is going to bring Mom back. If you can't deal with that then you need to let me look into putting her into a nursing facility where they can take care of her."

Her father had resisted all efforts to remove her mother from the home they'd shared for fifty years. Nor would he listen now. "It would kill her to be in such a horrible place. Like a prison they are," he said. "At least here, she recognizes her things and seems happy most of the time, even if she's on another planet. And those nursing homes . . . you hear stories about what they do to old people . . . sometimes alone at night . . . I can't let that happen to her."

"Dad, I know you want to keep looking after her," Marlene said. "But there's going to be a day when she's going to be better off in the hands of professionals who know this disease and know how to minimize the impact on her. I have plenty of money, and you've never let me help with anything, so let me help with this. We can find the best there is where those bad things don't happen. You can visit her anytime you want. But she'll get the care she needs, and you won't have to worry about her so much."

But her father shook his head. "I'm not ready," he said. "Sixty-six years we've been married. Sixty-six years of sleeping in the bed next to the same person. What would I do without her? No, Marlene . . . we do okay most of the time. Maybe later. You go home now; sorry you had to come all the way out here to deal with your crazy old parents."

Marlene looked at her father. He was a stubborn man; he'd ignored the prejudices and conquered the obstacles and built a good life for himself and his family. But that stubbornness could be hard to deal with at times, too.

"Okay, Pops, we leave it alone for now," she said. "But you can't let your frustrations get to you so that you end up hurting or yelling at Mom. She's already afraid of a world that is closing in on her; she needs your love and support, even when she's not all there. When the day comes when you can't deal with it anymore, you have to promise me that you'll tell me so that we can find a place. Promise me?"

The old man nodded and hugged her. "Yeah, yeah. Like I said, I don't know what came over me. I've never hit your mother in sixty-six years of marriage. So now it looks like I'll have to go have another talk with the priest."

Marlene kissed her father's cheek and patted him on the back. "You do that," she said. "But don't be too hard on yourself. You've been the best husband a woman could ever wish for . . . and the best dad."

That evening, Marlene was grateful when Butch and the boys got back home, and he told her about the note Guma had found in the file. "Regards some letter from a guy named Kaminsky about Villalobos that Breman apparently received and passed on to Judge Klinger." What made that even more interesting was that "an old friend" told him that he should pass on the name *Igor Kaminsky* to her as the former cellmate of Enrique Villalobos.

Marlene knew that more murderers had probably been caught because they opened their big mouths than because of all the detective work ever attempted. Prisoners were notorious for boasting about their crimes, if for no other reason than to make themselves seem tougher and meaner, so that maybe they wouldn't have to prove it physically. But their "friends" and cellmates were equally notorious for ratting them out to the authorities, hoping to work out some sort of deal in exchange for information.

The next morning, Marlene called a friend with the Department of Corrections, who told her yes, Igor Kaminsky had served time at Auburn and yes, Igor Kaminsky had been kept in a cell with Enrique Villalobos for a short time that past spring. "But he's not there now," said the friend, a middle-aged black woman she'd once helped protect from her abusive husband. "In fact, there seems to have been a screwup. He was paroled and let go but was supposed to be handed over to the INS to deport back to Russia. Instead, they just gave him some bus money, a suit, and let him go—we have no idea where. But a start might be Brooklyn; that's where he got arrested on the robbery charge that planted his ass in the pen. If they catch him, it'll be good-bye New York, hello Moscow. Hey, that's funny. . . ."

"What's funny?"

"Well, there's a federal BOLO for him. 'Consider armed and dangerous.' Pretty heavy-duty for a one-armed—"

"He's got one arm?"

"Yep, just like the bad dude in *The Fugitive*. Makes sense, don't it. Anyway, someone got a federal judge to issue a bench warrant for his arrest. They must want him back pretty damn bad for a one-armed, small-time crook who, according to his dossier, was so bad at his job that he let a Korean shopkeeper take his gun and nearly blow his ass away."

"Not exactly Public Enemy Number One, eh?"

"Not exactly."

"Who was the judge?"

"Let's see . . . Marci Klinger. Hey, ain't she the one presiding over the Coney Island case?" There was silence from the other end of the line. "Marlene? You there?"

"Yeah, I'm here. Just . . . writing this down. Um . . . I don't suppose there's anything else in that file of interest—like maybe Igor was the second shooter on the grassy knoll in Dallas? Igor's Russian, right? Maybe Oswald *was* working with the Soviets."

"Too young," her friend said with a laugh. "But as a matter of fact, I was just about to tell you . . . your Kennedy assassin was almost assassinated himself. Shortly before his parole, he got stabbed in the stomach by another inmate named Lonnie Lynd. And that's even more interesting because—this part ain't in Kaminsky's file 'cause it happened after he left, just four days ago as a matter of fact—if I'm remembering this right, I saw a report that an inmate named Lonnie Lynd got his neck snapped by some Russian dude named Svetlov."

"Snapped his neck?"

"That's what it says, but there ain't a lot of detail. Just that they were playing basketball."

"Full-contact sport."

"Yep. You might talk to Dr. Ron Jendry; he's the gang

counselor at Auburn. This gang ball project is his pet. He probably knew both guys."

"Anything else?"

"Nope. That's pretty much it. Oh, one last thing . . . it says here that he listed his brother, same DOB, as his next of kin in case anything happened to him in prison. The brother's name is Ivan. Igor and Ivan, the Russian twins."

"Any address for Ivan?"

"No. But it says to contact Ivan through a Father Stefan Sarandinaki with the Russian Orthodox Church in Brighton Beach, and I suppose that's a start."

"It is indeed," Marlene said. "Thanks, I got to run, but I owe you big."

"How about we go dutch for lunch next time I'm in the city?"

"Nope. Like I said, I owe you. I'm paying or don't bother to call."

"Okay, okay," the woman said with a laugh. "You're paying. See you soon, honey."

Marlene hung up and whistled. When her friend named Marci Klinger as the judge who'd signed off on the bench warrant, Marlene's hesitation to respond had a lot more to do with shock than because she was writing something down.

She knew from Butch that some sort of message or letter had apparently gone from Kaminsky, a potential material witness, to Breman to Klinger. Yet nothing had been said about the letter to Corporation Counsel.

So what is up with the judge? Marlene wondered. Did Breman receive the information and, not knowing what to make of it, went to the judge for guidance? The Kings County DA had just announced that her office would be settling with the defendants for an undisclosed amount—

believed by the press, who'd probably been tipped off by Louis, to be in the neighborhood of twenty million dollars. But that wasn't even a tenth of what Louis was suing the city of New York for, and he'd filed the papers intending to go after the ADAs and cops individually.

Breman must have made a sweetheart deal, she thought. Louis never even tried to squeeze that turnip for any more than he got.

After talking to her friend, Marlene had hung up and immediately called Auburn and asked to speak to Jendry. The man answered his telephone but was reluctant to say anything until she mentioned that she was the wife of the district attorney of New York.

"Butch Karp?" Jendry perked up. "He probably won't remember me, but I was a freshman on the Brooklyn High basketball team when he was a senior. . . . Terrible what happened to his mother that year. . . . But man, could he post up and drain the bucket. I'd hoped to follow his career in the NBA, but at least I've been able to keep track of him at the DA's office. He's not exactly flying under the radar down there, is he?"

"No, Butch is pretty much flying where everybody can launch missiles at him," Marlene said, amused at the man's still-evident hero worship.

"It's funny they still call him Butch," the psychologist said. "Tell him hi from Birdlegs Jendry."

"I certainly will, and if you're ever in the city, you ought to look him up," Marlene said. "He loves to talk about the good old days with old friends." Actually, Butch rarely talked about the "good old days"; he wasn't one to live in the past, but the thought of Birdlegs Jendry, whom he'd never mentioned, dropping in on him unexpectedly was too rich for her to miss the opportunity to set him up.

"I will," Jendry said, sounding extremely pleased. "Wow! Now, that's what I call serendipity. So, what was it you needed, Marlene? I hope you don't mind me calling you Marlene, but I feel as if I know you."

"No, not at all," Marlene said. "Any friend or former teammate of Butch Karp is a friend of mine. I insist . . . Ron. It's nothing much. I'm just trying to find out what I can about a former inmate named Igor Kaminsky, who was apparently stabbed by another inmate named Lonnie Lynd."

"Oh, yes," Jendry sighed. "Terrible business, these gangs. So much violence, most of it traceable back to their dysfunctional families and growing up without male role models in the ghetto. Such a hard pattern to change."

Gag me, Marlene thought. Rehashed sixties psychopablum. She doubted Butch would have had much to do with this former teammate. "I'm sure you're making a real difference," she said.

"Well, I'm trying, but to be honest, some days I just want to throw my hands up and go work for McDonald's," Jendry said with a great theatrical sigh. "The ones like Lynd and Svetlov . . . they're incorrigible. Lynd's dead, you know. Svetlov broke his neck like you'd snap a pencil, and Lynd was a big guy."

"What started the fight?" Marlene asked.

"That's just it, who knows? One minute they're playing a game of basketball, the next there's a riot with the Bloods and Russians going at it like a pack of wild dogs."

"Bloods? The gang?"

"Yes, yes. The Bloods gang. Hard-core gangbangers, but the Russians are just as rough and better organized. Anyway, Lynd gets his hand on a knife of some sort, but Svetlov, a hulking brute if I've ever seen one, just sort of grabbed him and *pop*, Lynd's dead."

"Svetlov say what started it?" Marlene asked.

"Nope. The snitches we have in the general population are saying that it was planned retaliation for the attack on Kaminsky. He seemed to have some sort of pull with the Russian mob. But Sergei's not talking, except to note, correctly, that Lynd pulled a knife on him. Self-defense, he says. But we got him in lockdown anyway."

"So what do you think my chances are of getting Svetlov to talk to me?"

"None and none," Jendry replied. "He's a stone-cold killer. The Russian mob's main muscle, and absolutely loyal to his bosses. He doesn't say anything they don't tell him to say."

Marlene hung up. Well, won't hurt to ask, she thought. Several hours later, she wasn't so sure when, with a buzz and a metallic snap, hidden bolts slid into place and the steel bars of the gate in front of her slid open. "Please step forward," said a monotone male voice whose owner she assumed was behind the dark window of the control booth. She did as told, stepping into what amounted to a cage large enough for one, and fought a momentary urge to retreat before the gate slid home behind her.

Silly, she thought as the gate closed, they have to let you out. She thought of the "release from liability" form she'd had to sign just to get this far, especially the part that said if she was taken hostage by the inmates, the Department of Corrections would not negotiate for her release. She'd be on her own.

There was more buzzing and metallic clicks, and the next gate in front of her slid open. "Step forward, please," the voice said again. Ever since she'd been escorted beyond the waiting room, which at least made an attempt at softening the scenery with a few magazines, a television set to CNN, and a motley collection of children's toys in a corner, every sound seemed magnified, as if unable to find anything to absorb its energy in all that steel and cement. God, I'd go insane if I was locked up, she thought. A good reminder to stay on the straight and narrow, Ciampi.

As soon as she stepped into the hall beyond the cage, she was met by a hard-eyed, square-jawed corrections officer. He handed her a Visitor badge. "Place this somewhere visible and keep it on you at all times," he instructed. "Follow me." Without waiting for a reply, he turned and led the way down a long, brightly lit hallway of gray-painted cinder blocks.

Reaching a row of doors, each marked with a letter of the alphabet, he opened the one marked B. She looked inside and saw that it was a tiny interview room with a single mushroom-shaped metal stool bolted to the floor in front of a window she was sure was probably capable of stopping an automobile. This was max at Auburn State Prison—not the most hard-line in New York's prison system but no joke, either.

"Have a seat, he'll be here in a minute," the guard said and closed the door behind her.

Marlene sat down on the stool and picked up the telephone receiver from its place on the wall to listen. Nothing but a slight buzzing noise. The walls were white and glossy; there were no nooks and crannies, no place to hide anything, even if they hadn't confiscated her purse and searched her before letting her proceed. A horrible place. Then again, she thought, it's designed to secure and punish pretty horrible people. She looked up and saw the eyes of a camera gazing down at her. Nothing would go unnoticed, not that she had any intention of trying.

A door in the room opposite her opened and the largest human being Marlene had ever seen shuffled in. His massive wrists were cuffed to a chain that ran around his belly and between his legs. She assumed the shuffling was because he was shackled. He stood blinking in the bright light, looking at her as a guard unlocked the fastener holding the handcuffs to the belly chain while two more guards looked on. He waited for them to back out of the room before he took a seat on the stool.

Marlene picked up the telephone. When he made no move to do the same, she indicated he should do so with her head. He gave her a bored look but reached up and plucked the telephone off the wall with his manacled hands.

"*Da?*" the big man said.

"Sergei Svetlov?" Marlene asked.

"Depends. Who vants to know this?" His baritone voice seemed to rumble up out of some deep dark well.

"Marlene Ciampi . . . I'm a private investigator working for Corporation Counsel in New York."

Svetlov shrugged. "Means na-think to me."

"It does to me," Marlene replied. Jendry was right—Svetlov wasn't likely to be very helpful. But it couldn't hurt to ask. "I was wondering if you could help me find Igor Kaminsky?"

Svetlov pursed his lips and said, "I don't know this man."

Marlene tried a different tack. "He's not in any trouble with the law. In fact, his life might be in danger, and I might be able to help."

"I tell you, I don't know this man," Svetlov said again.

"But you killed the man who tried to kill him," Marlene said. "Those people might try to kill him again."

Svetlov, whose big, round, scarred head reminded her

of a jack-o'-lantern, shrugged and said, "I killed the shitty man who tried to stab me . . . is self-defense."

Marlene looked at the man, who looked impassively back at her. "Well, thank you, Mr. Svetlov, for agreeing to meet with me," she said. "If you remember anything that might help me, you can contact Dr. Jendry and he'll be able to reach me."

Svetlov smiled, and she was surprised how pleasant it made his face. "Is not often I have visit from a beautiful woman. This pleasure is mine."

Hmm, a ladies' man; maybe a little of the old Ciampi sex kitten will turn the trick, Marlene thought. She smiled shyly and brushed a strand of her hair from in front of her eyes. "If you remember something important about Igor Kaminsky, I could come back up and talk to you again."

"Perhaps," Svetlov said in a way that let her know that he was on to her game and had, in fact, expected it. "But unfortunately, I do not know this man."

Ten minutes later, Marlene stepped outside the prison, relieved just to be beyond the clanging doors and metallic voices. It was only sixty miles down the road to the next stop in her Department of Corrections tour but a world of difference in attitude. The Roxbury Prison Farm was considered a model of humane and progressive incarceration for model prisoners. There were a few lifers at the farm, who for one reason or another had managed to get transferred there, but most were inmates who were expected to return to society as changed men.

The looming walls of Auburn were topped with razor wire and watched over by men with rifles in guard towers. But there was only a fifteen-foot-high chain-link fence between the inmates at Roxbury and freedom. There were no guard towers or men with guns in plain sight of the inmates. The guards patrolled in cars around the perimeter, but most of the security work was done by cameras.

The grounds of the prison farm were immaculately kept and appeared to have been professionally landscaped with bushes and trees. Beyond the campus, there were rows and rows of crop fields—barren now, but plowed and furrowed for the spring planting.

Hell, if they had a pool and a bar, I could almost live here, Marlene thought after a cursory check of her identification at the front gate. She pulled up to the building with the pretty painted sign that read Administration.

Again she had to invoke her husband's name to get the superintendent, an officious little mouse of a man named Andrew Vundershitz—an unfortunate but appropriate name—to cooperate. Vundershitz had a guard escort her to a waiting room with overstuffed chairs and a well-stocked magazine rack. The guard disappeared and a couple of minutes later reappeared with Enrique Villalobos, who was even uglier in person than the mugshot she'd seen.

The prisoner was wearing jeans and a clean blue prison shirt, but it was the only thing clean about him. His yellow, jaundiced eyes held hers for only a moment before drifting down to her breasts. The purple scars of a childhood bout with measles looked hideous against his ocher-colored skin. There was something about the way he combed his greasy black hair back from his pointed face and his rodentlike teeth that made her think of a large rat she'd seen once in the alley next to the loft building on Crosby.

The creature had seen her too—it was broad daylight—and rather than scurry away, stood on its hind legs and hissed at her. Marlene was no coward but there was something about the hissing rat that unnerved her and she'd turned and ran.

"You want me to stay in the room, ma'am?" the guard asked. He looked like a big, strong farm kid, probably from one of the neighboring farms, who was supplementing his income with a job at the local prison. He evidently thought it was a good idea if he remained.

"No, that's okay, officer," Marlene said. "I'll be fine."

"Yes, Officer Richardson," Villalobos sneered. "She'll be just fine. I'll treat her real good."

Officer Richardson pointed a thick finger at Villalobos. "You behave or if this lady complains, you and I will have a little discussion out by the toolshed."

Villalobos feigned a hurt look. "I wouldn't hurt a fly, Officer Richardson. You got no call to talk to me like that." Then he turned and leered at Marlene. "Obviously, this fine-looking bitch has heard that Enrique Villalobos is a stud and wants to find out for herself."

Marlene felt grateful that she was no longer carrying a gun. Otherwise, she thought, I might be tempted to wait for Officer Richardson to disappear, then put a hot one in this piece of shit's brain.

When she first agreed to take the case, Marlene had looked at Villalobos's PSI, the presentence investigation report done on every prisoner to give the judge some guidance on the appropriate place and severity of incarceration. The psychiatrists who'd examined Villalobos had recommended maximum security because of the likelihood that he would reoffend if he escaped. The psychologist had noted that Villalobos both hated and worshipped his mother, with a strong possibility, though it had been denied by both, that the mother had had sexual relations with her son from an early age. "It is felt by this board," the examining physicians wrote, "that the crime perpetrated on his victims was a way of acting out repressed anger at his mother. Yet, publicly at least, he professes a great love for her."

When Richardson left, closing the door behind him, Marlene smiled at Villalobos. "Mr. Villalobos, I'd like to talk to you about a friend of yours."

"Oh, yeah?" he said, placing his hand on his crotch. "I got lots of friends. Like the women I fucked. They always want more from their 'friend,' Enrique."

"Yes, I'm sure," she said sarcastically, but it didn't affect his smile or what he was doing with his hand. "But I'm here to talk about another man . . . Igor Kaminsky."

Villalobos's smile disappeared and his hand returned to the arm of his chair. "I don't know no fuckin' Kaminsky."

"No? The DOC's records say he was your cellmate at Auburn in February. About the time you 'confessed' to the rape of Liz Tyler."

"I remember sweet Liz, all right," Villalobos said, regaining his composure. "I always remember them tight asses I fuck. Um, um, it's so g-o-o-o-d."

Marlene again wished she was packing heat, or at least a Taser, but forced herself to continue. "Well, I just thought you might be interested to know that Mr. Kaminsky has been in contact with the Brooklyn DA's office."

Villalobos scowled. "Oh, yeah, now I remember that lying sack of shit. I think I fucked him, too, in my cell. That's what I do to liars and bitches."

"That's what you did until you had a 'positive prison experience' and found Jesus, right?"

The smile returned to the convict's face. "Thas right, bitch. Me and God is tight like this," he said, crossing his fingers.

"Yeah, Enrique, I'm sure God has something special

planned for such a good friend . . . someplace cold and dark and alone except for the voice shrieking in your head," she snarled.

The sudden turn in her demeanor shocked him at first. But he recovered and hissed, "Fuck you, bitch . . . when I get out of here—and you better believe I will—I'm going to come visit you and do what I did to sweet Lizzie."

Marlene fought to keep that other side of her—the one she'd been trying to conquer—from jumping up and ripping Villalobos's heart out through his throat. She only partly succeeded as she leaned forward. "Listen, you fuck. When I leave here, you ask some of your piece-of-shit friends, if you have any, if they know Marlene Ciampi. Ask them, ass wipe, if they think that there's maybe something not quite right about her, in fact, maybe something's quite wrong. I know a lot of really bad people in the world, and some of them owe me favors. And maybe before you can get out, I send a few of them to visit your mother—I believe she's still living over off West Fourth in Brooklyn—and I have them do to her what you did to Liz Tyler."

Marlene's threat to have the man's mother raped—one she would not have wished on any woman no matter what the provocation—had the desired effect on Villalobos. "You go near my momma, and I'll kill you," he hissed again only louder. "I will hunt you down and rape you, and slit you open like a chicken."

"I'll bet she screams like crazy when they do to her what you did to Liz," Marlene said. "I bet she cries and begs for her son Enrique to save her . . . but he won't be able to because he's locked up here."

"Fucking whore," Villalobos screamed and lurched out of his chair at her.

Out in the hall, Officer Richardson heard the scream

and rushed for the door. But before he could get it open to rescue the pretty woman inside, something had happened to the prisoner, whom he found lying on the ground gasping for air and clutching his sides.

"What happened to him?" Richardson said with an amused look.

"I think he hurt himself stumbling against the chair," Marlene said. "But you might want to get him to the infirmary." She tapped Villalobos in the side with the toe of her boot, which caused him to scream in pain. "I do believe he broke his ribs in the fall."

"Yeah," Richardson smiled. "Good thing I saw the whole thing or he might have tried to accuse you of beating the tar out of him."

Marlene grinned back at him. "Oh, my, yes, good thing. I wouldn't want something like that to hurt my reputation."

20

NO SOONER DID MARLENE WALK IN THE LOFT
door from her tour of New York's penal colonies than
she began to tell Butch, who stood in the dimly lit
kitchen, about her encounters with Svetlov and Villalobos. "That greasy piece of crap, Villalobos, is your proto-
typical prison braggart. It wouldn't surprise me in the
least that he said something to Kaminsky that he regretted later and told Sykes, who tried to have him killed by
Lynd."

She paused and pursed her lips in concentration as she
looked out the window. "Svetlov may have just been retal-
iating—after all, in the jungle you can't just let the other
guys go running around sticking shivs in your guys. You
have to answer. But I get a feeling that there's more to it
than that. We need to find Kaminsky."

Only then did she look back and catch the look on her
husband's face. "What's wrong?"

"Kaminsky's dead," he said.

Butch explained that he'd asked Guma to nose
around and see what he could find out about Kaminsky.

His old friend had connections in the criminal under-world that would have done any wiseguy proud. Butch occasionally wondered about the extent of those connections, but it had always been a sort of unspoken rule, like the army's "Don't ask, don't tell."

This time it wasn't Guma's mob sources that tipped him off, it was the Kings County Medical Examiner. Karp was just getting ready to leave his office that afternoon when Guma walked in and announced that he'd located "one I. Kaminsky. Or, what's left of him. He's down at the Brooklyn morgue. Apparently, some guy shoved him in front of a subway train. My friend at the ME's says it ain't pretty, but I'm headed over there to see if there's anything interesting in his personal effects."

"Well, that sucks—to use one of the twins' favorite expressions," Marlene said to her husband. "Whatever Kaminsky had to say about Villalobos—if anything—is now in the hands of Judge Marci Klinger. But for some reason, she's chosen not to say anything about it, although judging by the note in the file, she's had several months to consider it."

"So what's your next move?" Karp asked.

"Guess I need to visit Marci Klinger."

"Just going to walk up and ask her for the letter, eh?"

"Yep."

"Sounds like a plan," he said. "Maybe it will shake her honor up a bit if nothing else."

On Christmas Eve day, Marlene showed up at the federal courthouse on Centre Street intending to do just that. The building was only a block from the Streets of Calcutta where Butch worked, but a world apart in demeanor. The swirling, smelly mass of arguing, shouting, crying humanity was replaced by lawyers in thousand-dollar suits who quietly went about their business, sometimes conversing under their breath with equally well-dressed clients as if they were in a library.

When she reached the judge's office on the fourth floor, Marlene tried to breeze past the pretty, young black woman sitting at the reception desk. Nothing doing.

"May I help you?" the young woman asked as she stood to block the door to the judge's chambers.

"I hope so," Marlene said. "I'm here to see Judge Klinger."

"Your name?" The young woman glanced at the calendar on her desk.

"Marlene Ciampi, but you won't find me on the calendar."

The young woman frowned. "I'm sorry, but if you don't have an appointment—"

"I think the judge ought to hear me out anyway," Marlene said loudly, having decided on the bold frontal attack. Law clerks for U.S. District Court judges were used to the imperious nature of their bosses and tended to respond only when they believed that they were outranked. But this girl wasn't budging.

"A lot of people would like to speak with Judge Klinger," she said, her face still friendly but also indicating she was not going to take any grief. "Perhaps you'd like to make an appointment."

Marlene continued speaking as if she thought the clerk might be nearly deaf. "My name's Marlene Ciampi. I'm a private investigator working for Brooklyn assistant district attorneys Robin Repass and Pam Russell regarding the so-called Coney Island Four case. I believe the judge would like to hear what I have to say before I tell it to the press."

It was all a bluff—a course of action she'd decided on after she got the bad news about Kaminsky from Butch.

He'd suggested that she might shake up the judge but so far she wasn't even shaking up a young law clerk. "Look, Ms. . . ."

"Verene Fischer," the young woman said, holding out her hand. "I know who you are, Ms. Ciampi. I'd like to prosecute sex crimes someday myself, and I have great admiration for the program you set up with the New York District Attorney's Office. And, of course, everybody knows your husband. But I'm just a law clerk . . . the judge's receptionist is gone and I've been left with instructions that she's not to be disturbed. I hope you understand my dilemma."

Well, guess I just got taught a lesson in diplomacy by a child, Marlene thought. She liked this girl. "Yeah, I do, Verene . . . sorry, guess I was pushing a little hard," she said.

Verene grinned. "I would have been disappointed with anything less from Marlene Ciampi."

The law clerk was interrupted when the door to the judge's chambers opened. Marci Klinger stood framed in the doorway. "May I help you?" she said in a way that indicated that she was in no mood to be helpful.

Marlene's practiced eye did a quick assessment of the black-robed jurist. Klinger was in her late fifties and looked every day of it, although she was making attempts to stave off the inevitable. Her face had that stretched, brittle look of a woman who'd tried both face-lifts and acid peels. She'd tried to disguise the rest with too much blue eye shadow for a woman her age and a lipstick color that seemed to indicate she was color-blind. Klinger still wore her hair in a bouffant that had been popular in the early sixties and went to some lengths to keep it the same color it had been back then—a sort of wheat blond—and it was held in place with at least a can of hairspray.

Verene handled the introductions. "Judge Klinger, this is Marlene Çiampi. She dropped by and was asking if she could have a moment of your time," she said, hastily adding, "I told her you asked not to be disturbed."

"That's all right, Verene," Klinger said coolly. "Ms. Ciampi and I met many years ago, although most of what I know about her is her reputation . . . something of a mixed bag, that reputation, eh Marlene?"

Marlene felt like punching Klinger. "I guess that depends on who you ask . . . the people I've worked for . . . or the people I've put in prison, or . . . killed."

"Yes, yes, all sorts of allegedly bad men have met an untimely end at your hands," Klinger said. "But to be honest, vigilantes don't impress me. In fact, I think they're just as deserving of a prison sentence as the people they go after."

"You may be right," Marlene responded. "Then again, I've known a few jurists who deserve a little time in the big house as well."

Klinger glared at Marlene, then made a face as if she'd tasted something sour. "Might I ask what was so pressing that you didn't feel it necessary to call like any other person and ask for an appointment?"

Although she was seething, Marlene kept a half-smile on her face because she could tell it was irritating Klinger. "Well, I do apologize for just showing up, your honor. But I've been retained as a private investigator by two of the named defendants in the Coney Island Four case that your honor is presiding over. As you know, there's only a month before trial starts, and I needed to ask you a question."

"Then ask," the judge answered. "I have about thirty seconds."

"Thank you," Marlene said. "It's come to our attention

that a letter from a former cellmate of the alleged sole perpetrator of the sexual assault on Liz Tyler, a disgusting individual named Enrique Villalobos, was sent to Brooklyn District Attorney Kristine Breman. We have reason to believe that this letter was then forwarded on to you. Of course, Corporation Counsel, for whom I work at least officially, would consider any such correspondence to be discoverable and withholding that letter a violation of our clients' right to due process. I'd like a certified copy of that letter, your honor. I can wait here or in your chambers."

Klinger's face flushed. "How dare you? Are you implying that I would withhold evidence? I have no idea what you are talking about. Your question does not really even deserve an answer . . . but for the record, I have not received any such letter from District Attorney Breman. Now, Ms. Ciampi, if you are quite through with your fishing expedition, then I would suggest that you remove yourself from the premises before I call security and have you escorted out of the building."

Marlene hesitated. She considered egging the judge on to see if she could make her go ballistic. But she decided on prudence and turned to leave, only to stop when she saw the look on Verene's face. "Are you okay?" she asked the young woman, who looked as though she'd developed a sudden case of nausea.

Verene nodded her head. "Yes, sorry, I haven't been feeling well today. I think I ate something funky for breakfast."

"Verene," the judge interrupted, "if your illness allows, would you come into my office please. Good-bye, Ms. Ciampi. I'm sure you'll understand if I don't wish you a Merry Christmas."

Marlene was steaming when she walked out of the judge's office. But she felt better once she hit the cold but fresh air outside the building and trotted down the granite steps. She didn't get what she'd come for, but in that regard, the judge was right—she had been on a fishing expedition. She'd landed something she hadn't expected either. She was absolutely sure that the law clerk, Verene Fisher, wasn't ill until the little exchange between herself and Klinger. She knows something.

Unknown to her, Marlene just missed running into Hugh Louis, who walked into Klinger's office and demanded to see the judge. But Verene immediately pressed the intercom and announced, as she'd been told in this case, "Mr. Louis is here and would like to speak to you."

"Show him in, please."

Verene stood and opened the door to the judge's chamber and stepped quickly aside. She didn't like Hugh Louis or the way he was always mopping at the sweat on his face with his big white handkerchiefs. Nor did she like the way he undressed her with his eyes and suggested that they have dinner and talk about the possibility of her working for him after she passed the bar exam. "I'm always lookin' for good, young talent to nurture," he said to her once, in a way that left no doubt what he meant by *nurture*.

"Thank you, Mr. Louis," she'd replied. "But I want to be a prosecutor and work for the New York District Attorney's Office."

"Be my guest," he said. "Work in a thankless, dead-end job with no money . . . the hardworking little black girl who thinks she's going to get somewhere in the white man's world. What are you going to do when they tell you to look the other way when injustices are done to your black brothers and sisters?" In that moment, her distaste for Hugh Louis turned to hatred.

Louis took one last leering look at the law clerk as he moved past. But when the door was closed behind him he wasted no more time getting to the point of his visit. That morning he'd received a call from Enrique Villalobos and wasn't happy about what he heard.

"Some bitch named Maria Champi was up here asking questions," Villalobos told him. "She wanted to know where to find that fucker Kaminsky. When I wouldn't tell her, she sucker-punched me when I wasn't looking and broke two of my ribs. I plan to file a lawsuit, but that lying piece-of-shit guard, Richardson, is backing up her story that I fell against a chair. You need to do something about her and Kaminsky, or this whole thing could get fucked up."

Louis had weighed his words carefully. He knew that the prison sometimes monitored the calls of inmates. "I believe the woman you talked to was Marlene Ciampi, and once again, you are talking when I have advised you as your legal representative to remain silent. You understand?"

"Yeah, that was the bitch's name," said Villalobos. "I didn't say nothin' to her 'cept maybe someday I might get out and do to her what I did to that other bitch at Coney Island."

"That's good," Louis said. "But from now on, and this is only a suggestion, but I'm sure my clients—especially Mr. Jayshon Sykes—would appreciate it if you did not speak with representatives of the racist regime that has persecuted them."

Villalobos was quiet. He understood the threat. "Ain't nobody got to worry about Enrique Villalobos. I told the truth," he said just in case the conversation was being recorded. "I was the only one that raped sweet Lizzie."

"Good, good," Louis said, "and I appreciate that you

called and let me know that the Ciampi woman was up
there trying to find a smokescreen to spread over the
truth. Let me know if you hear from her again, but
remember, silence is golden."

Louis had hung up the phone, mopping at the sweat
that had popped out. He'd worried when he learned from
Lindahl that Ciampi had signed on to help the ADAs.
She had a reputation for tenacity that could prove trou-
blesome, especially if she located Kaminsky or that damn
note he wrote to Breman.

Having Ciampi nosing around asking questions about
Kaminsky was alarming. Damn that moron Sykes. Too
stupid to notice that his victim had both arms. Well, now
Sykes and his gang were going to have to find Kaminsky
and take care of the problem before Ciampi did. And that
could be tough. The gang had been trying to keep an eye
on the streets in Brighton Beach, but black gangsters in
the Russian sector stuck out like sore thumbs, and the
Russian mob wasn't going to tolerate their presence for
long. He'd have to get on Olav Radinskaya to pull some
strings, flush Kaminsky out.

In the meantime, Louis had decided that there were
too many loose ends. He wanted the letter that Kaminsky
had written to Breman in his possession. He and the
judge had an "understanding," but he had to tread lightly.
No one pushed a federal judge around.

"Marci," he beamed as he waddled toward her, his
hand extended. "Damn, you lookin' good, girl. You been
working out?"

Klinger returned the smile and shook his hand though
in truth it made her cringe to touch that sweaty palm, and
it was all she could do not to wipe hers off on her robe.
The man sweats like a whole herd of pigs, she thought.

The two exchanged pleasantries and wished each

other a Merry Christmas and noted that they ought to get their families together for dinner "one of these days, real soon."

"So, Hugh," Klinger said, "what brings you here today? I'm sure it wasn't to pass on a Yuletide greeting."

"Well, heh-heh," he chortled, "I did want to pass that on, but you're right, this is a business call. I've been thinkin' that maybe I should have that letter that lying piece of crap Kaminsky sent to Krissy. Heh-heh. I think we all agree it's just another inmate trying to get a deal. But if it was to fall into the wrong hands, someone might use it to confuse the issue and upset the applecart, so to speak."

So that's what the fat tub of goo wants, Klinger thought. He doesn't trust me. She decided to let him sweat it out, literally. "That letter has certainly become a popular item for being a collection of lies," she said.

"How do you mean?" Louis asked, pausing in mid-mop.

"Well, just a few minutes before you arrived, Marlene Ciampi was here with the same request," she replied, satisfied to see that the news shook Louis. "In fact, I'm surprised you didn't run into her in the hall."

Louis felt his overworked heart skip a beat. "All the more reason for me to have the letter," he said. "It needs to be destroyed before it causes problems for all of us."

Klinger could have clapped her hands in glee; the letter was her insurance policy in case he ever turned on her. "Well, I don't know that I'm prepared to do that, Hugh," Klinger said. "It was given to me in confidence by my dear friend Miss Breman."

Louis stopped mopping his brow; all pretense of friendliness disappeared from his face. "Okay, let's cut out the crap," he said. "We both know that letter is dangerous. What if Ciampi can convince another judge to issue a search warrant for your office?"

"Preposterous," Klinger said, waving a hand in dismissal. "Ciampi was fishing. She knows something but not enough. No federal judge is going to give her a warrant to search the office of another federal judge based on guesswork."

"Maybe not," Louis said. "But I don't like taking that chance. Let me sweeten the pot. There're going to be changes in the administration in Washington, D.C., after the new year. It could be your ticket to the U.S. Justice Department, maybe even the new—and prettier—version of Janet Reno. But you need your friend Hugh Louis to put in a good word."

"Cut the bullshit, Louis," Klinger replied. "You don't like me, and I don't like you, and neither of us trusts the other. However, I do agree that we have a mutually beneficial relationship. I can control the outcome of this trial, if it comes to that, and you know the right people in Washington. But that letter is my insurance policy that after the trial, you don't drop me like a hot rock."

Louis felt a hatred boil up in him like bile. He would have liked to reach across the desk and slap the ugly old bitch. But he smiled and nodded as if she'd made an excellent point. "All right, you got me. If not a friendship, then a partnership. You just need to make sure that letter doesn't fall into the wrong hands. Or, well, you've seen my clients, they might take it personally."

"Don't threaten me, Louis," Klinger said. "You just get this thing settled with Lindahl so that we don't have to go to trial. And I'll do my part if we do. In the meantime, the letter stays in my safe where it belongs."

Louis stood up to leave. He didn't bother to shake the judge's hand and she didn't bother to stand up.

Louis left the judge's chambers without saying anything to the law clerk, who had her nose planted in a book of New York statutes. Verene was happy to see him go, but her mind was in turmoil. The button on the judge's intercom had locked in the open position, so she'd heard every word of the conversation.

Two hours later, the judge emerged from her chamber to go home for the day. "Staying late, Verene?" she asked.

"Yes, ma'am, if you don't mind," she said. "It's nice and quiet here when everybody's gone and I can get some good studying in. I'll get the guard to lock up after me if that's all right with you."

"Suit yourself," the judge said and left.

Verene waited another half hour to make sure the judge wouldn't have forgotten something and decided to return. Then she stood up and went into Klinger's chambers and walked quickly over to the wall safe. She figured that the judge had probably forgotten that she'd once called and given Verene the combination so that she could fetch some documents to bring to her courtroom. And Verene never forgot a number or a conversation.

Verene opened the safe and removed the unmarked file with the letter and envelope with the return address to Auburn State Prison. She took out the letter and began to read. By the time she finished, tears were rolling down her cheeks; she was young and idealistic. She'd hoped when she started to clerk for Klinger that she'd found a role model in the judge. But now she knew better. She took the letter out to the copy machine in the office and made several copies. Placing the letter and envelope back in the file, she returned it to the safe.

With the copies tucked into her purse, Verene picked up her law books, turned out the lights, and left.

21

IT HAD BEEN A PRODUCTIVE AFTERNOON. MOST everyone at the office had gone home at noon for an early start on Christmas Eve, which had allowed him to sit down with Repass and Russell to discuss the case. He'd hoped Guma would be there, too, but his old friend had called to say he had good news but would have to tell him later at a dinner party Marlene was throwing.

So it was only the two assistant DAs who had sat in stunned silence when he told them what Marlene had learned about Kaminsky and Klinger.

"I can't believe a federal judge would do this," Russell said.

"Why not? It's a corrupt world." Repass added, "But how do we prove this little bit of corruption?"

"Let's not worry about it now," Karp said. "The letter would be nice, and I'd like to be able to get that judge removed because of it. But we need to concentrate on winning this case. We still have an advantage. They think this thing is going to be settled without a fight. I heard that Lindahl has even drafted a proposed agreement."

"What!" the women exclaimed. "If he does that, we're on our own," Russell said.

Karp held up his hand. "But I've been assured by Denton that there'll be no deal. The city council would have to approve, which could happen, but it would take some time. Then the mayor has to sign off on it. It ain't going to happen between Christmas and New Year's, after which Denton will be sworn in. He's been doing a bang-up acting job with Lindahl, giving all the signs that he's willing to go along just to not have it hanging over his head at the start of his administration. So the opposition's been in no hurry. So let's just get our own ducks in order and give them a little surprise come January 24 and our opening statements."

The rest of the afternoon had been spent formulating their strategy, looking for holes and filling them. They'd knocked off at five and Karp had hurried home, looking forward to a little time with the kids and Marlene before the guests arrived.

He walked in through the front door of the loft and froze at the sight of the young man with the gun in his hand. The gunman was wearing blue jeans and cowboy boots, a holster slung from his thin hips like a gunfighter in a Western movie. He was facing away from Karp, who thought he might just be able to take him out before he was noticed. Then he heard the twins shout.

"Cool! Do it again! Do it again!"

As Karp hesitated, the gunman holstered his weapon, then after a brief pause drew the gun and "fired" in the proverbial blink of an eye. The sound of applause and more delighted shouts from his sons convinced him that no one was in any danger. Which meant that someone was playing with guns in his home.

"What the hell?" he said, walking into the loft, where

he saw that the twins, Lucy, Marlene, Jojola, and Gilgamesh were all smiling at the man with the gun.

"What the hell," he repeated himself just in case he hadn't been heard the first time. The gunman turned as he holstered his .45 Colt—the very pistol that a young Butch Karp had dreamed of owning someday as he'd watched the Saturday afternoon matinees with his buddies, dreaming of being a cowboy—and stuck out his hand as he walked across the floor.

"Mr. Karp, sir," the young man with the tan, thin face and piercing blue eyes said. "Ned Blanchett, I'm . . . a friend of your daughter. Sorry if I startled you."

"He's my boyfriend, Daddy," Lucy said, jumping into Karp's arms. "You be nice."

"I'm always nice," Karp groused and tried not to wince when Ned shook his hand. He was no slouch and regularly hit the weights, but damn if the kid doesn't have a grip that could crush a two-by-four. "I just don't like guns."

Ned's smile disappeared. His face crumbled into that of the boyfriend who knows that he's made a bad first impression on his girlfriend's father and might never recover. He hurriedly fumbled at the gunbelt buckle. "I'm sorry, sir. You're absolutely right, sir. I should have asked your permission. I'll put it away, sir."

Sir? Karp thought. Next thing I know, he'll be asking for permission to marry my daughter.

"No reason to apologize to Mr. Grumpy," Marlene said, who joined her daughter in hugging Karp. "We asked you to demonstrate. Or, more accurately, if you include the twins, begged you to demonstrate."

"Ned's in the Wild West Exposition at the Garden, Daddy," Lucy said. "He's going for the national title in the quick-draw contest."

"He's really fast," Zak chimed in. "Less than a second to clear the holster and fire."

"Ned won the regional contest in Denver last month," Lucy added. "There's a hundred-thousand-dollar purse and a sponsorship contract as a motivational speaker with Colt if he wins."

Ned was turning beet red from all the praise. "I've just practiced a lot," he said. "Some days there ain't much else to do as a ranch hand."

Lucy detached herself from her father and reattached herself to Ned. "He's being modest," she said, and let go the kind of sigh only a young woman in love can give. "My very own cowboy."

"Ranch hand," Ned corrected her.

Karp used the moment to study his daughter as if he were seeing her in an entirely new light. She'd never had many boyfriends, not until young Dan Heeney from West Virginia, but even that was a sort of puppy love. This was different and, he realized with a pang, part of the change he'd seen in her. It wasn't just that she'd gained weight and filled out; she was a woman. He made a mental note to ask Marlene if . . . he hated to even consider it and forced any images out of his mind . . . she'd asked Lucy "the question." Not my daughter, he prayed. Not yet. She's too young.

Then his gaze shifted to Ned, who was looking down into Lucy's eyes with adoration. Something passed between them, and Karp knew then that he was no longer the most important man in Lucy's life. He fought off the jealousy by being overly friendly.

"Well, Ned, I'm glad to finally meet you. From everything I've heard, you're practically the reincarnation of every matinee idol of my childhood." The boy turned beet red again. Oh, man, ten bucks he says Aw shucks, Karp thought.

"Shucks."

Close enough.

"I'm just a ranch hand," Blanchet said, then wondered if that sounded too unmotivated for the father of the woman he hoped to marry someday. He quickly added, "If I win the contest, I'm hoping to use the money to go to college."

Good recovery, son, Karp thought. It's pretty tough to dance around the old man. He smiled, thinking about how he'd had to do a similar waltz with Marlene's father, a good Italian Catholic who'd resisted the idea of her marrying a divorced Jewish lawyer whose only ambition was to remain a poorly paid prosecutor for the New York District Attorney's Office.

Marlene had finally sat Mariano down and told him, like it or not, she intended to marry Karp, bear his children, grow old with him, and die in his arms. After twenty-five years, three grandchildren, and a lot of pushing by Concetta, Mariano had pretty much come around, though he couldn't help but occasionally grouse—loud enough for all to hear—that it just wasn't going to be right when the family met in heaven and his son-in-law wasn't there because he didn't convert, confess his sins, and accept Jesus Christ as his savior and the Catholic faith as the one true church.

"Well, I should warn you that carrying a gun without a license for it in New York City is a felony," Karp said, wondering why he felt like the school tattletale.

"But he does have a permit, Daddy," Lucy said. "I already talked to Clay Fulton and it was here when Ned arrived."

"Clay did what?" Never much of a drinker, Karp decided he needed an eggnog with plenty of rum.

"I suggested it," Marlene said. "Ned's awfully good with that thing and this family—your daughter—tends to need protecting."

"Well, I don't know how much use I'd really be, ma'am," Ned said. "I've never had to shoot anything except targets and bottles. And to be honest, I'd just as soon I never had to, neither."

"I need a drink," Karp said, heading for the kitchen. He saw Jojola standing off to one side grinning at him.

"What are you smiling at?" Karp scowled. "What's next, now that Buffalo Bill's Wild West show has come to town with a cowboy and an Indian. Knife throwing? Scalping lessons?"

"That's easy," Jojola said, grabbing Zak and pulling his long curly hair up in a fist. "You just make a cut across the front and yank it off."

"Cool," Zak squealed.

Karp blinked twice and continued on to the kitchen, where he poured himself that eggnog with rum. Nothing like discussions about shooting people and scalping lessons to bring out the holiday spirit, he thought. I wonder what normal families talk about on Christmas Eve. He gulped the first drink down and just managed to pour another before he was dragged off to the bedroom by Marlene.

"I know that was a little bit of a shock, but now we need to get ready," she said. "People will be here soon."

"Couldn't we close the blinds and turn off the lights, then not answer the door?"

"Come on, Scrooge. Quit with the bah humbug and lighten up." She draped her arms around his neck and kissed him. "And if you're nice, I'll let you open your Christmas present early."

"I'm always nice," he said but was distracted by trying to imagine what his present might be. He chugged the second eggnog, then dutifully climbed into the dark gray turtleneck and khaki slacks his wife laid out for him.

One and a half more eggnogs later, he was feeling in the Christmas/Hanukkah spirit when the first guests, Murrow and Stupenagel, arrived. Murrow was wearing a red silk shirt with a green bow tie with red plastic holly berries attached, and a red-and-green-checkered vest. Stupenagel was dressed to kill in a slinky green satin dress cut almost to her navel to expose as much of her milk-white breasts as legally possible and a slit up the side to expose her mile-long legs.

Stupenagel walked over to Karp and held up a piece of mistletoe she was carrying in her hand. He tried to duck but was too late and she planted a long, firm kiss with just a hint of tongue on him. "I'm Jewish and that's not a Jewish tradition," he complained.

"Yeah, but you're at a Christmas party, Butch, so get used to it," the journalist said and held the plant up again, which sent him scurrying back to the kitchen.

Clay Fulton and his wife, Helen, showed up next, but Marlene had not even closed the door before V.T. Newbury and his blue-blooded girlfriend, Katrina Hairsmith-Dupont, "of the Massachusetts Duponts, of course," stepped out of the elevator across the hall.

Katrina sniffed twice and hurried past Marlene, muttering something about "some people." Marlene then learned that "some people" were Ray Guma and a boozy blonde half his age who emerged from where they'd been making out against a wall of the elevator, unseen at first.

Guma saw Marlene and grinned. "Marlene Ciampi, I'd like to introduce you to my date and possibly the next Mrs. Ray Guma . . . Crystal ummm . . . Crystal, what is your last name?"

"Vase," she said, and giggled. "Crystal Vase, you big

dummy. Of course, dat's my stage name. Sort of catchy don't ya tink?" She stuck out her hand to Marlene. "My real name's Breanna Buchowski, but I don't like it much. Pleased ta meet ya, I'm sure."

Crystal Vase, aka Breanna Buchowski, wiggled into the apartment, stripping her coat off and handing it to Karp. She was wearing a blouse that exposed cleavage that had Stupenagel turning green with envy, and her skirt was so short that Karp wondered if she could even sit down without revealing the color—or even presence—of her panties.

She looked up at Karp. "Oh, my, you are certainly one tall drink of wadda," she giggled. "Now you'll have to excuse me, I have ta find the liddle girls' room ta tinkle. Ray's been pouring drinks down me all afternoon, and I'm about to pee on your floor."

"Down the hall, first door on the left," Marlene said hastily.

As soon as she was out of sight, Marlene and Karp turned and looked at Guma.

"What? What?" he said. "She's an actress."

"Off-Broadway I take it," Stupenagel said, walking up. "Any show I might have seen?"

Guma stuck his tongue out at Stupenagel, a former lover and longtime mutual antagonist. "Well, she's not really an actress. She's more of a dancer." He looked around at all the raised eyebrows. "Hey, she once tried out for the Rockettes at Radio City Music Hall." There were more raised eyebrows. "Okay, okay, I met her last night at the Manhattan Gentleman's Club on Forty-second. You wouldn't believe what she can do with a—"

"Guma!" Marlene hissed, nodding at the twins who had joined the group. "Young ears."

"Aw, Mom," Zak complained. "Uncle Ray's already told us about the three Bs."

"Three Bs?"

"Yeah, the birds, bees, and broads," Giancarlo said innocently.

Ducking Marlene's glare, Guma headed back "to check on my future ex-wife."

By now everyone was listening to the conversation at the door and laughing except for Hairsmith-Dupont, who had maneuvered herself over to the bookshelf, where she pretended to be vastly interested in the Karp-Ciampi collection. V.T. joined her with two glasses of wine.

Last to arrive was Harry Kipman. His wife had died of ovarian cancer five years earlier. They'd been sweethearts since their high school days, and he'd still not gone out with anyone after her death, to Karp's knowledge. He'd initially turned down this invitation until Marlene called and begged him to come.

"Well, okay, but don't be trying to set me up with anybody," he said. "I'm not ready."

Two hours later, well lubricated on a half-dozen bottles of red wine and eggnog and fueled by Marlene's famous veal parmesan, roasted Italian sausage with sautéed red and green peppers with onion, and gnocchi, as well as several loaves of bread, the conversation was roaring right along. Even Katrina had loosened up to the point of asking Crystal, who, when not dancing for folded dollar bills, was a hair colorist, what she recommended as far as putting highlights in her blond-going-to-gray hair.

"Oh, honey, let me do you in copper—with those green eyes, you'll have every man in New York wanting a go at that cute little chassis of yours," Crystal promised.

Katrina, whose "chassis" resembled a surfboard with two peas on it about breast high, blushed but looked pleased. "Well, I don't know," she said. "I've never been a redhead."

The twins had been ordered off to their room a half hour earlier. They'd gone under protest and only after their dad, who'd had a couple more than his usual, had very nearly given his permission for them to hold Ned's Peacemaker in the morning. To their delight, John Jojola had gone with them. "Come on guys, I'll tell you some stories about Christmas at my pueblo," he said.

When Marlene tried to get him to stay, he shook his head. "It's really not a good idea for me to be around alcohol," he said. "It's not that I'd take a drink. But I don't like the feeling of wishing I could have one."

"We've had enough," Marlene said. "We'll stop. Just stay." She reached for his arm.

Jojola smiled and patted her hand. She sensed the almost electric bond that there'd been between them from the first time they met. It wasn't a man-woman thing. It was more like two old souls who recognized each other.

"Go back to the party," he said. "I need my rest anyway." He hesitated, then added, "I have something I need to do. So if I disappear for a couple of days, don't worry about me."

"This have to do with your dream about David Grale?" She shivered saying the name.

Jojola nodded. "It may be nothing. But I can't ignore the spirits."

"What if it's more than a couple of days?" she said and tried to smile but just managed a small one.

"Send the cavalry." Jojola smiled. "Or better yet, send the Sioux."

When Marlene walked back into the living room, Lucy and Ned were getting up from the couch where they'd snuggled in to listen to "the old folks." They put on their coats, as Lucy explained, "We're going to Rockefeller Center to see if we can ice-skate if the crowds aren't too bad."

"Hey," Karp pouted. "I wanted to take you and the boys ice-skating under the Christmas tree. That's *our* tradition." He hadn't meant to sound so petulant, but, by God, a father just didn't have to let his daughter start breaking family traditions with the first cowboy who came along.

Lucy walked over and kissed him on the cheek. "We're going to be here for at least three weeks. There'll be plenty of time to go ice-skating as a family." Then out the door they went.

Karp turned to find Marlene smiling knowingly at him. "Daddy's having trouble letting go," she said, wrapping an arm around his waist and leaning her head on his shoulder. "Come on, deep breath."

"I am not," he argued, mostly because there was something else on his mind. "By the way, where's he going to sleep? John's on the futon in the boys' room. Out here on the couch?"

Marlene gave him an amused look.

Then he understood what that meant. "Oh no . . . they're not . . . you're not thinking it's okay for them to . . . ," he sputtered. "Not in my house."

Marlene gave him a squeeze. "It's her house, too," she said. "In Ned's defense, he offered to sleep on the floor of the boys' room—said he sleeps on worse when he's riding herd. But Lucy won't hear of it."

Maybe it was the wine, but Karp felt like crying. This is why I don't drink, he thought, it turns me into an idiot.

Marlene steered him back into the living room. Guma was sitting on the love seat next to Crystal, who'd passed out and was snoring like an old man. Green thong, Karp thought, his theory about the skirt having been borne out by the physical evidence. Marlene noticed too and tossed an afghan over the sleeping woman. "She looked cold," she said when she noticed that now he was the one with the amused look on his face.

Murrow and Stupenagel occupied a single overstuffed chair, though it was difficult to see him with her on his lap; they were talking to Kipman, who'd done a number on the brandy and swayed as he stood next to them. Meanwhile, Fulton, Newbury, and their female counterparts were engaged in a lively discussion about the war in Iraq.

Looking for something less meaty than politics, Karp glanced at Guma. "So what was the big secret you couldn't make our meeting for?" he said.

Guma extricated his hand from under Crystal's ass and got up. "Well, maybe this isn't the place, but since the new love of my life has already embarked on her beauty rest, and I'm feeling generous, I guess I'll give you an early Christmas present," he said loud enough that the other conversations stopped and everyone turned to listen.

"I'm Jewish, but go ahead, it can be a late Hanukkah present," Karp said.

"Well, it's not true that I've been pouring drinks down my beloved's throat," he said. "I didn't even get over to the club until four o'clock on my way over here. I've been working. And as it turns out, the I. Kaminsky down at the morgue is not the I. Kaminsky we thought he was. It's his brother, Ivan; as far as I know, Igor Kaminsky is still alive."

"Good work, Guma!" Marlene exclaimed.

"Thank you," Guma said, giving a little bow. "But to be honest, it didn't take any great detective work. I knew that our boy was missing an arm. But the guy in the morgue had both of his . . . or at least he did before he got slammed by the train, but most of the pieces were present and accounted for."

"Wow, just like in *The Fugitive*," Stupenagel said. "I just love Tommy Lee Jones."

"Hey," Murrow complained. "I thought you loved me."

"And you're right, my little sugar plum," she cooed. "I love you lots more than Tommy Lee Jones, Honey Buns."

"Sugar Lips," Murrow replied.

"I think I'm going to be sick," an awakened Crystal said before Karp could voice a similar sentiment.

"It is pretty icky," Karp said.

"No, I mean I'm going to be sick for real," she said, scrambling to her feet and wobbling down the hall to the bathroom from which loud retching noises emanated.

Guma hurried after her but soon returned. He had a sheepish look on his face. "Uh, sorry, Marlene," he said.

Marlene patted him on the shoulder. "Don't be. She's a nice kid. Probably too nice to be hanging out with a lecherous old fart like you. I believe I've had my own intimate conversations with the porcelain god in my younger days. Anyway, back to the fugitive. Anything else?"

"A little," Guma said, nodding. "According to witnesses, the dead man, Ivan Kaminsky, was shoved off the platform by a young black man, who, with several other young black men, then chased another man who was the spitting image of the victim."

"Ooooh, so maybe what we got here is a case of mistaken identity," Stupenagel said, her mind already working on the story. "The killers—and I'd bet any amount of money it's Sykes and his gang—decided that Igor knew too much, but somehow they went after the wrong brother first."

"But that would mean that someone told them that Kaminsky represented a danger to them," Marlene said.

"But Villalobos wouldn't have told them he'd been stupid."

"The letter," Karp said. "The letter Kaminsky wrote to Breman, who passed it on to Klinger."

The room was silent as the implications of what he'd just said hung in front of them. "Breman or Klinger or both told Louis," Kipman finished the thought. "Which makes them accessories to murder and attempted murder."

Guma whistled. "That's real big-game hunting . . . a U.S. District Court judge and the Brooklyn District Attorney."

"So what's the next step?" Fulton asked Karp. "You want me to round up Sykes and his cronies and see if the witnesses in the subway station can pick them out of a lineup? It would put a pretty good damper on their lawsuit if they were in prison."

Karp thought about it for a moment, then shook his head. "Let's see if we can get recent photographs of Sykes & Co. and let the witnesses pick them out of a photo lineup and, if they do, put them in front of a grand jury," he said. "But I want this kept quiet. This isn't just about the murder of Ivan Kaminsky. Right now, we can't prove that Breman or Klinger or Louis had anything to do with it." He looked pointedly at Stupenagel. "I am assuming that this was all off the record."

Stupenagel protested. "Why is it that you naturally jump to the conclusion that I'm the only one in the room who can't be trusted? Never mind, don't answer that. But you don't have to worry. In fact, you might remember that I'm the one who talked Marlene into looking into this because Robin and Pam are friends of mine. But the old deal still stands. When it's time, I get first crack."

Karp nodded. "Fair enough. The problem now is that we need Kaminsky and . . . if we can figure out a way to get it, the letter." That reminded him of another missing link in the case. He turned to Fulton. "What about Hannah Little?"

Fulton shook his head. "She disappeared from her neighborhood after the trial. She and her family put up with a lot of crap from the 'solid citizens,' who apparently thought it was worse to be a snitch than a rapist. They even burned her mother's car one night. Then her brother got shot out in California and that was it. Hannah and her mother packed up in the middle of the night and left Bed-Stuy. I tracked her to Ohio from a letter she wrote back to a friend, but that was the last anybody heard from her."

The group was silent, contemplating the extraordinary turn of events. Murrow cleared his throat. "Well, I hate to be outdone when it comes to handing out Christmas presents, but Ariadne and I have another. Okay with you, my love?"

"Say that last part again, you silver-tongued devil, and you can pretty much say anything else you want and I won't care."

"My love," he said again.

"Would someone throw cold water on them?" Karp said. "Okay, Murrow, it's going to be pretty tough to top Guma, but you can try."

Trading narration duties, Murrow and Stupenagel recounted their adventure at the Sagamore Hotel. When they finished, Karp groaned.

"I knew it was too much to hope that everybody was doing this by the book," he growled, wondering if the sudden indigestion was from too much rich food and wine or the story he'd just heard. "You do realize that not a word of what you overheard would ever make it into a court of law, right? Not to mention—which you also seemed to have been aware of when you made your escape—that you could probably be prosecuted for assault on a police officer and trespass."

Karp looked at Murrow and frowned. "Don't you think that maybe I should have heard about this a little sooner?"

Murrow looked hurt, but Stupenagel came to his defense. "To hell with that, Karp. The only reason that story's not splashed across the cover of the *New York Times* under my byline is because Murry talked me into waiting. . . . Now, you want to shut up and apologize to a man who is absolutely loyal to you, or do you need me to kick your ass?"

"All right, enough," Karp said. "You don't have to convince me about Mr. Murrow's loyalty, which I return, by the way, in full measure. But you and I, and by the nature of his job, Gil, have different obligations. Yours is to inform the public. Mine is to protect the public by prosecuting criminals, but I also have to follow the rules . . . and that's protecting the public, too."

"Oh, bring out the fife and drum," Stupenagel said. "I thought we'd heard enough speeches this past fall from the two losers we had running for president. Jeez, Marlene, I thought you liked the strong, silent type."

Marlene shrugged. "No comment. I have to sleep with him and if he's cranky, I won't get any . . . know what I mean?"

"I give," Karp exclaimed. "Why does everybody pick on me? Okay, Stupe, as Paul Harvey would say . . . now, the rest of the story."

"I should make you squirm, Karp, but because my other good friends here are waiting, I'll tell you," Stupenagel said. "I went back up to Bolton Landing the Monday after Honey Buns and I were up there playing secret agents . . . and doctor, but I won't go into that. I stopped in a local real estate office and asked what a place like that cute little fishing lodge costs where Ewen keeps the beautiful but dim mistress. Well, when the place got bought two years ago, it went for 2.4 million smackers, which is pretty stiff on a union boss's salary . . . but even tougher if you're twenty-four years old and working at the local Quickie Oil & Lube."

"What's that mean?" Karp asked.

"I was about to tell you. Sheesh, Karp, you have no sense of story pacing," Stupenagel said. "Let me remind you that I am one of the finest nonfiction writers of the twenty-first century. I was trying to build in a little suspense."

"As you can see, we're all already on the edge of our seats," Marlene said, getting a little impatient herself.

"Good, just where I like my audiences at this point," Stupenagel said. "What it means is that the house was purchased not by Ed Ewen but by his sister's son, Michael Mason, a good-looking kid in his midtwenties who makes his living in oil . . . changing oil in other people's cars, that is. He couldn't have bought that house if he'd saved every penny since childhood. Besides, he doesn't live there; he's got a live-in girlfriend and they're shacked up in a one-bedroom in the woods."

Stupenagel looked around, pleased that she had everybody's undivided attention. "Anyway, I dropped by the house after first calling union headquarters and finding out that Ewen was in but unavailable. Anyway, the door gets answered by this blond bombshell who could be the separated-at-birth twin of our own Miss Crystal Vase."

"Oh, please, God," Guma prayed earnestly. "Let me be the one who reunites them."

"Oh, please, Guma, try not to make me ill," Stupenagel said. "That poor girl is going to wake up tomorrow, take one look at you, and swear off drinking for the rest of her life. . . . So anyway, before I was so rudely interrupted by the Italian Scallion—"

"That's Italian Stallion."

"I asked the blond bombshell if 'Mr. Ewen' was at home. At first she was a little suspicious—I'll tell you why in a moment—but I gave her the business card of the real estate woman I'd talked to, a LeAnne Dalton, which seemed to reassure her. Anyway, I told her that I was just in the neighborhood because I had a buyer who was interested in the property and was willing to pay top dollar. I asked her if she was Mrs. Ewen, which made her all giggly. She said, 'Not yet,' so either Mr. Ewen is stringing her along, or the current Mrs. Ewen is about to be turned out to pasture. The bastard. Anyway, the next part of the story I'll turn over to my sweetie."

Karp looked at Murrow. "Okay, sweetie, spill the beans, and I can only hope that you kept the felonies to a minimum."

Murrow grinned sheepishly at Karp. "Uh, my part was to see if I could track down Captain Carney's property in Florida. Fortunately, he's either not as clever as Ewen or just figures that he doesn't have to be as careful because of the distance. He's got a real nice beachfront condominium in Key West. Again, a call to a real estate agent revealed that I could get a similar condominium in that building on the same floor for a cool 1.5 million."

"Must have shook down a lot of hookers when he was walking the beat," Guma said, to general laughter.

Karp could feel the wine wearing off and the beginnings of the headache he knew he'd be battling while the twins were ripping open their presents and screaming with Christmas greed. He looked at Newbury, who was scribbling notes on a napkin. "Well, V.T., looks like you may have your smoking gun."

Newbury looked up and grinned. "You'd burn your hand if you grabbed the barrel. When I can think clearly again, we can strategize who to put the screws to in that lot and blow the lid off this baby."

Marlene hurried off to the kitchen and returned with a magnum of champagne. "I was saving this to get my own sweetie good and liquored up for New Year's Eve," she said. "But I think this calls for a celebration."

Karp winced. The champagne would force the headache to retreat for a little while, but it would be back with a vengeance. But he raised his glass to toast with the others. "Merry Christmas and a Happy New Year."

"Hey, what does a girl hafta do to get a little drinky around here?"

Crystal Vase stood wobbling in the hallway. She teetered like a tree about to fall in the forest, and then went over. She hit the ground with a dull thud and didn't move.

Hairsmith-Dupont was the first to reach her. She knelt beside the young woman and felt her neck. "She's got a pulse," she announced.

"That's all Guma needs," Stupenagel said. "Poor girl."

"Very funny," Guma replied, pulling Crystal into a sitting position and then, with the help of the other men, lifting her to her feet. She woke up again as they were putting her in a chair.

"Ray," she mumbled so low that he had to lean forward to hear her. "Ray, take me home." She then threw up on him.

"Okay, show's over," Marlene said. "Ray, shall I call you a cab?"

22

Saturday, December 25

KARP WOKE UP WITH WHAT FELT LIKE ALL OF Santa's reindeer stampeding around in his cerebellum. Marlene, on the other hand, cheerfully jumped out of bed to make sure Santa hadn't messed up after the guests left the night before.

The wrapped presents had needed name tags, and faux Santa, feeling no pain from the champagne, was sure to have messed up at least a few. The unwrapped presents—those that the real Santa had hand-delivered straight from the North Pole, even those clearly stamped Made in China—needed to be sorted into clearly recognizable piles that demonstrated Santa did indeed know that the boys had been equally good. As much good as could be expected of Zak, anyway.

Returning from her inspection tour, Marlene didn't appear to be suffering from any ill effects of alcohol. In fact, she was humming a Christmas carol and making loud sighing noises to encourage him to get up. When that didn't work, she invited the boys—who were bouncing off the walls in their bedroom waiting for him to rise so that the yearly greed fest could begin—to instead bounce on the bed.

"AAAHHH," he'd cried. "I'm getting up. I'm getting up. Please, I think my brain is hemorrhaging."

The twins stopped, concerned looks on their faces. "Don't worry, guys, Daddy's just a little hungover," said Marlene, demonstrating none of the Christmas spirit she professed to have in spades. "Giancarlo, find his slippers and bathrobe. Zak, go wake up Lucy and Ned . . . but don't go in their room, on pain of death, just knock."

Zak ran out. A moment later, there was a shriek, then Lucy's outraged voice. "Get out of here you little brat! MOTHER!" Marlene trotted out of the room to carry out the threatened sentence on Zak, who apparently dodged the axe and ran back into the bedroom to jump on the bed. "They're naked in there, you know," he said, peering down at his father, who groaned and rolled over to plant his face in the pillow.

When Karp finally shuffled into the living room, Marlene handed him a cup of hot herbal tea—"chamomile and peppermint with some ground-up Tylenol, perfect for a hangover"—and then forced him to drink when he growled that he didn't want it. Jojola smiled and lifted a cup. "It's good, even without the Tylenol. Merry Christmas and belated Happy Hanukkah."

Karp just stared at him until Jojola decided to join the boys, who were salivating next to the piles of unwrapped presents, waiting for the starting gun from their mother. Lucy got her revenge on Zak by taking extra time "to fix my hair" before emerging from the bedroom with Ned, who got the evil eye from her father.

Not that he would have admitted it to Marlene, but Karp felt better after a half hour or so of sipping the tea while sitting on the couch, laughing at the twins, who were practically hyperventilating with avarice. The boys shredded expensive wrapping paper without a second glance and fell upon their presents like lions on a gazelle. Over by the door, Gilgamesh happily gnawed on his Christmas present: a big soup bone from the kosher deli that had moved in on the ground floor, replacing a Chinese restaurant-supply store.

Meanwhile, Lucy carefully pried open the tape and unfolded the paper on her presents as if she intended it to be used again. One of her gifts was a lacy, red negligee from Victoria's Secret, with a matching red thong. Instead of the embarrassment such a present might have caused her in the past, she held it up against her body and asked Ned what he thought.

"I think I might die when I see that on you, but what a way to go," he replied with enthusiasm until he glanced over at Karp, which put an immediate end to any further comments.

"It's from your father and me," Marlene said.

"I had nothing to do with it," Karp insisted.

Marlene next brought out a large box for Ned, which he accepted shyly, complaining that he didn't need "anything more than what you've already given me." Inside the box was a two-thousand-dollar Neiman-Marcus version of the Marlboro Man's fleece-lined coat. "It's made of buffalo hide," she said.

The young man sat stunned, stroking the baby-soft skin. "I don't know what to say. It's the most beautiful thing—outside of my horse and Lucy—that I've ever seen in my life." He stood and retrieved a box from beneath the tree and handed it to Marlene, who sat down next to Karp to open it.

"It ain't much," he said. "But there's a story to it."

Marlene opened the wrapping and then the box.

Inside was a crucifix with Jesus on the cross that had been carved out of a single, gnarled piece of light-colored wood.

"Tell her where you got the wood," Lucy said.

"It's from that old piñon tree that you were hung up on over the gorge," he said, referring to the tree that had prevented her and Lucy from plunging seven hundred feet into the Rio Grande Gorge that summer. "There wasn't much left of it—most went to the bottom with your truck—but enough for this here carving."

"The idiot climbed down that cliff to get it," Lucy added.

"I had a rope on me, tied to my horse."

"Good idea," Lucy teased. "What if the horse decided to take off before you were ready, or maybe came to see what you were doing. . . ."

"She's too smart for that," Ned said in defense of his horse.

"But it's what I get for falling in love with a cowboy," she concluded. "They can't ever do anything the easy way. It's like they're always in a movie."

Love? Karp thought. Get me my shotgun; I'll shoot the sneaky bastard.

Marlene examined the crucifix. It was simple—the work of someone with only a pocketknife for a tool—yet the simplicity gave it grace and power, and it had obviously taken Ned many hours to carve.

"It's beautiful, Ned," she said and walked over to give him a kiss on the cheek.

Blushing, Ned said, "I thought something carved out of that tree might still have some luck left in it for you and your family."

There's something wrong with this kid, Karp thought. Nobody's this nice.

"Trees have spirits, too," Jojola noted as he emerged from the boys' bedroom with an armful of presents. There were two small bone-handled knives for the boys, who looked with puppy dog eyes at their father, who in turn rolled his but nodded. Jojola gave Lucy and Ned matching silver bracelets—"made by one of the best silversmiths in the pueblo"—and a beautifully woven rug to Marlene. "It's Navajo," he shrugged. "But they're okay people once you get to know them. A little full of themselves."

The last present Jojola handed to Karp in a small box. Inside was a stone carving of a bear. "It's a fetish," he explained. "We believe that every human being has a kinship with an animal spirit guide with whom they share personality characteristics. Mine is the eagle. Marlene's is the cougar."

"Figures," Karp said. "Something with claws that bites."

"Independent, courageous . . . a giver of life to its cubs, and a bringer of death, but only to feed or protect her family."

There was an awkward silence that followed the word *death,* so Jojola moved on quickly, "I asked the spirits to show me your totem. A bear appeared to me in my dreams and he spoke with your voice, saying something like, *'Wa a leak come salon.'* I don't know what that means—it's not Tiwa, my people's language, but it's probably important."

"Wa alaikum salaam," Lucy corrected him. "It's Arabic and means 'And unto you peace.' It's a traditional response to the greeting *'A salaam alaikum,'* which means 'Peace be unto you.' I wonder where you would have picked that up."

"I don't know," Jojola said, "but when bears talk, I listen." He turned back to Karp. "The bear is a very special animal to most Native American tribes. He is the most powerful animal in the wild, but he doesn't rely on just brute strength. He is clever and will try to solve a puzzle before turning to force as a last resort. The bear is thought to be wise and contemplative because for four months of the year he hibernates and thinks deep thoughts before emerging in the spring to put those thoughts into action. Sometimes he appears to be moving so slow that you cannot imagine he has another speed, but if he charges, he can outrun a horse. Oh, and if someone is stupid enough to tangle with an angry bear, the bear usually wins."

Karp turned the fetish over in his hand. It was crudely chipped out of some sort of quartz or a similar mineral he couldn't identify. He liked the feel of the stone; as small as it was, the figure did seem to imply a creature of power. "Thank you, John," he said. "For the bear and the thought."

Marlene handed Jojola a box. He opened it and lifted out a strange-looking headset with what looked like small binoculars attached.

"Cool!" Zak shouted. "Night-vision goggles!"

"A Rigel 3250 with built-in infrared for illumination even in total darkness," explained Giancarlo, who'd helped his mother pick it out at the Sharper Image and knew all the details by heart. "It weighs less than a pound, which makes it one of the lightest on the market."

Karp thought that Jojola's bronze face looked sad for a moment—the lines around the eyes and mouth deeper, his brown eyes seeing something not in the room. But then the Indian smiled and said, "It is a wonderful gift."

Marlene started to reply, then choked up a little before finally shrugging as if she'd given him a pot holder. "You said that it's dark where you're going."

"What do you mean by that?" Karp asked.

"Yeah, where's John going?" Giancarlo wanted to know.

"He just got here," Zak complained.

"It's nothing," Jojola said. "I just have some business to attend to for a few days. I'll see you after that."

"Cool," Zak exclaimed. "Commando stuff like when you were in Vietnam?"

"Nah, nothin' like that . . . just looking around. We'll talk about it some other time. This is Christmas morning, and I think there's more presents under the tree."

Lucy and Ned then exchanged gifts. She'd bought him a new pair of boots and he gave her a silver heart-shaped locket with a photograph of his face inside. "So you never forget what I look like," he said and kissed her gently on the lips, a gesture that sent a spasm of pain clutching at Karp's frontal lobe.

When all the other gifts had been handed out, Karp gave Marlene a small box. She opened it and found a key. "What's this?" she asked.

"Why, it's the key to my heart," he replied.

"Oh, honey, that's so sweet. . . . But come on, what is it really?"

"Can't tell you yet," Karp said. "You have to wait until after the New Year."

"I'm supposed to wait until after the first to learn what the mystery key for my Christmas present fits?" she said. "That's not fair. I'll go crazy wondering what it is."

"Sorry, can't tell."

The twins and Lucy all giggled. Marlene glared at them all, one at a time. "Okay, I get it. This is a conspiracy to drive me insane and lock me up in some looney bin so Karp can bring his little Trixie into my bed, and you kids can run amok with no parental supervision."

"Guilty as charged," Karp said.

"Can Ned and I take Gilgamesh back to New Mexico?" Lucy laughed.

"Who's Trixie?" asked the twins.

Marlene swore that she would catch them when they were alone "and yank fingernails until someone cracks." But no one seemed to be giving in to fear at the moment, so they moved on to a simple brunch of pastries and juices.

Afterward, Karp lay down on the couch, determined to have a little quality family time watching the twins play with their new toys. But the games had beeped, pinged, and chimed until he felt as if he'd been chained to the floor of a Las Vegas casino, right next to the nickel slots. Finally he couldn't take it anymore and demanded that all electronic "anythings" be banned from the living room for the rest of the day.

The boys complied and took the games back to their room. But then the little monsters returned with their nonelectronic plastic samurai swords and armor—a gift from Uncle Ray, whom Karp intended to beat over the head with a law book when he saw him again—and commenced to hack at each other and then feigned loud, protracted, yet heroic deaths by ritual seppuku.

When Ned mercifully offered to show the twins the Peacemaker, Karp didn't put up a fight. "Anything to keep them quiet for a few minutes," he moaned. "But no firing blanks. No shouting. And no death scenes."

There'd been a blissful hour of lying on the coach with an ice bag on his head, while the twins and Ned talked quietly and practiced their quick draws. But twelve-year-old boys cannot help but occasionally shriek with joy at the heft and feel of a real cowboy gun, so he'd finally given up any pretense of quality time with anyone and retreated to his bedroom.

A little while later, Marlene popped her head in long enough to say that she and the boys were going to her parents' house to drop off presents. "I'll give them your holiday wishes."

He must have slept because the next thing he knew, she was back opening the door again. She walked in and closed it behind her. Kicking off her shoes, she crawled up on the bed next to him and curled up against his chest.

"How'd it go?" he asked.

"Well, if you don't mind the woman who gave you life referring to you by your sister's name . . . or watching your father try not to cry as he watches his wife disappear inside of the shell of a woman he no longer knows . . . it went as well as can be expected."

He felt her body trembling and realized that she was crying. He wished that he could cover her with his own body and shield her from the pain, but there was nothing he could do except hold her.

At last she stopped crying and sat up. "Let's go see the kids," she said. "You up for it, Lazarus?"

"Sure," he replied, sitting up and wincing as someone stuck a needle in his cerebral cortex.

In the living room, he looked around. "Where're Lucy and Ned, and John, for that matter?" he asked.

"I don't know," Marlene replied. "They were gone when I got back."

Karp turned his attention to the twins, who were sitting somberly on the couch. He wondered if they were crashing from their sugar buzz of the morning. "How were Pops and Grammy?"

"Grammy didn't know who we were," Zak said dejectedly.

"A lot of people confuse you and Giancarlo," he'd replied.

"No, I mean she didn't know who any of us were," he said, angrily wiping at the tears that rolled down his cheeks. "She kept calling Mom 'Josephine' and thought we were the neighbor boys from down the street."

"She asked if we were the naughty kids who ripped up her flower garden yesterday," Giancarlo said, his lip trembling. "She didn't know it was Christmas. She saw the presents and thought it was her birthday. She even opened Grandpa's presents. Why is this happening to her?"

Karp's heart suddenly ached for his children. Concetta Ciampi was the only grandmother they'd ever known. She'd been there for their births. She'd watched over them when their busy parents had been too consumed with work, changing their diapers and reading bedtime stories. Now she was being taken from them in the cruelest way imaginable. The outward appearance was the same, but the woman inside was leaving them.

"I don't know," he said. "But you need to know that she can't help what is happening to her."

"Is she dying?" Zak sniffled.

"In a way," Karp replied. "But her mind is dying before her body is ready. We've just got to do our best to let her know that we still love her—that we understand that she's still in there somewhere—and support Grandpa, too. This is very hard on him."

Later that night, the boys had settled onto the couch with him and Marlene to watch *It's a Wonderful Life*. He sent a silent thank-you to Frank Capra, wherever he was, for the film's life-affirming message.

The credits were rolling, and the twins had been sent off to bed, when Lucy and Ned—whom Karp thought looked a little like Alan Ladd in the movie *Shane* with his new coat and old cowboy hat—returned.

"Where's John?" Marlene asked.

Lucy looked troubled. "Gone . . . for now."

"What do you mean gone?" Karp asked. "What was all that heart-of-darkness stuff about earlier?"

"He went to find David Grale."

"David Grale is dead. He bled to death at the altar in St. Patrick's Cathedral."

"I know, Daddy," Lucy said. "He knows it, too. But he's been having this dream, and, well, he says he needs to at least try to locate Grale."

"Why? What's supposed to happen if he doesn't?" Karp asked. He didn't like all this spiritual mumbo jumbo; it bothered him in a way he didn't understand, which made him irritable.

"He won't say . . . not exactly," Lucy said as Ned stepped behind and wrapped his arms around her.

Karp tried to ignore the way his daughter seemed to melt into the cowboy. "Well, what did he say inexactly, then?"

"Oh, just that tens of thousands of people might die. A little Armageddon, New York style."

Karp made another mental note to talk to John about doomsday prophecies around his spiritually impressionable daughter. "Where was he going?"

"I don't know, and I don't think he did either. Just that it was going to be dark. . . . Sorry, Dad, I don't know any more than that and I'm tired. It's been a long day, and I want to go to bed. I love you."

Lucy then led Ned off to her room. Karp looked away rather than watch the pair disappear down the hallway. *They're naked in there, you know.*

Karp asked Marlene if she knew where Jojola was going. But she either didn't know much or she didn't want to talk about it. All in all, it's a strange way to end

Christmas Day, he thought. But the pathos wasn't over yet.

As he and Marlene lay in bed that night, the conversation had again turned to her parents, especially her father's growing frustration and instability.

"I'm worried about what he's going to do," Marlene said.

"You mean when she dies?"

"No. I'm worried that he may snap and hurt her. He's going crazy with the fear that something is going to happen to her on one hand, and the guilt of wishing that she'd just die on the other."

"Maybe it really is time to put her in a nursing home," Karp said.

Marlene shook her head. "I asked him again today, pleaded with him. But he won't hear of it. It's the guilt. He said, 'What if she's in there somewhere, waiting for me to come and get her out, but she can't tell me how. I can't just take her from the home she loves. I can't be that cruel.' So he just sits there hating what she's becoming, and hating himself for it."

She turned to Karp and put her hand on his chest. "If I ever have Alzheimer's and I can't do it myself," she said, "I want you to shoot me before you start to hate me."

"I could never hate you."

"I'm sure my father would have said the same thing."

23

Sunday, December 26

JOHN JOJOLA JOINED LUCY AND NED AT A SMALL
Thai bistro on Bayard and Bowery. He'd dressed for
dark work over his thermal underwear—black water-
proof boots, black pants, black turtleneck. He carried
a small black knapsack containing the Rigel 3250 goggles, a small flashlight, black gloves, a black ski mask,
and his fourteen-inch, razor-sharp hunting knife. Marlene had tried to give him a gun before she left with the
boys, but he turned her down. "I'm going to find a
man," he said, "not kill one. My knife should be sufficient for the rats."

The meal ended when an immense hairy man
appeared in front of the restaurant and pressed his
incredibly filthy face against the window in an effort to
see in. His brown-button eyes found the trio and locked
on Jojola.

"There's Booger," Lucy announced and turned to
Jojola. "It's not too late to stop this and just come home."
She didn't sound as if she thought she'd convince him,
and she was right.

"I can't, Lucy," Jojola said. "I had the dream again last night. Charlie said I'm running out of time."

The dream was always the same, with only minor variations. In it he was running, crouched over through low, narrow tunnels like those he'd encountered in Vietnam when he was pursuing the Vietcong into their underground lairs. As he ran, he passed sudden openings leading off into the dark, any of which could hide an enemy who waited to leap out and kill him.

In the dream, Jojola was pursuing a Vietcong leader he had faced during the war, known only by his Vietnamese nickname Cop, which meant Tiger. A former teacher, Cop blamed the South Vietnamese government for the murder of his family, and was the most ferocious and intelligent of the men he and his childhood friend and army recon partner, Charlie Many Horses, had been assigned to track and kill. Always, Cop had managed to stay a step ahead of them.

Once, during the war, Jojola and Charlie Many Horses had been dropped by helicopter into a valley where villagers had reported sightings of the guerilla leader. The two split up to reconnoiter the area when Jojola jumped a Vietcong soldier who was preoccupied with trying to disguise the entrance to an underground bunker. Prodded by Jojola's knife, the man pointed into the hole and said, "Cop."

Unable to deal with a prisoner, Jojola had been forced to slit the man's throat and drag him into the bush before returning to the hole. He knew he should wait for Charlie. He also knew Cop was near but rarely stayed anywhere for long.

Jojola had hesitated outside the hole. He'd tracked men into these lairs—some, simple holes in the ground, others, extensive labyrinths built to withstand U.S. bombs—to hunt them like black-footed ferrets hunted prairie dogs back home. His hesitation wasn't so much due to a fear of dying; he'd faced death many times since arriving in-country nearly two years earlier, during his first tour. But Sergeant Jojola didn't want to die underground where his soul would be trapped in the dark, away from the open skies and sun.

Yet, Cop was in there, and so that was where he needed to go, too. What he didn't know when he plunged into the opening and found himself in a maze of tunnels, dimly lit by the occasional small candle in recesses in the walls, was that in the not-too-distant future Cop would be responsible for the massacre of a village of Hmong whom he and Charlie had befriended. And that one day Cop would kill Charlie.

In the tunnel he lost his flashlight and gun. In shock, he waited for his enemy to walk up and finish him, but instead he heard the sound of someone staggering away in the dark. I hit him, too, he thought, he's escaping! He twisted onto his back and tried to rise, but the pain struck him like a lightning bolt and he passed out.

How many hours he'd lain there he didn't know. But he woke when someone grabbed him by the shoulders. He tried to reach his knife in its sheath, but a hand restrained him.

"Goddammit, John, if you stab me I'll never get your dumb ass out of here," whispered a voice.

Charlie Many Horses was probably the only other man in Vietnam who could have tracked him into the hole and through the maze of tunnels. He hauled Jojola, who passed out from the pain twice along the way, out of the lair and then to a rice paddy, where by prearrangement they were met by a helicopter.

Cop had escaped to continue his guerilla efforts. The villagers would die and so would Charlie. Jojola had sworn to kill Cop, but his second tour of duty had ended with his friends unavenged.

Jojola's experience in Vietnam continued to haunt him after he returned to the pueblo—impervious even to drowning in alcohol—until he'd learned to accept it and the fact that no matter how fast he ran through the tunnels, or pulled the trigger when the face appeared, they would all die. He would live and try to be a good man, a police officer to serve and protect his people, and a good father to his son, Charlie, named for the long-lost brother.

And so Cop had lost his power to frighten Jojola. Until recently, when Jojola had a different dream, this one about David Grale.

Grale said, *"It's a bomb, John Jojola. A dirty bomb. And behold, a pale horse. And the name of him who sat on it was death. . . . Thus begins the final battle, John, thus begins Armageddon."*

Then Grale lifted his hand and in the dark a gun flashed. Again Jojola felt the bullet punch into him as he spun and fell. In the darkness, he was grabbed by the shoulders and turned over to find himself looking up into the gentle, sad eyes of Charlie Many Horses, who cradled him on his lap. *Sorry, my brother, there is no time to rest. You must return to New York. Find Grale . . . or all the villagers will die.*

But what will I do if I find him? Jojola asked his dream friend, but Charlie was gone and he lay awake in the dark of his bedroom.

"There's no more time," Jojola told Lucy and Ned as they all left the restaurant and met up with Booger.

"Hi, 'ucy," the giant said and hugged her; she was

probably the only human being on the planet who would have tolerated the filth.

"Hi, Booger," she said. "This is my boyfriend, Ned."

"Hi, 'ed." Booger beamed and stuck out a big greasy paw, which Ned shook trying not to remember that he'd just seen the man picking his nose with it.

"You know John Jojola," Lucy said.

Booger looked at Jojola and nodded his head. "Yes, 'e wants to fin' Grale."

Jojola also shook the extended hand. He wasn't repulsed by the odd man. In fact, with his huge mane of curly dark hair and beard that covered most of his face, as well as the dark brown eyes and rounded hump of his massive shoulders, Booger reminded him of a buffalo. A good sign, he thought. The buffalo was one of the most sacred animals to Native Americans. Even his people, who had settled in the area at Taos to grow crops a thousand years before the Spanish found them in the sixteenth century, used to ride out on the plains east of their holy mountain to hunt buffalo in the land of the Comanche.

"Where's Warren?" Lucy asked.

"Right here . . . fucking bitch blow job," Warren replied, peeking out from behind a Dumpster where he appeared to have been keeping an eye out. "We need to . . . twat whore . . . move fast. Roger won't wait."

No one seemed to know or want to say who Roger was, only that he might be able to help Jojola learn what had happened to Grale after that night at St. Patrick's. Ever since Jojola and Lucy had arrived in New York, they'd gone out at night trying to learn from the street people if Grale was alive. Lucy had called into sewer drains and yelled into subway tunnels.

Most of the street people they met who knew of

Grale said they believed that he was dead. But others muttered that perhaps there was a connection between Grale and a shadow army of Mole People who roamed the subterranean depths beneath the city—and sometimes the streets at night—hunting evil men. But no one seemed to know for sure if Grale led them, much less how to find him.

Until one evening, shortly before Christmas, Booger and Dirty Warren had suddenly appeared. "Why . . . turd face . . . do you want to find a dead . . . fuck you . . . man?" Warren asked.

"My friend here, John Jojola, had a dream," Lucy replied.

"Ah, the brave Indian . . . piece of shit . . . oh crap, oh crap," Warren said with a little bow. "But you know Grale died . . . suck my cock."

"We know," Lucy said. "But John thinks he may still be alive."

"It could be a dangerous journey, and all for nothing."

"I still have to try," Jojola interjected. "Can you help?"

Booger had stepped in front of him and bent over until his face was mere inches from Jojola's. The stench of the man's body and the foulness of his breath nearly made him gag, but there was intelligence in the small dark eyes that peered into his. "Es 'oo dangerous," the man said as he straightened again. "Es 'adness and 'eath."

"Madness and death," Warren translated. "But if that is your fate . . . motherfucker piss breath . . . who am I to stop you." He'd then told them to meet at the Thai bistro.

Outside the restaurant, Warren took Jojola aside. "It may be too late," he said. "Take Lucy and her family and flee to New Mexico."

"If it's so dangerous," Jojola replied, "why don't you leave?" He searched the man's face and thought, If the other one is a buffalo, then this one is Coyote, the Trickster, with his curious affliction. I should be wary of him, but on the other hand, Coyote has helped me in the past.

"Because . . . dumb shit . . . this is my home," Warren replied. "If the beginning of the end starts here, then here I will be."

Booger had then quickly led the way across Bowery and Canal to Chrystie. Few people were out on Christmas night and those who were gave Booger a wide berth. Every once in a while, the giant would stop his shuffling gait and look around, sniffing the air, as if he worried that they were being followed. He plunged through Sara D. Roosevelt Park and across Allen Street until he reached a row of old brick tenement buildings on Orchard Street and stopped outside the one with a sign: Lower East Side Tenement Museum.

Booger and Warren both looked around nervously; then, motioning for the others to follow, they hustled up the stairs and rang the doorbell. After a minute a light appeared inside the museum and came toward the door as if someone were carrying a candle. As was the case, when the door opened and a small, bald man wearing smeared round glasses appeared, holding the candle up to each of their faces.

"May I help you?" he asked, apparently not concerned that a filthy giant, a man muttering obscenities, an Indian, a cowboy, and a girl were standing on the doorstep of a museum that was closed for the holiday. At least that's what the sign on the door said.

"'Behold, a pale horse,'" Warren said. "Shit."

"'And the name of him who sat on it was Death,'" the little man replied. He pointed a finger at Jojola and said, "Only him. I'm sorry but the rest of you must leave."

Lucy started to object, but Jojola stopped her. "It's all

right, Lucy. This is the part I need to do on my own."

"Let me come with you," she cried. "I know David better than anyone. If he's alive he wouldn't let me be hurt."

Jojola shook his head. "Can't do it, Lucy. I have a feeling we all have a part to play out in this, but this journey is mine." He looked at Ned. "Take her home, son. And Lucy, if something happens and I don't come back . . . tell my son that I love him and will see him down the trail."

Lucy nodded and allowed herself to be guided back down the stairs. The little man closed the door and locked it behind them. He looked up at Jojola's face, searching for a moment, then turned and led the way back through the museum.

They reached a stairway and headed down into the basement, past an ancient boiler and coal furnace, until they came to a wall. Jojola wondered why they'd stopped but then the little man tapped on the wall with a small stick. A portion of the wall then moved outward, and another man, only slightly bigger than his guide and dressed in a long, hooded robe, jumped out.

"This is Roger," his guide said and turned to go.

When he was gone, the new man looked up at Jojola from beneath the hood, which shrouded most of his face in shadow. "So, you're the up-worlder who killed the demon Lichner," he said. "Nice work. You must be pretty handy with the pig-sticker you have in your bag. You might want to keep that handy where we're going."

"Where are we going?" Jojola asked.

The man grinned. "Why, down under, don't you know."

"Is that where I'll find Grale?"

The man shrugged. "Who knows what you'll find. Maybe only death." With that the man turned and went back through the secret passage.

Jojola hesitated. He didn't want to follow this man. He didn't want to die where the sun would not find his soul. Pulling open his backpack, he removed the night-vision goggles, which he placed on his head, and his knife, which he attached to his belt.

"You coming?" a voice said from beyond the hole in the wall.

"Right behind you, Roger," he said and plunged into the dark.

They'd marched for several hours in the dark—Roger using a small flashlight, Jojola with his goggles. The paths they took varied. At first they seemed to follow some sort of passageway between buildings, with old bricks beneath their feet and lining the walls.

Then Roger squeezed through a crack and Jojola followed him into what appeared to be an ancient sewer system. "Built in the 1800s and abandoned," his guide explained. "This whole island is honeycombed with passages and sewers and subway lines—some of them working, some of them not and long forgotten. Some we have no idea who built them or why."

For a time they'd followed a subway track. "Stay away from the third rail," Roger warned. "Touch it and you'll disintegrate."

That path had led to a hole that went down a rickety old ladder that had obviously been taken from somewhere else—it looked as if it had once belonged on a fire escape—and into a narrow, damp passage carved from the rock. The passage plunged down, turned corners, rose again. Sometimes there'd be a roar and a subway train would pass overhead or to one side. Other times they'd march along with no other sounds than the dripping of water and the scurrying of rats.

At least Jojola thought they were rats. Roger sometimes paused when the scurrying grew louder in side passages. He seemed concerned, but all he'd say was, "We
need to keep moving."

Although at times they kept up a good pace, other times
the going was slow as they wound their way through the
maze of tunnels, and even seemed to double back. At one
point, after they'd plunged for what Jojola estimated to be
a half mile, Roger called a halt.

"Sorry, need to catch my breath," he'd panted.

"You okay?" Jojola asked.

"Not really," Roger replied. "My liver's giving out on
me. Used to be a stockbroker in the up-world, you know.
Had a wife and kids, nice home in Mount Vernon. But,
man, did I love the bottle. Lost everything, including my
self-respect. Now look where it got me." The man laughed
bitterly.

"Yeah? I had my own love affair with tequila and
whiskey," Jojola said. "Spent a lot of time in gutters and
jails. But why live down here?"

"Too hard to stay sober up there," Roger said. "And I
guess this is my self-imposed purgatory to atone for
abandoning my family, as well as myself. I did some
pretty terrible things up there. At least here I'm doing
some good."

"How's that?"

"Why, trying to keep the hounds of hell at bay so that
the rest of the world can enjoy their Christmas dinners
and PlayStations," Roger said with another bitter laugh.
"Demon hunting, Mr. Jojola."

"Demon hunting?" Jojola asked. But instead of an
answer from Roger, he was struck by a rock that came out
of the dark, and then another.

"You're about to find out, Mr. Jojola. I suggest you get

out that knife," Roger shouted, pulling aside his robe to produce a long knife of his own.

Then Jojola saw them. A dozen pale human figures with luminous eyes, flitting from crevice to crevice toward them. They brandished sticks and metal bars; occasionally one stooped to pick up a rock and hurl it in their direction.

"Show them no mercy, Mr. Jojola," Roger said. "They'll show you none." With that he shouted, "In the name of Jesus Christ, I commend your souls to hell," and ran to meet the attackers.

Jojola followed and found himself face-to-face with a large man in tattered clothing with fingernails like talons. "Stop, I don't want to fight you," Jojola said.

The man opened his mouth in a horrible leer but just hissed as he swung a huge club at Jojola, who ducked and stabbed for the man's chest. The blade sank deep and the man screamed and fell to the ground writhing.

Before he could turn, another of the attackers jumped on Jojola's back and sank his teeth deep into his shoulder. Reaching up, Jojola grabbed the man by the hair and pulled him off. Still holding him up, he slashed with his blade and nearly severed his assailant's head from his body.

The attack was over as suddenly as it began. Jojola and Roger had backed themselves against a wall with their blades out when one of the group barked some command and they retreated—though not before clubbing the first of Jojola's victims to death and dragging him and the other dead man off.

"Something for the old stew pot tonight," Roger said and laughed mirthlessly.

"What in the hell was that?" Jojola said, rubbing his shoulder where he'd been bitten.

"We like to call them morlocks, you know, after the creatures in H. G. Wells's book *The Time Machine*,"

Roger replied. "But really they are evil men—murderers, rapists, pedophiles, the criminally insane possessed by demons—who have fled into these lovely depths, though they venture out on dark nights to prey upon up-worlders. These, and others even more dangerous, are the ones we hunt, Mr. Jojola. . . . What's wrong with your shoulder?"

"One of the bastards bit me."

"Hmmm, that's not good. They don't have the best dental hygiene, you know, and their bites tend to cause infection. We'll have to have it treated when we arrive."

"And when will that be?"

"Soon, Mr. Jojola. But I should caution you, we are in a very dangerous spot and not just from our hungry friends. We will have to go very slowly and carefully."

The troop of armed men had proved Roger right, but they'd run into no further problems by the time they reached their destination. Jojola's guide led him down another ladder, at the bottom of which stood a half-dozen men and women, all armed with a variety of weapons, from knives and spears to one or two guns.

"Your knife," said the largest, stepping up to Jojola with his hand out.

Jojola stepped back. "Sorry, no one touches my knife while I'm alive."

"Suit yourself," the big man said, lowering a sawed-off shotgun.

A moment later, the shotgun clattered to the ground, and Jojola straddled the man, who lay on his stomach, and pulled his head back by the hair, the knife at the man's throat. The man's stunned comrades, who'd hardly had time to react when the Indian disarmed their leader, pointed their weapons but seemed unsure of what to do next.

"If they don't back off, you'll die before I do," Jojola snarled.

"Stop!" a loud voice commanded from off to the side. "We are all friends here."

A tall, hooded figure entered the tunnel from behind a curtain of burlap sacks sewn together. He threw back his hood and Jojola found himself looking at the face that had haunted his dreams recently.

"David Grale," he said, releasing the leader of the guards.

"John Jojola, I presume," Grale said and laughed, which caused him to suddenly bend over and gasp in obvious pain. He straightened again and, his voice weaker, said, "My friends tell me that you and Miss Lucy Karp have been inquiring about my health, which is sadly lacking, I'm afraid."

Jojola pointed to Grale's midsection. "The knife wound?"

"Yes," Grale agreed. "I'm afraid the demon Lichner has done for me, although it will take a bit more time than he would have hoped."

"But I felt for your pulse . . . the blood . . ."

"Why am I not dead?" Grale asked with a solemn look. "I believe it is because God has more tasks for me before He calls me home. That and our wonderful little medical clinic we've established here in my . . . kingdom. But come, let me show you."

Grale turned and passed through the burlap sack curtain, expecting Jojola to follow. They walked quickly down another tunnel, then climbed another ladder into a large hall.

Jojola was surprised to see that the gymnasium-size hall was illuminated by electric lamps.

Grale caught his glance and smiled a little sheepishly. "We've several electricians among our brothers and sisters here in down-world, and I'm afraid we've been naughty and tapped into New York public utilities."

Looking around, Jojola took in the "brothers and sisters," who walked through the hall or conversed in small groups. Some were obviously mentally troubled, meandering around, talking to themselves. One half-naked woman ran past, shrieking, "They've taken my baby! They've taken my baby!"

Grale watched her disappear out of the hall and turned back to Jojola. "My apologies; Helen's five-year-old disappeared on the way home from school some ten years ago and she's never recovered. Some of our brothers and sisters among the Mole People take more looking after than others. But it's our Christian duty and we're happy to help."

"Who are the Mole People?" Jojola said. "I take it there is some difference between them and the morlocks or demons Roger and I met."

"Ah, so you met those we hunt . . . and who sometimes hunt us," Grale said.

"Yes, I had to kill several, and one bit me on the shoulder."

Grale frowned. "We'll need to see about antibiotics. Those wounds are common and they tend to cause nasty infections. Anyway, in answer to your question: yes, the difference is that between day and night, good and evil. The Mole People are—as Lady Liberty might say if she could speak—the wretched refuse of New York, the unwanted, the sick, the despairing . . ."

"Homeless . . . street people?" Jojola asked.

"One more step farther down the ladder of acceptance in our society," Grale said. "Those who for one reason or another—shame, loathsome physical deformities, up-world desires that they would prefer to avoid—have found their way down here. But they are not homeless. This is their home. They were a bit unorganized and were set upon by the evil ones who lurk down here as well until I arrived and brought with me the light of Jesus Christ Our Savior . . . as well as that of New York Electric. But now, as you can see, they have a place to call their own."

Grale pointed and Jojola saw that the hall was lined with small alcoves. Some were closed to view by more burlap sacking. But others were open and revealed beds and other furniture—obviously recycled from the up-world—and personal effects. Some were occupied by a single person, but others housed what appeared to be entire families.

"How do they survive?" Jojola asked.

Grale shrugged. "Scrounging, begging—and I'm afraid a certain amount of stealing, though we try to discourage it except in cases of survival—in the up-world."

Leading him to one of the larger alcoves, Grale pulled back the curtain to reveal an amazingly well-equipped medical clinic. "Sorry, appears that the doctor is out," he said. "But here my life hung in the balance for some weeks. I guess I needed four complete blood transfusions. But come, John Jojola, you did not make this journey to ask questions about people the rest of the world has forgotten, or my health."

Grale led Jojola to an alcove, spartan except for a crucifix on the wall and a straw mattress on the ground. "My humble abode. So tell me, what brings you?"

A half hour later, Jojola finished his story—both the Vietnam version and the dream version.

As he spoke, Grale's already haggard face looked even more tired. He sighed. "I think I can explain some of your dream by showing you something."

Grale swept out of the room and was joined by two

bodyguards and Jojola. They walked for perhaps a quarter of a mile—apparently paralleling a subway track, judging by the regularly interspersed roars as trains went past on the other side of the wall. As they walked, Grale filled him in.

"I don't suppose you've ever heard of a man named Alfred Ely Beach? Well, in 1870, Mr. Beach, a real dreamer, secretly built a small prototype of a pneumatic subway that would run a short distance under Broadway. He figured, correctly, that Boss Tweed and his cronies in Tammany Hall would have extorted huge sums from him to build his experiment, so he did it under their noses by renting the basement of Devlin's Clothing Store at Broadway and Murray and then, over a period of fifty-eight days, having his men dig out a tunnel."

Grale stopped his story and climbed a ladder to a wide but low-ceilinged tunnel that required they crawl as he led them in. "Quiet, please, from this point on," he whispered to Jojola. "Anyway, most New Yorkers know the story of Mr. Beach and his clandestine subway, which worked, but due to Boss Tweed's machinations never went any farther."

Reaching a spot twenty yards in, Grale carefully lifted a sheet of metal from the ground and scooted it to the side. "What only a few know is that Mr. Beach built another, somewhat longer prototype—two blocks long that runs almost directly beneath the triangle created by the intersection of Broadway and Seventh Avenue from Forty-fifth to Forty-seventh Street—Times Square," he whispered. "He died before he could put it to use and his team sealed it off; his grand project was forgotten. However, someone has discovered this long-lost tunnel and is planning to put it to their own less-benign uses. Here, have a look."

Jojola crawled to the place where Grale had removed

the metal sheet. He looked down, letting his eyes adjust to the dimly lit interior of another large tunnel.

Now he understood the presence of the armed troop of men in the tunnel. More than a dozen such men were below him no more than twenty-five yards away—some of whom appeared to be Middle Eastern, including some in traditional headgear wrapped to hide their faces; others were young blacks. They carried weapons, and the Arabs were obviously training the black men on how to conduct a defensive delaying action to protect whatever was at the other end of the tunnel.

Grale tugged on his sleeve and motioned him to follow as he crawled farther up along the top of the other tunnel. Behind them the bodyguards slid the sheet metal over the viewing hole.

At the far end of the tunnel, Grale removed another cover and motioned for Jojola to look through the opening. Below him more men were rolling fifty-gallon drums into place, hundreds of barrels it seemed, though it was tough to tell in the light thrown by the workers' lanterns. Above the center of the drums, a scaffold had been erected on which several foot-locker–size boxes had been placed.

Jojola backed away from the view port; then he and Grale retreated until they stood again in the access tunnel. "What are they doing?" he asked.

"We suspect that the barrels contain fuel oil to be mixed with those bags of ammonium nitrate you could see stacked up in that far corner," Grale said. "As best we can tell, there's between three and four hundred fifty-pound bags, which is about four times the amount Timothy McVeigh and Terry Nichols used to blow up the Alfred P. Murrah Federal Building in Oklahoma City. As I told you, that tunnel runs directly beneath the north end of Times Square."

"They're planning on blowing up Times Square?" Jojola said, alarmed.

Grale nodded. "I'd guess on New Year's Eve," he said. "The blast, according to one of our former engineers—a good man but a cocaine addict who suffers from extreme paranoia and simply can't handle the up-world—should be enough to blow through the other subway lines that bracket Times Square and create one hell of a hole. And I mean that literally: fires, buildings collapsing, and tens of thousands of people trapped in the middle of it. The initial blast will probably cause the most casualties, but it's not necessarily the worst of it."

Stunned, Jojola heard himself ask, "What would that be?"

"Two weeks ago, we found two dead men—bearded, obviously Arabs—at the bottom of a pit," Grale said. "They showed all the signs of having died of radiation poisoning. We believe they were probably the couriers who brought the material into the country."

"The material?" Jojola asked. Then the answer dawned on him. "The dirty bomb in my dream. They're planning on blowing up Times Square and releasing radiation into the air."

"Yes, killing thousands more and making Manhattan unlivable for the next hundred years," Grale said. "Of course, the real purpose of the atomic weapon is to sow fear. The use of such a weapon on a city in the United States will cause widespread panic."

As he spoke, Grale's voice grew increasingly prophetic, and he began to pace. The change disturbed Jojola. He's losing it.

"The economy will plunge," Grale continued. "Our allies will be afraid to do business with us for fear that it could happen to them."

"You've got to tell the police," Jojola said.

Grale stopped short, his eyes blazing as he turned toward Jojola. "I'm sorry, my brother, but we can't do that."

I was afraid this is where that was leading, Jojola thought. "Why not? As you said, thousands will die. How can you let that happen?"

"We are aware of that," Grale said. "But if we tell the police, they will discover our down-world and that will be the end of us."

"What does that matter when so many lives are at stake?" Jojola said, aghast.

"Maybe not much to you," Grale said. "But everything to those who live here."

"But they'll all die, too, if that bomb goes off."

"If we don't succeed in stopping them ourselves, then yes," Grale said. "We don't have the strength of arms to take them on. So we've been trying to narrow the odds a few at a time."

"The beheadings."

"Yes, those and others down here where our little life-and-death struggles go on unnoticed by the up-world. We kill them. They kill those of us they catch. The beheadings are our attempt to terrorize the terrorists into abandoning their plans and hamper their recruiting efforts. Some of the more superstitious have even taken to calling me Shai-tan; I think it's rather ironic that such evil men would call *me* Satan. Or sometimes they use the fallen one's true Islamic name, Iblis."

Grale sighed as if talking about recalcitrant school bullies. "They are right about one thing: they refer to the 'others'—the so-called morlocks, though I prefer the term demons—as *rajim,* the cursed ones. Unfortunately, they have been led to believe that our efforts in the up-world are the work of a few racists, and their plans are going forward."

"Then you have to go to the police, get help. Surely, something can be done for your people."

"Like all the wonderful things that are done for the homeless and insane now?" Grale said. "No, my friend, we will defeat them ourselves, or we will all die. As the Muslims say, *In sha' Allah*, 'God's will be done.' "

"What do you mean?" Jojola said angrily. "How could God want such an evil thing?"

"It isn't a matter of what God wants, but it is all according to *His* plan. It's the beginning of the end . . . of Armageddon . . . the United States will react to this act by lashing out and attacking Muslim countries that have any link at all to Islamic extremists. Other western countries will either join them or, fearing a U.S. hegemony in the Middle East and a threat to their oil supplies, will support the Arab nations. Muslims around the world will react, entire generations will dedicate themselves to suicide bombings. Starting with the Middle East, the world will convulse in flames and death. As it foretells in the Bible, the nations of the world will divide along the lines of those on the side of God and those on the side of Satan. The temple will be restored in Jerusalem and the Messiah will return to establish his kingdom on Earth."

"You're insane," Jojola said.

"Probably," Grale said. "But I might also be right."

"If you won't go to the police, I will."

"I thought you'd probably say that, John," Grale replied. "But I'm afraid I can't allow it."

Jojola heard the sound behind him, but too late. A blow struck him on the side of the head and then the world went black.

24

KARP STOPPED AT DIRTY WARREN'S NEWSSTAND outside 100 Centre Street and regretted it immediately when the man shouted, "Morning, Karp. Did you have a . . . damn shit . . . great Christmas?"

"Great, Warren. And you?" He really wasn't in the mood for light, epithet-filled conversation. Kipman had called Sunday, apologized for bothering him at home, then asked for a meeting between just himself, Karp, and Rachman. The way old Hotspur said it, Karp knew it wasn't going to be pretty. So he'd decided that they'd meet Monday. It was officially a legal holiday because Christmas had fallen on a Saturday, but he preferred that the rest of the staff not be around if things got ugly.

"Went and saw my . . . oh crap . . . mother in Queens. Thanks for asking."

Karp turned to go, but Warren called out to him. "Okay, smart guy, in *It's a Wonderful Life*, what film is showing at the movie theater in Bedford Falls as George runs down the street?"

Answering Warren's film trivia questions had been an

ongoing contest between the two of them for years. Warren had yet to stump him and wasn't going to with this question. "Too easy, pal, you're slipping," he said. "I just watched *It's a Wonderful Life* with the family Christmas night."

"So what's the answer . . . bitch?"

"The Bells of St. Mary's," Karp replied. He expected Warren to be disappointed and launch into one of his expletive-enhanced tirades, but instead the little man just smiled.

"Okay, genius," he said, "but what's the other connection between the two films?"

"Now that's a good one," Karp admitted. "How many tries do I get?"

Warren grinned. "No way, Karp. This isn't some . . . piss shit . . . guessing game. You either know or you don't."

"Oh, well in that case . . . Henry Travers, who played Clarence the Angel in *Wonderful Life,* also starred in *Bells* as Horace P. Bogardus."

"Goddammit!" Warren howled. "It's not . . . fuck you . . . natural for someone to have all that crap swimming around in his head."

"Have a great day, Warren," Karp said.

"Don't look so smug," Warren grumped. "Son of a bitch."

"Warren . . ."

"Can't fucking prove nothin'."

Inside the Criminal Courts building the Streets of Calcutta were deserted. The eighth floor was even quieter, and there was no one in his office when he walked in. He breathed a sigh of relief. At least at the office he could get a moment's respite from the twins' haul of new Game Boys, PlayStations, and Xboxes and their never-ceasing electronic noises that he was sure had been invented to drive parents insane.

The day after Christmas had dawned bright and clear, which seemed a good thing until Karp felt the bitter cold that accompanied it as he led his clan to Rockefeller Center to skate beneath the tree.

The outing proved to be just the ticket to shake the family's melancholy over Marlene's parents and the disappearance of John Jojola. They'd gone home and feasted on leftovers from the party, then called it an early night.

Karp was already in bed when Marlene walked in from the bathroom in a new silk robe. "I just remembered," she said, "that I forgot to give you that early Christmas present."

"It's never too late," he said.

Marlene let the gown fall open. Apparently she'd spent quite a bit at Victoria's Secret. "Care to unwrap one more?" she asked.

"I think I might die . . . but what a way to go," he said.

"Hmmm," she murmured, stalking him across the bed like her totem mountain lion. "I suggest you lie back then and let me do all the work. I wouldn't want to overtax that poor old heart."

The next morning as he was putting on his coat to leave for work, Marlene had slipped up to him and kissed him a little longer and a little warmer than the standard good-bye buss. "I love you, Butch Karp, and don't know what I'd do without you."

"Feeling's mutual, Marlene Ciampi. And, God willing, we'll never have to find out what it means to be without each other."

Walking to work, he'd wondered why he'd added, "God willing." That wasn't the sort of thing he normally said. He'd never believed that God would react one way or another based on superstitious addenda to conversations. Must be the season, he told himself.

In his office, Karp pulled the bear fetish Jojola had given him out of his pocket and placed it on his desk. He hoped it might make him feel wise, but mostly he felt grouchy as a grizzly when he walked into the conference room a half hour later.

Kipman and Rachman were already seated on opposite ends of the table, not speaking, just staring off into space. Karp took his usual seat.

"Okay, Harry," he said. "Talk to me."

Kipman adjusted his glasses and cleared his throat but did not look at Rachman. "In light of what just occurred with the Columbia basketball players' case, I spent the weekend down here looking over the case of the People v. Alexis Michalik."

"YOU WHAT!" Rachman seethed. "What gives you the right to second-guess—"

"Actually," Kipman interrupted, "as this office's chief appellate attorney, I have the right to vet cases where I might have concerns about future grounds for appeal. And you know that. After all, better to correct a problem before it's a problem."

Rachman sputtered she was so angry. "Concerns about future appeals? You sneaky little—"

Karp rapped on the table with his knuckles. "Rachel, please, Harry does have the obligation to prereview cases that he may have to defend later." He asked Kipman to go on.

"Well, I have to say that I have some real concerns about the Michalik case."

"Oh, my God." Rachman started to say more but shut

up after she looked at Karp, who gave her all the warning she needed with his legendary glare.

"For one thing, during a follow-up interview with the police, the complainant, Sarah Ryder, told a detective that when she 'woke up' from an apparently drug-induced sleep, she was naked and tied by her wrists to the legs of a couch. In that interview, she says it was at that point that Michalik removed his pants and, as she begged him to stop, he'd raped her. However, in her initial interview with the police, Ms. Ryder told the officer that Michalik was already raping her when she woke up. Nor was there any mention of attempts to dissuade the defendant."

"Please," Rachman sneered. "This is your big concern? She's mixed up about at what point Michalik actually raped her? And did you ever think that maybe the first officer didn't ask her if she'd told Michalik to stop?"

Kipman shrugged. "Perhaps, perhaps not. If I may continue . . . I am also wondering why we haven't heard from you, during discussions of cases in this very room, that the complainant has a mental health history that may be relevant to these allegations."

Rachman snorted. "Because it's not relevant."

"This includes having made false sexual assault allegations against another man in the past."

"A mixed-up child, angry over her parents' divorce and the mother's subsequent remarriage to a man she didn't like."

"Also, apparently Ms. Ryder used to date a member of the New York Rangers hockey club. But when he broke up with her, she attempted suicide by swallowing a jar of pills."

"A cry for help," Rachman interjected, "from a young woman who'd been led to believe this man loved her.

Then when he said it was over, she gave in to despair. Is that a crime? You want to talk about something that's relevant to the case? How about an eyewitness who sees her in the building, disheveled and in tears? Then she tells him that she's been raped. Or how about the roofies in the beer glass and in her blood tests? How about the doctor who says she has injuries consistent with forced sexual contact? And the rope burns on her wrists? All of it relevant, admissible in court, and consistent with her story."

Kipman nodded. "No one disputes that there was probable cause for the arrest and that you have a strong case. And you're right, the complainant's medical history will probably . . . probably . . . not be allowed into evidence. However, it is relevant to us as we decide whether to go forward, if it is clear that this complainant lied to the investigating officers and to you."

Rachman frowned. "What do you mean she lied? About what?"

"You'll recall that during the rape examination the doctor took swab samples from her body, and the investigating officer collected her clothing to be tested for body fluids. You'll also recall that the complainant stated that she had not had any sexual relations with any other man, except the suspect, for a period of several months."

"What about it?"

"Well, the reason I asked for this meeting is that the DNA test results came in late Friday afternoon," he said. "The stain on the victim's blouse was a match for the suspect."

"You're surprised?" Rachman smiled.

"Not about that," Kipman said. "However, there was a small stain in her panties, almost too small to test, but enough. It was another semen stain . . . but not the defendant's."

Rachman sat silently for a moment, then slapped the table with her hand. "Doesn't matter," she said. "Her prior sexual history is not relevant."

"No, but it is relevant that she lied," Kipman said. "The defense will have copies of her statements, and they will have copies of the DNA reports. At the very least, they will have an argument in pretrial motions that if the victim lied about her sexual history, this information can be used to impeach her on the stand. It also gives them an opening to get into her mental health history, if they can demonstrate that she has established a pattern of false accusations and lies about sexual assaults."

"The shield laws would never allow it," Rachman countered.

"The shield laws are not absolute," Kipman said.

"The very reason the shield laws were created was to make inadmissible these distractions," Rachman said.

"Maybe, but the table's been set," Kipman said. "And we now have a complainant who we know has a history of making false accusations and lying. She lied about this case. It's not just a question of what we can fight in court. As Butch says, we have an obligation to prosecute only when we have a moral certainty that we are right. I think there's a real question of whether we have that moral certainty."

"Whose side are you on, Kipman?" Rachman shouted. "So what if she had sex with a boyfriend and didn't want to have some cynical police detective thinking she was a slut. Maybe she forgot to wash those panties."

"The stain was recent, even post this alleged incident with Michalik," Kipman said.

"Doesn't matter," Rachman argued, her voice rising. "The only question—and I don't know why I keep having to explain this in the office of the New York District

Attorney—is whether she consented to have sex with Alexis Michalik. Women are being raped by men they know at epidemic rates, and this office would have us go back to the Dark Ages when it was the victim on trial. I'm sick and tired of it." As she finished, Rachman stood up and slammed her file down on the table.

She looked as if she was going to go on but Karp silenced her. "Sit down, Ms. Rachman. You will conduct yourself as a professional. Mr. Kipman has raised legitimate concerns that need to be addressed, not ignored. . . . Now, I want you to go home, relax, and then the next time I hear about this case from you, I want to hear your evidence—all the evidence—and then we will decide how to proceed. And if we go forward with the charges, Ms. Rachman, it will be with that moral certainty or it will not happen. Do I make myself clear?"

Whatever Rachman was going to say stuck in her throat and all that came out was a strangled, "Yes, sir."

"You've done a lot of good work for this office and on behalf of the people who count on you to protect them," Karp said. "But I am concerned that you are allowing your zeal for your work to interfere with your judgment. So just do as I ask."

Rachman dropped her eyes to the file in front of her. She quickly pushed the papers back into the folder and, averting her eyes from Kipman, walked stiffly and silently out of the room.

When she was gone, Karp turned to Kipman. "What do you make of the semen in the panties?"

Kipman shrugged. "It could be like Rachel says; the girl has a boyfriend but for one reason or another didn't want to tell the detective. Maybe she didn't want to look promiscuous, or was worried that it might impact her credibility. But the fact is she lied, and we better be ready to have a good explanation to give a judge, and if he doesn't buy it, a jury."

Both men jumped a little when the telephone in the conference room rang. Karp answered it.

"Hey, Butch," Clay Fulton said. "Marlene said you decided to get a jump start on the week."

"Yeah, Clay, what's up?" The detective had been around too long to get too worked up over news that could wait for the usual work hours.

"Well, maybe nothing," Clay said. "But one of the detectives on that case with the Russian professor was over yesterday visiting with his wife and we got talking. He has some concerns about the way the information they've come across is being handled by our Sex Crimes Bureau."

Karp felt a headache coming on, the little brother of the beast he'd had Christmas Day. He pressed the conference call button so that Kipman could hear. "Yeah? Such as?"

"Well, he said there's a second eyewitness who was at the building that night. He interviewed a janitor who says he was outside having a smoke when he saw the complainant leave. This witness doesn't exactly describe a distraught young woman who'd just been sexually assaulted. In fact, and I quote, 'She laughed and did a little dance spin at the bottom of the stairs.' "

"Did the complainant see the janitor?" Kipman asked.

"Oh, hi, Harry, didn't know you were there. He didn't think so . . . he was sitting on a bench off to the side in the dark. He just figured she was a happy college coed and didn't think any more about it until he saw the newspapers."

"Sure he saw the right woman?" Karp said.

"Apparently he was positive when my friend showed him a photograph."

"Maybe at that distance he was confused about whether she was laughing or crying," Karp suggested. "Maybe the 'dance' was because she tripped."

"Yeah, maybe," Fulton said. "But after my friend read the report from the other investigators, he called the janitor back and asked why he didn't mention the first witness bumping into the complainant at the top of the stairs. The janitor's reply, and again I quote, was, 'What man? There wasn't nobody else around.' The janitor even went back and checked the after-hours sign-in book."

"There's a sign-in book?" Karp said. An angry midget was banging on the inside of his head with a ball-peen hammer.

"Yep," Fulton said. "I guess you've got the picture—no one else signed in after the complainant. But here's what was bothering my friend. His report about the second witness never made it into the case file. He checked. And he knows he gave it to Rachman."

"Aw, Christ," Karp swore.

"You okay, boss?"

"Uh, yeah, sorry, Clay. Just getting a headache."

"Guess this didn't help."

"Forget about it. Thanks for calling."

Fulton hung up, and Karp turned to Kipman. "I don't want a word of this to get out," he said. "If Rachel's going to hang herself, she's now got plenty of rope."

25

Tuesday, December 28

MARLENE TRUDGED UP THE CREAKING STAIRS OF the nineteenth-century apartment building on Minetta Street in the Village. Reaching the fourth floor, she walked down the hall until she found what she was looking for, apartment 4C. Vivaldi's *Four Seasons* and the cloying odor of marijuana drifted out from under the door. She knocked. Footsteps approached and the peephole darkened as the occupant looked out.

"Who is it?" a man's voice asked.

"Marlene Ciampi. I called."

A dead bolt was pushed to the side and the door opened to reveal Ted Vanders in faded blue sweatpants and a NO MORE YEARS anti-Bush T-shirt that looked as if it had doubled as a napkin. His red-rimmed eyes flicked to her face and down to the ground as he stepped back. "Come on in."

"Thank you," Marlene said. Inside, she looked around the tiny living room. A stained and faded couch whose springs had long ago given up offering support sat against one wall, while a La-Z-Boy recliner of equal vintage and a littered coffee table between them completed the furniture. An ashtray on the table overflowed with butts; a freshly lit cigarette was smoldering on top of them, an apparent and not very successful attempt to hide the heavier pot smell. A cheap stereo sat on the ground beneath the window leading to the fire escape.

"I already told the cops everything I know," Vanders said, sinking into the chair.

"Yes, I'm sure they were very thorough," Marlene said. "But sometimes they miss something, and I just want to review a few questions I have. After all, a man's freedom and career are at stake here, and I'm sure you want him to have a fair trial."

Vanders seemed to have a hard time following the question and it took him a moment to realize he was expected to reply. "Uh, yeah, sure," he said. "I just have a lot to do to get ready for the next semester, and I've been up since five working on my master's thesis. But if I can answer a couple of questions, I'm happy to help."

Marlene smiled. "Thank you, Ted. I know you're busy so I'll keep this short. Maybe you could just sort of walk me through that evening."

Vanders picked up the burning cigarette and took a drag. "Sure. Uh, let's see, I was heading into the building to use my adviser's computer. Dr. Hurley lets me have a key so I can use her office when she's not there."

"Does that key get you into the building, too?" Marlene asked.

Vanders hesitated and took another puff. She could almost see the wheels spinning in his head as he analyzed the question.

"Um, no, usually I have to buzz for the janitor, but I was just walking up the stairs to the entrance when Sarah,

I mean Miss Ryder, came out of the door. I asked her to hold the door; then I noticed she was crying."

"Was there anybody else around?"

Vanders hesitated again but shook his head. "No. I guess the janitor must have been on break or cleaning one of the other offices."

"Okay, so go on . . . Miss Ryder was crying. . . ."

"Yes," Vanders said. "And her hair was messed up, and her blouse was sort of out of place."

"So what happened next?"

"I asked her if she was okay, and if there was something I could do. At first she wouldn't say anything . . . just kind of stood there crying. So I asked her again and she said, 'I was just raped by my professor.'

"I asked her who, but she wouldn't say. She seemed sort of disoriented. Like she was on drugs."

"Had you ever met Miss Ryder before?"

Vanders shook his head emphatically. "No. We don't exactly travel in the same social circles." He tried to laugh.

"You've never met her but you can tell that she's disoriented. How do you mean?"

"Well, she was wobbling around a little and just seemed high or something."

"And this stranger confides that she'd just been raped?"

"Yes."

"Did you go call the police?"

"She asked me not to. She said she just wanted to forget about it."

"So why did you come forward later?"

"I read an article in the newspaper that Professor Michalik had been arrested for raping a student. I put two and two together and figured that the girl I saw had gone to the cops. I thought it was my civic duty to come forward."

"Your civic duty," Marlene repeated. "Of course. And again, you met her at the front entrance to the building?""

"Yes, the front," Vanders said. He was growing more nervous, alternating putting the cigarette down and picking it up but not always putting it to his lips. "Is that all? I really do have to get back to studying."

"Yes, for the moment," Marlene said, "but could I impose on you to use your bathroom. I had a venti caffe latte at Starbucks and my bladder isn't what it used to be. Then I'll be out of your hair."

Vanders practically leaped to his feet. "Yes, of course." He escorted her to the bathroom.

Marlene noticed that the door to what had to be the bedroom was closed. He saw her glance at it and almost shoved her into the bathroom. "There you go," he said. "Sorry it's a mess."

Once inside, Marlene shut the door. She noticed that the toilet seat was down. Sure sign of a woman in the house, she thought. Someone's training him. Everything else about the room was, as he said, a mess. A tube of toothpaste was open on the counter, its contents oozing out, and the mirror looked as if it hadn't been cleaned since Nixon was in office.

She flushed the toilet to disguise the sound of her opening the medicine cabinet. A quick survey of the contents yielded what she hoped to find. Bingo, roofies, she thought, and opened the pill container. She removed two pills and then replaced the cap and put the bottle back in the cabinet. Running the water down the sink, she closed the cabinet door, and then listened for her cue.

Outside the door of apartment 4A, two men began arguing. Vanders looked out the peephole to see who was yelling, but the men were just out of sight. He banged on his door. "Hey, quiet down out there. I'm trying to study."

The voices got louder. Vanders opened the door and saw a large, horribly filthy man tussling with a smaller man with a long nose, who was swearing with an expertise the likes of which Vanders had never heard before.

" 'Ooh gonna get it 'ow!" the large, filthy man shouted.

"Yeah, you and . . . motherfucker shit face . . . what army, crap," the little guy yelled back.

"Hey, you guys get out of here or I'll call the cops," Vanders threatened. "You don't belong in this building. And, oh, God, one of you smells like something crawled up inside of you and died. Get out!"

" 'crew 'ooh," the filthy man said to Vanders.

"Yeah, screw you, cock vagina mouth," his opponent added, before turning and pushing the big man, who roared something unintelligible and swung his fist. The smaller man easily ducked the punch, which carried past and struck Vanders squarely in the nose.

The blow knocked Vanders back into the apartment and to the ground just as Marlene emerged from the bathroom. She ran over and looked out in the hall. The two antagonists were hustling away in the direction of the staircase. They paused at the top and looked back. Booger flashed her the victory sign and then they ran down the stairs and out of sight.

Marlene ducked back inside and knelt next to Vanders, who was crying and trying to stop the blood that poured from his nose. She produced a large white handkerchief from her purse and started to dab at his face. "Oh, my God, are you all right?" she asked.

"My node, I dink dey broke my node," Vanders moaned.

"Lie back until the bleeding stops," Marlene advised. "Shall I call the cops or an ambulance?"

"No, I don't dink dat's necessary. Are dey gone?"

"Yes," Marlene said. "A couple of bums, by the looks of them. They're probably a mile away by now."

Vanders sighed and lay back. Marlene continued to sop up the blood and once "accidentally" gave his nose a poke.

Vanders screamed. "Wad did oo do dat for?" he cried.

"Sorry," she said. "I was just trying to see if your nose was broken. It doesn't look crooked." A minute later, she added, "The bleeding seems to have stopped. You can probably get up now."

Vanders sat up. "Yes, I dink I'm otay. Danks for da handkerchief. Sorry, I dink it's ruined."

Marlene looked at the bloody cloth in her hand and shrugged. "That's okay. I'll just take it home and wash it. I hear vinegar will get blood out." She stood up. "Well, if you're sure you'll be okay, I'll be going."

Vanders stood up and gently felt his nose. "Yes, danks, I dink I'll lie down for a few minutes."

When the annoying Ciampi woman left, Vanders wandered back to his bedroom and opened the door. Sarah Ryder was sitting on the bed with her arms crossed. "What in the hell was going on out there?"

Vanders explained. "How 'bout a kiss to make it bedder?" he said.

Ryder smiled back and tenderly patted his cheek. But instead of a kiss, she grabbed his nose between the knuckles of her fore- and middle finger and twisted as he yelped.

"Fuck, you know I hate kissing smokers," she said. "I might as well lick an ashtray."

"I did what you tol' me," Vanders complained.

"Yes, Ted, you were a good dog, like always. Just keep it that way or I'll really break your beak," she said; then, more to herself, she added, "I wonder what that bitch was up to."

Vanders shrugged. "She's just fishing for any-ting."

Ryder looked at Vanders. What a pathetic weakling, she thought, too bad he's so perfect for my plan. "Yes, you're probably right. Now you just be a good boy and maybe Sarah will give you a doggy-style treat one of these nights. . . . But first you'll have to brush your teeth for an hour and gargle with Listerine. I really can't stand cigarette smoke. In the meantime, I got to go. I need to call my friend Rachel at the DA's office and see if they're ready to press charges against dear professor Michalik."

A few minutes later, Ryder left the apartment and headed down the stairs. She didn't know that a large man in apartment 4B across the hall was watching through the peephole in his door. Milan Svetlov was not quite as immense as his brother, Sergei, but he was just as loyal to their boss, Yvgeny Karchovski, whom he now called on his cell phone.

Yvgeny had rented the apartment after one of his men, who'd been assigned the task of following the Ryder woman, saw her visiting the "witness." Milan had been given the job of watching Vanders's apartment and reporting any unusual activities. A visit by the woman Milan had seen at Alexis Michalik's loft two weeks earlier certainly qualified, especially with the little bit of street theater he'd just watched.

After the Ciampi woman arrived, he'd kept watching and saw the big man and his small comrade tiptoe up the apartment stairs and start their "argument." What followed was better than American television. He'd wondered about its purpose, however, until he saw the woman emerge from the apartment and carefully place the bloody handkerchief in a large Ziploc bag, which she then deposited in her purse.

When a man answered his call, Milan spoke quickly in Russian, listened, chuckled at a joke, and then went back to his post at the peephole in time to see the good-looking whore come out. You're confident now, he thought, but justice is coming.

In his office at 100 Centre Street, V.T. Newbury was also thinking about justice as he sat across from Captain Tim Carney of the New York Police Department. The captain had been invited to the meeting ostensibly for some minor internal affairs questions, only to learn that he was the one under investigation.

So far, Carney was in denial. He looked over at Clay Fulton, who sat with his arms crossed and a scowl on his face. "Come on, Clay, we've known each other twenty-five years," he said.

"Yeah, and I never liked you for even one of them," Fulton responded. "Now I like you even less. In fact, I'd like to take you out back and beat the snot out of you."

Newbury grinned. "I don't think that will be necessary, Clay," he said. "Mr. Carney's in plenty of hot water as it is. Now, Tim, would you rather explain to me or to a grand jury looking to indict you how it is that a police officer, even a captain, with a mortgage on a modest little home in Yonkers and three kids in expensive colleges can afford a condominium in Key West for . . . ," Newbury knew the number but enjoyed the dramatic effect as he studied the papers in front of him, "one and a half million dollars?"

Carney chewed his lip. He considered saying something snappy like, "By being a careful saver" but realized prudence might be the better part of valor. But he wasn't just going to flop over and said, "Am I being charged?"

"No, not yet," he said. "If you were, I would have already asked Clay here to read you your Miranda warnings. In fact, I want to make it clear and on the record—and by the way, this conversation is being tape-recorded—that you are free to leave. You don't have to answer my questions at all. But tell you what, you have until January 2 to think it over, after which time I will see who—Olav Radinskaya, Shakira Zulu, Hugh Louis, Ed Ewen, or Sam Lindahl—might be more willing to chat."

Carney blanched at the roll call of names. "Why was I your first choice?" he said.

Newbury shrugged. "Call it sentimentality or a choice between a half-dozen evils. You served the NYPD with distinction at one time—four commendations for bravery. I guess you looked ahead and saw penny-pinching in your golden years, and I can understand that wasn't a thrilling picture. But let me be clear—we're talking shades of gray. You might be the lightest shade, but you're still guilty as sin. So I'm giving you a chance to minimize the damage, but you're not going to get entirely off the hook. And by the way, if we hear that you ran back to the Rat Pack and tried to warn them—and let me assure you we will hear, just like we heard about the place in Key West—there will be no mercy."

The police captain swallowed hard and nodded. "I . . . I want to talk to a lawyer."

Newbury closed the file. "Fine, talk to a lawyer. But do it before January 2. After that we start working our way up shade by shade."

26

Friday, December 31

JOHN JOJOLA WILLED HIS TIRED FEET TO SHUFFLE TO *the tempo of a dozen hide-covered drums. Sweat dripped into his eyes beneath the elaborate kachina mask of painted wood, leather, and feathers that he wore to represent one of the ancestral spirits of his people. The pounding of the drums reverberated off the rectangular, salmon-colored adobe homes of the Taos Pueblo and throughout his body. As he danced, he prayed to the spirits of his people while the drummers sang to the spirits, asking for their help, the repetitive chanting broken occasionally by a ululating cry.*

Jojola became aware that someone was talking to him in the waking world, but he wasn't ready to wake up. He knew he was running a fever; the spot on his shoulder where he'd been bitten felt hot and throbbed with the beating of the drum; the old bullet wound he'd received from Cop in Vietnam ached. He didn't know how long he'd been handcuffed to the old wrought-iron bed in a small alcove just outside of Grale's main hall.

Days, he was sure, but it was always night in down-world.

The drummers and dancers had been at it since dawn. Sweat glistened on the bare parts of their bodies in the afternoon sun or ran in rivulets through the layer of dust that covered them from head to foot. He and the other exhausted dancers moved trancelike as they willed the beating of their hearts to become one with that of the drums and carry their tired bodies on into the night.

"John Jojola, can you hear me?"

The voice was that of David Grale. When he'd first come to after being knocked unconscious, Jojola found himself handcuffed to the bed and Grale standing over him. "I'm sorry to have hurt you and that you must now remain my guest," the madman said. "But I'm afraid it's necessary."

Grale had explained how he and the Mole People were preparing for "the last battle." On New Year's Eve, even as the terrorists prepared their bomb, they would attack.

"We have numbers on them and have created several access points behind their lines by loosening the bricks in Mr. Beach's old tunnel so that at the right moment we might surprise them. But I don't hold out much hope for success. They are much better armed and trained. And there is always a man standing by the fuse to the bomb; they rotate the guard, but I suspect that whoever's sitting there with his hand on the lighter has orders to blow it if something goes wrong. Their leader has prepared a well-protected egress from the site, so I suspect that he plans to be gone before the apocalyptic moment—a delay that may be our only chance to reach the bomb before it goes off."

"And if you don't, thousands of people will die," Jojola had replied. "Millions, if your prophecy is allowed to come true."

"It's not my prophecy." Grale shrugged. "It's in the Bible."

He had been dancing since the ceremony began without water or food and was entering the phase when exhaustion, deprivation, and the mind-numbing thudding of the drums produced hallucinations. A kachina in a headdress meant to represent a bear danced next to him. They locked eyes. It was his friend Charlie Many Horses. "Wake up, John. If you don't wake up the villagers will die. I will die because there will be no one to invite my spirit into this life; it will be as though I never lived. Wake up, John."

"Wake up, John," Grale said. "I'm going to give a special mass now. If you'd like to attend and receive absolution before the end tonight, I can have you brought into the great hall."

"You're not a priest," Jojola murmured, still locked in the dream by his fever.

"No," Grale admitted. "But I'm all they've got. I'll stop by before we start tonight and see if you'd like to confess and be saved."

"What day is it?"

"Why, I thought you knew. It's the morning of New Year's Eve day . . . December 31."

He was back dancing next to Charlie in his bear kachina outfit. "Remember what I said. Remember what the bear said. Remember what I said. Remember what the bear said," Charlie chanted to the rhythm of the drums. *"Wake up, John. Wake up, John. Wake . . ."*

". . . up, John Jojola," a voice whispered in his ear. Someone fiddled with the handcuff that held his wrist to the bedpost. Then his arm was free. Lifted into a sitting position, he was cradled by someone who spoke rapidly but quietly in a foreign language. Vietnamese? He wondered if his dream, or maybe it was real life, had shifted back to Cop's tunnels. "Charlie?" he asked, opening his eyes.

The light was dim and it took a moment to adjust but the face looking down at him with a half-smile was not Charlie's. But it was a familiar face . . . from a dream or the here and now?

"Tran?" he said.

Tran Do Vinh, a former schoolteacher, Vietcong leader, and current head of a Vietnamese tong, or crime syndicate, smiled more broadly. *"Em vui ve gap lai,"* he said.

"It is good to see you, too," Jojola said, then winced as someone on his other side stuck him with a needle.

"Penicillin," Tran explained quietly. "Dr. Bao Le, who sometimes accompanies me and my men on these little excursions, believes your fever is due to an infected bite wound on your shoulder. You apparently ignored the Do Not Feed the Animals signs." He laughed, as did the two armed Vietnamese men—one young, one middle-aged—standing guard at the entrance to the alcove.

"You should feel better quickly," the doctor added.

Jojola looked at the young man's face. "Aren't you . . . ," he began to ask.

"Yes, the son of my cousin, Thien, who you may

remember from the restaurant-supply store beneath the Karps' residence," Tran answered. "Alas, after our last little adventure together, we felt it necessary to remove our 'operations' so as not to compromise Mr. Karp's duty to uphold the law. But we are still watching out for them, which is how Lucy contacted me."

"Lucy?"

"Yes, the indomitable Lucy Karp became worried when you did not return—apparently with good reason, though she waited almost too long—and she sent me to find you. Fortunately that is not as difficult as it might have been. In the past, we have had dealings with the Mole People; they need such things as medical supplies and clothing, and we find them to be useful for spying on our 'competitors,' as well as the police. We've lost contact since Grale was killed—"

"He's alive," Jojola interrupted.

"What?"

"Yes, he's giving Mass in the big tunnel."

Tran made a motion with his head to one of his men standing guard in the opening to the alcove. The man ran off.

"Hmmm . . . well, then, I guess more accurately since Grale was wounded, they've grown more secretive. We haven't been welcome down-world, as they like to call this place, but at least we had a good idea where to look."

Tran's man came back and nodded. "He's giving communion but it may not last much longer."

"Yes," Tran said. "We should be going if you're up for it."

"I'm ready," Jojola said. His head felt light and the wound still throbbed, but just the idea of escaping the dark invigorated him. And there was the little matter of . . .

"There's a bomb set to go off below Times Square tonight," Jojola said.

Tran furrowed his brow as Jojola explained. Helping Jojola to his feet, the bandit chief said, "I don't have the men with me to take on these terrorists, just these two. All the more reason for us to leave this place."

They started to leave when Jojola turned back. "My knife," he said and retrieved the blade from a box in the corner along with his night-vision goggles. He'd turned back around and was looking at Tran's back when one of the other men returned and said, "Cop, the ceremony is over. We must hurry."

Both Jojola and Tran had frozen at the use of the nickname. "Cop . . . ," Jojola repeated it as if he'd just been informed of the death of a child. "I thought I recognized your face last summer . . . I just couldn't place it. You killed those Hmong villagers and my best friend." He slid the knife from its sheath. "I am sworn to kill you."

Tran didn't turn around. "You are wrong, but this isn't the time or place to debate with you. Kill me, my men will kill you, and this bomb will kill many thousands more. Or leave it until another day. Which will it be?"

Jojola felt the weight of the heavy knife in his hand. He imagined sinking the long blade into the kidney of his old enemy and cutting through his spine to the other kidney. "We leave it for another day."

Tran nodded and headed out of the entrance. Jojola followed, stepping over the body of Roger, who he supposed had been left to guard him. He hoped the Vietnamese had not killed him—his guide had not been a bad man—and took it as a good sign that there was no evidence of blood.

They fled down the tunnel until they reached a ladder that led down into a sewer. There they splashed on for a block before reaching another ladder down which light streamed. Another Vietnamese man waited for them at the bottom of the ladder. He quickly handed them all workman's coveralls and orange hard hats with New York Street Department stenciled on the side.

"Can you climb?" Tran asked after they got into the clothes.

"I could fly if it meant reaching the sun," Jojola said.

They emerged from a manhole in the middle of a street around which a crew of Vietnamese "workmen" had erected a traffic barrier. A white van roared up and its side door slid open. They scrambled in and the van took off, only to screech to a halt again, having very nearly struck a young black man crossing the street.

"What the fuck, dawg! I'm walking here," the young man yelled, then continued on his way without looking back.

Jojola looked at the street signs on the corner. West Forty-fourth Street and Sixth Avenue. The van then lurched forward; at Fifth Avenue it turned south.

A block away, Khalif carefully moved down the sidewalk, ready to duck into a store entrance or behind some other pedestrian in case Rashad turned around. He'd just about given himself away shouting out a warning as his friend stepped out in front of the white van. But the screeching of the car's tires and the honk of an irritated cabbie who'd also had to pull up short covered his voice.

A half hour earlier, he'd been at the basketball courts, playing H-O-R-S-E with the Karp twins, when Rashad entered the gate and said he wanted to talk. "Away from these two," he'd said, indicating the boys.

When they were out of earshot, Rashad hugged his

friend. It was a long hug, accented by strong slaps to Khalif's back.

"What was that for?" Khalif said with a grin. It had been a while since they'd talked much. Rashad was always off with his new friends—Khalif assumed that meant the Arabs—and his anti-American rhetoric had grown until Khalif wasn't comfortable around him anymore. But he still loved Rashad like a brother and was hoping the hug was a sign of a thaw in their relationship.

"Just . . . just that I'm going away for a while," Rashad said, his voice hitching a little. "And I just wanted to say I love you, man. Whatever happens, I wanted you to know that."

"Now hold on, dawg, you're scaring me," Khalif said. "What do you mean you're going away? And what's this shit about whatever happens? Are you in trouble?"

Rashad shook his head. "No, not anymore," he said. "My trouble, our trouble, is behind us. There ain't nothin' I can do to change the past, but there is something I can do to change the future."

"What in the hell are you talking about, homes?"

"I can't talk about it. At least not now, maybe someday. I got to go, but I just wanted to say . . . later, my man."

Rashad left the court and began walking north up Sixth Avenue. As Khalif watched him go, the twins came up.

"Is everything all right?" Giancarlo asked.

At first Khalif didn't answer. Then he shook his head. "I don't think so, G-man," he said. "I know that man better than I know myself. He just told me good-bye—like a forever good-bye—and I don't know why but it scares me." He was quiet again, then turned to the boys.

"Sorry, homies, I got to find out what he's up to. I'll catch you on the flip-flop."

Khalif had followed Rashad all the way up Sixth Avenue to Forty-fifth Street and then west across Seventh Avenue at Times Square.

Rashad had continued to a theater under renovation. He looked around and then hurried across the street and up the steps into the building.

Khalif waited across the street, watching from a nearby doorway. Two men in hard hats loitered outside; they didn't do much more than smoke cigarettes and check out the other men, like Rashad, who arrived one at a time and in pairs. In the time since Rashad had gone into the building, seven or eight others had followed him. But the strange thing was that nobody was coming back out.

It was even stranger that Rashad had not mentioned getting a new job with a construction company. And what did renovating a theater have to do with Rashad's statements at the basketball courts? Khalif also thought the mixture of workmen outside and those entering the building was odd. Everyone looked either Middle Eastern, Asian, or black. Not a Hispanic or a white among them.

When Rashad still hadn't come out, Khalif made up his mind to go in. He didn't want to; in fact, he was scared to death without knowing why. But he couldn't abandon his friend to whoever had manipulated him into doing whatever it was that had Khalif so frightened and Rashad sounding like he was going to his death. He owed him.

When they'd been freshmen in high school, Khalif had been the one hanging out with the wrong friends, gang members who wanted to bask in his basketball glory as a status symbol. He'd started hanging out at their crib, where one night he saw some things having to do with drugs and guns that he wished he hadn't. But he was too afraid to leave. Then Rashad showed up—just walked in the door, told Khalif to "stand the fuck up and walk the fuck out of here," and when two members of the gang got in his face, stared them down until they told Rashad "get your faggot friend out of here and don't come back."

He owed him.

Khalif crossed the street, going past the loiterers and up the steps. He had just entered the door, however, when a large, dark-skinned man with an African accent stopped him. "*A salaam alaikum,*" the man said without smiling.

"*Wa alaikum salaam.*" Khalif's response had been automatic. He'd had no idea how he was going to get past the guard so he was surprised when the man nodded toward the interior of the theater and said, "Hurry up, you're late."

Khalif swallowed hard and walked in.

Meanwhile, Zak and Giancarlo crouched behind a car. After watching Khalif follow after his friend, Giancarlo turned to his brother. "So what do you make of that?"

Zak shrugged. "Only one way to find out."

"Oh no, you're not going to—"

"My thoughts exactly." Zak stood up and walked quickly down the sidewalk. The hard-eyed loiterers watched him approach and then start to pass in front of the theater. Halfway across, he suddenly turned and ran up the steps.

"Hey, you, boy!" one of the loiterers yelled, but Zak was already through the doors. He was smiling until he looked up and saw the large guard.

"What are you doing here?" the man demanded.

"I was looking for a bathroom," Zak said. "I've got to go really bad." He danced from foot to foot to prove his need.

"There's no bathroom here, now leave," the guard said.

"Wait!" a man yelled from behind the guard. "Grab him!"

The guard lunged for Zak, who easily dodged him and turned to run out the door. He might have made it, too, except for one of the loiterers, who had run up the steps and caught him just as he was exiting.

Zak launched himself at the surprised loiterer. He stomped on the man's foot and punched him in the groin before being grabbed by the neck from behind by the big guard.

"Get ya' hands off me," he yelled as he was dragged, kicking and punching back, into the theater, where the man who'd ordered the guard to catch him stood. He found himself facing an olive-skinned man with a pock-marked face who looked at him like a snake studying a small bird.

"Let me go," Zak said, swinging wildly at the guard, who held him at arm's length to avoid the blows. "My dad's the district attorney."

The man bent over until his face was inches from Zak's. He smiled—as unpleasant an expression as the boy had ever seen. "I know," he said. "I saw you and your brother at the basketball court."

27

THE DECAPITATION MURDERS INVESTIGATION HAD taken an alarming twist that began when Karp received a visit from three men, all of whom seemed to have been struck from the same mold of clean-cut, square-jawed athletic types, an impression they added to by wearing the same dark glasses and nearly identical dark suits. He recognized the oldest of them, the one with the gray crew cut, as Agent in Charge S. P. Jaxon, Espey to his friends.

"Espey, my man," Karp said, breaking from his conversation with Mrs. Milquetost in the outer office. "What brings the FBI to my neck of the judicial jungle?"

"Good to see you, too, Butch," Jaxon said. He gestured toward Karp's inner office. "Got a minute?"

"Sure," Karp said, the radar going up. Jaxon, an old friend who now headed up the FBI's New York office, was a man of few words, but he wasn't abrupt unless time was of the essence. "Mrs. Milquetost, see that we're not disturbed."

"Milquetost?" Jaxon said under his breath as he and the other two men preceded Karp into the room.

"Don't ask," Karp said just as quietly, closing the door behind them. He walked around his desk and sat down, indicating that they should do the same. "Okay, Espey, where's the fire?"

"I'm afraid that's the million dollar question," Jaxon replied.

The way he said it sent a chill down Karp's spine. Something serious is about to go down, Karp, my man, he thought.

Jaxon introduced the other two men as Kris Kluge of the CIA and Gary Albert of National Homeland Security. "We may have a very serious situation on our hands," the FBI agent said.

Karp spread his hands. "Go ahead. Whatever I can do to help."

Jaxon smiled and then gave him the rundown. "Thanks, I knew you'd say that. We've identified two of the three heads found recently in Manhattan," he said. "Two of them are on just about everybody's terrorist watch lists. Both Al Qaeda, and we expect the third was, too; he was with one of the other guys, just another one we haven't seen before."

It already didn't sound good, but Karp could tell from the way Jaxon was laying his story out that the worst was yet to come. "I'm waiting for the other shoe to drop," he said.

Jaxon looked at him steadily for a moment with his deep-set, coffee-colored eyes, then turned to Albert. "Here it is," Albert said with a slight Texas twang. "When we X-rayed the heads at Quantico to help with the ID, the film came out overexposed. They were hot as charcoal briquettes at a barbecue."

"Radiation?" Karp asked.

"Yep. Probably would have killed them sooner than later if our friend with the knife wasn't around."

"You know it was a knife?"

"Yeah, probably a big hunting knife, judging by the length of the slash marks and the nicks on the vertebrae."

"What about the radiation?"

"Isotopes from the heads of the three stooges indicate a below-weapons-grade plutonium. They'd been around it for quite a while."

It dawned on Karp what they were driving at. "You think they brought a dirty bomb into New York City," he said.

Jaxon nodded his head. "They'll use a conventional bomb and essentially put the radioactive materials on top of it. When the real bomb blows up, the nasty stuff gets thrown into the air, sucked into lungs, sipped in water . . . you get the picture."

"Most of the casualties, especially at first, would probably be from the initial blast," Kluge said. "Maybe thousands of lives. But they're almost secondary to the terrorists. The real thing is to, well, cause terror. Panic the population. Destabilize the economy."

"Make us afraid," Karp finished for him. "So who killed these guys?"

Jaxon shrugged. "We don't know. The Mossad says they didn't do it—not that they'd necessarily tell us the truth, though in this case I believe them. Could even have been a splinter group that wants to get credit. But I doubt the current story that it was a bunch of redneck good old boys. The two guys we know were no slouches; they were trained, effective, cold-blooded killers. Bubba wouldn't have stood a chance."

"Say you don't catch the rest of these assholes," Karp said. "When and where with the bomb?"

Kluge looked out the window. Albert stared at his feet. Jaxon twisted his mouth, then said, "If I was a betting man, tomorrow night, Times Square."

Karp rubbed his face with a hand. "I was afraid you were going to say that."

"We've intercepted a lot of radio and Internet traffic in the last few days," Kluge said. "It's jumped threefold and it seems clear that an Iraqi by the name of Hussan is coordinating the event. He also goes by several aliases— Ibn Abdul, Mustafa, Al-Sistani—and if we're correct about him being here we're in big trouble."

"We think he was on the ground in Manhattan on 9/11, coordinating and maybe checking out how the city reacted to a big disaster," Jaxon said. "He likes going for big spectacular splashes . . . airlines, embassy bombings, car bombs in crowded marketplaces, and, ironically, made-for-TV beheadings on Al Jazeera."

"Maybe we should shut it down," Karp said. "New Year's Eve on Times Square. Shut it down. Call it off."

The other three men glanced at each other. "Can't," Albert said.

"What do you mean 'can't'?"

"Comes from the top," Jaxon said. "The man in the Oval Office. And to be honest, he's got a point. Can you imagine what will happen if we suddenly go on high alert and someone finds out it's because terrorists have atomic weapons in this country and are preparing to use them? The media would go apeshit. It's one thing to screen airline passengers and make everybody feel safer again. But what if the public suddenly has to confront the fact that these guys can just load up a truck with ammonium nitrate, toss in a suitcase full of plutonium, drive it into the middle of their city, light a match, and turn it into a dead zone for the next hundred years?"

The room was quiet, as thoughts about the potential consequences settled around them like dust. "What do you need from me?" Karp replied.

"Just that if the NYPD or your own investigators turn up anything on who might have committed these three homicides, give us a shot at them," Jaxon said. "Obviously, whoever did these killings knew what they were doing and what's more, knew where to find the bad guys. We've been looking for the two dead ones for three years, and they turn up without their heads right under our noses."

"I'll do what I can," Karp said, "which doesn't seem like much given the circumstances. Does the NYPD know?"

"They know that they need to button down the place as tight as possible," Jaxon said. "They're keeping unauthorized vehicles away from the crowd; have plainclothes and uniforms all over the subways; and have swept the tunnels beneath Times Square. Airspace will be kept clear by armed Apache helicopters and F-16 fighters. But you can't account for everything or everyone. If we want to be sure, we need to find the bad guys and their bomb, but we don't have much time. I've got a SWAT team—the best of the best—ready to move; the problem is where."

Jaxon and the other two didn't linger. "I know that I don't need to tell you, but this has to stay strictly between us," the agent said as he opened the door. "And hey, maybe we'll get lucky. Maybe whoever killed these guys has already dumped the shit in the ocean."

"Yeah, and maybe tomorrow night's not New Year's Eve."

After the agents had left his office and he'd wrapped up the day, he went home where Marlene was waiting to fill him in on the Michalik case. By the time she finished, his stomach was in a knot. He immediately got on the telephone and told Kipman and Rachman they'd be meeting the next morning to discuss the case. Rachman, who thought it was to discuss bringing charges against Michalik, insisted that Ryder and her attorney, Schmellmann, be allowed to sit in. He didn't tell her that Marlene would be there, too.

The next day, as the others entered the conference room and sat down, Rachel Rachman pointedly remained standing with a hand on the shoulder of Sarah Ryder, who sat between her and Harvey Schmellmann. When everyone was settled—Karp turned from his conversation with Harry Kipman and Marlene, who sat on the opposite side of the table, and Schmellmann stopped trying to catch a glimpse of himself in the window—Rachman cleared her throat.

"I want it on record that I am opposed to the presence of Marlene Ciampi at this meeting," she said stiffly. "She is not only the attorney of record for the defendant—and this meeting was called to discuss filing formal charges— she is also your wife, which smacks of a conflict of interest." She didn't look at Marlene as she spoke but kept her eyes on Karp.

"Duly noted," he replied, at the same time wondering, Whatever happened to Rachman? When Marlene had recommended her to head the Sex Crimes Bureau, she'd been one of the best attorneys on the staff, dedicated and aggressive but not a zealot. Maybe it's my fault, he thought. Maybe I should have recognized the psychological toll of handling those kinds of cases all the time and reassigned her to something less . . . emotionally draining . . . white collar crime maybe, though I doubt she would have gone willingly.

Karp looked over at Clay Fulton, who lounged against a wall, lost in his own thoughts. Clay still walked with a bit of a limp, courtesy of a bullet he caught in the leg that past summer, but refused to take it easy on himself.

The night before Karp couldn't sleep. He tossed and turned and finally got out of bed and went to the living room and stood looking out the window at the empty sidewalks. He wanted to wake Marlene, tell her to get up, grab the boys, Lucy, Ned, and Gilgamesh and get the hell out of the city.

"Why?" she'd ask.

"Oh, because terrorists are planning on blowing up Times Square with atomic weapons," he'd reply.

But he couldn't tell her. It wasn't just that Jaxon had sworn him to secrecy—for all he knew, Jaxon, Kluge, and Albert had already put their families on planes for some place like Wisconsin. However, there was something about having insider information that the people who would gather to celebrate on Times Square didn't have. No, once again, New Yorkers would face the future together. But he was glad that it had been years since anyone in his family had wanted to go watch the ball drop.

"You okay?"

Karp turned and saw Marlene. She looked beautiful standing in the moonlight that poured in from the skylights. He thought about what he was going to have to do that day—bomb or no bomb. The only answer to terrorism was to continue living out their lives as best they could.

"I will be as soon as I tuck you back into bed," he said.

"You sure you meant to say tuck?" She laughed and

turned back for their bedroom. He followed like a hound after the fox.

"Having noted your exceptions," he continued, "I'll explain why I asked for this meeting. First, and you know this full well, it is not unusual for this office to agree to meet with defense attorneys who request the opportunity to present reasons why their clients should not be charged with crimes. You will remember that it is this office's policy to seek justice, and if information is volunteered that might help us decide what is just, then we should listen. This is an informal meeting, which, by the way, is also why I agreed to allow Ms. Ryder and Mr. Schmellmann to attend."

"And we appreciate that, Mr. Karp," Schmellmann said. "We are confident that after we've heard this 'new information' you will feel comfortable going ahead with formal charges."

"Thank you, Mr. Schmellmann, for the vote of confidence," Karp said and turned back to Rachman. "Now, except for your duly noted objections, is there anything else or can we proceed?"

As an answer, Rachman sat down and whispered something to Ryder, whose eyes never left Marlene. Karp saw the look, turned to his wife, and said, "Okay, Marlene, go ahead."

"Thank you," Marlene replied. "I've gone over the evidence and along with some things we've turned up in our own investigation, I believe it is not in the best interests of justice for this office to pursue charges against my client. In fact"—she hesitated and looked pointedly at both Rachman and then Ryder—"not only is my client not guilty of sexual assault, I believe there is good reason to charge the complainant in this case with crimes."

Schmellmann and Rachman both jumped to their feet. "This is an outrage," Schmellmann roared.

"As I suspected," Rachman added, "you're just going to let your wife put the victim on trial and . . ."

Karp rapped his fingers on the table. "Mr. Schmellmann and Ms. Rachman, have a seat. This isn't *Perry Mason* and we're not in a courtroom, so save the theatrics. Let her finish and you'll get your opportunity to respond."

"Our new information comes from a police detective who interviewed one Marcus Cook, a custodian at the building who was working on the night Ms. Ryder claims she was attacked. For some reason, the detective's DD5 report didn't make it into the file, though I believe any judge in New York County would determine that it is exculpatory evidence."

Karp glanced at Rachman, who sat forward at the mention of Cook's name and now flushed angrily. "How did you get that report?" she demanded.

Karp ignored her and turned back to Marlene. "Go on."

"According to the report filed *at the beginning of this case* by Detective Scott Richardson, Mr. Cook contends that he was outside the building smoking a cigarette when he saw a young woman he later identified from a photograph as Ms. Ryder exit the building. He described her as neither distraught nor crying as reported by another witness, Mr. Ted Vanders. As a matter of fact, and get a load of this, Cook said that Ms. Ryder did a 'little dance' at the bottom of the stairs."

Rachman snorted. "Maybe I should point out that the reason why that report file is still on my desk is that we have serious questions about Mr. Cook's reliability as a witness."

"In what regard?" Karp asked.

"The man has two misdemeanor arrest records for possession of marijuana. He's also an alcoholic who's been suspended twice already from the university for drinking on the job and is essentially working on his third strike."

"So why not turn the evidence over to the defense—as is clearly required—and then impeach him at trial?" Karp said. "When did you get the DD5?"

Rachman shrugged. "A couple of days ago. We were preparing to turn it over, but before the defense could get to him and try to confuse the issue, we wanted to interview him again and see if his story didn't change, as might be expected from a drug addict and alcoholic. For all we know, he didn't have the right night or see the right woman."

Karp looked over at Fulton and nodded his head. "Just a moment," he said as the big detective left the room. A few seconds later, Fulton returned with another man.

"Good morning," Karp said. "Everybody, this is Detective Scott Richardson, who I believe is the detective who filed the DD5 regarding Mr. Marcus Cook. Is that correct, detective?"

Richardson, a compact, balding man with dark intense eyes, nodded. "Yes, sir."

Karp looked at Rachman, whose face had drained of color. "When did you file that report, detective?"

"I'd have to look at it for the exact day," the detective said. "But months ago . . . about a week after the alleged incident."

"Do you have any reason to believe one way or the other that Mr. Cook might have confused which night he was talking about, or the identity of the woman he saw?"

"I suppose it's possible," Richardson replied. "But I doubt it. Mr. Cook was quite clear about the night—it was the last night he worked that week and he has the time cards to prove it. And while he was sitting on a bench in the dark, he had an unobstructed view of the steps and door. I know because I went and sat there myself. He distinctly remembers seeing Ms. Ryder emerge but . . ."

"Yes, detective, you were about to say something?" Karp asked.

"He says he never saw Ted Vanders or anybody else that night strike up a conversation at the front door with Ms. Ryder."

"That's ridiculous," Sarah Ryder scoffed. "It may not have been quite at the front door, I was too upset to remember all of the details. It could have been inside the doors where this guy, Cook, might not have been able to see us."

"Again, anything's possible," Richardson said. "However, the evidence indicates that no one other than you and Professor Michalik entered the building that evening."

"How do you know that?" Rachman asked.

"The after-hours sign-in book," Richardson said. "Ms. Ryder's name is on it, and so is Professor Michalik's. But no Ted Vanders."

"Doesn't prove anything," Rachman said. "Lots of people would walk right by a sign-in book, especially if the janitor's not around to see that they do."

"Well, that might be true," the detective agreed, "but Mr. Vanders couldn't have entered the building and met up with Ms. Ryder further down the hall."

"Why not?" asked Schmellmann, who was beginning to look a little pale himself.

"Because you need a key to get in that door," Richardson replied. "Only the custodial team has them. Not even the professors have those keys. After hours, you have to be let inside by someone else."

Karp interrupted the next question. "Thank you,

detective. If you wouldn't mind remaining. We may have more questions. But let's move on. Marlene?"

Marlene stood and turned off the lights. She then pressed the button on the slide projector set up on the table. The first slide appeared on the screen. "These are the photographs taken of Ms. Ryder's wrists the day after the crime occurred," she said. "Ms. Ryder, if I may ask you a question, you struggled even though you were bound, am I correct?"

"I object to this," Schmellmann said. "My client is not the one on trial here."

"She doesn't have to answer," Karp said. "In fact, she's free to leave."

"It's okay, Harvey," Ryder said. She turned back to Marlene. "Yes, of course I struggled. I did not want to be raped."

"No, I'm sure you didn't," Marlene said. "But what I'd like to direct everyone's attention to is how the rope burns are perpendicular to her wrists; they look like bracelets." She hit the button and another slide came up. "This photograph was taken from a case I did ten years ago of a woman who was tied up in the fashion described by Ms. Ryder. Notice how the burns don't go directly across her wrist, but travel at more of a diagonal toward her hand, as though she was trying to pull her hand free of the ropes."

"Oh, so now you're a forensic contusions expert," Rachman scoffed.

"No," Marlene replied evenly, "but I have retained someone who is and that will be his testimony."

"Weak," Rachman said. "We have an expert who will say that the contusions on Ms. Ryder were consistent with her story."

"Maybe so," Marlene said, "but do you also have an expert who is going to explain how Ted Vanders's semen got into the panties Sarah Ryder wore to the rape examination?"

Sarah Ryder stiffened and turned white. Schmellmann began to sputter about miscarriages of justice. And Rachel Rachman screeched, "What? What kind of bullshit trick is this?"

Karp interrupted again and turned to Richardson. "Detective, are you aware of anything that might shed some light on the current discussion?"

"Yes, sir," Richardson replied. "We've been aware for some weeks now—as has Ms. Rachman because I personally forwarded the information to her—that semen had been found in the panties of the complainant that did not match that of the accused."

"Yet, if I'm remembering this correctly," Karp said, "Ms. Ryder claims that she had not had sexual contact with another man for a period of months before the alleged rape?"

"All we know is that the semen was not a match for Michalik," Rachman interjected. "And once again, am I the only one here who recalls that the victim's sexual history is not relevant?"

"Well, first of all, the shield laws are not absolute," Marlene said. "What is relevant is that the blood type of the person whose semen was left in the panties is a match for Ted Vanders. We're still waiting on DNA testing to be sure, but if I was a betting woman, I'd mortgage the house to get to Vegas with this one."

Marlene explained how she'd obtained a blood sample from Ted Vanders—leaving out that she knew the combatants in the hallway. "It was just a couple of bums brawling in the hall and Ted stuck his nose in there and got it punched," she said.

"Your sample was illegally obtained. It would never

stand up in court," Schmellmann said. "You didn't have a warrant and I'm sure Mr. Vanders did not consent."

Marlene shrugged. "It was my handkerchief. I can do anything I want with it, including having it tested."

Rachman's eyes narrowed. "You set that up. You were ready with your little handkerchief. The judge will see that and throw out your 'evidence,' and you'll be lucky he doesn't throw the book at you, too."

"You want to bet?" Marlene replied. "You want to bet that I can't get a judge to order a blood test on Vanders even if my 'evidence' isn't admissible? And you want to bet that I can't make that worm Ted squirm on the witness stand until he cracks and tells the jury how he entered a conspiracy with that woman"—Marlene pointed a finger at Ryder—"to frame Alexis Michalik for sexual assault. When I'm done with him, it will be your 'victim' who'll be hauled off in handcuffs."

Marlene took her eyes off Ryder and looked over at her husband so she didn't see the danger until it was too late. With a shriek, Sarah Ryder pulled a pair of scissors from her purse and launched herself over the table at Marlene. "You fucking bitch," she screamed. "You ruined my fucking plan."

Marlene would have been too late to avoid the attack. But Kipman saw Ryder coming and turned in front of Marlene to shield her, presenting his back to the assault. He took the scissors in his shoulder. The three—Marlene, Kipman, and Ryder—then tumbled to the ground as Karp, Rachman, and Schmellmann looked on in shock.

The two women sprang to their feet while Kipman lay gasping on the ground with the scissors protruding from his back. The confrontation didn't last much longer. Marlene, who'd been schooled in the "sweet science" by older brothers since childhood, tagged Ryder with two quick, hard left jabs, which rocked her head back, and then turned out the lights with a right cross. Ryder went to the ground like a sack of rice.

Just as suddenly, Karp shouted to Fulton to cuff Ryder and ran over to Kipman. Fulton ran over and picked the still-groggy woman off the floor, placed her hands behind her back, and put on a pair of bracelets.

Kipman was lying on his side, bleeding through his shirt. The bloody scissors were off to one side.

When Harry's eyes met Karp's, Kipman said with righteous indignation, "So much for the shield law."

After Kipman was hauled off by the paramedics, Marlene said, "Well, except for poor Harry, I'm glad we had this little meeting. What can I tell my client?"

"I guess you can tell him that he will not be charged," Karp said.

Marlene popped up out of her chair like a kid being released for summer vacation. She walked over and kissed Karp. "I'll see you at home. I'm going to go call the Michaliks and tell them the good news, then suggest a good civil attorney to bring a lawsuit against the university . . . oh, and I wouldn't be surprised if there's a good case against the city for Ms. Rachman's behavior."

"Gee, thanks," Karp said. "We're closing shop at noon today, so I'll see you in about an hour?"

When Marlene scooted out the door, Rachman stood and quietly swept her papers into a pile and stuffed them into her briefcase without looking at Karp. She started to move toward the door.

"Detective Richardson, do you have your handcuffs with you?" Karp asked.

"Sure do."

"Then would you kindly place Ms. Rachman under arrest."

Rachman blinked at him several times, and then her face flushed angrily. "You can't arrest me," she said. "What for? All that stuff about the janitor is crap. He's a drunk. And who cares if she had sex with someone? Besides, how was I to know that Ryder had a screw loose. I was just doing my job."

Karp held up a hand. "You disgraced this office. You've forgotten what your job is. At the very least, you'll be indicted for obstruction of justice, false imprisonment, and withholding evidence in a criminal case. Your zealotry cost a man his job, his reputation, enormous embarrassment and pain, and very nearly his freedom. I will also personally see to it that you are disbarred. You are going to swing for this one, Rachman, big time."

He looked at the detective. "Now do me a favor, Scott, and get her out of my sight."

An hour later, he walked up the stairs to the loft, hoping that the federal agents were wrong and that he could just spend a nice, quiet, safe New Year's Eve with his family. He knew that wasn't going to happen when he walked in the door and saw Jojola lying on the couch, Ned and Lucy tending to him, while Tran stood next to Marlene, who was holding a sobbing Giancarlo.

"What now?" he asked.

Marlene looked up at him with fear and rage in her eyes. "Terrorists have Zak and they're planning on blowing up Times Square tonight."

28

KARP AND MARLENE SQUARED OFF IN THE MIDDLE of the living room. Tran and two of his men stood by the door as if ready to flee, while Jojola lay on the couch. Ned sat in one of the easy chairs with Lucy on his lap, her head nestled against his chest. Giancarlo had been given a mild sedative by Dr. Le and was napping.

"I've got to call Jaxon," Karp said.

"No, please, let us do this," Marlene pleaded. "Our son's life is at stake."

"And if we don't stop these guys, thousands—no, make that tens of thousands—of other people could die," Karp said.

"You heard John, they're ready to blow it now if they have to," Marlene said. "Our only chance is to convince Grale to help. The Mole People are the only ones who know the sewers and tunnels well enough to get us close. But you get a bunch of feds crashing around down there—I don't care how good they are—and the Mole People will disappear. I'm betting there's a lot of them who don't want to be found by the police. And as soon as the terrorists get wind that there's something wrong, they'll light the whole place up."

"We can shut down Times Square and try to get everybody out of there," Karp argued.

"What makes you think that the terrorists aren't watching for that?" Marlene asked. "There's already a few hundred thousand people wandering around in Times Square—half of them drunk. If I'm a terrorist, I have someone watching the crowd; if the cops suddenly start moving people out, I take it as a sign that they're on to me, and I get however many I can by lighting the fuse before all the chickens have flown the coop."

Karp knew that what she was saying made sense in that twisted Ciampi way. Why else was he even entertaining the idea of not picking up the telephone and calling Jaxon? He was trying not to let his fears for his son enter into the equation, but between Marlene's arguments and the image of Zak in the hands of terrorists, he felt his resolve weakening. "So what makes you think you'd be any more successful?" he asked in a last-ditch attempt to stick to his guns.

Marlene felt the opening and went for it. "We'll go in as just a small group. Me, John, Tran, and some of Tran's men. The key will be contacting Grale and getting him to help."

"Wait a second. I also heard John say that Grale's gone off the deep end . . . or maybe I should say the deeper end," Karp said. "At best, he sees this as the forces of good—him and the Mole People—versus the forces of evil in some climactic underground battle that they either win or Times Square gets nuked. At worst, he imagines this as some biblical milestone along the road to Armageddon . . . 'the moment we've all been waiting for, folks.' He might even try to prevent you from interfering with the will of God."

"That's why I'm going, too," Lucy interjected.

"Like hell you are," said her parents.

"If David is losing it, I'm the only one here he might still listen to," Lucy insisted, getting up off Ned's lap. "You know as well as I do that he believes—as do I—that there's some preordained connection between us, some act in a play we're in that the curtain hasn't closed on yet."

"Very poetic," Karp said, "but no way do I risk losing my daughter as well as my son."

"It's not up to you, Daddy," Lucy said softly. "I make my own decisions. Zak's my brother, but even if he weren't in danger, a lot of other people are going to die if I don't get to David."

Karp was still trying to adjust to being told by his little girl that he wasn't responsible for her safety anymore when Tran spoke up. "She's right," he said. "Our best chance is doing this the Vietcong way. A small, fast group using stealth to get behind the enemy's lines and hit him when and where he doesn't expect it. Perhaps with a diversion to draw his attention elsewhere, but not so large—like your friend with the FBI would certainly do—that the terrorists panic and set off their bomb prematurely. We have to count on Grale's belief that the leader of the terrorists intends to be long gone before the bomb is set off—that's why he has the escape route."

Karp studied Tran for a moment. The wide face was still handsome though furrowed with lines of age, as well as joy and sorrow, the once jet-black hair now more of a gunmetal blue-gray. The teacher-turned-guerilla-turned-bandit chief was an interesting dichotomy. He'd been such a loyal friend to Karp's family, especially Marlene, whom Karp suspected Tran was in love with. But he was also the head of a crime syndicate and had no compunctions about using violence, even murder, to achieve his ends. He'd known the man for more than a decade, yet knew so little about what made him tick; he was sure, however, that the man's loyalties lay with Marlene and arguing with him wasn't going to accomplish anything.

Karp turned to Jojola, hoping that as a police chief, the Indian would side with the notion of calling in law enforcement. Two hours after Karp had arrived home to find that the world had just gone to hell in a handbasket, Jojola was already looking better. His wound—an ugly, festering bite—had been cleaned and treated; a second shot of penicillin seemed to have kicked the infection, at least temporarily, and chilled his fever. But instead of siding with him, Jojola suggested a compromise.

"I'm afraid I have to agree with Lucy and . . . ," Jojola started to say Cop, an indication of how his emotions had been warring since that moment in the tunnel. ". . . and Tran. We're going to need the element of surprise to take out the enemy's leadership, save Zak, and secure the bomb."

"What then?" Karp said. "So you're sitting on the bomb when these guys regroup and come to take it back. From what I've heard, these terrorists have trained men with them, too."

Jojola nodded. "Yes, that's where my plan would go a bit beyond what Marlene and Tran have already proposed."

"How so?"

"I'd say give us two hours, and then send in the cavalry." The others murmured their agreement.

Feeling that he'd reached the best settlement under the circumstances, Karp voiced his final objection. "Okay, you do it your way, for two hours only. But I still don't like the idea of Lucy going. John, you and Tran know what you're doing, and God only knows that my wife has a certain flair for this sort of thing, though I'd hoped we'd moved beyond that. But Tran has worked with the Mole People; maybe he can persuade Grale without Lucy."

Before Lucy could answer, Jojola spoke up again. "I'm also going to side with Lucy on this one. I know this might not seem like a logical reason to you. But my dream told me that Grale was alive and that I needed to find him. I found him and now we know what we're up against.

"Lucy also has had a dream of these tunnels and Grale's role in this. Our fates seem to be tied to each other—the three of us, and I suspect you, Marlene, Tran, even the boys. Now, it could be that the end result is only that we die together, and that these dreams and the coincidences that have played out are only the spirits' way of calling us home. But I have to think that there's something more to this. Some reason that goes beyond a common death. And I think Lucy is meant to be our link to Grale."

The room was quiet except for the panting of Gilgamesh. Then Ned, who'd stayed in the background listening to what sounded like some scene out of a Hollywood spy movie, spoke up. "I'm going too."

"Sorry, Ned, but no," Marlene said. "I know you want to protect Lucy, but this isn't a good idea. I don't like Lucy going, but at least the risk makes sense."

"I can shoot."

"Tin cans and rabbits," Jojola said. "There is a difference when the target is a human being and he's shooting back at you. I don't doubt your courage, but this is not a Wild West show."

"Then I'll follow you," Ned said. He pointed to Lucy. "Wherever she goes, I go. Try to stop me, and we'll find out whether I'm any good at shooting human targets."

The older of Tran's men laughed. "Americans are all such cowboys," he scoffed. "They think they can ride in, bang, bang, the bad men are all dead. Then off into the sunset."

Tran cut him off. "Perhaps, but there is something about their cowboy mythology that you don't realize and that is they don't believe they can lose, even when they're beaten. If you haven't completely forgotten our own history, you might recall what happened to us at Khe Sanh. Yes, we eventually won our country—only to see a new tyrant take the old tyrant's place—but it wasn't due to the lack of courage or fighting ability of these American cowboys."

"And Indians," Jojola said. "When you talk about cowboys, don't forget the Indians." He meant it lightly, but Tran's face grew sad.

"No," he replied. "I will never forget the Indians, especially those who hunted us."

Jojola's face darkened. "At least we didn't murder almost every man, woman, and child in the Hmong village, or cut off their ears for the sin of 'listening to the Americans.' At least the men we hunted could defend themselves."

Tran furrowed his brow. "You think that was my doing?" he said. "I was told that was an atrocity committed by a traitor among you—a South Vietnamese officer and his men—because he suspected that the Hmong were helping us. It wasn't true, by the way, but my men and I left them alone." A light dawned on Tran's face. "Ahhh, now I know why you and your partner began taking the ears of my men. It did not seem like your way at the time."

"And what about my friend—his name, by the way,

was Charlie Many Horses," Jojola said. "You killed him."

"How can you blame me for that?" Tran said. "He was trying to kill me."

Jojola was quiet. "I will need to ask Charlie what he wants me to do," he said at last. "I have lived with the hatred of Cop for so long; it is a tough thing to realize that my old enemy is also my new friend."

"In the meantime, we have a whole new set of enemies for you two," Marlene said. "When do we go?"

"We will have to wait until dark—four hours from now," Tran said. "The police are all over the area now, and a bunch of people running around with guns is going to attract more than the usual amount of attention. I have two men watching the theater now; with the two I have here our little band of sappers comes to nine."

"Ten," Karp said. "Zak's my son. I'm going, too."

"Sorry, Butch, but we need you here to call in the cavalry," Marlene said. He started to argue but she put her fingers to his lips. "Please, my love, you know I'm right. Besides, if . . . if something happens, Giancarlo will need you. But I think we will need a tenth member."

"Who?" Tran asked.

"Oh, I think Gilgamesh would like a little outing," she replied.

For the next three hours, the loft was turned into a staging area for guerilla warfare. Tran's two men disappeared and then returned with several suitcases, which, when opened, revealed Mac-10 submachine guns with silencers and nightscopes. Another suitcase yielded K-bar knives, Rigel night-vision goggles, and headset radios. Lucy and Marlene returned from another shopping trip with black turtlenecks and black pants. "Afraid we had to pay top dollar at Macy's," Marlene said.

As the others dressed and prepared, the older of Tran's men saw Ned cleaning his Peacemaker. He walked over to the younger man and tried to hand him a Mac-10. "You'll need a little more firepower," he said.

Ned shook his head. "I don't know the first thing about that gun," he said. "And probably couldn't hit the broad side of a barn."

"It fires a hundred rounds in the time it would take you to empty your gun," the man said.

"It only takes one to kill a man."

The man shrugged and left the cowboy inserting the .45-caliber rounds into the chamber.

They were ready with an hour to spare, a time each spent lost in his or her own thoughts, except for Lucy and Ned, who disappeared into her bedroom. Karp watched them leave but this time didn't resent it. The young will find a way to celebrate life, even in the darkest times, he thought. He glanced over at Marlene, who stood looking out the window. He walked over. "Got that key?"

"What key?"

"Your Christmas key," he said. "Get it, I want to show you something."

When Marlene returned from their bedroom with the key, Karp led the way out of the loft, down the stairs, and to the building across the street. He punched in a security code to get in and flicked on a light switch.

"Oooh, now this is mysterious." Marlene laughed as he led her to the elevator and hit the button to take them to the top floor. "So you've been keeping a little pad on the side for your mistresses, and now that we may all die, you were feeling guilty and wanted to show me, eh?"

"Would you stop with the mistresses," Karp said, suddenly peeved.

Marlene realized she'd chosen the wrong moment for levity. "I'm sorry, Butch, I'm trying not to think about what's happening with our son, or what could happen in the next few hours."

"That's okay, I shouldn't have snapped," he said. "I'm scared to death, too, and if I think about it too much, it might overwhelm me. I know I should be worried about all those people up at Times Square, but the only people on my mind are my family." He tried a smile. "Anyway, enough of this; come on, I have something to show you."

He led the way down a corridor to a door on the south end of the building. "Go ahead, use your key," he said.

Marlene inserted the key in the dead bolt, turned it, and then opened the door. Karp put his arm around her waist to hold her back for a moment as he reached inside to turn on the lights. "It's not quite finished," he said. "But I hope you'll like it."

He let her go and heard her gasp as she entered. Essentially the inside was one large room with a tall, vaulted ceiling. The part away from the windows had been set up as a reading area with a couch, overstuffed chairs, and a stereo. But most of the room was empty, except for an easel that stood over by the big picture windows that Marlene had admired from her own home across the street. The sun had set but the twilight bathed the room in a soft glow as though gold dust had been sprinkled in the air.

"I don't understand," she said, turning back to Karp. "You kicking me out or something, buddy?"

Karp laughed. "Not in a million years. It's just an art studio where you can get away from the hustle and bustle of the family and really concentrate on your painting. And over there," he said, pointing, "is a sink and shelves for working in clay. In case you decide to expand on your artistic endeavors. It was supposed to be done at Christmas, but you know how construction goes in New York."

Marlene was speechless for so long that Karp began to wonder if he'd messed up. *Maybe I should have just stuck with the tennis bracelet idea,* he thought. Then he really grew concerned when she began to cry.

"Oh, my God, Butch, I must have been a saint in my previous life—took care of lepers and fed the poor—to have deserved you as my husband," she said. She walked over and flung her arms around his neck and began kissing him with an urgency that carried them over to the couch.

A half hour later, Karp and Marlene walked back into their loft holding hands. "We were beginning to think that perhaps you'd decided to go get Zak on your own," Jojola said.

"How do you like your studio?" Tran asked.

"How did you know?" Karp asked.

"Easy. It's my construction company doing the work."

"Well, in that case, I'd like to talk to you about completion dates . . . missed completion dates, that is."

"Maybe if you weren't so picky with the paint colors and carpeting we might have—"

"Gentlemen," Marlene interrupted, "can we take this up some other time. I believe we have a son and a city to rescue."

Ten minutes later they were ready to go. The guns and other equipment had been repacked and taken to a van that was waiting outside. While the others trooped off down the stairs, Marlene said good-bye to Karp and Giancarlo, who'd emerged sleepy-eyed and in tears.

"Don't go," Giancarlo wept.

"I have to go get your brother, honey," Marlene said.

"He sent you to get help; we can't let him down, can we?"

Giancarlo shook his head and crowded in against his father, who wrapped his arm around his son's shoulders. "Just promise me you'll come back," he sobbed.

Marlene looked up and into her husband's eyes. "I promise," she said. She turned to go, giving a silent hand signal to Gilgamesh, who jumped up and bounded out the door ahead of her.

"Momma!" Giancarlo yelled, but she was gone.

Fifteen minutes later, a white van pulled up in an alley across the street from the theater. Nine people and one very large dog jumped out and headed into a side door of the older apartment building that faced the theater and had been opened by a young Vietnamese man in the uniform of a New York City police officer. A few minutes later, they were all safely in a dark room looking out at their target.

"Two men out front," said a second young Vietnamese man, who was also dressed as a cop. "We don't think they are using radios to communicate with those inside because we've seen them using hand signals. There is another man just inside the doors. He apparently asks those who enter for a password, which may be problematic as it makes sense that they have some sort of video surveillance unit inside the theater to watch the front. Once someone goes in, they don't come back out, at least not this way, so this must be their access to the tunnels."

"Well done, Minh," Tran said. He turned to the others. "So it appears we will have to fight our way in, which will take our element of surprise."

"Maybe not," Jojola said. He'd been thinking about his dreams. Charlie Many Horses rarely spoke to him unless there was a good reason. "Remember what the bear said," he said aloud.

"What?" Marlene asked.

"What the bear said," Jojola repeated. "Lucy, what was that Arabic response?"

"Wa alaikum salaam?" Lucy replied.

"Yes, now give that to me again," Jojola said.

After he'd repeated it until Lucy gave him a nod, Jojola turned to the others. "Okay, here's my plan; if you have a better one, speak up."

A few minutes later, the two men outside the theater watched an old bum who stood across the street facing them. The man's long hair and beard were matted and he wore a filthy Santa Claus suit with high-top tennis shoes. He'd been standing there for an hour, just watching them; their shouts telling him to move on had done nothing. Only now did he say something, and in a voice that seemed to bounce off the nearby buildings:

"AND BEHOLD, A PALE HORSE. AND THE NAME OF HIM WHO SAT ON IT WAS DEATH, AND HADES FOLLOWED WITH HIM. AND POWER WAS GIVEN TO THEM OVER A FOURTH OF THE EARTH TO KILL WITH SWORD, WITH HUNGER, WITH DEATH, AND WITH THE BEASTS OF THE EARTH."

"Go away, crazy man," one of the guards shouted, but he was distracted when his comrade tugged on his elbow and nodded to a man who was walking toward them. Their job was to watch for sudden increases in interest from people watching the theater or police activity. They'd grown more nervous as people filtered toward Times Square, but most of the celebrators had skirted the construction zone cones and yellow tape in front of the theater by crossing to the other side of the street.

The stranger ducked under the tape, nodded to them conspiratorially, and hurried up the steps and into the theater.

"Must be a brother from the Philippines," one of the men said to the other. "An ugly people, if you ask me."

"Maybe. I saw some who looked like him when I was fighting for the jihad in Chechnya," the second man replied. "But he looks like a fighter, so I'm glad to have him on our side. Can you see if he made it past Ahmad?"

"He's giving him the password now."

Inside the theater's front door, Ahmad, the same large Yemeni who'd confronted the twins, stepped in front of John Jojola. *"A salaam alaikum,"* he said.

"Wa alaikum salaam," Jojola replied.

The big man relaxed. "Why are you so late?" he asked.

"I'm supposed to report on the crowds," Jojola said, nodding in the general direction of Times Square.

"Well, you better hurry; they're almost finished with our little surprise for the infidels."

Jojola hurried in, glancing at his watch. He had three minutes to find the surveillance equipment. He saw a door marked Employees Only and, on a hunch, opened it and went up the stairs. Sitting at a monitor in what would otherwise have been the theater's technical booth were two sleepy Middle Eastern men.

"A salaam alaikum," he said.

"Wa alaikum salaam," they replied. "What are you doing here? You should be in the tunnel. There're only three hours left."

"Charlie Many Horses sent me with a message," Jojola said.

"Charlie who? What message?"

"Charlie said to say, 'Fuck you, you scumbag,'" Jojola

snarled, drawing his knife from its sheath and lashing out with a foot that caught one of the men in the throat, propelling him into a wall.

The second man reacted by reaching for the radio headset he'd removed after Jojola got past Ahmad. But Jojola pinned his hand to the table with the knife. The man's scream was cut short by the bullet Jojola put in his temple with the small .380 handgun with silencer he'd secreted in a boot.

Jojola turned to the other man, who sat with his back against the wall, trying to breathe through a crushed larynx. "Happy New Year," Jojola said, pumping two rounds into his skull. He then whipped out the radio headset from his pants pocket, flipped the switch, and said, "Let's go."

Outside, a woman accompanied by a large dog came jogging down the sidewalk toward the two men out front. "Go around," they shouted and waved.

"I don't want my dog to get hit by a car," Marlene shouted back, ignoring the fact that there were no cars on the street.

The two men looked at each other and shrugged, stepping back to allow the dog and woman to pass. "Nice doggy," one said just as the woman made a movement with her hands. The next thing the man knew, the nice doggy had him by the throat. But there was hardly time for him to be frightened as with a shake of his head, the dog tore his throat out.

The second man backed away in horror but there was little to do but scream once before the dog was on him. Gilgamesh's powerful jaws smashed through the arm the man had thrown up to protect himself, then bore in at the man's neck. With a crunch, the man's neck snapped.

Marlene looked up the steps just as a large black man

emerged from the doors drawing a gun. "Help me," she cried. "My dog's gone crazy."

"Stand back," the man yelled, waving her out of his line of fire at the ferocious beast that was killing his comrades. Then a surprised look came over the man's face and his gun clattered to the ground; he groped once at the hunting knife that protruded from his back and then collapsed.

Jojola appeared and wrenched his knife from the dying man and dragged the body inside. At the same moment, the white van pulled up in front of the theater and the rest of the team jumped out and hurried up the stairs, carrying several suitcases, except for the two Vietnamese "police officers" who quickly hauled the bodies of the two guards into the van.

"Nice doggy," one of them said to Gilgamesh, who wagged his tail as blood dripped from his jowls. There was a sharp whistle and the dog turned and ran up the stairs, following his mistress and the others into the theater.

The two faux police officers set up traffic cones around the front of the theater and van, which they then festooned with crime scene tape.

The two officers then sprinted into the building.

The group made their way into the basement, Tran's sappers easily taking out two guards at the entrance to a hole that had been dug in the foundation and led into an older sewer line. Electric lights had been strung along the main route, past side tunnels and holes in the walls where the brickwork had collapsed. Jojola noted tracks from many men as well as motorized vehicles. "Carrying something heavy," he said, "probably how they brought the barrels into the tunnel."

The electric lights ran out at a particular large hole in the sewer line but the tracks led through it into a large, dark cavern. The team put on their night-vision goggles and proceeded through with Tran's men, Jojola, and Gilgamesh on point.

The team had stopped to discuss their next move when Gilgamesh began growling at the dark space in front of them, and then at places on each side. Where there had been no one, suddenly the goggles' infrared sensors began picking up figures moving in the shadows.

"We're surrounded," Marlene said. The team formed a circle, guns bristling and pointed at the people moving in the dark.

"There must be a hundred of them," Ned whispered. "Do we shoot?"

"No," Lucy said. "I think we've found who we're looking for . . . or he found us."

The figures closed in around them and now the team could pick out individual faces—strange, emaciated, hollow-eyed faces, many disfigured or covered by sores—and made more ghastly by the green imaging of the goggles. They wore an assortment of clothing that appeared to have been scavenged from Dumpsters as well as more primitive robes and sackcloths. They carried weapons although these, too, were makeshift—a few guns, spears, knives, and even clubs.

Two of them, both wearing hooded robes that covered their faces, stepped forward. "So we meet one last time at the end of all things," the taller of the two said and threw back his hood.

"David," Lucy cried.

"Hello, Lucy." He smiled but only briefly before his face grew grave again. "You shouldn't have come, unless it is your wish to die here with us."

"We might die, but first we have to stop these evil people from setting off that bomb," Lucy replied.

"I'm afraid I can't let you do that," Grale said. "I . . . we've decided that this is the will of God. Jesus's kingdom on Earth cannot be established until the last battle and this will be the beginning of it."

"How can you say that when it means tens of thousands of people will die?" Lucy asked. "Innocent people, David. What happened to the good man who used to work in the Catholic soup kitchens and championed the poor?"

"Every man has to follow the path God has set for him," Grale replied. "I am just an instrument of the Lord. I have hunted the demons in the depths below the Sodom of our times, but they are gathering in ever greater numbers. This explosion will also destroy them. I know it may be hard to understand, dear Lucy, but what is it if thousands die but the world and mankind are saved?"

"You're crazy, David," Marlene said. "Who are you to say what God intends?"

"I know what I know, Marlene," Grale said. "We will not try to stop these men."

"Then step aside and let us pass," Marlene replied. "If we succeed then that, too, would be God's will."

Grale shook his head. "I will not allow it. This is the moment the Bible speaks of."

"Then you and your people will die. My son is in there, and I'm going to go get him."

"Did you ever wonder why you named your child Isaac? The child born to be sacrificed to God," Grale shouted. He raised his knife like Abraham at the altar and his eyes flashed insanely. "Leave now, while there is time to enjoy your family and lives before the end of days. But this is my kingdom and it is my will that shall be done."

The small band raised their guns and prepared to be charged by Grale and his people. But Lucy walked up to

Grale and slapped him so hard the sound echoed in the cavern and dropped him to a knee in front of her.

"That's my baby brother in there, David," she screamed into his shocked face. "If you don't help, I'll hate you forever." She slapped him again, which knocked him to his hands and knees and set the Mole People to muttering and looking at each other and their downed leader for some sign of what to do.

At first there was no response. Grale's head remained down. Then his thin shoulders started to shake and a strange sound came from him. It took Lucy and the others a minute to realize that it was the sound of laughter.

Grale looked up and rose to his knees with tears streaming down his face. He was laughing so hard that he grabbed his old wound in pain. But the mad light was gone from his eyes. "Oh, God, Lucy," he said. "I tell you we're standing on the edge of the abyss, the end of the world, and you tell me you're going to hate me forever? The irony is just too delicious." He looked around at the Mole People nearest to him, who fidgeted, unsure of whether they were supposed to join in the laughter or kill the up-worlders. "Well, I certainly can't have that weighing over me for all of eternity. Now can I?"

The Mole People decided it was their cue to cheer. "No!"

Grale stood up and turned to Tran and Jojola. "Okay, before Lucy hits me again and removes the teeth I have left, what's the plan?"

A block away and ten minutes later, Al-Sistani stood as near to the bomb as he dared—not wanting to risk radiation poisoning. From above he could hear the thudding of rock bands and the faint cheers of the people gathering on Times Square. He looked at the boy, whom he'd had tied to one of the barrels, and then took a photograph on his digital camera. An award-winner for Al Jazeera, he thought happily. I'm sure his parents will appreciate knowing where their son spent his final moments.

"How are you doing, boy?" he said. "Feel honored that you will be the first to die?"

"Shove it, asshole," Zak replied. "I know why you're doing this."

"Oh?" Al-Sistani smiled. "Tell me."

"Because you're so ugly, the girls you dated wore their veils across their eyes so they wouldn't have to look at your face."

Enraged, Al-Sistani walked over to the boy and picked him up by his hair. The kid hadn't shut up since they'd caught him. At first he'd wondered if the boy had been able to alert the authorities. But after they found the tall, young basketball player—the friend of the recruit, Rashad, lurking in the theater—he realized that the boy had simply followed his friend. Now it didn't matter; the bomb was nearly ready. At eleven-thirty he would give a signal to the martyr, who was working on the fuse beneath the scaffolding. The man would then wait for a half hour to allow Al-Sistani's escape, and while every television station in the world was broadcasting the New Year's Eve festivities in New York, the city would die.

"What's the matter, Pizza Face, the truth hurts?" the boy said and kicked him in the shins.

Al-Sistani pulled his gun and was going to shoot the boy.

"Leave him alone!" The challenge came from the basketball player, Khalif, who lay on the ground, tied up next to one of the rows of barrels.

Al-Sistani whirled and walked over to Khalif, whom he

kicked in the stomach. "Maybe I should shoot you instead?"

"Allah curse you, you son of a pimp!"

While somewhat tame by American standards, the traditional curse was one of the worst in the Arabic language, akin to saying, "Fuck you." Al-Sistani pointed his gun at Khalif's head and was about to pull the trigger when there was a burst of gunfire immediately behind him. He turned and saw Rashad pointing an assault rifle at the ceiling.

"Khalif, dammit, what the fuck you doing here, dawg?" Rashad said.

"Looking for you, brother."

"Shouldn't have done that . . . we're about set to blow up the New York Stock Exchange and this whole place is going to come down."

"Is that what you think? Is that what this motherfucker told you? Don't you hear that cheering up above, brother? That's Times Square. They're planning on killing all those people up there."

Rashad, whose hands shook as he pointed the weapon at Al-Sistani, asked, "Is that true? Is that what this is all about? What was all that crap about destroying the economy but not killing people?"

Al-Sistani shrugged. "This will destroy the economy . . . and kill infidels. But you have proved yourself not worthy of joining our glorious cause." In the blink of an eye, he raised his gun and fired. A small hole appeared in the forehead of Rashad and then a trickle of blood as the young man collapsed to the ground.

"Rashad!" Khalif cried out. "Oh God, you fucking murderer . . ."

Al-Sistani silenced the young man with a kick to the head. He considered killing him and the boy. Not yet, he thought, they may yet be valuable as hostages. He listened again for the celebrations above and smiled. Firecrackers, he thought. The fools will soon have a much larger explosion to add to their celebration. Then a frown crossed his face. The sounds he thought were firecrackers came from the far end of the tunnel.

Just then one of his men ran up. "We're being attacked," the man yelled.

"Police?" Al-Sistani shouted back, ready to give the order to light the fuse as soon as he had time to get away and then flee.

"No," the man said and laughed. "Not unless the New York police are using old weapons and spears. We think it is that rabble we have seen in the tunnels. The *rajim.*"

"Quit saying that," Al-Sistani said angrily. "They are not *rajim,* or *jinn* . . . they are filthy infidels—murderers and thieves—who live in this cesspit because even other infidels will not tolerate them. Kill them and be done with it, or are you incompetent?"

"I'm sorry, sir, but they do seem to have a few trained men among them," the man reported. "But we still outnumber them and have better weapons. We will deal with them shortly."

Al-Sistani thought about it for a moment. Neither federal agents nor the police were likely to enlist the scum who lived in the sewers and attacked with spears. He looked back at the man working on the fuse. "How much time before you are ready?" he yelled.

"Fifteen minutes," the man shouted back.

Al-Sistani decided to go see what was occurring himself. But first he cut Zak loose from the barrel and dragged him up by his arm.

"Let go of me, you dirtbag," Zak said.

Al-Sistani struck him in the face with the back of his

hand. He expected the boy to cry and was surprised when he spit out blood and looked at him coolly. "You'll pay for that." He yanked the boy and began to march with his two bodyguards toward the tunnel entrance. The man who had reported on the battle with the *rajim* fell in with him.

Back at the mouth of the tunnel, Marlene and Tran hunkered down as the wall behind them was hit by another spray of bullets from the men twenty-five yards beyond them. They knew where the men were because they received regular reports from Lucy, whom Grale had taken to the viewing area above the tunnel.

Before launching their attack, Jojola had asked Grale, "Is there a way to come at them from behind?"

"The leader's escape tunnel," Grale said. "It comes out in the basement of the Red Sea Lebanese restaurant on Sixty-fifth. But it is well guarded, and not just by the terrorists."

"Who else?" Jojola asked.

"The only way to come at the escape route other than from the restaurant is to swim through a flooded sewer and beneath an iron grate," Grale said.

"That doesn't sound pleasant but I've done worse," Jojola said.

"Yes, but it passes through what we call an unsecured tunnel," Grale said.

"What's not secure?" Tran asked impatiently.

"The others . . . my people refer to them as morlocks . . . or *rajim*, the cursed ones, as our Muslim friends like to call them. For some reasons known only to them, they seem to guard certain areas in down-world more than others, and that is one of them. We know about the sewer and grate, but no one can go there."

"I did it once," a small man in a hooded robe said, stepping forward.

"Roger, I'm glad they didn't kill you," Jojola said.

"I am too tough though I've had a headache ever since."

"No more than you gave me."

"Call it even," Roger said. "Back to this, I've been to that end before. It was some time ago, when the others weren't as numerous, but I know the way."

Jojola smiled. "Are you willing to be my guide again?"

"Six of one, half a dozen of another," Roger said and shrugged. "There are going to be a lot of ways to die down here tonight. It's pick one, and this is as bad as any."

"Take one of my men," Tran said. "In case you have to fight your way through."

Jojola shook his head. "You're going to need all of them if you're going to have any chance. The Mole People may be brave, but they're going to be up against well-trained fighters and a superior force. You'll have to at least keep them occupied long enough for Roger and me to get through."

"I'll go," Ned said. "I'm not going to be any more good here than I would be there, and besides, us cowboys and Indians need to stick together."

"I'm going, too," Lucy had said.

"No, you're not!" Tran, Jojola, Ned, and Grale shouted.

"Then what am I supposed to do?"

Five minutes later, Lucy found herself lying on top of Beach's tunnel peering down as the terrorists made their preparations. Jojola patted her on the arm and left. *"Hasta la vista,"* he said.

"Hasta luego," she replied. "Until we meet again."

Jojola left her alone with Ned. "I love you, Ned Blanchet," she said. "You be careful."

"I love you, too, Lucy Karp. See you a little ways down the trail."

Lucy let herself sigh loudly. "You're such a cowboy."

"*Vaya con dios.*"

"Yes, go with God."

For some reason there'd been no word from Jojola shortly after he and Ned left. Now things were looking bleak. Tran's men were dead, as were the Mole People who hadn't already faded away. Even Gilgamesh, who'd accounted for several terrorists, lay bleeding from a gunshot wound in his side.

The terrorists apparently had a side entrance to their tunnel and had used it to come around behind Marlene, Tran, and the remaining Mole People. Grale crawled over to Marlene and Tran. "There's still time to flee. We can get Lucy and retreat to our cavern where we can wait for the end."

Marlene shook her head. "We have to hold out here as long as possible and give John a chance to get to the bomb."

"He may already be dead," Grale said.

"I know, but as long as there's a chance, I have to remain."

Just then Lucy's voice came over the radio. "I see the leader; he's got Zak with him. He's almost right below me."

Marlene looked at Grale, who answered the look. "I'm going. If I can save Zak, I will." Then he was gone.

Tran popped up to give him cover, shooting until his clip was empty. He dropped down again. "I have one clip left."

"I have most of one," Marlene replied.

"Well then, I guess this is it, my friend," Tran said. "The end for you and me."

Marlene smiled and leaned over to kiss him on the cheek. "I could not wish for better company to take this path with."

Tran nodded. "There is one good thing. As a Buddhist, I believe we will be reborn in forty-nine days, and since we will die at the same time, we will be reborn together. I can only hope that this time you return as a Vietnamese woman."

"I think you'd make a pretty cute Italian," Marlene laughed.

"Well, shall we do this," Tran said.

"Ready when you are."

On the far end of the tunnel, John Jojola, Ned Blanchet, and Roger were also fighting for their lives. At first their trip through various tunnels large and small had progressed without incident. But as they neared the end where Roger said they would come to the sewer, they'd suddenly been attacked by the others.

The first warning had been the sound of scurrying in side tunnels and the occasional glimpse of luminous eyes through holes in the walls and thin white arms that reached out for them as they passed. They'd conserved their ammunition until a large group suddenly blocked the tunnel in front of them, charging them with spears and clubs.

Jojola's Mac-10 had killed the first three with a sound like corn popping, and Ned's .45 had accounted for two more, by comparison blasting away like a cannon. The others had melted away, but the sound of scurrying and the shrieking of insane voices grew behind.

They rounded another corner only to find the way blocked by more. Spears jabbed at them from the sides. Looking behind, they saw a large crowd—some of them gamboling forward on all fours, others sort of hopping. Jojola shot those in front, and Ned two more who reached at them from a side entrance, but it was clear that those coming from behind were gaining.

"Go on," shouted Roger. "The sewer is just ahead. Jump in and dive down about five feet until you reach the end of the grate. There is just enough room to get under. I'll hold them off."

Jojola looked at the small man and noticed that part of a spear protruded from his side. "I'm finished," Roger said. "But don't worry, I'm going to meet my God."

"Take the gun," Jojola said. "I will see you on the other side someday."

Roger smiled and took the machine gun. "I've always wanted to shoot one of these," he said. "Now go."

Jojola and Ned ran forward and had just reached the edge of the sewer when they heard the gun go off behind them. It fired over and over again until it fell silent.

"Go," Jojola shouted to Ned who plunged into the water and disappeared beneath its fetid surface. He waited a moment and jumped in after. Feeling along the grate, Jojola squeezed beneath the bottom when he felt a pair of hands and then another grab him from behind and start to pull him back. He felt himself running out of air and suddenly he saw his body floating in dark, filthy water . . . away from the sun.

"Come on, Jojola, are you going to let some half-wit morons finish you after all we went through," Charlie Many Horses said. *"I believe you have a son waiting for you to come home."*

Well, how about a hand, Jojola thought back. He

extended his arm and felt a strong grip take his hand and pull him beyond the grasp of his would-be killers.

He came up on the other side, held firm by Ned Blanchet, gasping for air. "I thought you'd decided to go back and help Roger," the young man said.

"Roger's beyond our help," Jojola said, standing and drawing his knife. "But I believe he's at peace. Now, let's finish this."

Lucy jumped when Grale touched her leg. "Just your friendly local madman," he said with a smile. "They still below?"

She nodded and moved aside to let him look. He peeked through. Almost directly below him was one of the terrorists, and behind that one were three more, one of whom was holding Zak by the arm.

Grale carefully slid the rest of the cover back, revealing a three-foot-square hole. "What are you doing?" Lucy whispered.

Grale looked at her and put a finger to his lips. "Going to make like Batman, my little Robin."

"What . . . ?" Lucy began to ask but there wasn't time to finish her question as Grale looked down once more, then leaped through the hole.

Lucy scooted back to the hole just in time to see Grale stand and lift the man he'd landed on to his feet. The other surprised terrorists had jumped back and looked on in terror as Grale spun the man around and, with a vicious slash of his long, curved knife, decapitated the hapless man, who stumbled forward before collapsing into a puddle of water.

The remaining terrorists—including the one leading the way, who pulled Zak—retreated. She could hear them beseeching Allah for protection.

Lucy scrambled up and crawled as fast as she could to the next viewing spot. She looked down as a terrorist turned and tried to shoot Grale, screaming, "Shaitan!" But he panicked and his shots went wide. He had no time to shoot again.

In a fury Grale closed, his knife arced through the area, and the man's head rolled from his body. "Hurry, he's coming," shouted the leader to the last man behind him.

However, the third man stumbled and fell against an opening in the tunnel that gave way to a dark space. Suddenly, thin white arms reached out and grabbed him. "Help me, the *rajim* have me!" Then the man was pulled back into the dark space where he screamed again. There was the sound of scurrying and a whispering, excited voice; then the screaming stopped.

The man with Zak retreated back to the end of the tunnel and turned to face Grale. "Stay where you are, Iblis," the man shouted.

Lucy could see the muscles of the man's pitted face twitching with fear; his eyes, as wide and luminous as twin full moons, were almost insane with hatred and terror. He pulled Zak's head back with one hand and with the other pulled a knife from his belt.

Lucy screamed, "Zak!" But no one heard her.

Grale advanced toward the man, his knife held loosely in his hand. He tensed to pounce, but a shot rang out and instead he fell to his knees.

To Lucy's horror, several more terrorists ran up and surrounded Grale.

Down on the tunnel floor, Al-Sistani smiled and shoved the boy down to the ground. "Good work, men," he said, recovering from his own fear of the dark-robed man. He walked up to Grale and kicked him in the head, sending him sprawling, unconscious.

"What news from the tunnel entrance?" he asked the men surrounding the wounded man.

"Allah be praised, only two still lived when we left," one man said with a grin. "They are warriors, and fighting fiercely, but our men were preparing to rush their position. We heard firing just before we arrived. They must be dead by now."

"Excellent. Now see how the enemies of Allah die," he shouted and turned to shoot Zak, but the boy was nowhere to be seen. Then he looked over to where the basketball player knelt facing him. Al-Sistani could see the boy hiding behind him.

"Murderer," Khalif spat. "You shouted for Iblis. Well, he waits for you in the eternal fires."

Al-Sistani laughed and raised his gun. But suddenly there was the sound of a dozen angry bees and his men crumpled to the ground. Al-Sistani looked up and immediately knew that his chances of escaping had evaporated.

Advancing in short runs up the tunnel, black-clothed men wearing bulletproof vests came toward him. "Hands up," shouted their leader, a middle-aged man with short gray hair. "Get your fucking hands where I can see them."

Al-Sistani whirled toward the man with the fuse. I hope it's true there are seventy-two virgins in paradise for every martyr, he thought, then shouted, "Light the fuse!"

Then to his shock, the man beneath the scaffolding pulled the mask off his face. "Sorry, *pendejo*," the man said, "no can do." He held up a man's head. "You looking for this guy, maybe?"

Another, younger man walked out from behind the scaffolding. Al-Sistani couldn't believe what he was seeing. The young man wore his handgun slung low like a stupid American cowboy.

"My friend John just called you an asshole, you asshole," the cowboy said.

"Yep, looks like it's over . . . asshole," a tall man said, coming out from behind the line of federal agents.

A wild cheering and the sound of explosions came from above the tunnel. Karp looked up and smiled. "Sounds like the ball just dropped."

A short woman with dark hair also pushed through the federal agents. "Hey, Butch, how about my New Year's Eve kiss," she said and embraced the tall man. "Even if you lied."

"Only a little," Karp said. "I waited a good half hour before I called Jaxon."

"Good thing you did," Jaxon said. "Marlene and her pal were just about toast, not to mention the rest of the city. By the way, where is the Vietnamese guy? Man, he could teach us a few things about guerilla warfare."

"He's gone," Marlene said. "And you're right, he could. Now, don't you think someone should disarm that creep?"

Al-Sistani still stood with the gun at his side. He considered, for a moment, surrendering; then he thought of a lifetime spent in a federal penitentiary. Kill the Karp boy. Make his Jew parents suffer, he decided and quick as a snake turned to where Khalif was shielding the boy and lifted his gun.

A shot rang out, but it wasn't from Al-Sistani's weapon. So fast that the federal agents and others who saw it later said there was no discernible moment between when Ned Blanchet's gun was in its holster and when it blew a hole the size of an orange in the terrorist's head.

"Holy shit, nice shooting, cowboy," Jaxon said.

A small voice came down from the ceiling. "My hero." The group looked up and began to laugh at the adoring face of Lucy Karp as she looked down on the group like one of the angels in the Sistine Chapel.

29

Monday, January 24

BY THE TIME KARP SAW STUPENAGEL MOVING toward him through the lobby of the U.S. District Court building, it was too late to give her the slip.

"Good morning, Butch," she said cheerfully, clip-clopping quickly across the granite floors in her high heels to get a pace in front of him. "Want to tell me what you and Special Agent in Charge Jaxon were talking about yesterday? Along with the two other suits who smelled like more feds, only different?"

Karp knew better than to issue a flat denial. Stupenagel's sources were too good. So he dissembled. "You can smell the difference between feds?" he said, making a feint to one side, then dodging to the other to get ahead as he moved toward the elevator.

Stupenagel recognized the ploy as she cursed herself for wearing too tight a skirt this day for good maneuvering and had to fall in behind. "Yeah, they use different kinds of soap," she replied sarcastically. "I once slept with Jaxon way back when he was just a junior agent, though still pretty damn special, if I remember right—

and don't you ever tell Murrow I said that or I'll rip your balls off. He was a Lifebuoy type; those other two, I don't know, maybe Dial, which makes them . . . you tell me . . . spooks?"

Although their relationship had improved over the past year or so, Karp knew not to trust the reporter entirely, especially when there was a big story she wanted. Still, he was always impressed by her deductive reasoning, which ranked right up there with the best detectives he knew.

"So you going to tell me what's up?" she asked.

Karp shrugged. "Just a post–New Year's Eve briefing about the heightened alert status. But it turned into a pretty quiet night, so just a courtesy call . . . that's all."

Stupenagel rolled her eyes. "Only one problem with being the most honest man in this city, Karp, and it's that you couldn't lie your way out of a paper bag."

"Well, that's my story, and I'm sticking to it," he replied as he reached the elevator door and punched the up button.

"I don't suppose it had anything to do with those three heads?" she asked as the door opened and they got on with a small Chinese woman. "Little bird told me that a couple of them were on the most wanted list of terrorists. . . . Another little bird told me that a whole gang of feds rushed into a Broadway theater under reno-vation over on Forty-fifth Street an hour or so before midnight on New Year's Eve and that certain members of the Karp family were seen being led out and whisked away. That entire block was shut down for two weeks after that."

The Chinese woman gasped at the word *terrorists* and punched the button that would let her off on the next floor. A bored-looking lawyer and his client, a thin white teenager with tattoos on his neck and hands, got on. "She told me she was fifteen," the teen said. "How was I to know she was twelve?"

Stupenagel started to say something but Karp grabbed her by the arm. "Ow, that hurts," she complained as he led her off the elevator when they reached the fifth floor.

"So does the truth, and half-truths can hurt even more," Karp growled. "Hasn't anybody ever told you that your mouth runs nonstop?"

"All the time." Stupenagel grinned. "In fact, you do. But look, it's my job to ask questions. Can I help it if people like to tell me things even if they shouldn't? So I get the word that these three heads belonged to Islamic terrorists. Good. Somebody's doing the world a favor. But who? And what were these guys up to? Then there's the feds in your office . . . things are adding up, Karp, but I'm still missing a few numbers. Come on, help a lady out here."

"I might if I could find a lady," he retorted, saw the hurt look on her face, and softened. "Sorry. Look, Ariadne, you are the best there is at what you do—and I hate to admit this but I'm impressed with your integrity as much as your talent—but this isn't something I can tell people about, and maybe you shouldn't either." He was surprised to see Stupenagel's eyes get wet.

"Did you know that was one of maybe three times you've ever called me by my first name or said anything nice to me about me and my work? So okay, for now anyway, I'm going to quit pestering you and Jaxon. But I won't stop digging; it's my job. And I know you know that and respect me for it."

"Don't get carried away with this buddy stuff," Karp growled. Then he grinned and gave her a wink. "Now, if you'll excuse me, Ariadne, I got a trial to win."

"No problem," she said. "I've got to go check in with the press pool. I'm covering the trial so you better be good, Karp, or I'll fry your ass."

Walking off, Karp heard her laugh. He chuckled himself. He hadn't been lying . . . not entirely. Jaxon, Kluge, and Albert had dropped by his office as a courtesy call to fill him in on the final details of the New Year's Eve escapade.

A Haz Mat team had been flown up from the FBI campus at Quantico to dismantle the bomb and dispose of the nuclear material. "They had enough to level most of Times Square, not to mention throw up a cloud of radioactive dust that might have covered half the island. The leader was that guy I told you about, Al-Sistani. Professionally, I wish we could have captured him and seen if we could get him to talk. Personally, I'd pin the Congressional Medal of Honor on the cowboy," Jaxon said.

All told, twenty foreign terrorists, as well as two dozen American recruits, had been killed. "The bodies of twice that many—what I can only call *street people*—"

"—You might try *patriots;* they didn't have to fight," Karp interjected.

"You're right, patriots, though I'd like to know how they got there, but . . . ," he said when he got a sharp look from Karp, ". . . we stuck with our deal and didn't go looking for anybody. Your boy's 'kingdom' . . . what was that guy's name . . . Grale? Yeah, Grale . . . anyway, his little kingdom is off-limits as far as we're concerned. I just hope you know what you're doing there, the guy is bonkers. And the grapevine informs me that he still may be breathing—how they do it down there is beyond my comprehension."

"Yeah, maybe," Karp said, "but not all that bad by New York standards."

Jaxon laughed, then pursed his lips. "I'd also like to ask

you about the Asian guys with all the high-tech gear who fought with the . . . patriots," he said, "but I'm guessing you won't say much there."

"I didn't know them," he said truthfully. "But they did a good thing."

"And the Asian guy who was with Marlene but slipped away?"

"What Asian guy?"

"Thought you'd say that. What about the Indian and the cowboy?"

"An old friend and Lucy's . . . ," he hesitated, the word coming hard, "fiancé out here visiting for Christmas. They've all three gone back to New Mexico. Guess you could try to talk to them there."

"Already have; they aren't saying much about the street people and Asian commandos, either."

"Vietnamese."

"What? Oh really? Anything else?"

"Didn't know them . . . except that they were Vietnamese and their bodies should be turned over to the Vietnamese community."

"I'll see to it," Jaxon said, standing up and shaking his hand. "Well, if you see any of these guys, tell them thanks. A lot of people owe them their lives and this country owes them a debt of gratitude."

"If I see them I'll tell them that."

Walking toward the courtroom, Karp reflected that all in all the incident had turned out surprisingly well. As he'd told Marlene, he'd only waited a half hour before he called Jaxon and, after making him promise that he'd give his wife and the others another hour, filled him in.

Jaxon had at first been angry for the delay. But when he listened to the plan, he'd conceded that "Ciampi's

Commandos," as he called them, might have been right. He then summoned his SWAT team and picked up Karp on the way to the theater.

The FBI agent tried to get him to wait in the command truck but Karp shook his head. "No way," he said. "That's my family in there. I'll stay out of the way, but give me a gun; I'm going."

They reached Marlene and Tran, who'd taken up a defensive position behind a pile of rocks just as the terrorists were closing in. They'd run out of ammunition and drawn their knives for a last stand when the SWAT team arrived and routed them.

"Well, if it ain't John Wayne and the Seventh Cavalry." Marlene grinned. "But come on, the job's not finished. The rest of them are up the tunnel . . ." Marlene paused and listened to her headset. She took off running, waving the SWAT team to follow. "We have to move fast . . . the leader is retreating toward the bomb, he may blow it!"

Meanwhile, after climbing out of the sewer drain, Jojola and Ned had found the going easy until they'd almost reached the tunnel entrance, where Ned had to shoot two guards. Jojola told them, "The guy was just finishing the fuse—little electric hookup—didn't see me until I slit his throat. We were trying to figure out how to get to Zak with all those armed guys when Grale flies from the ceiling like some kind of vampire, then goes after them."

When it was over, Marlene rushed back to her dog. Gilgamesh turned out to be as tough as his namesake and survived, but not everyone was as fortunate. They'd attended the funeral for Rashad Salaam at the twins' insistence. Afterward, Khalif had come over to shake Karp's hand. "Rashad wasn't bad," he said. "He died saving me."

"So what are you going to do now?" Karp said.

"Funny you should ask," Khalif said. "My lawyer is filing papers on your ass—nothing personal—and I'll use the money to go to college. Maybe someplace where I can walk on and play ball."

Marlene had been upset about the death of the street people and especially Tran's men. "I know the older one had been with him since Vietnam," she said. "And one was his cousin's son, a doctor. They all died heroically."

Well, that's one wild story that Stupenagel will never get . . . at least not from me, he thought. But he really did owe Stupenagel, and for more than just keeping her mouth shut, or at least keeping a story out of the newspapers—although that was partly due to the deal they'd struck that she'd get the whole Coney Island Four story first. When it was appropriate for him to talk about it, he'd give her the inside scoop.

Sometimes you have to trade with the devil, he thought, to get a deal made in heaven. And this deal was working out to be just that.

With the New Year, Bill Denton had been sworn in as the mayor of New York City. One of his first acts was to fire Corporation Counsel Sam Lindahl. Having served through a half-dozen administrations, Lindahl was completely caught off guard and hardly had time to stand up—much less remove anything from his office—when Clay Fulton walked in, told him the mayor wanted to see him, and then to come back to "remove personal effects only."

Denton had then named his own Corporation Counsel, a quiet but extremely competent civil attorney and Columbia law professor named Randall Canney. Then Canney's first public act—in concert with the timing worked out with Karp—announced that the District

Attorney of New York County had been appointed by the governor to defend the city from the "spurious" lawsuit filed by the Coney Island Four and their attorney.

Hugh Louis had a nuclear meltdown on *Brooklyn Insider* with Natalie Fitz. He was so hot that the pint of pomade he'd combed into his hair for the show ran in greasy-looking rivulets down his neck as he mopped furiously at his face. "It's all part of the white racist military-industrial complex's conspiracy to undermine justice when it comes to the black man in this country," he said. "They pull out the biggest white man they got to stomp on my clients yet again."

"And you, Jayshon, what do you think?" Fitz asked the young man at Louis's side.

That I'd like to stick it up your white ass, he thought. "Mr. Karp has characterized me and my friends as 'vicious animals' and 'thugs' in newspaper articles," he said, placing a hand on his chest as if grievously wronged. "I'd just like to remind him that I was my class valedictorian that spring when I graduated from high school. I was also president of Young Businessmen of America—Brooklyn Chapter and the debate team. I planned to go to college to become a doctor so that I could return to my neighborhood and establish a clinic. But I guess Mr. Karp believes that all black people are animals and thugs. If that doesn't say 'racist,' I'm not sure what does." Word was that the television station had to cut to an unscheduled commercial break because Natalie Fitz was crying and couldn't continue for several minutes.

Louis had appeared at Karp's office in a more conciliatory mood. "Listen, Mr. Lindahl and I had reached a settlement . . . pretty much everything except the signatures," he said. "We were willing to accept a flat $100 million—"

"No," Karp said flatly.

"However, considering things have changed, I believe my clients would consider $40 million—that's only $10 million each—to have this little matter go away."

"No."

"Now, look here, Karp, you're going to be running for office next year, and I don't think you want the black and Hispanic communities pegging you for a racist—"

"No. Not one red cent," Karp said, trying to keep his voice level and to resist the urge to stand up and kick the shit out of Louis. "I'm busy. I think you can show yourself out."

"Enjoy the year, Karp," Louis said as he stood up. "It's the last one you'll spend in the NY DAO."

Karp had then thrown another brick at Louis at a pretrial hearing a few days later when he didn't ask for a continuance. "We're happy with the current trial date, your honor," he said to Klinger. "In fact, if you'd like to move it up that would be fine with us."

The tumblers were all falling into place. The day after Louis's visit, Police Captain Tim Carney's lawyer called and left a message with Mrs. Milquetost asking for a meeting. He had Newbury call with his response. "Come on down. We'll listen to what he has to say."

"What about a deal?" the lawyer said. "What can I go back to him with?"

"Nothing," Newbury shot back. "We'll hear him out and decide where to go from there."

Carney showed up with his young lawyer, Christopher P. Ferguson III, a cheap ambulance chaser in a Sears coat, who immediately began making demands. "He gets complete immunity or we walk."

"Walk," Karp said and pointed at the door. "You know the way."

The lawyer started to bluster, but Carney said, "Sit down, Chris, and shut up. They got us bent over a barrel." He turned to Karp and Newbury. "Sorry, my wife's sister's kid, just out of law school. Okay, here's the part you get for free; you don't have to give me a deal to listen. But if you think it's worth something to you and would like me to testify, then let's talk. And I'll throw in something you'll like a whole lot on an unrelated but very big case."

Carney then laid out how Lindahl had been steering the big-enchilada cases alleging police malfeasance and corruption to a few big law firms for years—"mostly Louis, Zulu, and Radinskaya."

Newbury shrugged. "We already have that."

"Yeah, but do you have proof that Lindahl was taking kickbacks for his kindnesses, as well as when he signed off on the payments and forwarded the No Prosecution files to your office?"

"We're listening," Karp said. He could almost feel the excitement boiling out of Newbury, though his old friend hadn't moved or said a word. The smoking gun is a friggin' cannon, he thought.

Carney smiled and said, "Yeah, I bet you are. There's more. Shakira Zulu was also paying some of her fellow city councilmen to sign off on the settlement payments, which, as you know, is required by law."

"So where do you and the esteemed union boss, Ewen, fit in?" Newbury asked.

"I'd advise you not to answer that," Ferguson said. "Not until we have a deal."

"Shut up, Christopher, you got a mouth on you like

your mother," Carney said. "Essentially, I was paid to look the other way and make sure that Internal Affairs didn't poke our noses into certain cases and rubber-stamped whatever these law firms said. Some bad cops got off, the 'victims' got big settlements—part of which would also go to these firms that were supposed to be representing the cops. So they were double-dipping right there."

"And Ewen?" Karp asked, thinking he'd never liked the toadlike man.

"He kept the PBA membership in line if they started asking questions about the bad apples and made sure they were protected and kept on the force. No matter what anybody thinks, good cops don't like dirty cops."

"Dirty cops like you," Newbury said.

Carney looked down at his hands. "Yeah," he said, his voice breaking, "like me. I ain't got no good excuse, but I guess I was looking at the end of the line for my career, and what did I have except mortgage payments and college tuitions for five kids. I wanted more for my family . . . and, yeah, more for a dirty cop like me."

Karp felt sorry for the man. He knew Carney had a half-dozen medals for heroism, and Newbury's research seemed to indicate that he'd come to this point only within the past five years. Still, you agree to accept the pay when you sign up, he thought. You want to make more money, sell real estate. "It was still a crime," he said.

Carney nodded. Ferguson cleared his throat, and, when no one told him to shut up, proceeded. "I think now would be a good time to talk about a deal if you want my client to testify to what he just told you, as well as supply you with a sizable amount of documentation to back up these allegations."

"What do you want?" Karp said, looking at Carney, whose eyes were glued to the floor.

"No prison time—I wouldn't last two minutes in the general population. Whatever else you may think of me, most of my career was spent putting bad guys behind bars. A lot of them are still there."

"What else?"

Carney cleared his throat but at first couldn't speak, then muttered, "I'll sell the place in the Keys and give the money, and everything else I got through these deals, back to the city."

"That would happen whether you said so or not," Karp said.

"I'd like . . . I'm begging to be allowed to retire from the force, the way I imagined when I first went to the academy," he said. "I'll need my pension to support my family and make sure my wife can stay in our little place in the Bronx. She's a good woman who doesn't deserve to be hurt because I fucked up—pardon my French."

"You'll be required to testify at the trials," Newbury said, "which means the press is going to be all over you. You're not going to be able to protect her from what comes out."

"Yeah, I know," Carney croaked, tears running down his face. "I figure if it gets bad, we can sell the place and move to Seattle, where our oldest daughter is living. She's been after us to move out there. Says it's safer."

Karp had already made up his mind to agree to the deal, but he wanted the information on the other "big case." Feeling like a hard-ass, he said, "The price is too steep."

"That's outrageous!" Ferguson sputtered. "Uncle Tim is a good man. He made a mistake. . . . I guess this is why they refer to you in the public defender's office as Saint Karp."

Karp ignored the young lawyer and kept his eyes

fixed on Carney. "I think you know as well as I do that holding back for a deal is not going to help relieve the guilt that's sitting on your shoulders."

"I'll never be out from under it," Carney said, "but you're right, I have to tell you. It's about the Coney Island case. Some of the guys on the force who are getting screwed by Breman are old friends. I wasn't sure what I was going to do about it. We were going to make a bundle from our share of whatever those fuckers won. But it didn't feel right, so I had some of my specialists plant a bug in Breman's office. I got her on tape telling that pile of crap Hugh Louis about some letter a guy named Kaminsky sent her from prison. It said Villalobos was lying about being the only one there who raped that woman."

"So, we got a deal?" Ferguson asked.

"Shut up, Christopher," Carney and Karp said at the same time. The two looked at each other for a long moment until Karp at last spoke. "I hear it rains a lot in Seattle."

"Don't I know it," Carney replied. "It'll be hell on the arthritis."

"There are worse things."

"Don't I know it."

A week later, Karp whistled as he entered the courtroom and saw Murrow and Kipman sitting in the row behind the table where he'd be sitting. Behind them were Robin Repass, Pam Russell, and Dick Torrisi. He exchanged little nods as he walked past and placed his briefcase on the defense table.

There were very few other people sitting on his side of the aisle, mostly those who looked as if they wished they were sitting on the other side, which was packed with spectators and the press. Louis was chatting amiably with that worm of a reporter for the *New York Times,* Harriman, who lorded his exalted position over his colleagues in the press with a disdainful smile as he bent his head toward Louis and laughed over some private joke.

The four plaintiffs were sitting at their table, all of them watching Karp with baleful looks. He smiled at them until they looked away.

The nest of reporters went nuts when Brooklyn DA Kristine Breman entered the courtroom, walked to the front row behind the plaintiffs' table, and took a seat. The reporters ran up to her or leaned over the other benches to ask her questions. But she demurely shook her head no. "Not at this time, please," she said, obviously enjoying the attention. "I'm just here to see that justice be done."

The press quickly lost interest when a police officer entered with a frail, frightened-looking woman with gray hair. Her eyes locked on Karp's and she looked nowhere else as she walked to her seat next to Torrisi, who took her hand and patted it between both of his. She gave Karp a thin, wavering smile.

"Thank you for taking the case, Mr. Karp," Tyler said. "I know this isn't your job."

"I wouldn't say that . . . but you're welcome. And please, call me Butch. How are you doing with all this?" he asked, waving at the crowd of press who hovered on the other side of the aisle, hoping to catch her attention.

"Okay," she replied. "I just want this to be over with . . . again. My nightmares have grown worse; my psychologist says it's the stress."

Karp was the consummate prosecutor. And one of his strengths was that he could put aside the emotional aspects of a case and concentrate on what he would need to convince a jury. However, this case had his stomach tied in knots. He knew that it was a load of crock, and he was reasonably sure he could persuade the jury to see it that way. However, the two things he needed to make it a lock were still missing. He knew that Kaminsky sent a letter to Breman impeaching Villalobos that had then been handed on to Klinger. But he couldn't prove it, didn't have a copy of the letter, and Kaminsky had disappeared.

He would also have liked to find Hannah Little. Louis was sure to attack the confessions as coerced—big, bad racist cops browbeating poor little black teenagers. Hannah's testimony that Kwasama Jones told her he'd held Liz Tyler down while Sykes and Davis raped her would put the nail in the coffin. Jones was certainly not under any duress from cops when he talked to her on the telephone.

"Oyez, oyez, all rise, U.S. District Court Judge Marci Klinger presiding." As the crowd rose to its feet, Klinger swept into the courtroom. She hardly bothered to sit down before she fixed Karp with a fierce glare. "Before we begin, Mr. Karp, I want to repeat my opinion that your appointment to this case smacks of theatrics and politics. If I so much as sniff such I'll—"

"I assure you that there will be no such sniffing necessary," Karp said. "Certainly nothing to equal the daily circus of news briefings my opponent conducts regarding this case, despite your gag order."

"I object to this characterization," Louis said, rising to his feet. "I cannot be held responsible if the members of the journalism profession approach me in public places and ask questions."

Karp started to reply, but Klinger slammed her gavel down. "That's enough," she said. "Mr. Karp, I will decide what does or does not meet with the spirit of my ruling regarding a gag order. And now, since I will assume that nothing more need be said on this matter, I will ask that the jury be brought in."

The members of the jury filed in quietly and took their seats as Louis stood, smiled, and nodded to every one as if each was a long-lost friend. Sykes also smiled at the jurors and nudged his coplaintiffs to do the same.

The jurors, most of them, smiled back at him. It made him laugh inside at how gullible people were. He'd been fooling them all of his life. Teachers had loved him. The mothers of his friends adored him and told their sons to be more like him. The mothers of his girlfriends hoped they'd marry him—not that women really attracted him *like that;* he liked to rape them and make them cry out in pain. Only once—because of those assistant DA bitches sitting across the aisle near that bitch he raped and beat the shit out of—had his streak of people liking him been broken. That other jury didn't like him, that other jury sent him . . . brilliant, personable, whole-life-in-front-of-him Jayshon Sykes . . . to that horrible place for the rest of his life. Well, when this is over, he thought, I'm going to pay a little visit to them bitches, and after I've done every filthy fucking thing I can think of to them, they won't live to tell no one about it.

When they were seated, Klinger invited Louis to give his opening statement. He rose slowly, carefully, from his chair as if lost in deep thought. Patting at his forehead, he began to speak, his shoulders slumped as if he carried a great weight.

"Ladies and gentlemen of the jury . . . friends . . . I come before you today with a heavy heart. Heavy because I am a firm believer in our justice system. Despite its failures in the past to protect people of color, I still believed that it was the black man's best hope for this country to live up to that last line in the Pledge of Allegiance, 'and justice for all.' "

Louis sighed. "But years ago, justice was manipulated, and in a rush to judgment, four young black men were convicted of a crime they did not commit. That system—represented by two assistant district attorneys for Kings County, as well as police officers and detectives of the New York Police Department—conspired, yes, conspired to steal, as surely as someone putting a gun to their heads and pulling the trigger, the flowers of these young men's youth."

Suddenly, the big man whirled and pointed a finger at Karp. "Oh, I'm sure the defendants in this case will point out that these were not totally 'innocent' young men. And yes, they were teenagers who did stupid teenage things, like fighting with people on the boardwalk at Coney Island. Pranks for the most part, until one elderly man decided to fight back and threatened to harm one of my clients, Mr. Jayshon Sykes—who, afraid, lashed out. Unfortunately, Jayshon was a strong young man and the elderly man was frail and should not have been so belligerent. It was a tragic accident, something Jayshon has regretted every moment since, and you did not hear him or his companions complain about doing their time in prison for that infraction. And I don't need to remind you about what hideous dens of depravity our prisons have become."

Louis walked over to his table and took a sip of water before turning back to the jury. "I ask each of you, could you cast that first stone? Are you without sin? These boys, now men, committed a sin, surely. But a much greater sin was about to be committed. Because early that next morning, long after these boys had finally gone home to bed . . . a sin so monstrous that it grieves my heart to even think of it . . . was committed when a lovely young woman was brutally raped and nearly killed by a vile and despicable man named Enrique Villalobos. You will hear, my friends, from Mr. Villalobos, who, with nothing to gain for himself by this confession, will tell you that he and he alone committed this horrible sin."

Karp listened to Louis drone on about the horrors of prison and the abused, poor, neglected backgrounds of his clients until he felt somewhat nauseous. As expected, Louis launched into a long diatribe about how his clients were "beaten down by The Man" and confessed out of fear and exhaustion. "And being told that they could fry for this one, go to the electric chair . . . suffer a million, a billion, volts of painful electricity boiling their organs in their own blood and their brains into mush." It was the plaintiffs' turn, as well as some of the audience, to turn green.

After an hour-long, meandering opening, Louis wrapped it up by pleading with the jury "to find for my clients . . . to the tune of $250 million dollars . . . yes, a lot of money but what price tag would you put on freedom? What price would you attach for being scooped off the street like so much dog feces as a teenager and then spending the best years of your life rotting away in a prison cell? What price would that be worth? You need to send a statement, a strong statement, to the government that this sort of injustice will no longer be tolerated. Thank you for listening."

With that Hugh Louis sank into his chair like an electric toy running out of juice. Sykes reached over and patted him on the shoulder, and, loud enough for the jury and audience to hear, said, "Thanks, Hugh, thank you for telling the truth."

"Mr. Karp," Judge Klinger said. "Are you ready to proceed?"

Karp glanced up from his notes and nodded. He rose from his seat, wincing a little as he placed weight on his bum knee. He walked calmly to the podium, where he put his notes, and then looked at the audience.

"An interesting opening statement by Mr. Louis," he said. "In fact, if I didn't know anything about this case and was listening, I might be inclined to believe him."

At their seats, the plaintiffs nodded and smiled. "That's right," Sykes said. "The truth shall set you free."

"Except," Karp said, "it was a pack of lies and utter nonsense."

Louis erupted from his seat, spilling the cup of water he'd just poured. "Objection, your honor! Argumentative and . . . um . . . unprofessional."

Klinger was glaring. "Mr. Karp, you've been at this a long time, and you know as well as I do that was inappropriate."

"Since when is the truth inappropriate, your honor," Karp replied.

Klinger's face colored angrily. "You've been warned, counselor."

Karp looked back down at his notes as Klinger instructed the jurors to "ignore that last statement by the defendants' attorney." He smiled back at the jury—secretly pleased that he'd planted the seed. Now it was time to move on.

Calmly and matter-of-factly, he ran through the events of the night before Tyler was attacked. The assaults on Coney Island. The attack that nearly killed the elderly Korean man "by Jayshon Sykes, who had a piece of steel rebar in his hand and cracked an elderly man's skull like it was an egg. And before you hear Mr. Louis tell you again about this fight that ended badly, the ninety-three-year-old victim was five foot four and weighed 120 pounds, Jayshon Sykes was six foot three and close to two hundred. I don't think he was afraid."

Louis jumped to his feet. "I object, your honor, this is not a criminal trial with my clients facing charges. They have been exonerated. This is a civil trial to determine whether the conduct of the agents of the City of New York, that is, the police, rose to the level of malfeasance that would entitle my clients to remuneration."

Karp paused and waited for Klinger to sustain Louis's objection. When she did, he continued. "Well, Mr. Louis is correct—this, unfortunately, is not a criminal trial. But I will demonstrate to you, the jury, that the convictions of these men were valid and therefore, the assistant district attorneys and the police officers who worked on this case did their jobs correctly, ethically, and well. That other jury wasn't mistaken—they knew that there was a missing defendant whose semen had been found on the clothing of Ms. Tyler—but they also knew the truth. Those four men"—he pointed at the plaintiffs' table—"raped and nearly murdered Liz Tyler in a way so heinous, so depraved, that it defies any hint of human compassion."

Karp walked out from behind the podium with his hands in his pockets as he strolled over by the jury. "But I will do more than prove the first jury was right. I will show you how ludicrous the plaintiffs' case is. Heck, they haven't even thought through how the cops could have conspired to frame the plaintiffs when they, the cops, didn't even know if Liz Tyler, who was in a coma, would wake up. And if she did wake up, would say, 'Hey, you got the wrong guys.' So are the cops going to frame people knowing the victim might very well come out of her coma and expose them as frame artists? Further, I will demonstrate to you—through videotapes and witnesses—that these four . . . what did Mr. Louis say, 'innocent young men' . . . didn't behave like browbeaten, frightened teenagers. Far from it, they actually bragged in front of numerous witnesses about what they did."

Karp turned around, meaning to gather his thoughts, but caught Liz Tyler looking at him. Tears trickled down her cheeks, but she had a slight smile on her face. He smiled back.

"If this was just about money, and there was any chance that they'd been wronged by the system, I'd say give it to them," Karp said. "But there are a few problems with that. First, they weren't wronged. Second, it goes much deeper. If you let them get away with this, it could destabilize the entire justice system that Mr. Louis professes to champion. Never again will a jury believe a police officer when he takes the stand. Nor will a jury accept as trustworthy a confession offered into evidence. All the good detective work will just be thrown out the window.

"And third . . ." He paused and glanced sideways at Tyler again. "This is about justice. Not for four bloodthirsty, depraved thugs. It's about an injustice they did to a young mother and wife. She was the one who had her youth and everything she loved stolen from her. She is the one owed a debt that can never be repaid."

30

After opening statements, the plaintiffs' case had taken only the remainder of the day for Louis to present, which demonstrated to Karp that his strategy had worked. It was obvious that Louis had expected to settle and was unprepared for the trial.

Largely his efforts consisted of calling his clients to the stand to talk about their disadvantaged childhoods and how they had been intimidated and threatened into confessing to the rape and attempted murder of Liz Tyler.

Cross-examining each of the first three plaintiffs—Davis, Jones, and Wilson—Karp was satisfied merely to establish that none of them had been questioned without the presence of an adult family member. "And at what point were you intimidated or threatened or coerced?" he asked. None seemed to have a better answer than "the cops scared me."

Otherwise, they sullenly denied making comments in front of the police or to other witnesses that indicated their guilt. He let it be for the time being; he'd return during the defense part of the trial with his witnesses and the videotapes of the confessions.

When Louis called Sykes to the stand, the young man nearly bounced out of his seat as though eager to tell his story. Sitting back down in the witness box, he smiled broadly at the jurors. However, he allowed his demeanor to crumble almost to tears as he described, at Louis's request, the years he'd spent in prison. "They . . . they do horrible things to you," he said, his voice cracking. "I'm sorry, I can't talk about it."

Louis then asked about the night twelve years earlier on the Coney Island boardwalk. "Mr. Karp in his opening statement described your behavior as 'wilding.' Would that be accurate?"

"No. I'm afraid the police came up with that term, which would be an exaggeration," he said. "It was mostly just pushing and shoving people—admittedly not very nice—but we were just a bunch of poor kids and were trying to get people to give us a little change so we could eat a hot dog. But the Korean man grabbed my arm . . . he had his hand in his coat pocket and I thought maybe he had a gun. I was scared and hit him just to get him to let me go." Sykes paused and shook his head sadly. "I guess I hit him harder than I intended."

"And you were convicted of that crime," Louis said, "am I correct?"

"Yes," Sykes replied dutifully. "I did the crime."

"And did you do the time?"

"Yes. I was sentenced to six years to serve concurrently with my other sentence. With good time, I could have been out in four years."

"Good time?" Louis asked. "Can you tell the jury about that?"

"Yes," Sykes answered. "I stayed out of trouble and did

my time. I was reborn again as a Christian and tried to spread the good word among my brothers in prison."

Louis moved on to Sykes's confession to the police. "I was scared," he said. "I was just a big kid and they kept threatening me. They said I could get the electric chair. They talked about how hard it would be on my momma if I was to be executed."

"So what did you tell them?"

"Actually, I told them what they told me to say for the camera."

"Thank you, Mr. Sykes. Your witness, Mr. Karp."

"Good afternoon, Mr. Sykes," Karp began.

"Good afternoon, Mr. Karp," Sykes replied and gave the jury a small, frightened smile.

"I understand that you struck Mr. Kim with a piece of steel rebar, is that correct?"

Sykes shrugged. "I believe you are right. I don't really remember. . . . I've tried to block that out. I've felt so terrible about it."

Karp walked over to his table and picked up a plastic bag marked with an old evidence tag. Inside was a fourteen-inch piece of rebar. "Did it look like this?"

"Could be," Sykes said. "It was just something I picked up from a construction site."

"Any explanation why it would be found under the pier at Coney Island?"

"Not at all," Sykes responded, looking bewildered. "I dropped it after I hit Mr. Kim. I suppose Mr. . . . um . . . Villalobos could have picked it up. . . . Or maybe the police just *said* they found it under the pier."

"Let's move on," Karp said. "You just told the jury that you felt threatened by the police officers and detectives after your arrest. Did anybody do anything to you physically?"

"What do you mean?"

"Did anybody hit you or push you or touch you in any violent way?"

"No."

"So the threat was a verbal one."

"Yes, they sort of hovered over me like they might hit me and said those things to me."

"Do you recall saying to a female police officer, 'I want to lick your pussy'?"

Sykes hung his head as if in shame. He'd been told not to deny this one because it had been taped by the jail's surveillance camera. "I . . . I may have. I was scared—there were a lot of bad men around me in the jail—and I wanted them to think I was tough so that they wouldn't bother me later."

"I see, and was that the same reason your prison indicates that you were placed in solitary confinement no less than six times for assaulting other people, including a guard?"

"Yes," he said. "You have to understand that in prison, if the other inmates think you won't fight back, they'll do . . . horrible things to you. Fortunately, I found Jesus and reading the Bible taught me to turn the other cheek."

"Mr. Sykes, did you know Mr. Enrique Villalobos before he confessed to assaulting Ms. Tyler?"

"No."

"Really? All that time spent in the same prison and you never met him?"

"It's a big place. You sort of hang out with your own kind."

"And what might your own kind be, Mr. Sykes?" Karp asked.

Before Sykes could answer, Louis objected. "Your honor, may we approach the bench?"

Klinger nodded. "Please, Mr. Louis."

In front of the judge but out of earshot of the jury, Louis angrily whispered, "Your honor, Mr. Karp knows full well that we . . . I mean you . . . already ruled that any reference to my clients' alleged gang ties would be unfairly prejudicial and is off-limits."

Karp snorted. "Alleged? Does the truth ever matter to you, Mr. Louis? Your client is the one who just made the statement that he hung out with his own kind, which I take to mean murdering, raping scumbag pieces of human crap."

"Your honor!" Louis complained.

Klinger pointed a finger at Karp. "You've been told to steer away from this subject, Mr. Karp. I won't warn you again."

When they returned to their places, Karp resumed his questioning. "So, your answer is that you never met Mr. Villalobos?"

Sykes nodded. "That's right."

"What about Igor Kaminsky?"

Sykes looked like he was concentrating for a moment then shook his head. "I'm sorry but I don't recall the name."

Karp studied Sykes for a moment, just long enough for the young man to start to fidget in his seat. "No more questions."

Louis then called a psychologist to the stand. William Randolph Florence, a portly, balding man, entered the courtroom and was sworn in. He testified that "even if the police detectives didn't physically or verbally assault the plaintiffs, they were psychologically intimidated into giving the detectives what they wanted . . . confessions."

Florence noted that he'd conducted a study in which he'd interviewed 110 incarcerated African-American males who told him that "the mere presence of someone in uniform or in a position of authority was enough to prompt this psychological intimidation response. I call it the Florence Psychological Response Syndrome, or FPRS . . . Fippers, ha ha."

"So let me get this straight," Karp asked on cross-examination. "You talked to a number of men who had been arrested and incarcerated by other men who were wearing uniforms and/or were in a position of authority?"

"Yes. One hundred and ten to be exact."

"So essentially, convicted felons told you that cops and prosecutors make them nervous? Seems to make perfect sense to me." The jurors and the audience laughed.

"Objection," Louis said. "He's mischaracterizing what the witness said."

"Sustained."

"No further questions for this witness, your honor."

Louis had, of course, saved his "big gun" for last. Enrique Villalobos slunk into the courtroom wearing an orange jail jumpsuit. He took the stand and leered at the women in the jury through his red-rimmed and yellow-jaundiced eyes, his lips pulled back from his brown-stained rodent teeth in what was intended to be a smile but looked like a grimace.

Under Louis's questioning, Villalobos recounted how he was standing beneath the pier that morning when he saw a young woman jogging toward him. "I hid in the shadows until she was close, then I jumped out and hit her. She was out of it pretty good and just lied there sort of moaning," he said, licking his thin purple lips, which sent a shudder of revulsion through every woman in the courtroom. "But I jumped on her and punched her in the face and stuff like that."

"What did you do then, Mr. Villalobos?"

"I decided that I was going to fuck her," he said, smirking. "I took off her shorts and then I did her dirty."

"What do you mean 'did her dirty,' Mr. Villalobos?" Louis asked.

"I fucked her in the ass," he replied, winking at one of the female jurors who quickly looked down at her notepad.

"And when you were finished raping Mrs. Tyler?"

"I hit her again a couple times to kill her so she couldn't identify me."

"Then why after all this time have you come forward now, Mr. Villalobos?"

Villalobos did his best to assume a look of shame but it came off more as constipation. "Well, it was like this," he said. "I have lived a life of sin. I raped women and even some children. But one night in prison, I had a dream that my soul was in danger and that innocent men were in prison because of my sin. The only way I could be saved was to accept Jesus Christ as my Lord and Savior and to confess.

"So I talked it over with the prison chaplain and he encouraged me to talk to the prison superintendent and he told me to write to the Brooklyn District Attorney. And, well, you know the story from there."

"Were you offered any deals for this? Did you get something for this information?"

"Only a clear conscience," he said. "I'm what they call a lifer. The only way I come out of prison will be in a pine box."

"Thank you, Mr. Villalobos," Louis said, mopping his face. He turned to Karp. "Your witness."

Villalobos waited like a man facing a firing squad as Karp approached and said, "Mr. Villalobos, you testified that you hit Ms. Tyler repeatedly . . . hard enough to crack her skull in three places. Can you tell the jury what you used to hit her?"

Villalobos looked at Karp suspiciously. He'd been warned to be careful when answering, but this wasn't one of the questions he'd gone over with Louis. He looked over at the fat lawyer for guidance, but Karp stepped into his line of sight.

"Yes," Villalobos said and tried to smile. "It was a piece of driftwood I found under the pier."

"I see," Karp said. "And did you bite Ms. Tyler on the breast before or after you hit her with this piece of driftwood?"

"After," Enrique said, then looked at the women in the jury, "after I fucked her."

"Thank you, Mr. Villalobos," Karp said. "I have no further questions at this time for this witness—"

The remainder of his statement was interrupted by a murmur of astonishment from the audience. Even Louis looked surprised. But Sykes turned his back toward the jury and smirked, first at his colleagues who struggled to keep their faces noncommittal, and then at Liz Tyler. When he caught her eye, he smiled and made a kissing motion with his mouth.

"—however, I ask the court to hold Mr. Villalobos over so that I can recall him during the defense portion of the trial," Karp said.

Villalobos stopped smiling and looked over at Louis, who looked worried but offered no guidance as he rose to his feet. "Your honor, that is the plaintiffs' case."

31

Tuesday, January 25

THE NEXT MORNING, KARP WAS SURPRISED TO SEE
Liz Tyler standing outside the courtroom without her
police escort.

"I told them it wasn't necessary," she said when he
asked. "I said it was fine if they just got me past the
crowds at the screening area. They have better things to
do than shepherd me around like I was in kindergarten. I
don't know, maybe I'm starting to feel stronger."

"Have you given any thought to what you'll do when
this is over?"

Tyler looked surprised, as if the question had never
occurred to her. "I don't really think that far ahead, Mr.
Karp. I know I must seem so weak to you. I know other
women have survived what I went through and gone on
with their lives, whatever that means. But if my life
ended tomorrow, I wouldn't be sad. I'm tired of being
afraid all of the time, Mr. Karp."

"Butch," he said.

Tyler smiled. "Butch. . . . I think that's why I couldn't
deal with resuming my life with my husband and child. I

was afraid—not of what might happen to me, but that something might happen to them and I'd be powerless to do anything about it. Just like I was powerless that morning when Jayshon Sykes and the others raped me."

"You remember?" Karp asked.

Tyler hesitated. "I won't take the stand, if that's what you mean," she said. "I couldn't . . . and it probably wouldn't help you anyway. I'm sure Mr. Louis would soon have me confused. And to be honest, I still have a hard time differentiating what is nightmare and what was reality. But I remember Sykes was the one who first grabbed me and dragged me under the pier by my hair. And I remember . . ." She started to cry. ". . . I remember him on top of me but he couldn't . . . he couldn't finish, so he hit me again. The others . . . I remember faces and being raped, but it was as if I were crawling into a shell . . . they could have my body but they couldn't have me."

The last statement came out as a sob. Hesitantly, Karp put his arm around her, felt her tense and then relax against his chest. After a minute, she pulled back. "I'm sorry, but I think I needed that," she said and gave him her tiny smile. "I've never been able to find my way back out of that shell, Mr. . . . Butch. It's like I'm living in a body that doesn't belong to me anymore."

As he began to present the defense case that morning, Karp briefly touched the damp spot on his jacket where Tyler's tears had soaked in. "Your honor, the defense calls Jack Swanburg to the stand."

Karp looked toward the back of the courtroom where a short, rotund man wearing bright green suspenders to hold up his pants entered. Swanburg looked a little like Santa Claus with his flowing white hair and beard, merry blue eyes, and a round belly that Karp suspected did, indeed, shake like a bowl full of jelly. However, Karp knew that the man's mild appearance belied his reputation as one of the country's foremost forensic scientists, a freelancer from Colorado who made his living examining forensic evidence for both prosecutors and defense lawyers.

On the witness stand, Karp quickly established that the man was a doctor of pathology with expertise in a variety of forensic disciplines, "including blood-splatter analysis, bitemark identification, forensic photography, ballistics, and dactylography . . . better known as fingerprint analysis."

"Is there anything you're not an expert in?" Karp asked with a smile.

"Well, you'd have to ask my wife, Connie," Swanburg replied with a chuckle. "I'm not too handy around the house."

"Doctor, can you tell the jury how many cases you've testified in?"

"Nearly three thousand."

"For the prosecution or defense?"

"Both. I like to think that I testify on behalf of the truth," Swanburg said. "There have been times when my testimony has worked against my employer. They all know going in that I will report my findings as a man of science—without prejudice."

"Dr. Swanburg, have you studied the evidence in this case?"

"I have looked at everything—the reports and photographs, as well as the physical evidence—that I was given," Swanburg said carefully.

"Fair enough, Dr. Swanburg," Karp said, approaching the witness stand and handing Swanburg "a photograph marked as People's Exhibit 24 J from the criminal trial of the plaintiffs. Can you tell the jury what it depicts?"

"Yes, I can," Swanburg said. "It's a photograph of a bite mark on the left breast of a woman. And according to the tag on the back that woman was . . . Mrs. Liz Tyler."

"And what can you tell us about what it shows?"

"Well," Swanburg said, speaking to the jury, "in some ways, a clear bite mark such as the one in the photograph can be used like a fingerprint to identify who it belonged to, especially if there are particularly significant characteristics."

"Thank you, Dr. Swanburg," Karp said, retrieving the photograph and handing it to the jury to look at. "Now, did you get a chance to match the bite mark in that photograph with the dental records of Mr. Enrique Villalobos?"

"Yes," Swanburg said. "I examined the X-rays taken in the prison dental office during a routine checkup."

Louis almost knocked over his chair standing up. "Objection. Whatever tomfoolery is going on regarding this bite mark, these records were obtained without a proper search warrant or notification to counsel."

Karp silently thanked Harry Kipman. "To the contrary, your honor," he said. "We obtained the records with a subpoena duces tecum and notified counsel, all as part of our pretrial motions. However, Mr. Louis made no objection at that time. I guess he must have missed it."

"I'll allow it," Klinger said, though it was clear she wasn't happy.

Karp handed Swanburg a set of X-rays. "Are these the dental records you examined?"

Swanburg nodded. "Yes. You'll notice that Mr. Villalobos has protruding incisors—somewhat rodentlike."

The courtroom erupted with laughter as Louis again jumped to his feet. "I object to that characterization— obviously planted by the defense."

Before Klinger could respond, Swanburg apologized.

"I'm sorry, your honor, I did not mean to disparage Mr. Villalobos. I was just trying to characterize . . . describe the sort of bite pattern his teeth would leave. I withdraw the comment." He smiled so innocently that even the judge smiled back.

"Very well, Dr. Swanburg . . . but do try to limit your comments to less . . . uh, disparaging descriptions . . . and stick to the science."

"Good advice, your honor, I should know better," Swanburg said and turned to beam at the jurors. "So let me rephrase that. . . . Mr. Villalobos's incisors protrude, which would give an elongated bite pattern."

"Could he have created the bite mark on Ms. Tyler's breast?" Karp asked.

"Objection," Louis said. "Calls for conclusion."

Karp rolled his eyes. "Your honor, Dr. Swanburg has been admitted as an expert witness in this field. Of course, he's going to reach a conclusion."

"The witness may answer the question."

"Yes, certainly. No, Mr. Villalobos could not have created that particular bite mark."

"Thank you, Mr. Swanburg," Karp said. "Let's move on." He walked over to the podium where he flipped a couple of switches, darkening the courtroom and starting a slide projector that pointed to a screen off to the jury's side. A photograph appeared showing the side of a woman's head. The face was swollen and discolored, a large white patch over her eye. "Can you identify this photograph for the jury, please."

"Yes," Swanburg said. "It is a photograph taken of Mrs. Tyler's head, I believe the day after the assault."

Karp used an electronic pointer to indicate a long, straight purple mark on the side of Tyler's skull just above her ear. "Can you identify this mark?"

"Yes, it is a severe contusion—a bruise, in layman's terms," Swanburg replied. "It is approximately five inches long and a half-inch wide. It is the result of a blow with a blunt object that also fractured the victim's skull, somewhat like tapping an egg with a butter knife to crack it open."

Karp pressed the projector button and another photograph appeared on the screen. "And this?"

"It is a blowup—greatly enhanced and sharpened with the aid of the equipment at my lab in Colorado."

"What can you tell us about this photograph that we perhaps could not see in the first version?" Karp asked.

"Well, the most significant thing is the pattern of ridges along the main contusion," Swanburg said. "Notice their regularity."

"And what does that tell us?"

"It tells us that to a high probability, the object used to administer the blow was man-made," Swanburg said.

Suddenly realizing the implications, Louis, who'd all but ignored Swanburg's reports in the pretrial hearings, objected as he wiped furiously at his face with his handkerchief. "Your honor, what is this high probability? Sounds like guesswork to me."

The judge turned to Swanburg. "Care to answer?"

"Well, yes," Swanburg said, sounding somewhat miffed that Louis had referred to his efforts as guesswork. "Very little in this world, even the world of science, is 100 percent sure. I'd say this is about 98 percent."

"I'll allow it," Klinger said with a sigh and a disgusted look at Louis.

"Could this contusion have been caused by, say, a piece of driftwood?" Karp asked.

The judge looked at Louis as if she expected him to object. But he just waved her on.

Swanburg shook his head. "No . . . very unlikely. The contusion is too straight, the pattern of ridges too regular to have been created by Mother Nature."

Karp picked up the bag with the piece of rebar he'd shown Villalobos and handed it to the witness. "Dr. Swanburg, are you familiar with the object contained in this bag?"

Swanburg looked carefully at the bag and the evidence slip on the back. "Yes, I am. It is a piece of half-inch steel rebar, approximately thirteen and a half inches long."

"How are you familiar with it?" Karp asked.

"Well, I have one just like it."

"Oh? And why is that?"

"Because I was asked to see if I could duplicate the injury to Mrs. Tyler, using an exact copy of the piece of rebar in the People's exhibit."

"How did you go about that?"

"My associates and I used our copy of the rebar to strike the sides of pigs."

"Pigs, Dr. Swanburg?" Karp said as though surprised. "Why pigs?"

"Well, we use pigs quite a bit in forensic testing," Swanburg said. "It might be a bit embarrassing to some of us, but pigs are nearly identical to humans in the chemical makeup of their bodies, as well as certain physical characteristics. For instance, their skin is nearly hairless and reacts to injury much like ours."

"Now, Dr. Swanburg, I'm noting that some of our jurors are looking a bit squeamish," Karp said. "Did you hurt these pigs?"

Swanburg looked worried. "Well, in the sense that delivering a blow hard enough to cause a contusion, which means the breaking of blood vessels and injuring the skin—I guess you could say we hurt the pigs. However, the pigs were anesthetized during the procedure, and then given painkillers until the bruising went away. We take good care of our little piggies. They spend most of their time wandering the grounds and eating."

Karp smiled. "So then, doctor, what was the result of your experiment?"

"Please turn to the next slide. Ah yes, there . . . this is a photograph of a contusion caused by striking a pig with our piece of steel rebar. Note the long, straight bruise with the evenly spaced ridges."

"Dr. Swanburg, in your expert opinion, could an object such as the People's Exhibit have created the contusion we saw on the side of Ms. Tyler's head?"

Louis roared as he jumped to his feet. "I object. Why was I not told of this experiment? I demand that this so-called evidence be thrown out and the defense counsel censured for attempting to sneak false evidence into this trial."

Karp smiled. Here was the reason for not asking for any adjournments. Louis was lazy and now he was going to pay for it. "Your honor, I believe if plaintiffs' counsel will refer to his notebooks, Defense Exhibits 30–45, he will see that he received this evidence nearly two weeks ago. Again, he made no objection in any one of a half-dozen pretrial hearings after that date."

Stunned, Louis turned to his notebooks. "Give me a moment, your honor." Turning to the specified pages, he mopped at his face, then smiled broadly. "Oh, yes," he said. "Now I remember. We didn't consider this important at the time, nor do we now. Please continue, doctor."

After the lunch recess, Swanburg returned to the stand. Karp looked back at the row of benches behind his table.

Repass, Russell, and Torrisi were in their seats but Tyler was missing. Good, he thought. He'd told her she might want to miss the afternoon's testimony, and she'd taken his advice.

The reason was soon clear as he put up on the screen a frontal photograph of Tyler's nude body taken after the attack. Swanburg pointed out the bruising on her arms and legs.

The next photograph was a close-up of the bruising on Tyler's legs. "Can you give us an opinion, doctor, on what caused these marks?"

"Yes, you can see the pattern left by hands as they held her down. She must have struggled quite hard."

Karp put another photograph on the screen. A close-up of Tyler's chest—with the bite mark clearly evident—as well as her upper arms. "What can you tell us about these bruises?"

"Again, you can see the marks of hands on her arms as though she was being restrained."

"Thank you, Dr. Swanburg, I have no further questions."

Klinger invited Louis to cross-examine the witness. He stood and smiled at the jury, then shook his head as if they'd all been witnesses to some sort of card trick.

"Good afternoon, Dr. Swanburg. I won't keep you or these good people long, but let's review by starting with the bite mark. Is it possible that more than one person in this world might have teeth like that?"

"Well, yes," Swanburg said. "There are any number. However, given that one of—"

"Thank you, Dr. Swanburg, I'd appreciate it if you'd just answer the question I ask rather than try to continue to testify for the defense."

"I was trying to answer the question completely."

"And I can appreciate that but it's also true the defense hired you to appear here today, isn't that so?"

"Yes."

"And they—or I guess I should say the taxpayers of New York—are paying you the handsome fee of $550 an hour, plus expenses."

"Well, yes, but my fees are in line with—"

"Just a yes or no will suffice, doctor."

"Yes, that's all true."

"Thank you. Now, let's move on to the object that was used to strike Ms. Tyler. I believe you testified that it is 'unlikely' that something created by nature, such as a piece of driftwood, would have caused that bruise. But it doesn't rule it out, now does it?"

"No."

"And is there anything on that piece of rebar from the trial that links my clients—who by the way are not on trial here—to it?"

"No."

Karp let Louis make his little speeches and asides without objecting. He was hoping that the lawyer would gain confidence and walk into his trap. Come on, baby, keep walking, he thought.

"Dr. Swanburg, let's for a moment revisit the photographs of the arms of Ms. Tyler," he said. "Now, couldn't these be the marks left by one man who was raping a woman as he held her down?"

"No."

The smile on Louis's face disappeared and reappeared on Karp's.

"No? And why not?"

"Because if you look carefully, you will see that the finger marks were not made by a man having sexual intercourse while lying on top of a woman. They're inverted and were made by someone who was leaning or kneeling at her head and holding her down."

Louis turned away from the jury so as not to reveal that he knew he'd been had. He looked up at Karp and saw the smile. "No further questions."

Karp rose for redirect and the coup de grâce. "Dr. Swanburg, what conclusions can you draw from the bruises?"

"That at least three men participated in holding down the victim," Swanburg said. "One on each of her legs and one, as I said, at her head."

Karp nodded. "No further questions."

The rest of the day Karp spent playing the confessions of the plaintiffs. By the time he turned off the video machine, the jurors looked like they'd been beaten themselves. He'd refrained from commenting—if he felt it necessary, he could do that during closing arguments and summation—but for now, the videos demonstrated that the Coney Island Four were not browbeaten or intimidated. There were no big cops hovering over them or yelling in their faces. And he'd ended the session with Desmond Davis laughing about what they'd done to "the bitch" and Sykes shouting at the female police officer, "I want to lick your pussy."

Karp went back to his office feeling that he'd scored the major blows in the trial. But there were still some threads that worried him. The physical evidence placing Villalobos at the scene was irrefutable. Also, what if Louis tried to intimate that Kevin Little had assisted Villalobos—hence his reason for turning on the others—but that the remaining Coney Island Four had not participated? He needed Kaminsky. Kaminsky and the letter would be even better, because then he could go after Breman and Klinger for their participation in this travesty. If they could just have found Hannah Little the problem would have been solved, too.

That evening, Karp was looking forward to a little downtime with his family. Zak seemed none the worse for wear and enjoyed telling anyone who'd listen how he told the fearsome terrorist Al-Sistani to "shove it, asshole," until his father had said enough was enough. The only thing that seemed to truly be upsetting the boy was that he'd been warned that under no circumstances could he talk about the incident with anyone but family. Karp had impressed upon him the seriousness of the population of New York learning they'd come within a few minutes of having weapons of mass destruction used against them. For once his son understood the gravity of the situation, even if he had to remain disappointed that the further exploits of Zak Karp had to remain a secret.

Marlene also seemed to have dealt well with her excursion back into the world of violence. "It's how you look at it," she tried to explain. "In John's culture, a warrior avoids violence unless as a last resort, and I think that was about as last a resort as you can get."

Suddenly there was a buzzing at the security door. Karp sighed and went over to press the intercom button. "Yes, may I help you?" he asked.

A man's voice, heavily accented, answered. "You are being invited to a meeting with an old friend tonight."

Karp raised his eyebrows and looked at Marlene, who shrugged.

"And where am I supposed to meet this friend?" Karp asked with a laugh.

"Not just you . . . the presence of your wife is also requested."

"Well, that's even better. But as I said, when and where am I supposed to meet my old friend?"

"Midnight at Battery Park near the Staten Island ferry dock."

"Okay, I'm game. Who is this friend?"

"I can't say, other than he asks you to remember the pieces of candy he gave you as a child."

Suddenly Karp took notice. Uncle Vladimir? But why the secret midnight meeting? "Did he say why I might be interested in this meeting?"

"You wish to meet Igor Kaminsky, no?"

Marlene's jaw dropped as Karp said, "No, I wish to meet him, yes."

"Then midnight at Battery Park."

"Wait!" Karp yelled, but there was no other response. He and Marlene hurried over to the window and looked down. A large man jumped in the driver's side of a big, dark, but otherwise nondescript American sedan and immediately sped off.

"Well?" Marlene asked.

"I hear Battery Park is very romantic in the subzero cold on a dark night when the chance of frostbite is ridiculously high," he said.

"Karp, you sweet-talking devil, I'm in," she replied.

32

KARP LOOKED UP FROM HIS NOTES AND TURNED around as the courtroom spectators suddenly began buzzing. District Attorney Breman had entered the courtroom, although today she wasn't smiling or chatting with the press. The previous night's television reports, as well as that morning's newspapers, had jumped all over Swanburg's testimony and its implications for the plaintiffs' case.

The *New York Times*'s editorial board had even opined that "perhaps" Breman had moved too quickly to exonerate the Coney Island Four "and a more studied approach may have been called for." However, Karp noted, the *Times* reporter Harriman's "news" story had been slanted with words like "ambushed" and "sly district attorney for the County of New York" and "obviously slanted" testimony from the defense forensic expert.

"While the only undisputed fact is that Villalobos's semen was found on the victim's clothes," Harriman wrote. Meanwhile, "sources close to the plaintiffs" were sure that "the jurors are smart enough to see beyond the smoke and mirrors thrown up by Karp."

Harriman was now sitting in the row behind Tyler. In fact, quite a few members of the press, as well as the courtroom buffs, were now sitting on the defense side of the courtroom, apparently voting with their butts for whoever was winning the case.

Breman, however, walked down the aisle looking neither left nor right and took her customary seat behind the plaintiffs' table. Going down with the ship, Karp thought, as he looked at the plaintiffs and their attorney, who sat looking at his notes as he patted the moisture off his face.

Three-fourths of the Coney Island Four sat staring sullenly at the table. Sykes, on the other hand, was staring at him. Gone was the amiable valedictorian with the falsely imprisoned veneer he put on every day for the benefit of the press and jurors. The look he gave Karp now was of unabashed hatred.

"Are we ready to call the jury?" Judge Klinger asked. When she entered the courtroom that morning she'd actually given Karp a slight smile and nod, which left him somewhat nauseous.

"Well, actually, your honor, there is a matter I'd like to bring up first," he said loud enough to get the attention of everyone in the courtroom.

"Yes, Mr. Karp, please proceed," Klinger said nervously.

"Well, before we run into this issue in front of the jury, I wanted to inform the court that I may be calling Captain Tim Carney of the New York Police Department to the stand," he said.

"And I will object to that," Louis said, rising tiredly from his chair. "Captain Carney is not on any list of witnesses I have. Nor was he, to my knowledge, involved in the original case."

"Your honor," Karp said, "I may call Captain Carney

as an impeachment witness, and as we all know, such witnesses do not have to be on a witness list."

"And who and what will he be impeaching?" Klinger asked.

"Mr. Villalobos," Karp said. "Mr. Carney can testify to the veracity of a taped conversation between District Attorney Kristine Breman and Mr. Villalobos in which the former admits to having received a letter from another inmate named Igor Kaminsky, who contended that Mr. Villalobos admitted to him that the plaintiffs initiated and participated in the assault on Ms. Tyler."

Karp was gratified to see Klinger turn white as the courtroom erupted into bedlam. Breman stood and fled, with reporters after her like a pack of wild dogs after a deer. "That's ridiculous," she shouted over her shoulder at the questions thrown at her retreating form.

Klinger finally remembered to pick up her gavel and pound until the courtroom—at least those who hadn't run off to file stories or chase Breman—quieted down. "Is there anything else, Mr. Karp?" said the judge, the fear that she would be named next clearly in her eyes.

Let her stew, Karp thought, and wonder if I have a copy of the letter. "Yes, your honor, I ask that Kristine Breman be subpoenaed by this court and notified that she may be required to appear as a witness for the defense."

"Now, hold on a damn minute," Louis said. "I know nothing about these tapes. How were they obtained? Are they even legally admissible?"

"You can ask those questions of Captain Carney if I need to call him to the stand," Karp said. "But first let's see how Mr. Villalobos answers my questions. Perhaps he'll tell the truth, and there'll be no need for an impeachment witness."

"Well, Mr. Karp, unless we know how these alleged tapes were obtained I will not allow Captain Carney to take the stand," Klinger said. "So before that point, I expect that you will ask for an evidentiary hearing first. Now, if the theatrics are over, I'll ask the jury to be seated."

Karp was not particularly bothered by the ruling—he was mostly just stirring the pot, hoping the judge might "find" the Kaminsky letter, using some lame excuse as to why she'd kept it. On a personal level, it had been fun to watch Breman running from the jackals in the press, but he had a bigger bomb waiting in the wings anyway.

When the jury was seated, the judge gave him the nod and he recalled Villalobos to the stand. To warm up he asked the obviously nervous witness to repeat his testimony regarding how he alone had raped Ms. Tyler and that he'd used a piece of driftwood to assault her. He knew that the jurors would be comparing the disgusting persona of Villalobos and his statements to that of Jack Swanburg.

"Mr. Villalobos, do you recall telling anyone that this whole 'confession' was made up?" Karp asked.

"That's a lie," Villalobos hissed, looking at Louis.

"You never said that the plaintiffs were the first to assault and rape Ms. Tyler?"

"More lies. You lie," Villalobos shouted.

"Then, perhaps you've forgotten your former cellmate, Igor Kaminsky?" Karp fired.

"I had a lot of cellmates," Villalobos said. "I don't remember every one."

"Well, then," Karp said, looking toward the back of the courtroom where Clay Fulton, who had been waiting by the door, disappeared, "maybe seeing his face would remind you."

Fulton returned to the courtroom escorting a thin, white male with one arm. "Do you recognize Igor Kaminsky now?" Karp asked.

Marlene and Karp had shown up at Battery Park a few minutes before midnight, standing in the chill until an old man followed by a large younger man walked up to them. "Thank you for coming, nephew," Vladimir Karchovski said, kissing Karp on the cheeks. "Oh, and finally I meet your beautiful bride, the lovely and—so I'm told—quite inventive Marlene Ciampi."

"Marlene, I'd like to introduce to you my great-uncle, Vladimir Karchovski," Karp said.

"What? I didn't know you had a great-uncle Vladimir," Marlene said, extending a hand and blushing like a schoolgirl when the old man took it and raised it to his lips.

"Ah, unfortunately, we are an estranged family due to our . . . um . . . career choices," Vladimir said. "But come, it is cold outside and I'd like you to accompany me for a boat ride."

"Where?" Karp asked.

"Why, Ellis Island, of course," Vladimir said.

"Ellis Island? Why?"

"Please, just humor an old man. It is to make a point to you and to someone else important to me. And you know how we Russians love the dramatic gesture."

Vladimir and his bodyguard led the way to a small speedboat that waited at the dock. "Please, step aboard my steed," Vladimir said.

"Aren't you worried about the park or harbor police?" Karp said. "I don't believe that Ellis Island is open at this time of night."

"No," Vladimir said and smiled. "Perhaps not to the

general public. But the park police are poorly paid and they sometimes can be persuaded to let an old man visit when the crowds are not so large. Now please, I suggest you get down out of the wind. The ride over can be quite chilly."

The Ellis Island boat dock was empty when they arrived, but waiting on the steps leading into the museum was a tall, gray-haired man whose face had been scarred by fire. "Yvgeny Karchovski," Marlene said. "How nice to see you again. Karchovski—I take it you and Butch's uncle are related."

"He is my son," Vladimir said, turning to Karp. "Which makes him your father's first cousin. I get confused after that but you are cousins of some extraction."

"I don't understand," Karp said. "I've never quite understood the family's connections." He stepped forward and shook Yvgeny's hand. The two men were of almost the same height and build.

They could be brothers, Marlene thought. Although if I remember Alexis Michalik's comments, they would be oil and water, a gangster and a prosecutor.

"I'll tell you the story," Vladimir said. "But let us go inside. I'm, as the young say, freezing my ass off."

As they walked into the building and up the stairs to the great hall where millions of immigrant families had waited to be processed for entry into the United States, Vladimir told the story of another family. "It begins with two brothers, Yakov and Yusef, who were part of a large Jewish family living in the Galicia area of Poland when Imperial Russian Cossacks embarked on one of their periodic pogroms to terrorize and murder Jews.

"Yakov and Yusef survived because they were gone from the village that day, hunting. However, they returned to find their family slaughtered and their home burned to the ground. With many tears, they decided to split up. Yusef was tired of the old hatreds of Europe and dreamed of starting fresh in America, where even a Jew might hope to accomplish great things. He arrived on a ship filled with many other desperate people and waited in this very hall, where they changed his name to Karp for simplicity's sake and set him free to pursue his dreams.

"Meanwhile, Yakov burned with a desire for revenge, fighting first with the Germans against the Russians when World War I broke out; then when the Bolsheviks rebelled, he signed on to fight against the forces of Czar Nicholas. It wasn't so much that he believed in socialism, he just wanted to kill Cossacks. He met Lena, another revolutionary, who in 1918 bore him a son, Vladimir, who you see standing before you now.

"Unfortunately, my mother did not survive the Revolution and was killed outside of Yekaterinburg. An even more embittered Yakov fought on heroically, received the Red Star—the Soviet equivalent of the U.S. Medal of Honor—and was promoted to colonel, both relatively rare occurrences for a Jew, even in Lenin's new world order."

Vladimir took a seat as he continued his story about how he'd joined the Red Army, too, and fought at Stalingrad against the Germans in 1940. "I met a beautiful woman, Katrina, who also delivered to me a son, Yvgeny here. But I was captured on the front a year later and sent to a slave labor camp. The war ended, but those of us who survived the camps, we learned we were considered traitors in our Mother Country and I was not allowed back in, or to send for my wife and son, who believed me to be dead."

So he had joined the masses of displaced people wan-

dering Europe at the end of the war. The fact that he was
also Jewish did not help. "But I got a job working for the
Americans as an interpreter—it seems that me and my
great-great-niece Lucy share a gift for languages.
Through them, I was able to contact my Uncle Yusef who
sponsored my entry into this country. I, too, arrived like
so many before me and waited here—frightened, not
knowing what to expect."

With the help of Yvgeny, the old man rose to his feet
and began to walk to the far end of the hall. "I have
walked this path many times since," he said. "But that is
the one I will remember." They reached the end of the
hall. "Because at the bottom of these stairs there is a
smaller room, called the 'kissing post,' due to the fact that
this is where families were reunited after their long trips.
Waiting for me was your grandfather, Yusef. And waiting
for you now is someone you want to meet."

"Why all of this?" Karp asked.

"Because this man you seek, if he goes with you tonight,
he could very well lose the thing those of us who have
immigrated here treasure the most . . . freedom," he said.
"You spend your life putting bad men in prison, taking
their freedom, and that is as it should be. But I wanted you
to understand the sacrifice this man is making tonight."

Vladimir looked at his son. "At first, my son did not
want to assist with this, though he is not as hard as he
sometimes gives the impression. You may recall that it
was a man with a Russian accent who told your reporter
friend Ariadne Stupenagel about a certain meeting taking
place at the Sagamore Hotel."

Karp glanced at Vladimir, who nodded his head
slightly. "This was mostly a trade-off for Marlene's efforts
to assist his half-brother, Alexis Michalik. But in the
process he has learned a thing or two about the better

attributes of the American justice system, which may not always be perfect, but in the end, it tends to balance itself out . . . thanks in large part to people like his cousin. So when it came time to talk to this man you seek about your needs at this trial to keep those monsters from profiting by what they did to that poor woman, you had an ally."

The old man led the way down the stairs. "But do not forget the efforts some people make to secure their freedom . . . even if they are not always the best of citizens. Isn't that right, Igor Kaminsky?"

A young, one-armed man stepped from the shadows. "I am ready to go with you, Mr. Karp," he said. "I ask only one thing before I am deported."

"What's that?" Karp said, wondering what deal he might have to strike.

"That I am allowed to testify against the man who murdered my brother. Jayshon Sykes."

Karp held out his hand. "You can count on it," he said as they shook.

The appearance of Igor Kaminsky didn't work out quite in the manner Karp had envisioned. Villalobos had cracked, as he hoped, and started blubbering about how "Sykes and his gang, the Bloods, forced me to confess. They were the ones who attacked the woman and raped her. I raped her after they were through."

Once again, the courtroom had turned into a circus of reporters rushing for the door and shouting questions as Klinger banged away helplessly with her gavel. Kaminsky stood and pointed at Sykes, shouting, "That's the bastard who killed my brother Ivan. I demand revenge!"

Sykes seized the moment to strike the distracted bailiff and take his gun. He turned and fired first at Villalobos, the bullet striking him between the eyes and spraying

Judge Klinger with blood and brain. He next turned the
gun toward Karp but was bumped by a panicked Hugh
Louis, and the bullet instead struck the *Times* reporter
Harriman in the stomach.

Stunned by the pandemonium of his own making,
Karp stood still as Sykes re-aimed to shoot him. He was
pulling the trigger when a bullet spun him around,
knocking the weapon from his hand. He looked up and
into the eyes of the shooter, Liz Tyler.

Tyler had secreted the gun in her purse that morning.
The police officers who escorted her past the lines at the
security screening had not even considered checking to
see if she had a weapon. She'd intended to kill Sykes and
then herself.

"Fuck you," Sykes screamed at her. "You shot me, you
dumb . . ." He never finished the sentence as the next
bullet caught him in the mouth and exited out the back of
his skull.

Before the monster of her nightmares hit the floor, Tyler
pumped two more rounds into his chest. "Liar," she said,
and dropped the gun.

An hour later, Karp sat in the nearly empty courtroom
still trying to sort it all out. Only Clay Fulton remained,
mostly to keep him company. His thoughts were interrupted by someone behind him clearing her throat. He
looked over his shoulder and saw Verene Fischer, the
judge's clerk.

"How's Klinger?" he asked, not that he cared; she was
part of the whole corrupt mess.

"They took her to the hospital and gave her a shot to
calm her down, and the trial, what's left of it, has been
postponed until the day after tomorrow."

"Okay, thanks," Karp said. He waited for the young

woman to leave, but she remained standing behind him as if trying to decide what to do next.

"Yes? Is there something else?"

Fischer nodded. "Yes, there is." She handed him an envelope. "I think you've been trying to find what's inside," she said.

Karp opened it and pulled out a letter. Dated and stamped as received by the Kings County DAO was the letter from Kaminsky to Breman. He looked up at Fischer.

"Thank you," he said. "It took a lot of guts to give me this."

"You'll find the real letter in Judge Klinger's safe, if you can get a subpoena for it." The young woman turned to go.

"Wait, can I ask you why you're giving this to me now?" he said.

Fischer shrugged. "I guess I got tired of hiding."

"Hiding?"

"Yes," she said. "You see, Verene Fischer is not my real name. I changed my name ten years ago. My real name is Hannah Little."

Two days later, Marlene was getting ready to go to court to watch her husband's "grand finale," as he put it, though he wouldn't discuss the details. She was almost out the door when the telephone rang. Sighing, she picked it up.

"Marlene, oh, God, Marlene," her father sobbed.

"What is it this time, Dad?" she said. "Is she missing again?"

"No, Marlene," he cried, and began to sob and wouldn't speak.

Alarmed, Marlene shouted, "Dad, pull yourself together. What's happened? Is Mom all right?"

"No," he said in a voice that was almost a whine. "She's

dead. I woke up this morning and she wasn't breathing. Oh, Marlene, please, come help me."

"Dad, are you sure?"

"Yes, oh, yes, her eyes are open, but she isn't breathing and she's . . . she's cold, Marlene."

"Dad, I'm on my way," she said. "It will be okay. Just go down to the living room and sit down."

Marlene arrived at her parents' home in record time. She rushed into the house and up to her parents' bedroom with her father trailing behind.

"What am I going to do? What am I going to do?" he wailed.

Marlene stopped in the doorway when she saw her mother and then walked over slowly. Concetta Ciampi lay in the bed, her brown eyes fixed on the crucifix above the bed but no longer seeing it.

Marlene felt for a pulse, knowing there would be none. She was going to close her mother's eyelids when she noticed something and bent closer. Hardly noticeable, the small blood vessels in the eyes had ruptured. *A sign of asphyxiation.* She then noticed a crumpled pillow next to her mother's head. On one side there was a smeared lipstick stain, the same color her mother was wearing, and a damp spot.

"Oh, Marlene," her father cried. "What are we going to do?"

Marlene blinked back the tears, removed the pillowcase from the pillow, and closed her mother's eyelids. "I'm going to take you to my home, Pops," she said. "Then I'm going to come back and take care of Momma."

Karp looked at his watch and then at the back of the courtroom. He'd hoped Marlene would show but it was time to get the ball rolling.

That morning he'd met with Hugh Louis in his office. Louis had begun by blustering that the "mayhem" of two days ago didn't change the fact that his clients were still suing the city. "I'll get a new jury . . . we'll do it all over again . . . unless you want to settle this now."

"Shut up, Louis," Karp snarled. "And let me tell you how this is going to go down." He pulled out the Kaminsky letter and shoved it in Louis's face. "You're about to be indicted, but if you want to save your fat ass a few years in the big house, here's the deal."

An hour later, Karp was sitting in the courtroom wishing Marlene would show up when Klinger entered. She looked at the empty plaintiffs' table and demanded to know what was going on.

Karp, who had not bothered to rise, held a finger up—a sign for the judge to hold on for a minute.

"I beg your pardon, Mr. Karp," she sputtered. "Since when do you tell this court what to do."

"Hold on a moment, your honor, I'm waiting for some paperwork before we can begin," he said. "Ah, here it is now."

Harry Kipman rushed into the room flanked by U.S. Marshals and NYPD police officers. "Here you go, boss," he said, handing Karp two documents. "Everything went like clockwork."

Karp quickly looked over the paperwork and smiled as he rose to his feet. "Your honor, I have two applications," he said. "The first is that the attorney for the plaintiffs, Hugh Louis, has filed a motion to dismiss the case. I might add that Mr. Louis is now under indictment."

Klinger swallowed hard and nodded. "Very well," she said, her voice trembling, "case dismissed." She got up to leave.

"Your honor, I said I had two applications," Karp

replied. The judge turned slowly to face him. "The second application is that you're under arrest."

"This is outrageous . . . on what grounds?"

"We'll start with obstruction of justice. Based on the grand jury testimony from Verene Fischer, also known as Hannah Little, and Hugh Louis. Kristine Breman—who was arrested in her office earlier this morning—and you have been indicted by the grand jury down the street in the Criminal Courts building. The U.S. Marshals are present to take you into custody and hand you over to the NYPD."

"I want a lawyer," the judge said.

"You better get a good one," he replied as the marshals rushed past.

Epilogue

TWO WEEKS LATER, KARP MET WITH THE TEAM involved with the Coney Island trial at his office. It was a sort of celebration that had been delayed because of the death of Marlene's mother and her subsequent funeral.

Guma had furnished a cooler with beer on ice, and even Mrs. Milquetost was letting her hair down, so to speak, by sipping on a Coors. He figured they all deserved it as it had been a busy, as well as an emotionally draining, couple of weeks.

Breman and Klinger had been indicted for obstruction of justice and withholding of evidence. Between them and Rachman, he was sure that it wouldn't be long before the press started accusing him of being prejudiced against women in the justice system.

Newbury was in the process of adding on to the current indictment against Hugh Louis a host of charges, starting with conspiracy to commit murder in the death of Ivan Kaminsky. The now Coney Island Three were engaged in a competition for who could spill his guts—all

of it properly recorded in the presence of their lawyers—
to finger Louis as directing Sykes to kill Ivan.

Newbury had hoped that they might also nail Olav
Radinskaya on the conspiracy charge to go along with the
indictments facing Zulu, Lindahl, and Ewen for the No
Prosecution and Coney Island Four conspiracies, but the
Russian had disappeared a few days after the trial. His
body had subsequently been found floating beneath the
pylons of the Coney Island pier, an apparent victim of a
garrote.

In fact, there seemed to be something unhealthy in
the air for anyone involved in these most recent cases.
Ted Vanders, who, according to a note typed on his computer, was distraught over losing his beloved Sarah Ryder,
had apparently committed suicide by throwing himself
off the fire escape of his Minetta Street apartment.

The wheels of justice grinding away, Karp thought as
he looked around his office. Repass and Russell were
over in a corner laughing as they fended off Guma's
attempts to get them drunk "and let you take advantage
of us." Stupenagel and Murrow were arguing some point
with Kipman, while Newbury smirked.

Dick Torrisi walked into the office and was promptly
handed a beer by Mrs. Milquetost, who'd finished her
first and wondered "why a nice man like you isn't married. Perhaps you'd like to meet my daughter . . . she's a
little on the heavy side but . . ."

"I didn't get a chance to thank you in person after the
trial," Torrisi said, disengaging himself and walking up to
Karp with his hand extended. "Things got a little hectic
there with all the bullets and bodies flying around. So
thanks. And I wanted to add that your approval rating
with the PBA has gone through the roof. Arresting Rachman showed them that you'll go after anybody, even in

your own office, then taking down a federal judge and the Brooklyn DA . . . well, let's just say me and the boys, we appreciate you going to bat for us. I think you can count on the membership next fall."

"Thanks, I appreciate that, but I was just doing my job," Karp said.

"Nah, you might have been following your conscience," Torrisi said, "but it wasn't your job."

Their conversation ended when the others in the room started to clap. Karp looked around and saw Liz Tyler standing shyly at the door. She went around the room and shook everyone's hands and came last to Karp and Torrisi, who kissed her on the cheek and excused himself.

"Any idea what you're going to do now?" Karp asked.

Tyler looked up at him sideways with a shy smile. "Well, a couple of days after the trial, I got a call from my ex-husband. Apparently some guy with the newspapers got in touch with him to get a comment and told him what happened," she said. "Anyway, my ex suggested that I move to Arizona so that I can sort of get reacquainted with my daughter."

"Great idea. Any chance there's more to it than that?"

A shadow passed across Tyler's face. "No, not the way you're thinking," she said. "He . . . he remarried and has two more children. He's just being kind—he was always kind—and said he wants our daughter to get to know me."

"So are you going?"

Tyler bit her lip and nodded. "I bought a one-way ticket to Tucson yesterday," she said. "I'm pretty nervous. But I don't have anything keeping me here, and I don't want to go live with my parents in Iowa." She laughed. "Then I really would go crazy. I leave in the morning so this is good-bye, Mr. Karp." She stood up on her tiptoes and kissed him lightly on the cheek. "Thank you."

As Liz Tyler walked out the door, Marlene came in. The two women stopped, exchanged a few words and hugged. Then Liz was gone.

Those who hadn't attended her mother's funeral walked over to Marlene and expressed their condolences. Karp was glad to see her smile, even if she still looked a little weepy. It seemed she'd been crying since her mother's death.

There was something bothering her about her mother's death but when he asked about it, all she'd say was, "I'm not ready to talk about it." So he left it alone and didn't complain about the time she was spending across the street in her art studio. In fact, he enjoyed looking out the window and watching her as she painted. Sometimes she'd look over and wave. And just the day before, she'd flashed him her tits and laughed at his shocked expression.

Marlene broke away from the others and walked over to give him a kiss on the lips. "I saw you making out with that other woman," she said.

Her sense of humor is returning . . . a good sign, Karp thought. "You're mistaken; she kissed me in a moment of vulnerability. My lips are yours and yours alone."

"You'll keep it that way if you know what's good for you," Marlene said.

Just then his private line rang. They both looked at the telephone for a moment, neither wanting to answer it. Most everybody who had the number was already in the room, except for the kids and Clay Fulton, who was riding shotgun on the police escort transporting Andrew Kane to the upstate psychiatric hospital for his evaluations.

"I'll get it," Marlene said finally. "It's probably the boys wanting to spend the night with a friend or placing a dinner order."

She leaned over the desk and picked up the receiver. "Butch Karp's office," she said in her sexiest receptionist voice.

A moment later, her face turned ashen and her hand went to her stomach as if she was going to be sick. The other conversations in the room drifted to a stop as everyone turned to her. She looked up at Butch, and he knew that lightning was about to strike again.

"Marlene?" Oh, God, now what? he wondered. One of the kids? Her father? "That was Helen Fulton," she said as she started to cry. "Andrew Kane's escaped. Some people are dead, and Clay's been shot. He's in the hospital, and it doesn't look good."

Atria Books
proudly presents

COUNTERPLAY

The next thrilling novel
by Robert K. Tanenbaum

Turn the page for a preview
of *Counterplay*. . . .

Prologue

CLAY FULTON GRIPPED THE ARMREST OF THE BIG armored Lincoln like he used to cling to the safety bar on the Cyclone roller coaster at Coney Island when he was a kid. At six foot three and two hundred and fifty pounds, plus thirty-odd years on the New York Police Department, there wasn't a whole lot that frightened him. But zipping along a snow-patched country highway in upstate New York at sixty-five miles an hour made him nervous as a cat at the Westminster Dog Show.

You're just out of your element, he told himself. But something more than the drive had put him on edge. In fact, he hadn't felt quite right since waking up that morning.

What's the matter, Clay? his wife, Helen, had asked as he dressed for the day, sensing his disquiet.

Nothing, he'd lied. *Just don't want to mess this up . . . got to make sure my t's are crossed and i's dotted.*

Helen smiled and stretched languorously, making no move to prevent a breast from slipping out of the ancient nightshirt she wore. *Come back to bed,* she said, her voice suddenly husky—with sex or tears he couldn't tell. *Don't go today. Let one of your young guys and the feds handle it. I got a bad feeling, baby.*

Fulton felt a chill run down his spine at his wife's words. He wasn't particularly superstitious, but he was also careful not to tempt fate by ignoring gut feelings and a woman's intuition. Still, there was nothing he could do about it except keep his eyes open. *I've got to go, baby,* he'd argued. *You know I won't ask one of my guys to do something I wouldn't. Besides, I promised Butch I'd ride shotgun.*

Oh to heck with Butch, she'd pouted. *And to heck with your machismo. If you'd rather play cops and robbers than stir it up with your wife, then to heck with you, too.*

Helen had, of course, popped out of bed before he left to make sure he knew she didn't mean any of it. But her unease combined with his own had filled him with a sense of foreboding that he still had not shaken eight hours and more than four hundred miles later.

The road wasn't even that bad. The fields and wooded areas on either side were snow covered, but the potentially slick spots on the asphalt were few and apparently of no concern to his driver—a young, moonfaced FBI agent, who whistled tunelessly and looked back and forth at the countryside like a tourist on holiday.

Fulton wanted to ask the agent . . . his name was Haggerty . . . to slow down a bit, but he didn't want to come off as chickenshit. So he kept his eyes on the unmarked New York State Highway Patrol car on the road ahead of them and maintained a bored expression on his face.

Only normal to feel apprehensive, he thought. After all, a very dangerous individual was sitting in the backseat next to Special-Agent-in-Charge Michael Grover. If not the most dangerous man in America, the prisoner,

Andrew Kane, certainly ranked right up there. He was the most cold-blooded criminal Fulton had ever met over a long and "I've seen everything" career, and rich too, which made him even more dangerous.

Fulton glanced up at the mirror in the visor. Kane, the glib, handsome, and fabulously wealthy head of a Fifth Avenue law firm, stared out the side window, his hands cuffed together and locked to a chain-link belly-band. Six months earlier, he'd appeared to be headed for a landslide victory to become the next mayor of New York City. But that was before he'd been exposed by Fulton's boss, New York District Attorney Roger "Butch" Karp, as a homicidal megalomaniac whose tentacles went deep into the NYPD, the city government, and even the Catholic Archdiocese of New York.

Although technically a detective with the NYPD, Fulton worked as the head of the squad of detectives assigned to the NYDAO. He'd taken the job at Karp's request. The two of them had known each other for most of their respective careers, meeting when Fulton was a rookie cop and Karp a still wet-behind-the-ears prosecutor working for legendary DA Frank Garrahy.

Fulton and Karp had not always worked together. Karp had even gone into private practice for a short stretch before returning to the DAO where he'd been working as the chief of the vaunted homicide bureau when the governor appointed him to fulfill the remaining two years on the term of then–district attorney Jack Keegan, who'd been appointed to the federal bench.

The term was nearly up and now Karp was running for the office in November's elections. It was a thought that made Fulton chuckle. His old friend took to politicking about as well as a cat to water; he hated it and few things put him in a sour mood as did the necessity of what he labeled *kissing up to people you wouldn't spend two minutes with otherwise.*

"Are we there yet?" The mocking voice interrupted Fulton's recollections and brought him back to the moment. He glanced up at the mirror and into the smirking eyes of Andrew Kane.

Looking at Kane, it was hard to imagine him as a monster. Despite being approximately the same age as Karp and Fulton, the blue-eyed, blond-haired, and boyish Andrew Kane looked more like a well-preserved former fraternity president than a vicious crime boss charged with capital murder and a host of other major felonies. Nevertheless, they were on their way to a private psychiatric hospital in upstate New York to have Kane evaluated by doctors selected by his defense team, who hoped to have him declared insane and therefore not responsible for the crimes he'd been accused of.

The state's psychiatrists had already examined Kane and declared him fit to stand trial. Fulton had read their reports. Kane, they said, had an antisocial and schizophrenic personality disorder with strong narcissistic tendencies. In other words, he didn't give a shit about anybody else but himself.

Still, the important thing from the legal vantage of the prosecution was that he "knew and appreciated the nature, quality, and consequences" of his acts and that those acts were wrong. If the prosecution could prove that Kane possessed such a state of mind, he would be held accountable for his crimes, and any attempt at an insanity defense would be defeated.

Naturally, however, Kane's dream team of lawyers—the very best that money could buy—insisted that he be tested by their own doctors. The state's psychiatrists were obviously prejudiced, they argued, and the judge in the case, Paul Hans Lussman III, had allowed it. Like most judges, he was inclined to bend over backward on defense motions in a death penalty case so as to give the defendant every benefit of the doubt. Besides, no jurist likes to be reversed, especially on capital cases, which have a way of making it to the U.S. Supreme Court for the entire world to watch.

So now Fulton was riding shotgun on the transport security team. The New York City Department of Corrections was nominally in charge of getting Kane to and from the hospital for his evaluation. But Karp had asked him to oversee the security measures, which to Fulton meant he had to be there every step of the way.

"We'll get there when we get there," Fulton replied to Kane.

"If we get there, Mr. Fulton . . . if we get there," Kane laughed.

Fulton glanced at Haggerty, the driver, who smiled and rolled his eyes upward. They both knew that every precaution had been taken.

In fact, Fulton had taken a page from the past by re-creating a security detail he'd been on back in the late sixties.

Essentially, he was creating a diversion. To transport Andrew Kane, a five-car motorcade had wheeled up the driveway from the city jail known as the Tombs, and proceeded to the Willis Avenue Bridge. Crossing the East River, the motorcade converged with the Major Deegan Expressway, heading north toward Albany.

Meanwhile, an hour after the motorcade left, a hooded Andrew Kane was rushed out of the DA's elevator and into the armored Lincoln with Fulton and the two federal agents. A single unmarked NYPD sedan had escorted them up the West Side Highway and over the

George Washington Bridge, where the New York cops were relieved at the sight of two state patrol cars with four armed officers inside each, with one taking the lead while the other brought up the rear.

Not even Kane's defense lawyers had been told what day Kane was to be transported, nor was anyone informed that they would be avoiding the interstates and traveling north on small country highways and back roads. The biggest irritation for Fulton had been having to pass his plan through Special-Agent-in-Charge Grover, now blank-faced as he sat in the back next to Kane. The feds had insisted on participating—Kane had broken several federal, as well as local, laws, and the word was that after "the locals" were through with him, they wanted to talk to Kane about some of his international dealings with suspected terrorist organizations. Thus, the presence of Agent Haggerty and Grover, who'd essentially rubber-stamped Fulton's plan.

"Yeah, well, if something goes wrong, it'll give me a chance to shoot your ass and save the taxpayers a lot of money," Fulton said and looked again in the mirror. The humor was gone from Kane's face, replaced by a mask of such malevolence that the detective was suddenly reminded of one of his mother's old sayings about letting sleeping dogs lie.

"I'll remember that, Mr. Fulton," Kane said, and turned his head to stare out the side window again as he clenched and unclenched his jaw.

Fifteen minutes later, Fulton was grabbing the "oh shit" handle above the door as Haggerty jumped on the brakes to avoid colliding with the car ahead of them. They'd come around a corner and found that the vehicle in front had suddenly slowed to five miles an hour as they approached some obstruction on the road ahead.

Fulton grabbed the radio microphone. "What's the problem, Alpha?" he asked, calling ahead to the lead car.

"Mr. Fulton, there's been an accident," was the reply. "Damn, looks like a school bus turned over on its side. There's an ambulance on scene. Should we lend a hand?"

Fulton opened the window and stuck his head out. He could see the yellow bus and the ambulance; a paramedic seemed to be administering to several children standing near the bus, while a second paramedic trotted toward the lead car waving his arms.

Furrowing his brow, Fulton asked aloud, "How come we didn't hear about this on the scanner?" Each of the cars was equipped with a standard police scanner that should have at least picked up the call for help and the response from the ambulance crew.

Pulling his head back in, he yelled into the microphone and grabbed his gun out of his shoulder holster. "It's a setup! Back up! Back up!"

As Haggerty and the drivers in the other cars began to comply, Fulton looked in the rearview mirror just as a figure clad in black stepped from a wooded area behind and to the side of the rear car. He recognized the grenade launcher on the man's shoulder a moment before the rear state patrol car was struck and exploded in a ball of fire that lifted the vehicle off the ground and flipped it over onto its top.

"Get us the hell out of here!" Fulton shouted at Agent Haggerty, who sat with his mouth open looking in the rearview mirror at the burning vehicle behind them.

Up ahead, Fulton saw a paramedic dive in through the window that the driver of the lead car had rolled down. There was a blinding flash and then a full-throated roar as the man detonated a bomb attached to his chest. The suicidal act was so unexpected that Fulton was as stunned as Agent Haggerty, who looked like a man desperately trying to wake up from a nightmare.

Fulton quickly recovered and reached over to turn the steering wheel violently to the left. He jammed his leg across to hit the gas pedal, and the big sedan lurched off the road, striking another black-clad figure who was pointing an automatic rifle at them but did not fire.

"Drive!" Fulton yelled at Haggerty, who started to respond, but just then his head exploded from the impact of a bullet. A red mist filled the air as the agent slumped forward, his lifeless hands dropping to his sides.

The car continued for perhaps twenty-five more yards with Fulton trying to drive despite the obstacle of the dead man, but finally mired itself in the mud. It's over, he thought. Shoot Kane before they get to you.

Fulton started to turn but saw, in his peripheral vision, that Kane's hand was already moving toward him. He noticed that there was something in Kane's hand, but there wasn't enough time for him to wonder why his prisoner was no longer restrained. He felt a jolt on his neck from the stun gun and then everything went black.

When the lights came back on, Fulton was lying in the snow outside the car. He heard a man's angry voice . . . Kane's.

"You fucking moron!" Kane was shouting. "You could have killed me!"

"They were trying to escape." Fulton recognized this voice after a moment as Special Agent Grover's. "I had to shoot him. I knew the car would slow down in the field."

"Knew?" Kane hissed. "You knew the car wouldn't roll? You knew we wouldn't plunge into one of these frickin' ponds these hicks have out here? What do you mean, you knew?"

Fulton raised himself on his elbows, conscious that two armed, hooded men stood behind him with their guns trained on his back. They did not try to stop him from watching Kane berating the quaking Grover.

"You're an idiot, and I can't abide idiots," Kane said. He reached up with the stun gun and zapped the federal agent in the face, knocking him to the ground. He then bent over and picked up the shaken man's gun.

"No, don't!" Grover pleaded weakly as he struggled to recover from the shock.

"You're too stupid to live, Grover," Kane replied and shot him in the face, blood and brains splattering the snow.

Kane nodded in satisfaction as the body twitched once then stopped. He walked over until he stood directly in front of Fulton. "You owe me one," he said. "Saved you having to shoot him yourself, but I guess you won't be shooting me today."

"Fuck you," Fulton replied. He figured that there wasn't much of a reason for Kane to let him live, so he might as well go out cursing his executioner. Good-bye, Helen. Good-bye, kids. I love you.

Kane laughed and pointed the gun, but turned, hearing a shout from down the road.

Fulton looked that way as well. The hooded man up near the first burning police car yelled again. Fulton thought the words sounded Russian.

The smaller of the two guards behind him spoke—surprising Fulton because the voice was that of a woman—in yet another language . . . Arabic, maybe . . . to the guard next to her. This guard also proved to be a woman and replied to her comrade in Arabic, obviously translating what the man on the road was saying.

"He wants to know what to do with the prisoner," the first woman said to Kane in accented English.

Fulton looked at Kane and back to the scene on the highway. He could see one of the state police officers sitting on the ground, apparently wounded.

"Kill him, of course," Kane said.

The first woman shouted a command in Arabic, which the second woman translated to German or Russian, Fulton wasn't sure which, directing the translation back to the hooded man. She drew her hand across her throat for emphasis. The men on the road immediately shot the prisoner.

"Who's injured?" Kane asked the first woman, nodding toward the man who'd been run over when Fulton steered the car off the road. The man lay on the ground, propped up on an elbow and talking to one of his accomplices, who knelt to give him a cigarette.

"Akhmed Kadyrov," she said. "A Chechen."

"Hmmm . . . gives me an idea," Kane said. "Finish him and leave the body. We'll call our friends later and suggest that this presents an opportunity."

"And the infidel children?"

Kane scowled as though annoyed by one too many questions. "Must I tell you everything?"

"God, no!" Fulton shouted looking at the school bus where the children he'd seen earlier were now sitting, obviously crying.

The first woman shouted something else toward the men standing with the children. Apparently, one of the men there understood her and didn't need a translator. Immediately, there were several bursts of automatic rifle fire, which echoed across the fields. An eerie silence followed, which was broken by the cawing of crows and, after a moment, a bellow of rage from Fulton.

"God damn you, you murdering son of a bitch," he yelled. He tried to rise to his feet to go after Kane but was clubbed back to the ground by the two guards. Dazed, he rolled over onto his back. "Better finish it," he swore at Kane. "Or someday I'm going to kill you, you insane piece of crap."

Kane put a finger to his lips. "Oooooh. Down 'Shaft.' Always playing the hero, but it didn't do those children who were kind enough to participate in my little ruse any good, now did it? Or save any of these fine police officers and marshals? Guess being a hero didn't mean shit today."

Waving Agent Grover's gun at the detective, Kane said, "You know, I really should shoot you now. Isn't it always the way in movies: the bad guy doesn't kill the good guy when he has the chance and lives only long enough to regret it?"

Without warning, Kane rushed at Fulton and kicked him hard in the ribs, knocking the wind out of the detective. He kicked him again and again like he was punting a football. "You going to kill me, detective?" he raged. "You think a piece of shit nigger is going to kill Andrew Kane?" He rained more blows.

Finally, Kane tired and stopped. Panting from his exertions, he said, "However, no, Detective Fulton. As much as I would like to stomp you to death like a cockroach, I'm not going to kill you. Not yet. I want you to have to live with this fine job you did weighing on your conscience for a while, maybe you'll decide to suck on the end of your gun and blow your ugly head off because all those kids were counting on you to deliver crazy Mr. Kane to the hospital safe and sound. But first, I need you to take a message back to our mutual friend Mr. Karp."

"Fuck you," Fulton croaked, spitting blood out on the snow. "I ain't your messenger boy."

"Oh, I think you'll do as told," Kane said, kicking

Fulton again. "After all, ol' Butchie is going to want to know everything that happened here today. So tell him I said, 'The game is on.' And that I hope he's up to the challenge. I don't want this to be too easy when I kill every thing he loves—his bitch, his idiot kids, his imbecile friends, and even his fucking dog—before I come for him."

A black helicopter appeared from over the top of the trees and landed on the highway behind the last burning car. "Ah, my ride awaits," Kane said. "Samira, my love, would you do the honors?"

Fulton looked back and saw that the first woman had a handgun pointed at his leg. She pulled the trigger and the bullet tore into his knee. He screamed in rage and pain, and then screamed louder as a second bullet blew his other knee apart.

"Just a little something to remember me by," Kane said. "I think your chasing days are done, don't you?" He giggled and took off at a trot for the helicopter with Samira and the other female terrorist on his heels.

As the helicopter took off, Fulton lay in the snow wishing that Kane had killed him. Then he thought of Helen and his children and slowly, painfully, began dragging himself through the snow toward the overturned school bus.

UNFORGETTABLE BESTSELLERS FROM POCKET BOOKS

Blue Valor
Illona Haus
To solve a crime that defies the imagination,
a Baltimore cop must take a twisted journey into
the dark recesses of a killer's mind.

Saving Cascadia
John J. Nance
Washington state's Cascadia Island is a tranquil
Northwest paradise—until a disaster only one
man can predict threatens the lives of thousands.

The Pandora Key
Lynne Heitman
She's a tough, sexy private investigator—and
she's unlocking explosive secrets form the past.

Live Wire
Jay MacLarty
A high-stakes delivery and a high-risk courier
make for an explosive combination.

The Greater Good
Casey Moreton
Even in the top-secret world of Washington
politics, some crimes can't be justified.